THE HISTORIES OF SOME OF THE PENITENTS IN THE MAGDALEN-HOUSE, AS SUPPOSED TO BE RELATED BY THEMSELVES (1760)

CHAWTON HOUSE LIBRARY SERIES:
WOMAN'S NOVELS

Series Editors: *Stephen Bending*
Stephen Bygrave

FORTHCOMING TITLES

Stéphanie-Félicité de Genlis, *Adelaide and Theodore*
edited by Gillian Dow

Sarah Harriet Burney, *The Romance of Private Life*
edited by Lorna J Clark

E. M. Foster, *The Corinna of England*
edited by Sylvia Bordoni

*The Histories of Some of the Penitents in
the Magdalen-House, as Supposed to be related
by Themselves* (1760)

EDITED BY

Jennie Batchelor and Megan Hiatt

Routledge
Taylor & Francis Group

LONDON AND NEW YORK

First published 2007 by Pickering & Chatto (Publishers) Limited

Published 2016 by Routledge
2 Park Square, Milton Park, Abingdon, Oxfordshire OX14 4RN
711 Third Avenue, New York, NY 10017, USA

First issued in paperback 2016

Routledge is an imprint of the Taylor & Francis Group, an informa business

BRITISH LIBRARY CATALOGUING IN PUBLICATION DATA

The histories of some of the penitents in the Magdalen House.–(Chawton
House library series: Women's novels)
  1. Prostitutes – fiction
  I. Batchelor, Jennie, 1976 – II. Hiatt, Megan
823.6[F]

ISBN 13: 978-1-138-23592-2 (pbk)
ISBN 13: 978-1-8519-6860-2 (hbk)

Typeset by P&C

CONTENTS

ACKNOWLEDGEMENTS

In preparing this edition, we have accrued a number of debts to friends and colleagues. Katherine Binhammer and Laura Rosenthal, our fellow panellists on a round-table discussion of the novel at the 2006 American Society for Eighteenth-Century Studies conference, provided plenty of food for thought, as did our email exchanges and conversations with Sylvia Greenup. Mary Peace's knowledge and generosity have been a continual support throughout the editing process, and we thank her for very kindly making available her transcript of the Montagu-Richardson correspondence. Particular thanks go to Markman Ellis, who has helped with every stage of the project, from proposal to proofing, since it was originally planned.

We are grateful to Chawton House Library – an institution, like this novel, dedicated to the cause of female solidarity – for allowing us to use their edition as copy-text; and we also thank Stephen Bygrave and Stephen Bending at the University of Southampton and Mark Pollard at Pickering and Chatto for their enthusiastic response to the project.

INTRODUCTION

i

In a letter to Elizabeth Montagu, written on 1 December 1759, Elizabeth Carter wrote: 'I have not read the History of the Penitents, except a little extract, with which I was greatly pleased. It is much to be wished indeed that the general fashion of novel reading did not render such antidotes very necessary.'[1] Carter's account of *The Histories of Some of the Penitents in the Magdalen-House, as Supposed to be Related by Themselves* (published anonymously in 1759, but dated 1760) encapsulates eighteenth-century anxieties about the effects of reading – commonly figured as an illness in anti-novel discourse of the period – on young women.[2] She implies that novels are dangerous, communicating the immoral tendencies responsible for the epidemic of prostitution; but she also asserts that the right kind of novel can counteract the poison imbibed by promiscuous readers. According to Carter, *The Histories* is just such an attempt to restore the health of the body politic; it therefore participates in the public debate that produced the Magdalen House for the Reception of Penitent Prostitutes itself.

Rejecting earlier visual and literary accounts of the harlot's progress, from William Hogarth's famous six-plate series (1732) to John Cleland's *Memoirs of a Woman of Pleasure* (1748–9), proponents of the Magdalen House argued that women were driven to prostitution by economic necessity rather than personal inclination. *The Histories* reflects this ideological shift in the stories of four fictional Magdalen inmates, whose narratives are designed to serve both as warnings against extra-marital sexual encounters and as collective testimony to the necessity for the institution that would rehabilitate them. However, the novel – with its sentimental frame-narrative and radical communal emphasis – is also strikingly different from the other meditations on prostitution reform produced by campaigners for the charity. Like the Magdalen House pamphlets, *The*

---

1   Elizabeth Carter, *Letters from Mrs. Elizabeth Carter to Mrs. Montagu, Between the Years 1755 and 1800, Chiefly upon Literary and Moral Subjects*, ed. Montagu Pennington (3 vols, London: F. C. and J. Rivington, 1817), vol. 1, p. 69.
2   See, for example, Jacqueline Pearson, *Women's Reading in Britain, 1750–1835: A Dangerous Recreation* (Cambridge: Cambridge University Press, 1999).

Histories attempts to recuperate the prostitute by providing wide-ranging and detailed criticisms of the socioeconomic conditions that generated her predicament, but unlike the official publications, it also questions the motives of the institution's spokesmen, who would turn these penitent subjects into little more than 'Objects'.[3]

The opening of the Magdalen House in Goodman's Fields, London, on 10 August 1758 followed an energetic pamphlet debate sponsored by the Society for the Encouragement of the Arts, Manufactures and Commerce, although the need for 'an Hospital for Female Penitents' had been mooted some four years earlier by the exemplary eponymous hero of Samuel Richardson's *Sir Charles Grandison* (1753–4).[4] Robert Dingley, Sir John Fielding, Jonas Hanway, Joseph Massie and Saunders Welch all produced proposals detailing how the charity might be run and funded; Dingley and Hanway would go on to become members of its founding committee. Each writer identified different reasons for women's descent into prostitution. Sir John Fielding focused upon the problem of prostitution among the labouring classes and laid the blame upon the unreformed labour market, which fostered immorality among society's poorest members. Levels of prostitution, he argued, were a signal that 'Industry' was in just as desperate a state of 'Distress' as female virtue; his proposed solution was a public laundry in which women could find legitimate work and symbolically wash away their sins.[5] By contrast, Dingley, Hanway and Welch focused on women of the lower middling sort, identifying inadequate education and misplaced social ambition as the principal reasons for women's whoredom; these three pamphleteers were in broad agreement that the only way to prevent women from succumbing to the schemes of libertines and bawds was to ensure that they were given an education that would fit them for their respective stations in life. Without this vital resource, their moral health would remain precariously in the balance.

Although the pamphleteers differed in their accounts of the causes of prostitution, they were united in their conviction that dealing with the problem was a matter of urgency. Welch estimated that there were more than 3,000 prostitutes plying their trade in London, of which 2,500 were supposed 'barren' as a direct consequence of their 'infamous course of life'.[6] The accuracy, or other-

3   See, for example, Jonas Hanway, *A Plan for Establishing a Charity-House, or Charity-Houses, for the Reception of Repenting Prostitutes. To be Called the Magdalen Charity* (London: n.p., 1758), pp. 15–40.
4   Samuel Richardson, *The History of Sir Charles Grandison*, ed. Jocelyn Harris, (3 vols, London, New York and Toronto: Oxford University Press, 1972), vol. 2, p. 356.
5   Sir John Fielding, *A Plan for a Preservatory and Reformatory, for the Benefit of Deserted Girls, and Penitent Prostitutes* (London: R. Francklin, 1758), p. 3.
6   Saunders Welch, *A Proposal to Render Effectual a Plan, to Remove the Nuisance of*

wise, of such estimates is of less importance, perhaps, than the perception that prostitution posed an unacceptable level of threat to the nation. Such anxieties were by no means new, of course. The prostitute's trade had always, as Vivien Jones comments, called into question the 'boundaries between the public world of commerce and the private sphere of sexuality and domesticity' within which femininity was constructed.[7] But it was not only the 'private sphere' that was polluted by the streetwalker's commodification of sexuality and disregard for domesticity. As various early eighteenth-century commentators argued, the 'Trade in Sin' posed a grave threat to the nation's economy. Bernard Mandeville in his *Modest Defence of Publick Stews* (1724), a satirical attack on the Reformation of Manners campaigns, claimed that 'Whoring' disposed the 'Mind' of both the prostitute and the client 'to such a sort of Indolence, as is quite inconsistent with Industry, the main Support of any, especially a trading, Nation'.[8] Daniel Defoe's *Some Considerations on Street-walkers* (1726) similarly proposed that prostitution was a drain on the economy. Although prostitutes might be enthusiastic consumers of luxury items, Defoe suggested, their failure to engage in (re)productive labour – 'the great Use of Women in a Community' – rendered them little more than parasites.[9]

During the Seven Years' War (1756–63) the concerns expressed by writers such as Mandeville and Defoe were urgently refocused by philanthropists determined to reclaim the prostitute's un(re)productive body for a life of virtuous industry. As Donna T. Andrew has suggested, the war was the catalyst for the foundation of a number of philanthropic organizations in the mid-century, including the Foundling Hospital, Lock Hospital, Lambeth Asylum, the Marine Society and the Magdalen House. The decline in unemployment, which occurred as a result of both labouring-class men's conscription and the growth in trade during the period, enabled philanthropists to turn their attention away from the provision of work to other charitable endeavours designed 'to aid national policy'.[10] With this shift, the rehabilitation of prostitutes and

---

Common Prostitutes from the Streets of the Metropolis (London: C. Henderson, 1758), p. 13. As Tony Henderson points out, Welch's estimate was rather modest by eighteenth-century standards and impossible to prove with certainty. See *Disorderly Women in Eighteenth-Century London: Prostitution and Control in the Metropolis, 1730–1830* (London and New York: Longman, 1999), p. 178.

7   Vivien Jones, 'Placing Jemima: Women Writers of the 1790s and the Eighteenth-Century Prostitution Narrative', *Women's Writing*, 4:2 (1997), p. 204.

8   Bernard Mandeville, *A Modest Defence of Publick Stews: or, an Essay upon Whoring. As it is now Practis'd in these Kingdoms* (London: A. Moore, 1724), p. 4.

9   Daniel Defoe, *Some Considerations upon Street-walkers. With a proposal for lessening the present number of them. In two letters to a Member of Parliament* (London: A. Moore, 1726), p. 6.

10   Donna T. Andrew, *Philanthropy and Police: London Charity in the Eighteenth Century*

orphaned or deserted children became a vital part of the war effort, as vital even, in Hanway's words, as 'the *arduous* affairs of war'.[11] The motives for reclaiming these lives were only in part altruistic, however. In the short term, rehabilitated prostitutes could boost the economy by working in various manufacturing and service trades; in the long term, commentators argued, they might play a crucial role in repopulating the nation. These pressing socioeconomic concerns made the re-imagining of the prostitute as expedient as it was just.

The Magdalen House's disciplinary regime was designed to address these issues by reforming the bodies and minds of inmates and fitting them for a life of virtuous industry once they were released from the institution. The charity's published *Rules* were frequently revised during the early years of the establishment,[12] but at its inception, when *The Histories* was published, the hospital was organized along the following lines. To secure their admission, potential inmates had first to petition the committee, and then to undergo a medical examination.[13] The women were then given a uniform, and the rules of the institution were read to them before they were placed in one of two (later three) wards according to 'the education or behaviour of the person admitted'.[14] From then on, the women were subjected to a strictly regulated sixteen-hour daily routine of work and prayer, during which they were instructed in the skills needed to qualify them for service or to fit them for an apprenticeship in one of the dressmaking trades.[15] Once they had been in the Magdalen House for three years, the penitents were either released to friends or sent into service, to 'any housekeeper of sufficient credit' who would take them.[16]

(Princeton: Princeton University Press, 1989), pp. 56–7.

11   Jonas Hanway, *Thoughts on the Plan for a Magdalen-House for Repentant Prostitutes* (London: James Waugh, 1758), p. 18.

12   The second, but first extant, edition of *The Rules, Orders and Regulations, of the Magdalen House, for the Reception of Penitent Prostitutes* was published anonymously in 1759 (London: n.p., 1759). It was followed by further editions in 1760, 1769 and 1785. The rules were also included in a volume by William Dodd entitled *An Account of the Rise, Progress, and Present State of the Magdalen Charity*, which came out first in 1761 (London: W. Faden), with further editions in 1766 and 1770.

13   [Anon.], *The Rules, Orders and Regulations, of the Madgalen House*, 2nd edn, p. 18. Although each of the first three editions of the charity's *Rules* asserts the need for this examination it is not until the fourth edition that the charity makes clear that any women found to be suffering from venereal disease were refused entry into the institution and their applications considered again only once they had been cured. [Anon.], *The Rules and Regulations of the Magdalen-Charity*, 4th edn (London: W. Faden, 1769), p. 18.

14   [Anon.], *The Rules, Orders and Regulations of the Magdalen House*, 2nd edn, p. 18.

15   [Anon.], *The Rules, Orders and Regulations of the Magdalen House*, 2nd edn, p. 21, p. 20.

16   [Anon.], *The Rules, Orders and Regulations of the Magdalen House*, 2nd edn, p. 22. In practice, however, the Magdalens' fortunes varied. The 1766 edition of Dodd's report noted that of the 683 women admitted since August 1758, less than half (308) had been

It is noticeable that the organizational focus of non-fictional Magdalen House texts emphasizes the structure of the charity: who should run the institution, and how the penitents should be managed. Hanway's *Plan*, for example, opens with a twenty-six-page introduction justifying his interest in abandoned women, which is then followed by his vision for the institution, divided into neat subheadings. The third, 'The Government', is a list of those in authority: 'a president; four vice-presidents; a treasurer; a general court; a general committee of twenty-one; a sub-committee; governors in general; a chaplain; a matron; an assistant-matron; a physician; a surgeon; an apothecary; a steward; a secretary; a porter and a messenger.'[17] Hanway does not mention the penitents themselves until the twenty-first heading, under the title 'The Admission of proper Objects'.[18] The cumulative effect is, paradoxically, an absence: it is very difficult to glean a sense of the Magdalens' lived experience from all of this information.

The glimpse we do obtain of the inmates' lives illuminates the difference between the non-fictional and the fictional attitudes to prostitutes, as signified by their different approaches to autobiography. The *Rules* specifies that the women's '*true names* are registered, but if they are desirous of concealing themselves, they may have liberty to assume a *feigned name* ... neither is any enquiry into *names* or *families* permitted, but all possible discouragement given to every kind of discovery that the parties themselves do not chuse to make.'[19] The text of this regulation disturbs the notion that the Magdalens were not allowed to describe their experiences: in his 1917 history of the charity, the Rev. H. F. B. Compston claims that the wards of the Magdalen House were adorned with signs reading 'Tell your story to no one'.[20] However, as Compston does not cite his source for this detail, and the restriction is not mentioned anywhere else in the extensive contemporary literature on the project, it would be unwise to draw any conclusions about the Magdalen House attitude to autobiographical conversations based on this potentially apocryphal detail.[21]

'reconciled to, and received by their friends, or placed in services in reputable families, and to trades'. Of the remainder, 75 had left the charity of their own accord and 114 had been dismissed for 'Irregularities'. *An Account of the Rise, Progress, and Present State of the Magdalen Charity*, 3rd edn (London: W. Faden, 1766), p. 6.

17   Hanway, *Plan*, pp. 3–4.

18   Hanway, *Plan*, p. 15.

19   [Anon.], *The Rules, Orders and Regulations of the Magdalen House*, 2nd edn, p. 19.

20   See Rev. H. F. B. Compston, *The Magdalen Hospital: The Story of a Great London Charity* (London: Society for Promoting Christian Knowledge, 1917), p. 199.

21   Both Ann Jessie Van Sant and Donna Andrew incorporate Compston's claim into their analysis. See Van Sant, *Eighteenth-Century Sensibility and the Novel: The Senses in Social Context* (Cambridge: Cambridge University Press, 1993), p. 36; and Andrew, *Philanthropy and Police*, p. 125.

Yet the authorities' attitude to the penitents' identities is nonetheless striking: the women were required to register their true names, and we might speculate that this was designed to ensure the sincerity of the Magdalens' requests for admission and thus their repentance. But the fact that they were allowed to use aliases amongst themselves also implies that they could not be trusted with potentially sensitive information as they might at any moment slip back into their criminal ways. In contrast, the bona fides of those in charge were guaranteed by the benevolence of their endeavour. This confirms the impression that the pamphlets and the *Rules* convey of two distinct communities within the Magdalen House: first, the brotherhood of the governors, united by their charitable intentions, their wealth and their social status; and second, the sisterhood of the penitents, unstable in their commitment to virtue, in need of sequestration from the outside world and protection from each other. In contrast, *The Histories* submerges the institution's governmental fraternity, representing the Magdalen House instead as a sober sorority of virtuous and sympathetic individuals.

ii

The opening of *The Histories* places the reader in the feminocentric community created by the eponymous penitents, at a rare moment of relaxation in their busy schedule. The scene is set 'after the work of the day [is] past' (p. 10), and this is the only allusion that is made in the novel to an occupation that is not story-telling. Instead of emphasizing the penitents' productivity, a strategy that was central to the pamphleteers' programme for retraining the women and for maintaining the institution itself, the author characterizes the society as one of introspection and communion.

Emily, the youngest of the penitents, supposedly the first to enter the Magdalen House, is in tears; when asked the source of her grief, she replies that they are 'not tears of sorrow, but of joy and gratitude' (p. 10). This expression of exquisite sensibility develops into a genteel competition about the depth of the penitents' previous misery, which Emily resolves by agreeing to share her story with the group, in part to 'withdraw their thoughts from themselves' and give them 'some relief' (p. 11). As well as setting up the sentimental exchange that will enhance the reader's identification with the Magdalens, and the Magdalens' identification with each other, this tableau provides a rare description of their thoughts. They are all preoccupied with their histories, that is to say, with their sins and their subsequent salvation: as one of them explains, 'my heart is forever full' (p. 11). This produces a curiously static image of repentance: the Magdalens are permanently brimful of emotion; yet hearing Emily's story will provide a brief but necessary respite from the continuous contemplation of their own contrition, allowing them to consolidate their state of conscious remorse. The benefit of narrative to this community of listeners/readers is confirmed when, at the end of Emily's tale, she requests that they begin another cycle, and 'it was agreed that they should proceed in the order in which they arrived at the House' (p. 52). The relation of the penitents' histories thus becomes a revised history of the institution itself, one which obscures the role that 'the Beneficent Institutors of this charity' played in its establishment (p. 182).

Instead, the four narrators focus the reader's attention on 'the various stratagems used at first to corrupt them' (p. 3), and this narrative multiplicity creates a significantly different effect from that produced by later Magdalen novels, which relate the downward spiral of one woman only. The Rev. William Dodd's posthumous novel *The Magdalen* (1783) provides an instructive comparison: Dodd, preacher of the Magdalen House from 1759 through 1777, plagiarized the bulk of his text from Emily's narrative in *The Histories*, so the story itself is the same.[22] However, he recasts it as a series of letters, signed 'M.S.', to the lady of quality who sponsored her admission to the charity. The novel's didactic strategy thus directs the reader's attention away from the feminine community and towards the outside world, both through the figure of the benevolent patroness and the information that M.S. 'afterwards rose to an elivated rank of life; the particulars of which it is not permitted us to relate' (*sic*).[23] This reincorporation of the penitent into patriarchal society, presumably through marriage, contributes to Dodd's depiction of repentance as a finite individual endeavour, which is profoundly different from *The Histories*' representation of a never-ending, collective process that must be monitored with vigilance and that is characterized by a painful sense of obligation.

Yet this heightened feeling, combined with the enclosure of the penitents in the Magdalen House, produces a complicated and ambiguous effect. On the one hand, some critics have identified this sentimentalization of the prostitute as a divisive strategy, focusing the discourse of femininity and the charitable efforts of reformers on women from the middle stations in life. The narrators, with diverse but genteel origins, are equalized first through their degradation and then through their moral elevation; as Jones observes, 'This capacity for remorse signals the prostitute's actual or honorary middle-class status'.[24] On the other hand, this sentimental equality does assert that fallen women are capable of reformation; following Samuel Johnson's narrative of Misella in *The Rambler* (nos.

---

22   William Dodd, *The Magdalen, or History of the First Penitent Received into that Charitable Asylum, in a Series of Letters to a Lady with Anecdotes of Other Penitents* (London: W. Lane, 1783).
23   Dodd, *The Magdalen*, p. xvii.
24   Jones, 'Placing Jemima', p. 205.

170 and 171), this rejects the stereotype of the wanton whore who is complicit in her seduction.

The argument of *The Histories* thus diverges from the fundamentally misogynistic discourse employed by the male pamphleteers in their discussion of the need for the Magdalen House. Even for the enthusiastic Robert Dingley, the prostitute, a 'thoughtless' victim, is implicated in her seduction. She allows herself to be tantalized by the prospect of replacing 'Want, Confinement and Restraint of Passion' with 'Luxury, Liberty, Gaiety and Joy', terms which depict her initial situation as uncomfortable without being untenable and her desires as excessive, 'golden dreams'. It is only once she has lost her virginity that 'necessity' is mentioned; and this 'necessity' forces her into the typical cycle of prostitution: 'disease, death and eternal destruction'. But this is not simply her own personal tragedy; a viral metaphor equates the prostitute with the sexually transmitted disease that is spread throughout society: 'The same necessity, obliging them to prey on the unwary, diffuses the contagion, even through both sexes, propagating profligacy, and spreading ruin, disease and death ... almost through the whole species.'[25]

In contrast, the author of *The Histories* vigorously protests that the penitents are fundamentally innocent. Although some of the Magdalen narrators are vain or ignorant, not one of the women is held accountable for her fall. Emily may suffer from a certain 'weakness' of character, but it is her seducer's elaborate plotting, with which 'every servant' in the house colludes, that seals her fate (p. 20). The unnamed fourth penitent is similarly exonerated for her mistakes: the origins of her adulterous relationship with Captain Turnham are located in her parents' mercenary plot to coerce her into marrying a wealthy, 'battered rake' rather than in a propensity for vice (p. 133). Drawing a distinction between character and career that even the most sympathetic of pamphleteers struggled to sustain, *The Histories* maintains that its heroines are 'worthy objects of compassion' no matter how 'despicable and hateful' their profession might appear (p. 3).

One of the recurrent signals of the women's worth is their devotion to their children. The first, third and fourth penitents are mothers, and their maternal love for their sons – none of them have daughters – is transformative. Both the first and fourth penitents become prostitutes explicitly to support their children. When Emily has been tricked into entering a brothel, she only consents to receive clients when the bawd threatens to take her son; after this unscrupulous woman's death, she is reduced to streetwalking, the lowest form of prostitution, to gain enough money to feed him. She learns of the Magdalen House just when starvation threatens, and she is overjoyed 'for his sake' (p. 31) that the charity

25   Robert Dingley, *Proposals for Establishing a Public Place of Reception for Penitent Prostitutes, &c* (London: W. Faden, 1758), pp. 4–5.

will take care of both of them. Similarly, the fourth penitent is the mother of three sons, and after many adventures she realizes that only prostitution will allow her to provide for them. She places her two older children in a school, which she pays for with her earnings; and there the boys learn 'both the faith and practice of christianity' (p. 179). The eldest child dies, impressing his mother with his pious last words; she therefore repents and enters the Magdalen House, which also receives her two remaining children.[26]

However, it is the third narrative, the history of Fanny, which presents the most sustained meditation on motherhood. Fanny herself has multiple mothers: her biological mother; her foster mother; and Madam Tent, the bawd who pretends to be her long-lost mother. Madam Tent even uses her maternal authority to convince Fanny to have sex with her first client, Mr Mastin, who then removes Fanny from the brothel in order to have exclusive rights to her person.

When Mr Mastin tires of her, she is employed by his sister, Mrs Lafew, as a maid; and it is in the Lafew household that Fanny, from being a daughter, becomes a mother herself. Initially, this maternal role is figurative: when the family contract scarlet fever, Fanny nurses them back to health, nobly risking infection to reanimate the Lafew's four-year-old daughter according to the physician's instructions. In erotic language, the doctor asserts, 'if any thing could restore it, it would be going to bed to it' (p. 112), and Fanny accordingly shares her own bodily warmth with the little girl, giving her life. This act inspires Mr Lafew, whom Fanny has long admired, with a passion for his daughter's new mother; and they embark on an affair that, predictably, results in pregnancy. Fanny sets up her own establishment nearby, where she gives birth to a son.

Yet this history has a startling conclusion: Fanny contracts a serious fever, and the saintly but rejected Mrs Lafew, who is aware that Fanny is her husband's mistress, intervenes and saves her. An essential part of Mrs Lafew's curative is a religious education, which convinces Fanny of the need to cement her repentance far away from her seductive lover. Accordingly, she leaves her son to be raised by his father and his father's wife, and is received into the Magdalen House. In this history, the maternal Mrs Lafew enables Fanny to escape from the typical cycle of sexual indulgence, abandonment and starvation that describes the other prostitutes' narratives; inter-generational female solidarity thus triumphs over the domestic unit formed by the heterosexual pair.

Another significant feature of Fanny's story, which epitomizes the author's attempt to recuperate the figure of the prostitute, is her lack of sexual passion, distinguishing her from lusty, appetitive whores like her namesake, Fanny

---

26   Although these narrators claim that the children of penitent prostitutes were provided for by the Magdalen charity, this is not mentioned in any of the literature on the institution. Rather, this counterfactual detail emphasizes the fictional nature of the text: it is a fantasy of both penitence and charity, intended to generate reformation and sympathy.

Hill, whose story *The Histories* explicitly sets out to rewrite. When Fanny is convinced to have sex with Mr Mastin, it is not because she harbours any sexual feelings for him: he is 'horrid rude' and 'impudent' (p. 101). Indeed, even in her subsequent relationship with Mr Lafew, it is difficult to identify the moment when they become lovers; all we are told is that 'sickness gave rise to all tenderness of intercourse between Mr. Lafew and myself, instead of ceasing with it, it increased daily; and continued undiscovered till I proved with child' (p. 117). The details of their affair are cloaked in the narrative just as they are in the Lafew ménage; only with the incontrovertible fact of Fanny's pregnancy does the sexual nature of their 'intercourse' emerge.

The Histories' determination to write sexual desire out of the penitents' narratives is just one of the ways in which the novel, as Markman Ellis suggests, complicates the traditional 'seduction-into-prostitution' narrative that structures works such as *Memoirs of a Woman of Pleasure*.[27] More striking perhaps than the novel's challenge to this conventional framework is the insistence with which it distinguishes between the women's lack of chastity and their virtue, which remains curiously intact despite their transgressions.[28] Nowhere is this more evident than in the story of the second penitent, whose decline is triggered not by her illegal Fleet marriage, but rather by her failure to recognize the difference between private and public morality. Upon discovering that her marriage to Mr Monkerton is not legally binding as the couple were underage and had not obtained parental consent before marrying – a point of law dramatically proven when he sends her a copy of the 1753 Marriage Act – the penitent believes herself to be forever lost to 'infamy'. She explains, 'Virtue and reputation were for me synonymous terms; I therefore ... thought, that after having entered into that way of life, it was as impossible to go back, as if a point of honour had obliged me to fulfil the expectations which my former conduct might naturally have raised' (p. 73). As a result of this mistaken sense of 'honour', she agrees to become 'in reality, what [she] before had only appeared', a kept mistress (p. 73).

This penitent has internalized the advice of innumerable contemporary conduct-book writers, and indeed Magdalen House supporters, who

27   Markman Ellis, *The Politics of Sensibility: Race, Gender and Commerce in the Sentimental Novel* (Cambridge: Cambridge University Press, 1996), p. 183.

28   William Dodd, for example, wrote in uncomfortably racialized imagery that the project of the Magdalen House could not be likened to 'a scheme to wash *Æthiopians* white'. The women's virtue had not been 'obliterated', merely obscured by their prostitution. *Rev. Mr. Dodd's Sermon, Preached before the President, Vice-Presidents, Treasurer, and Governors of the Magdalen-House*, reprinted in *An Account of the Rise, Progress, and Present State of the Magdalen Charity*, p. iii.

equated virginity with virtue. According to Wetenhall Wilkes, author of *A Letter of Genteel and Moral Advice to a Young Lady* (1740), 'She who forfeits her Chastity, withers by degrees into Scorn and contrition; ... and the least Slip in a Woman's Honour is never to be recover'd.'[29] This unforgiving logic is targeted directly in the preface to *The Histories*. Although the author acknowledges that many of the real-life Magdalens' crimes 'have been owing to a want of steadiness in themselves in the practice of virtue, many of their subsequent vices have arisen from the affectation of too overstrained a chastity in others' (p. 4). Rather than safeguarding female virtue, *The Histories* argues, texts like Wilkes's *Letter* produce the vice they would eradicate by denying fallen women 'the means of reformation, by hunting them out of every way of obtaining an honest subsistence, till the only alternative left them, is, either to owe their support to a continuance in vicious courses, or to die martyrs to chastity' (p. 4).

Prostitution is thus as much a reflection of the failure of community as it is of morality or education. As Ruth Perry has recently suggested in a short but incisive reading of *The Histories*, heroines like the first penitent, Emily, 'deracinated [and] separated from her family of origin, unable to survive alone by waged labour', stand for the 'irony of the age of individualism, a necessary corrective to the myth of the socially mobile individual' produced by capitalism.[30] Almost everyone to whom Emily turns – her lover, the bawd who pays off her husband's debts and the potential employers from whom she desperately seeks work – betrays her. Even her sister, a successful, hardworking and uncharacteristically virtuous milliner, inadvertently abandons Emily by allowing her husband to have complete control of the shop's 'stock' and therefore of the profits which might have allowed her to support her fallen sister (p. 46). In a world in which both the labour and marriage markets conspire equally against women, *The Histories* looks to models of sentimental community for redress; the novel emphasizes the solidarity of this humble and grateful 'society' of women, who regard each other 'with an eye of pity' (p. 10). Yet this dynamic of sympathy is not limited to the penitential sorority: the preface instructs the reader to 'smooth the stern brow of rigid virtue, and turn the contemptuous frown into tears of pity' (p. 3). It is clearly the author's hope that readers will be spurred by these fictional narratives to change the society in which they live.

29   Wetenhall Wilkes, *A Letter of Genteel and Moral Advice to a Young Lady* (Dublin: E. Jones, 1740), pp. 75–6.
30   Ruth Perry, *Novel Relations: The Transformation of Kinship in English Literature and Culture, 1748–1818* (Cambridge: Cambridge University Press, 2004), p. 280.

iii

The identity of the author of *The Histories* remains undiscovered and the facts surrounding the novel's publication are few. We know that Lady Barbara Montagu presented the manuscript to Samuel Richardson in January 1759, claiming that its female author was a friend and neighbour whom she wished to help.[31] Richardson responded warmly to her proposal and agreed to print *The Histories*, suggesting that it needed a preface;[32] he then arranged for John Rivington and James Dodsley to publish the novel, after it was rejected by Andrew Millar and Robert Dodsley. Lady Barbara agreed to pay for the cost of printing.[33] To thank him for his efforts, Lady Barbara's brother, the second Earl of Halifax, sent Richardson some venison, a detail interpreted by Markman Ellis as an indication of the Montagu family's sense of kinship with the text, reinforcing his contention that Lady Barbara herself 'authorized (if not authored)' the novel.[34]

However, it is unlikely that Lady Barbara wrote *The Histories*, as there are no references to her authoring this, or indeed any other, text in the extant correspondence between her long-term companion Sarah Scott and Scott's sister Elizabeth Montagu.[35] Yet the formulation that Lady Barbara 'authorized' the novel is an elegant summary of the known facts. Richardson himself was unaware of the author's identity,[36] but would have known her to be one of the members of the Bath community in which Lady Barbara lived.[37] At the centre of this group

31   T. C. Duncan Eaves and Ben D. Kimpel, *Samuel Richardson: A Biography* (Oxford: Clarendon Press, 1971), pp. 463–5. The correspondence between Lady Barbara Montagu and Richardson is held by Cornell University Library.

32   At least one contemporary reader suspected that the preface was written by someone other than the author of the novel proper. Lady Echlin, the sister of Lady Bradshaigh, suspected that Richardson himself had written it on the grounds that no other author could 'so sensibly affect and touch the reader with the penitent's lamentable story' than 'the author of Clarissa'. Samuel Richardson, *The Correspondence of Samuel Richardson*, ed. Anna Laetita Barbauld, (6 vols, London: Richard Phillips, 1804), vol. 5, p. 98.

33   Eaves and Kimpel, *Samuel Richardson*, p. 464.

34   Ellis, *The Politics of Sensibility*, pp. 178–9; see also Eaves and Kimpel, *Samuel Richardson*, p. 464, for Lord Halifax's present.

35   Although Lady Barbara has occasionally been acknowledged co-author with Sarah Scott of *Millenium Hall*, the attribution is widely discredited today.

36   In a letter to Lady Bradshaigh dated 20 June 1760, Richardson wrote: 'To this hour I know not who was the Writer. It was sent me from a Lady of Quality as a Piece written by a Lady whom she patronized'. The National Art Library, Forster Collection, FM XI, ff. 268–9; Eaves and Kimpel, *Samuel Richardson*, p. 463.

37   It is clear from the Montagu-Richardson correspondence that the novel's author was living with, or at least in close proximity to, Montagu at this time, as she also reads with pleasure Richardson's letters. See, for example, Montagu's letter to Richardson dated 14 January 1760 held by Cornell University Library. We are grateful to Mary Peace for making available her transcript of this letter.

of like-minded women, who devoted themselves to various small- and large-scale philanthropic projects, were two of Lady Barbara's closest friends, Sarah Fielding and Sarah Scott, and they remain the two most likely candidates for the novel's authorship, although it is certainly possible that neither of them wrote it.[38]

Prior to its publication in late 1759, *The Histories* was circulated in manuscript and read by Elizabeth Carter, Elizabeth Montagu and Catherine Talbot. Significantly, all three women connected the novel with Sarah Fielding. In a letter to Carter, Talbot commented, 'it is at least a very good likeness of Mrs Fielding';[39] while Elizabeth Montagu recommended the novel to Carter as a work that she suspected 'to be chiefly written by your friend M[rs] Fielding'.[40] If Fielding had written the novel, it is certainly possible that Lady Barbara, her staunch supporter, would have helped her publish it.[41] However, it is hard to believe that Fielding would have needed an intermediary. A recognized author, she had an independent relationship with Andrew Millar, who published all of her novels except *The Cry* (1754) and *The History of Ophelia* (1760); in November 1758, during his visit to Bath, she sold him *The Countess of Dellwyn* for 60 guineas, and she wrote to Richardson on 14 December, asking him to print it.[42] Fielding and Richardson had been friends and correspondents since the 1740s; he printed her children's novel, *The Governess* (1749), *The Lives of Cleopatra and Octavia* (1757) and *Dellwyn*, which appeared in March 1759, when Richardson and Lady Barbara were corresponding about *The Histories*.[43] Indeed, this timing has lead Fielding's biographer, Linda Bree, to dismiss the attribution, as *The Histories* appeared immediately after *Dellwyn*, and before *Ophelia*, while Fielding was battling ill health and working on her translation of *Xenophon's Memoirs of Socrates* (1762).[44]

With Fielding's authorship in doubt a credible alternative might be found in Sarah Scott. Scott published all of her works anonymously, was notoriously

---

38   For a detailed discussion of the Bath community see Betty Rizzo, *Companions Without Vows: Relationships among Eighteenth-Century British Women* (Athens and London: University of Georgia Press, 1994), pp. 295–319.

39   *A Series of Letters between Mrs Elizabeth Carter and Miss Catherine Talbot, from the Year 1741 to 1770* (2 vols, London: F.C. and J. Rivington, 1808), vol. 1, p. 448.

40   Elizabeth Montagu to Elizabeth Carter, 22 September 1765, The Huntington Library, Montagu Collection, MO3154.

41   At her death in 1765, Lady Barbara left the financially straitened Fielding with an inheritance of £10 per annum. See Elizabeth Montagu to Elizabeth Carter, 22 September 1765, The Huntington Library, Montagu Collection, MO3154.

42   See *The Correspondence of Henry and Sarah Fielding*, ed. Martin C. Battestin and Clive T. Probyn (Oxford: Clarendon Press, 1993), pp. 139–50, especially pp. 144–50.

43   Eaves and Kimpel, *Samuel Richardson*, pp. 202–4, p. 464.

44   Linda Bree, *Sarah Fielding* (New York: Twayne Publishers; London: Prentice Hall International, 1996), p. ix.

secretive about her writing career, and is likely to have written more works than are currently attributed to her.[45] Her richly allusive fiction, like that of Fielding, explores the problems of arranged marriage, female dependence, inadequate education, poverty and male libertinism;[46] moreover, she frequently deploys the frame narrative as a structural device and pedagogic tool. Scott was deeply committed to providing for the poor and distressed, and pursued various philanthropic projects throughout her life, including the establishment of real-life communities, which resembled the female utopia she imagined in *Millenium Hall* (1762). Mary Peace has identified connections between the plot of this, Scott's best-known novel, and *The Histories*; and both Peace and Dorice Williams Elliott have noted *Millenium Hall*'s general indebtedness to the Magdalen House's ethos of rehabilitation, regulation and surveillance.[47]

Further anecdotal evidence can be found in a letter Scott wrote to Elizabeth Montagu in June 1760, only months after *The Histories'* publication; she requests her sister's help in placing a young woman of her acquaintance as a 'kitchen maid or house maid'. Such requests are relatively common in their correspondence, but the situation of this 'repentant sinner' is unique, as her life bears an intriguing resemblance to the story of Emily as it is described in *The Histories*. The young woman was 'bred up in ignorance' only to be 'debauched by her master' when she entered service; poor and pregnant, she received 'advantageous offers from another man', but successfully fended off further threats to her virtue. Despite wishing to help, Scott realized that to offer open support was potentially problematic and rejected the possibility of employing the young woman in her own household on the grounds that her servants might misinterpret this as a sign of 'lenity' to the 'offences' she had committed.[48] Scott may well have determined

45   Scott revealed her authorship of *The History of Gustavus Ericson* (1761) to her father (via Montagu) some two years after its publication, and only once she had learned of his approval of *Millenium Hall*. Sarah Scott to Elizabeth Montagu, April 1763, The Huntington Library, Montagu Collection, MO5301.

46   Joyce Grossman has identified 'stylistic, linguistic, and thematic affinities' between *The Histories* and Fielding's novels *Dellwyn* and *Ophelia*; however, the same could also be said of Scott's work. See Joyce Grossman, '"Sympathetic Visibility", Social Reform and the English Woman Writer: *The Histories of Some of the Penitents in the Magdalen-House*', *Women's Writing*, 7:2 (2000), pp. 247–66.

47   Mary Peace, '"Epicures in Rural Pleasures": Revolution, Desire and Sentimental Economy in Sarah Scott's *Millenium Hall*', *Women's Writing*, 9:2 (2002), pp. 305–16; pp. 312–3; Dorice Williams Elliott, *The Angel out of the House: Philanthropy and Gender in Nineteenth-Century England* (Charlottesville and London: University Press of Virginia, 2002), pp. 37–46.

48   Sarah Scott to Elizabeth Montagu, [20 June] 1760, The Huntington Library, Montagu Collection, MO5281.

not to disclose her authorship of *The Histories* for the same reasons that she refused to directly aid this fallen woman.

At present, it is impossible to solve the attribution conundrum. In time, further information may come to light which might resolve this issue, but even without a known author, the importance of *The Histories* is beyond question. The novel's revision of the harlot's progress marks not only an important historical moment – the founding of the Magdalen House charity – but also a decisive shift in contemporary thinking about women's sexuality and female community, which would continue to influence novels and polemics by women writers for decades to come.

SELECT BIBLIOGRAPHY

Primary Material

[Anon.], *A Congratulatory Epistle from a Reformed Rake, to John F—ng, Esq; Upon a New Scheme of Reclaiming Prostitutes* (London: G. Burnet, [*c.* 1758])

[Anon.], *The Rules, Orders and Regulations, of the Magdalen House, for the Reception of Penitent Prostitutes*, 2nd edn (London: n.p., 1759)

[Anon.], Review of *The Histories of Some of the Penitents in the Magdalen-House, Critical Review,* 8 (November 1759), pp. 373–9

[Anon.], Review of *The Histories of Some of the Penitents in the Magdalen-House,* Monthly *Review,* 21 (1759), pp. 449–50

[Anon.], *Life and Adventures of a Reformed Magdalen. In a Series of Letters to Mrs. B*** of Northampton. Written by Herself* (London: W. Nicoll, 1763)

[Anon.], *Spectacles for Young Ladies; Exhibiting the Various Arts Made Use of for Seducing Young Women … As Related by Themselves* (2 vols, Cork: n.p., 1767)

Dingley, Robert, *Proposals for Establishing a Public Place of Reception for Penitent Prostitutes, &c* (London: W. Faden, 1758)

Dodd, William, *An Account of the Rise, Progress, and Present State of the Magdalen Charity. To which are added, the Rev. Mr. Dodd's Sermon, Preached Before the President, Vice-presidents, and Governors, &c. His Sermon Preached Before his Royal Highness the Duke of York, &c. And the Advice to the Magdalens; with the Hymns, Prayers, Rules, and List of Subscribers.* (London: W. Faden, 1761)

—, *The Magdalen, or History of the First Penitent Received into that Charitable Asylum; in a Series of Letters to a Lady* (London: W. Lane, 1783)

Fielding, Sir John, *A Plan for a Preservatory and Reformatory, for the Benefit of Deserted Girls, and Penitent Prostitutes* (London: R. Francklin, 1758)

Hanway, Jonas, *A Plan for Establishing a Charity-House, or Charity-Houses, for the Reception of Repenting Prostitutes. To be Called the Magdalen Charity* (London: n.p., 1758)

—, *Thoughts on the Plan for a Magdalen-House for Repentant Prostitutes; With the Several Reasons for Such an Establishment* (London: James Waugh, 1758)

—, *Letters Written Occasionally on the Customs of Foreign Nations in Regard to Harlots: The Lawless Commerce of the Sexes: The Repentance of Prostitutes: The Great Humanity and Beneficial Effects of the Magdalen Charity* (London: J. Rivington, J. Dodsley and C. Henderson, 1761)

—, *Reflections, Essays, and Meditations on Life and Religion, With a Collection of Proverbs in Alphabetical Order, and Twenty-Eight Letters,* (2 vols, London: John Rivington; R. and J. Dodsley; and C. Henderson, 1761)

Kelly, Hugh, *Memoirs of a Magdalen; or, the History of Louisa Mildmay,* (2 vols, London: W. Griffin, 1767)

Lardner, Nathaniel, *A Letter to Jonas Hanway, Esq.; in which some Reasons are Assigned, why Houses for the Reception of Penitent Women, who have been disorderly in their Lives, ought not to be Called Magdalen-Houses* (London: J. Noon, 1758)

Madan, Martin, *The Magdalen: or, Dying Penitent, Exemplified in the Death of F. S. Who Died April, 1763, aged twenty-six years* (Dublin: B. Dugdale, 1789)

Massie, Joseph, *A Plan for the Establishment of Charity-Houses for Exposed or Deserted Women and Girls, and for Penitent Prostitutes* (London: T. Payne, 1758)

Walpole, Horace, *Horace Walpole's Correspondence*, ed. W. S. Lewis (48 vols, New Haven: Yale University Press, 1937–83)

Welch, Saunders, *A Proposal to Render Effectual a Plan, to Remove the Nuisance of Common Prostitutes from the Streets of the Metropolis* (London: C. Henderson, 1758)

Secondary Material

Andrew, Donna T., *Philanthropy and Police: London Charity in the Eighteenth Century* (Princeton: Princeton University Press, 1989)

Batchelor, Jennie, *Dress, Distress and Desire: Clothing and the Body in Eighteenth-Century Literature* (Basingstoke: Palgrave Macmillan, 2005)

—, '"Industry in Distress": Reconfiguring Femininity and Labour in the Magdalen House', *Eighteenth-Century Life*, 28: 1 (2004), pp. 1–20

Bree, Linda, *Sarah Fielding* (New York: Twayne Publishers; London: Prentice Hall International, 1996)

Compston, Revd. H. F. B., *The Magdalen Hospital: The Story of a Great London Charity* (London: Society for Promoting Christian Knowledge, 1917)

Eaves, T. C. Duncan, and Ben D. Kimpel, *Samuel Richardson: A Biography* (Oxford: Clarendon Press, 1971)

Elliott, Dorice Williams, *The Angel out of the House: Philanthropy and Gender in Nineteenth-Century England* (Charlottesville and London: University Press of Virginia, 2002)

Ellis, Markman, *The Politics of Sensibility: Race, Gender and Commerce in the Sentimental Novel* (Cambridge: Cambridge University Press, 1996)

Evans, Robin, *The Fabrication of Virtue: English Prison Architecture, 1750–1840* (Cambridge: Cambridge University Press, 1982)

Grossman, Joyce, '"Sympathetic Visibility", Social Reform and the English Woman Writer: *The Histories of Some of the Penitents in the Magdalen-House*', *Women's Writing*, 7:2 (2000), pp. 247–66

Jones, Vivien, 'Placing Jemima: Women Writers of the 1790s and the Eighteenth-Century Prostitution Narrative', *Women's Writing*, 4:2 (1997), pp. 201–20

Keymer, Thomas, 'Sentimental Fiction: Ethics, Social Critique, and Philanthropy', in John Richetti, ed., *The Cambridge History of Restoration and Eighteenth-Century English Literature* (Cambridge: Cambridge University Press, 2005), pp. 572–601

Lloyd, Sarah, 'Pleasure's Golden Bait': Prostitution, Poverty and the Magdalen Hospital in Eighteenth-Century London', *History Workshop Journal*, 41 (1996), pp. 51–72

Nash, Stanley, 'Prostitution and Charity: The Magdalen Hospital, A Case Study', *Journal of Social History*, 17 (1984) pp. 617–628

—, 'Social Attitudes towards Prostitution in London from 1752–1829', Unpublished Doctoral Dissertation (New York University, 1980)

Ogborn, Miles, *Spaces of Modernity: London's Geographies, 1680–1780* (New York: Guildford Press, 1998)

Peace, Mary, '"Epicures in Rural Pleasures": Revolution, Desire and Sentimental Economy in Sarah Scott's *Millenium Hall*', *Women's Writing*, 9:2 (2002), pp. 305–16

—, 'The Figure of the Prostitute in Eighteenth-Century Sentimental Discourse: Charity, Politeness and the Novel', Unpublished Doctoral Dissertation (University of York, 1995)

Pearce, S.B.P, *An Ideal in the Working: The Story of the Magdalen Hospital 1758 to 1958* (London: H.B. Skinner and Co., Ltd, 1958)

Perry, Ruth, *Novel Relations: The Transformation of Kinship in English Literature and Culture, 1748–1818* (Cambridge: Cambridge University Press, 2004)

Sale Jr., William M., *Samuel Richardson: Master Printer* (Ithaca: Cornell University Press, 1950)

Van Sant, Ann Jessie, *Eighteenth-Century Sensibility and the Novel: The Senses in Social Context* (Cambridge: Cambridge University Press, 1993)

NOTE ON THE TEXT

The first, and only, London edition of *The Histories of Some of the Penitents in the Magdalen-House, as Supposed to be related by Themselves*, a print run of 750 copies, appeared in November 1759. It must have sold reasonably well: on 12 December, Samuel Richardson was able to write to Lady Barbara Montagu, the novel's sponsor, that he thought book sales would satisfy his printing bill. The novel was positively reviewed in *The Gentleman's Magazine*, the *Critical Review* and the *Monthly Review* for November 1759.

Two other eighteenth-century editions of the novel were published, both in Ireland: the first, in 1760, by P. Wilson and J. Potts of Dublin; and the second, 'Printed by the Proprietor in Cork', in 1767, the year in which the Dublin Magdalen Asylum was founded. The Dublin edition combined the two-volume London edition into a single book; and the Cork edition adopts precisely the same format. Indeed, except for different printer's ornaments, pagination of the second half of the text – which would have been the second volume in the original – and title pages, it looks to be identical to the Dublin edition.

However, for the Cork edition the title has been transformed, presumably to meet the needs of the local market. It becomes the extremely elaborate *Spectacles for Young Ladies; Exhibiting the various Arts made Use of for seducing* YOUNG WOMEN, *and the dreadful Consequences of straying from the Paths of Innocence and Virtue, in a Stile that cannot offend the chastest Ear; and, at the same Time that it amuses with its surprizing Variety, conveys Instruction by the most effectual Method,* EXAMPLE. *Containing The most remarkable Histories of the Lives and Actions of those* YOUNG WOMEN, *who, conscious of their past Guilt, have dedicated the Remainder of their Time to the Service of* GOD, *and making Atonement, by Repentance, for their past Crimes, by retiring from the World to the* MAGDALEN-HOSPITAL, *London, erected for the Reception of Penitent Prostitutes. As Related by Themselves.* It also has a different epigraph on the title page: instead of the quotation from act III, scene iii of *Hamlet* that graces both the London and Dublin editions, the following lines, slightly misquoted from Thomas Otway's *The Orphan; or The Unhappy Marriage* (1680), appear: 'Trust not a Man; we are by Nature false, / Designing, cruel, subtle and inconstant: /

If a Man talks of Love, with Caution hear him; / But, if he swears, he'll certainly deceive ye' (II.i.286–9).

For this volume we have used the Chawton House Library copy of the London edition, intervening in the text as little as possible. We have retained the original spelling, punctuation, capitalization and formatting, with the following exceptions: changing the long *s* to the roman *s*; eliminating running quotation marks; and silently correcting obvious typographical errors. This includes incorporating the alterations suggested by Richardson in the list of errata appended to the last page of the second volume. We have also decided to retain the abbreviations of author's names after chapter epigraphs, as well as the misattributions, to maintain their similarity to their probable source, Edward Bysshe's *Art of English Poetry*, the eighth edition (1737), which contains all of the epigraphs except those for I.iv, I.vii and II.ii.

THE HISTORIES

Of Some of the

PENITENTS

IN THE

MAGDALEN-HOUSE,

AS

Supposed to be related by Themselves.

In **TWO VOLUMES**

In the corrupted Currents of this World,
Offence's gilded Hand may shove by Justice:
And oft 'tis seen, the wicked Prize itself
Buys out the Law: But 'tis not so Above;
THERE is no shuffling; THERE the Action lies
In his true Nature; and we ourselves compell'd,
Ev'n to the Teeth and Forehead of our Faults,
To give in Evidence. What then? What rests?
Try what REPENTANCE can: What can it not?

SHAKESP.

VOL. I.

LONDON:
Printed for JOHN RIVINGTON in *St. Paul's Church-yard*, and J. DODSLEY in *Pall-mall*.

M.DCC.LX.

PREFACE.

SOME apology may be judged necessary for a work which assumes real characters, tho' in the title-page it acknowleges itself to be a fiction.[1]

I have not indeed made free with the names of any of the Penitents; for tho'
some may imagine, that little ceremony is requisite towards persons who have
broke thro' all the forms of decency, and decorums of virtue, yet I cannot apprehend that *that* gives me a title to endeavour to bring those again on the stage of
the world, who have, for so good a reason, retired from it: But I may perhaps be
thought by others to have gone too far in making my imaginary persons assume
their characters; and if I can find any excuse for myself, it must be in the *motives*
which induced me to do so.

My first aim in the following work was to plead the cause of the Penitents
in the Magdalen-House, who by many are represented as persons too intirely
abandoned to guilt and infamy, to deserve relief, to which surely distress alone
is a sufficient title. Judgment is not intrusted with us: 'Every man must stand or
fall to his own master.'[2] Shall We be more rigid than HE who knoweth the heart,
and hath a right to our obedience? 'He maketh his sun to shine on the just and
on the unjust.'[3] Virtue alone can merit our esteem; but misery deserves our pity,
and indigence may claim our bounty.

Tho' the profession of a prostitute is the most despicable and hateful that
imagination can form; yet the individuals are frequently worthy objects of compassion; and I am willing to believe, that if people did but reflect on the various
stratagems used at first to corrupt them, while poverty often, and still oftener
vanity, is on the side of the corruptor, they would smooth the stern brow of rigid
virtue, and turn the contemptuous frown into tears of pity.

Tho' I do not pretend the following stories to be real facts, yet I think every
one will see so plainly, that the incidents are not only probable, but such as must
frequently have happened, as may lead them to acknowlege, that the first step
into that way of life oftener proceeds from weakness than from vice; and that if
the beginning of their misfortunes, or rather their crimes, have been owing to
a want of steadiness in themselves in the practice of virtue, many of their sub-

sequent vices have arisen from the affectation of too overstrained a chastity in others, who, unlike their Maker, ever ready to accept the repentant sinner, and to heal the contrite heart, exclude them from the means of reformation, by hunting them out of every way of obtaining an honest subsistence, till the only alternative left them, is, either to owe their support to a continuance in vicious courses, or to die martyrs to chastity: A martyrdom, which, I fear, many of their severest censurers would find difficult; and yet, surely, to none can it be so hard, as to those whose consciences are burdened with a heavy crime; for 'the sting of death is sin.'[4] Therefore, to them it must appear with accumulated horrors; and despair will drive them into an increase of guilt, to avoid so early an appearance before the Judgment-Seat, from whence is no appeal.

Example affects more than precept; the latter piques our pride, the former interests our passions on its side. This known truth suggested to me the form of the following work; and if, by relating a series of probable events, I shall incline any woman so effectually to pity the frailty of one of her own sex, as to forgive the past, and enable the offender to efface her guilt[5] by sincere repentance and a blameless life; if, I say, I can do this, I shall esteem myself extremely happy; nor shall I repine at the time I have bestowed on the following sheets, if I can only so far soften the obdurately virtuous, as to induce them to forbear the cruel endeavour of casting an odium on an institution which does so much honour to the present age; which will reflect never-fading glory on those who instituted it; and which will purchase for them rewards, that shall exist when time shall be no more.

That there can be no objects so miserable, consequently so deserving of compassion, as those for whose relief this institution is designed, is surely past dispute. I confess it is beyond the reach of my imagination to conceive a state of such absolute wretchedness as that of the prostitute. In most conditions, from the vicissitude of all worldly events, as prosperity is checquered with some painful hours, and for a time obscured by unavoidable afflictions, so wretchedness is interrupted by casual blessings, and its gloom enlivened by some gleams of joy. But the prostitute's life is divided between surfeiting riot, penury, disease, and infamy; continual transitions from one extreme to another, each almost equally distant from real happiness; surrounded with a variety of distresses here, and on the brink of eternal misery hereafter; their lives are a continual progression from one crime to another, and their deaths, in every circumstance, too horrible to relate.

Yet many appear unwilling to draw them out of this state of wretchedness; they shrink with horror at the mention of people so criminal, and hate them for the vices which should inspire us with a most ardent desire for their reformation. Were they less wicked, they would be less fit objects of compassion, and less require amendment.

A Being infinitely pure and perfect, was moved to pity by the sins of his creatures: Shall We then, whose offences are numberless, refuse our pardon and assistance to those, who may not more properly be termed fellow-creatures, than fellow-sinners, because their offences are of a deeper dye than our own? especially as the different degrees in which we rank our guilt and theirs may possibly proceed from self partiality: For if we take into our account their superior temptations, and inferior advantages towards the repressing them, the balance may not, to an All-seeing eye, appear in our favour. But if we are conscious of a real superiority in merit, let us be thankful to Him who gave it us, and by whom we have been preserved in that path wherein He first inclined us to walk; and while we lend our help to our stumbling fellow-creatures, let us petition Him who can turn the human heart, and change the will, to vouchsafe to guide them, during the remainder of their lives, in the road that leads to present peace, and future bliss. Let us not, by mean exultation, lose the benefit of our superior happiness; but rather increase our own, by imparting a portion of it to them; and not endanger our souls by pride, after having preserved them from sensuality.

The frivolous objections raised against the institution itself, have not given me much less concern. I have always been inclined to indulge an opinion, not peculiar to myself, that every one esteems virtue, tho' temptations may lead them to neglect the practice of it; and that both from the secret suggestions of conscience, and the desire of being thought to approve what is highly praise-worthy, no one would deny to merit its just tribute of praise: But the institution of the Magdalen-House has taught me, that this debt is often paid with an unwilling mind, and with-held as long as a possibility of cavilling at it remains.

Those who dare not boldly refuse their approbation to benevolence, with timid treachery endeavour to conceal their want of it, under objections, which, tho' void of force, since they are contrary to truth, still afford a lurking-place where malevolence hopes to hide itself, while it hangs forth the colours of prudence and sagacity, and sometimes assumes the name of rigid virtue. These pretend to fear, that this institution will prove an encouragement to vice, by offering the vicious an asylum: But this scarcely deserves an answer, being sufficiently confuted by this only consideration; that to be one of its inhabitants is certainly less eligible to a woman, who does not want to hide her head from shame, than the commonest service; and that to a person still viciously, or even gaily inclined, it would be the most dismal prison.

Others urge the improbability of a reformation. To amend the human heart, in opposition to its own inclinations, is indeed a difficult task; but whoever applies to this House, must, as far as their desire goes, and that is almost the whole way, be reformed already. If they are not led there by remorse, and some remains of unextinguished virtue, they are at least driven by a desire to seek shelter from the hatefulness of vice, or the horrors of its attendant miseries. Either motive is sufficient to reform the life, while secluded from temptation, and secured from distress and insult; and tho' they are brought thither, not by sorrow for their sins, but for the consequences of them; yet, when every distraction from reflexion, and every impediment to conviction, is removed, the whisperings of conscience will be heard; and she, whose design extended no farther than the reformation of her conduct, will find her heart amended, and, from a decent behaviour, will proceed to purity of mind.

An earnest desire after a thorough change of life can only induce persons to ask for admission into a place where every hour is spent in the utmost contrariety to their former practices. I need not urge, that the charms of decency, the sober satisfaction arising from regularity of conduct, and the delights of virtue, must win upon the heart, since their inclinations appear already fixed; and it is highly improbable that they should decline in a place where every thing is calculated for their increase.

I have met with some who ridicule the Magdalen-House as a fruitless undertaking, on a supposition that it is intended as a prevention of the vice to which it owes its inhabitants; and indeed, if, contrary to all reason, they imagine this to be the design of the institution, they may well apprehend it will prove useless.

I fear that is a vice which can never be suppressed, while he, who seduces a woman into guilt and shame, and abandons her to disease and poverty, obtains no other appellation by such villainy, than that of a man of gallantry; while he may be called a man of honour, tho' he breaks thro' ties of truth, faith, and humanity, in the destruction of one, whose greatest weakness was believing him incapable of the vileness to which she falls a sacrifice; too late perceiving, that the only charm he found in innocence, was the means it gave him to effect its ruin, by its unsuspicious credulity.

If the man who lives in the open profession of a sin, which is one of the most pernicious to society, and the most destructive to his own soul; for we are assured upon divine authority, that 'no such shall enter into the kingdom of heaven;'[6] if such a man shall be caressed by his own sex, whose rights he is ever ready to invade, and admired by the other, whose temporal and eternal destruction are his constant aim; can we wonder that he goes on, in uninterrupted schemes, to add to the measure of his iniquity; and to increase the number of wretches, whose souls and bodies are to be sacrificed to his dissolute principles, or meaner vanity?

The laws reach only part of the crimes which disturb society; public censure and discountenance is a punishment in which every one may be judge and executioner; and were they properly inflicted, would prove most powerful towards effecting a general reformation; but while we spend all our censure on folly, which should only excite our compassion, and suffer vice, the proper object of hatred and contempt, to escape with impunity, if it has rank and fortune to support it, we cannot hope to see the successfully wicked reclaimed. All that the best man can do, is, as far as possible, to repair the ravages *others* commit; and to endeavour to bring back to peace those souls whom *they* have involved in all the depths of misery.

This is the noble design of the institutors of the Magdalen-House: 'They have been eyes to the blind, and feet to the lame;'[7] for they have dissipated the worst of blindness, that of the mind; they have let in upon it the light of truth; and led the wavering wandering steps into the paths of peace and virtue. 'They have delivered the poor that cried, and those who had none to help them; the cause that they knew not, they have searched out. When the ear heareth them, it shall bless them; and when the eye seeth them, it shall witness to them.'[8] To whom can it more properly be said at the great and tremendous day of judgment, 'I was an hungred, and ye gave me meat; I was thirsty, and ye gave me drink; I was a stranger, and ye took me in; naked, and ye cloathed me; I was sick, and ye visited me:'[9] For inasmuch as these acts of humanity are done to the meanest of his creatures, we are assured our merciful Creator will accept them as done to Himself.

No person will dispute the use of Hospitals which are instituted for the relief of corporal distempers; but of much higher benefit is that intended to heal the soul; and not only to abate temporary pains, but to save from eternal torments.[10]

Amongst the greatest nation the world ever saw, the preservation of the life of a citizen was judged an action deserving public honour, and a crown was placed on the head of him who had thus merited the thanks of the republic. How much greater reward might these gentlemen justly claim; for they at once preserve great numbers from a pernicious life, and an untimely death, and, by restoring them to industry and order, render them useful members of society?[11]

With disinterested joy I behold their great desert, while I can only, at an humble distance, pray for their success, and please myself with hopes, that they will receive such contributions, as shall enable them to extend their charity to all who shall desire to partake of the benefits it offers.

And now, gentle reader; for gentle I must wish you to be, that from your good nature I may hope for a favourable reception of the following imperfect sheets; after I have declared that my design has been to write in defence of Penitents, give me leave to say, that I shall esteem myself peculiarly happy, if I can have any share in preventing one person from standing in need of penitence. To instruct, as well as to amuse, should be the highest ambition of the species of writers, among whom, by this attempt, I have ranked myself.

Many have given directions to the world how to read history; nor have the other branches of learning been left without rules for the method of turning them to greater advantage. If I may be permitted to be so methodical, upon that species of writing which seems generally to owe its rise to the wild wanderings of the wildest of things, the imagination; I will venture to give directions for reading of Novels.

Every fable has its moral. If Æsop could make birds and beasts teach by their actions,[12] can we suppose those of mankind are not equally intelligible and instructive? Though the facts be imaginary, the consequences drawn from them may be real; not only every story, but every incident, should have its moral; and that so obvious, that an observing mind shall readily perceive it.

The method therefore that I would recommend to those who apply themselves to this sort of reading, is, to attend to the Moral as much as to the Story. If in history our thoughts reach no farther than the facts, or in books of reasoning we stop at the first principles, not attending to the consequences arising from the one, nor the arguments deducible from the other, the mind will only resemble an index: It may prove of some use to those whose reflexions are less circumscribed, but can never contain any knowlege in itself. To such a reader, Livy or Tacitus[13] can give no greater improvement than the Seven champions of Christendom,[14] or the wonderful adventures of Guy Earl of Warwick:[15] The degree of probability in facts, is of no importance to those, whose thoughts never extend to the causes or the consequences.[16]

Novels should be wrote and read as books which are to teach by illustrating the moral by the facts, where precept is enlivened by examples, and imagination brought in to strengthen reason, not to confound it. If the writer loses sight of this design, still the reader may, if he pleases, keep it always in view; tho' such novels as require much effort in the mind to discover a good moral in them are certainly very pernicious; for works of imagination are fit only for the entertainment of an idle hour; when we should do by the reader, as indulgent parents act by their children, teach them in play, and blend instruction so closely with amusement, that the design shall be scarcely perceivable to the mind in that childish state of inactivity.

In defence of the following work I must observe, that I do not, under the term Amusement, include only that gaiety which plays on the imagination; for what interests the passions amuses the mind, however melancholy the subjects; and we are not less entertained at a tragedy, than at the more lively productions of the comic muse.

As these sort of books are most likely to fall into the hands of persons to whom fashionable dissipations leave little leisure for the perusal of any thing more serious, it is not blameable to wish, tho' it may be presumptuous to hope, that any thing They shall find in this performance may warn them against giving way to the emotions of vanity;[17] indulging the first step of indiscretion; or suffering their good principles to be erased by the dissolute or careless practices of others: But should it prove so fortunate, the author will, from a trifling labour, receive a satisfaction, which would not be dearly purchased by the application of a whole life.

THE
HISTORIES
Of Some of the
PENITENTS
IN THE
MAGDALEN-HOUSE

CHAP. I.

Let my tears thank you; for I cannot speak:
And if I could,—
Words were not made to vent such thoughts as mine.
DRYDEN.[18]

THE pleasure every one finds in talking of themselves, may serve to convince us, that so many persons as seek refuge in the Magdalen-House from guilt and infamy, cannot forbear giving some account to each other of their past actions, especially as they will contain much variety and adventure. That they must thereby call to remembrance all their distresses, is no reason against it; for we daily see people more inclined to dwell on the relation of their misfortunes, than on the happier events of their lives. Whether it proceeds from the satisfaction they receive in reflecting that the storm is over, or from the desire of being pitied, which seems implanted in our natures, He only, who knows all the springs of the human mind, can tell. That these penitents must by this means publish their own infamy, is as small an impediment; for that is sufficiently known by their being there; and their hearers have none of that obdurate virtue, which makes people not know how to pity weaknesses they never felt: All are in much the same state, tho' brought to it by different steps.

We have had examples of females, whose frailty has not been accompanied with half the extenuating circumstances that these persons can allege, yet have blazoned forth their crimes to a world, part of which, innocent of the like, must blame; and still a greater part, who having been more private, tho' not more virtuous, will certainly censure loudly, when they see

> — *Each fair advance,*
> *The luscious heroine of her own romance.*[19]

But in the society which I am speaking of, the case is different; Each looks on the other with an eye of pity: Equal distress, and equal relief, begets a sort of mutual affection; while their hearts overflow with gratitude to their noble benefactors, (noble, if not by blood or descent, intrinsically so from the generous benevolence of their worthy hearts) they rejoice not only in their own deliverance, but in that of all they behold; and, sufficiently humbled by former misery, they relate with compunction, from hearts overcharged with the remembrance of past wretchedness, and the comforts of present ease; not with vanity, like those I have mentioned, who exult more in their number of conquests, than blush at having themselves been so often conquered; and are more vain of their beauty, than ashamed of their vice.

When but a small number had flown for refuge to this blessed asylum, they were one evening sitting together, after the work of the day was past,[20] when one of them turning towards the youngest in company, who had long sat silent, observed that tears trickled gently down her cheeks. This young woman was not twenty years old; her person was extremely elegant, her hands and arms finely turned, her neck white as alabaster, and exquisitely formed. Her face expressed all the humble modesty of a Madona, with a countenance languishingly sweet. The young woman who observed her, asked, what sorrow could reach her in that comfortable retreat? 'for here,' continued she, 'what can we grieve for, except it be our sins? and such grief is accompanied with consolation, as it brings with it a hope of pardon, and a satisfaction in thinking we are come to a necessary sense of our own guilt, the first step to repentance.'

'You mistake the cause of my emotions,' replied the young woman: 'Mine were not tears of sorrow, but of joy and gratitude. When I beheld with what content, and innocence, that necessary ingredient to content, we sat here surrounded with all the comforts of this life, and all the assistances requisite to bring us to the blessings of the next, and compared it with the wretchedness from whence I was redeemed by it; my heart overflowed with gratitude to our excellent benefactors, who, like our blessed Lord, come as physicians to the sick, and call sinners, not the righteous, to repentance; who offer rest and refreshment to all those that are heavy laden with their miseries. From these worthy instruments of divine mercy, my grateful thoughts rose to Him who is the Author of all goodness, and consequently inspired them with this charitable intention; till, oppressed with my own sensations, they found some vent in tears, and wore the appearance of sorrow.'

'The liveliness of your gratitude,' replied the other, 'reproaches me for want of sensibility, who ought to feel so much more, and yet appear less affected. But my heart is for ever full, and how should it be otherwise? for I have suffered some years more of wretchedness than you can have done, who I imagine have scarcely seen your twentieth year.'

'You are right as to my age,' answered the young woman, 'but I am old in misery. Were I to measure my years by the pangs I have felt, my life would appear of an antediluvian length.'

'Your misfortunes must have begun early indeed,' said a third, 'and seem peculiarly affecting; they excite the curiosity of those who have enough to employ their thoughts at home, without concerning themselves about others; for idleness of mind is generally the parent of curiosity; but for all this, I confess myself curious.'

Many others expressing the same curiosity, the young woman told them she would not refuse to gratify them: If any thing she could say would withdraw their thoughts from themselves, it might be some relief, as we seldom feel other people's misfortunes so severely as our own.

Accordingly she proceeded, as the next chapter will shew.

CHAP. II.

How happy is the harmless country maid!
Who, rich by nature, scorns superfluous aid:
Whose modest cloaths no wanton eyes invite,
But, like her soul, preserve the native white:
Whose little store her well-taught mind does please;
Not pinch'd with want, nor clogg'd with wanton ease:
Who, free from storms, which on the great ones fall,
Makes but few wishes, and enjoys them all.

Roscommon.[21]

MY father was a clergyman in the West of England. He served two curacies and one living; all which together did not bring him in 100*l.* per annum; [22] but entirely engrossed his time, as he endeavoured to do his duty in each parish, to the utmost of his power, and obliged him to be at the expence of keeping a horse. This, with the continual repairs necessary to his parsonage house, which was much decayed, and the ill state of health wherewith my mother was afflicted for many years, made his income but barely sufficient for himself and his family, tho' it was not large; for of many children my mother bore him, one elder sister and myself only lived to grow up.

When I was near fourteen years old, my mother died, which occasioned my sister's return home. She had spent three years with an aunt, who was a milaner in a large town in that county; but, by the loss of my mother, became necessary to take care of my father's family, whose health declined so fast, that nursing him was her chief employ.

In a little more than a year, we lost my father; a great misfortune to us both, but particularly to me, who was thus left to my own guidance and support, when I was but fifteen. My appearance indeed was womanly; I had been bred up in religious principles, but at that age they could not be deeply grounded, nor so fixed as to stand against the temptations of the world, into which I was now thrown.

My father's effects, when sold and all accounts settled, yielded us but a few pounds. My aunt was dead, and we had no near relation who could assist us; but a Lady in the neighbourhood, who had always professed a great regard to my father, called upon us, when the first agonies of our grief were so far over, as to enable us to perceive the forlornness of our situation.

My sister applied to this Lady for her protection for me, for whom she was most uneasy; being, as she said, able to provide for her own support; but my youth and person, which perhaps she beheld with partial eyes, filled her with apprehensions for me.

The Lady assured us she would do her utmost to serve me; that if she had no sons, or I was less handsome, she would receive me into her house; but that was now impossible: however, she would enquire among all her friends, if she could find any thing proper for me, and hoped to succeed before we were obliged to quit the house.

This Lady was as good as her word; and not being so much afraid for other people's sons as for her own, she prevailed with a Lady of her acquaintance, who lived in the next county, to receive me as her woman. She had suffered me to assist in the dressing of her daughters several times, that I might be qualified for my place; and at the time appointed, gave me a letter of recommendation, to secure me still a better reception.

To take leave of my sister, was like losing my only parent; for such she was to me, tho' not above five years older than myself: I think I could not have felt much deeper affliction for her death, our separation appearing to us not much less grievous. I was frighted at the thought of going amongst entire strangers, and into a new employ; and my sister's apprehensions were such as were but too well verified in the sequel. She spent the last day we were together in warning me against the temptations which would perhaps fall in my way; of which I remember the following words were part, for they made a strong impression, tho' to little purpose; and the misfortunes into which I fell from disregarding them, fixed them stronger in my mind.

'My dear Emily,' said she, 'I cannot fear for your honesty, or sincerity, tho' I have said so much on those subjects. Your nature is superior to any offences of this kind; but my apprehensions are numerous in another respect. I would not attempt to tell you, you are not handsome; our own eyes in such particulars give us sufficient evidence, and we seldom doubt their truth; besides, the less persuaded you are of this, the more you will be pleased with those who tell it you, which all will be ready to do. Such a person as yours, in your situation, will attract many admirers; for while the one charms, the other will excite hopes; which I would flatter myself will be disappointed; but I confess my apprehensions arise as much from the tenderness of your heart, as from the snares that will be laid in your way. If that does not betray you, all the rest may be easily baffled: but what can I say that will steel your heart with indifference! Alas! it is above my power: He only who made it can correct it. To him, my dearest Emily, you must apply; and bear constantly in mind, that your present and eternal happiness depend on the proper regulation of your affections.'

Advice to this purpose she repeated the whole day, with many tears, and anxious prayers for my preservation.

The next morning parted us, never to meet again with so much satisfaction, melancholy as that last interview appeared to us.

One day's journey brought me to the house of Lady Markland, my new mistress. I was immediately introduced into the parlour, where she then was sitting with Sir George Markland her husband, their son Mr. Markland, a young gentleman of about twenty-five years old, and another Lady and Gentleman who were then with them on a visit. My confusion was so great, I was scarcely able to answer the questions she put to me, or even to deliver the letter with which I was charged.

While her Ladyship was perusing the epistle, my distress increased; for the rest of the company fixed their eyes so entirely upon me, that I could find no place for my own, and began to think the questions which had before distressed me, were a great relief, in having taken my attention. I have reason to believe the Lady took compassion on me; for she called me to her, asked me how I had performed my journey, and such sort of questions as seemed to have no other intention but to encourage me; then, turning to Lady Markland, said, 'I perceive, Madam, you are not of a jealous disposition.'

'No indeed,' replied her Ladyship, 'but if I was, it would be no reason why I should be plagued with an ugly face about me; for Sir George must see handsome ones abroad, if I suffered none but Hottentots[23] at home.'

This short dialogue increased my confusion; and no words ever sounded more acceptable than the orders Lady Markland gave to the servant who introduced me, to shew me to her house-keeper.

This house-keeper was one who had lived a great many years in the family, and, as I afterwards found, was held in great estimation. She understood all the necessary parts of a house-keeper's office, and none better than flattery; which, perhaps, gave a great charm to her other qualifications, for she was not without defects. Tho' she was an useful director in the kitchen, and an assiduous watch over the other servants, yet her first attachment was to her own interest, of which she was never neglectful. She was no bigot to truth; and in her Lady's absence, made herself amends for the flattery she thought proper to bestow on her before her face; falling as much short of what she deserved at one time, as she went beyond it at another. Nor did she excel more in chastity than in other virtues; for she had for some years been suspected of an intrigue with Sir George's valet-de-chambre; but being both thought excellent servants, it was winked at, tho' all the family were certain that it was well known to their master and lady. Indeed, being often present when they conversed freely, I found they made a jest of it, not from disbelief, but from thinking it of no consequence.

This greatly shocked me at first; and the familiarities between these two lovers, who were my only companions at meals and on evenings, were very distressing; however, as they gave me reason to think my absence would not be disagreeable, I sat with them as little as I could.

CHAP. III.

DRYDEN.[24]

MY Lady was very good-natured and indulgent to all her servants, and to me among the rest; tho' I had no hopes of becoming a favourite, when I saw, by her house-keeper's practice, how much she loved flattery. She would often say, when I omitted an opportunity of imitating her, that I was dull; and sometimes, that she fancied I could think nothing commendable in any one but myself; but all this without any bitterness.

I seldom saw Sir George, but in his Lady's presence; he would often talk to me and compliment me, called me Lady Markland's Venus; and when I entered the room, would cry, Here comes your goddess, my dear; but all with so much mirth, and so little design, that in time I learnt not to mind it, and answered to the name of Venus, as readily as to that of Emily.

Mr. Markland was much less free, but more attentive; he treated me with such respect, that his mother would sometimes tell him, she believed he thought I was a goddess in reality. He would answer, that a fine woman was a better thing; that no situation in life should make a man fail in politeness to one of the other sex; and that really there was a modesty in my appearance, which was truly respectable. These sort of compliments he would make me before his parents; and often gave the conversation such a turn, as afforded him opportunities of applying others to me by his eyes, which were unobserved by every one else. He found excuses to come into the house-keeper's room, where he would rally her and her lover on their mutual passion, taking occasion from it to vent some libertine sentiments, wherein they were sure to second him; and sometimes to behave with a tenderness and gallantry to me, which I ought with shame to say, rather alarmed than offended me; so little was I the better for my sister's good advice.

I wrote her an account of all the family into which I had entered; but at first, for fear of increasing her apprehensions, and afterwards from the conscious weakness of my own heart, did not tell her how very amiable Mr. Markland was, both in person and manner; in both of which he has seldom been equalled; nor of his addresses to me. But I communicated to her one circumstance, which sur-prized me; That were it not that they sometimes attended the parish church on Sundays, I should not know whether the family I lived in was Jew, Mahometan, or Christian; for there was never any sign of worship among them. I never heard the name of a Superior Being uttered, but as a word of course, or by way of strengthening an assertion. While the Gentleman and Lady I have mentioned remained there, cards employed the Sundays as regularly as the other days; and when they failed to do so after their departure, it was for want of a party.

I was much surprized at a manner of life, which I thought could be found only amongst the reprobate; whereas Sir George and my Lady appeared uni-versally respected; she behaved with good humour to her servants, and he with humanity to his tenants; that is, he did not require more of them than they could possibly pay, and chose rather to turn them out of their farms, than support them in gaol. In short, they committed no vices, and had constitutional good-nature; their characters might be well drawn by negatives; but as for positive virtues, they thought them unnecessary; they would declare they never did any harm, and did all the good they could: A strong assertion, and difficult to be made good by the best people: For as every action is an example to somebody, and has numerous consequences, many that the actor esteems innocent, will prove pernicious. Thus Sir George and my Lady, by winking at the intrigues of their servants, and speaking lightly of religion and virtue, banished both from their family, and became not only answerable for their own faults, but for those which their examples encouraged in their domestics.

My sister was as much vexed with the account I sent her of the family, as I was surprized at what I related. She wrote me word she wished me in a worse place, if I had but a better example. She had been taken into a milaner's shop in the town, where her aunt had lived, and where her conduct had recommended her.

I had not been above a month at Sir George's, before Mr. Markland began to make real love to me; he took every opportunity of finding me alone, which my practice of avoiding the house-keeper's room rendered more easy. I was sensible of a new-born partiality for this gentleman; and not having forgot what my sister had said to me, resolved to endure more of the house-keeper's company, that I might be less alone. This did not make much alteration; for Mr. Markland was too quick-sighted not to know that interest had its due weight with the house-keeper. He began therefore by making her presents, which his behaviour to me explained the reason of; and she, willing to deserve his bounty, multiplied oppor-tunities for his coming into her room, and was continually in his absence telling me of his passion for me, of my good fortune, and how much it might turn out to my advantage, without my understanding in what manner she meant. I could comprehend no other method of being benefitted by his love, than marriage; every thing else to me appeared attended with guilt and ruin.

I was now much at a loss how to avoid Mr. Markland; and what was worse, my heart was ready to furnish me with excuses for not doing it. My religious principles grew weaker every day; piety was treated as enthusiasm, strictness of manners as folly; for 'our Maker was merciful, and designed to make us happy; which we could be only by following our pleasures: that our tastes and passions were given us as benefits, that we might receive happiness from gratifying them.'

My Lady having found me several times reading in a religious book, at last snatched it out of my hand; and throwing it down, said, 'The girl would turn her head: She never knew a puritanical servant, who did not turn out a whore or a thief; and that she wanted not to have her jewels stolen, to feed methodist parsons; or her cloaths pawned, to furnish out their weekly contributions.'[25] As I had never seen her so angry, I began to think there must be some crime in religion, which I did not know, to make it appear so offensive.

The house-keeper one day caught me at prayers. This was told in the house-keeper's room, as a most ridiculous circumstance. Much laughter ensued. She asked me, if I was praying for a husband. Mr. Markland called me his fair saint; told me, I mistook the matter; for I was made not to pray, but to be prayed to.

To find religion both the object of serious censure and of ridicule, made me think there was something very uncommon in it; and that in having it, I was certainly guilty of a great peculiarity. My religion was rather founded on habit than reason. I had been told *what* I should do; but my father's continual occupation abroad had prevented his teaching me *why* I was to do so. Thus I was unprovided with reasons for my practice; and Mr. Markland, whose understanding furnished him almost at one view with all that could be said on every subject, was diligent in removing what he called the prejudices of education.

Every frailty that had been committed by any person who professed some regard for religion, if it had come to their knowlege, was repeated by them with triumph: But I was not weak enough to think this availed them much; for I had never been taught to believe that any common degree of piety would always conquer natural disposition, or be a certain defence against the temptations of the world; nor that the most religious were infallible. While they were mortal, they must be frail; and none pay so great a compliment to religion, as those who imagine every one who professes it must or should be a saint: But often wide is the profession from the practice!

In this manner we went on for near half a year that we continued in the country. Mr. Markland grew more assiduous and more open in his courtship, and I listened to it every day with more pleasure, and fewer fears. Nor did my companions suffer his cause to lose in his absence; they continually contrived to leave us alone together; when he would lavish all the vows and oaths that ever lover broke,[26] with such tender importunity, that I sometimes wondered how, with a heart so filled with frailty, I had resisted. But principle still got the better of my passion, tho' it was risen to the utmost excess of tenderness.

Mr. Markland was too well acquainted with the human passions, and I too little with the arts of concealment, for him to remain ignorant of the state of my heart: And had he not perceived it, his faithful assistants would have informed him of it; for they would in their discourse wind me in such a manner, that sometimes my blushes, and often my tears, explained it more fully than words could have done. On the knowlege of my weakness, Mr. Markland built his hopes of success. He often wondered at my resistance, but for ever expected it to fail. I sometimes had nothing but tears to answer to his tenderest professions. I wept for shame at listening to them, and for grief at thinking it necessary to reject them.

CHAP. IV.

Where more is meant than meets the ear.
MILTON.[27]

WHEN we were in London, Mr. Markland had still more opportunities of seeing me. Sir George and my Lady were always abroad, or engaged in company. They seldom enquired after their son, thinking it the duty of polite parents to suffer him to take his own way; or if they happened to ask any questions, the servants knew what to answer. Thus almost all his time was passed with me. While I was busy in attending my Lady at her toilette, he made his necessary visits, that the rest of the day might be his own.

I confess I was not always desirous of avoiding him; but if I had, I could not easily have contrived it, for every servant was bought to his interest. I desired the house-maid, who had leisure in the afternoons, to come and work with me, thinking thereby either to prevent his coming, or at least to put some restraint on his addresses. But he no sooner entered, than she retired; and I found, upon questioning her, that every servant had felt his bounty, either to procure their secrecy, or assistance.

Sensible of my own weakness, and how far every one was combined for my destruction, I had still virtue enough left to wish that I could find some refuge against myself; but could see none, unless I could obtain it of my Lady. Filled with this thought, I determined to apply to her for advice and assistance, acknowledgeing my own excess of passion, and giving her as little reason as possible to be angry with her son.

I waited with impatience for a summons to attend my Lady at her toilette, and took no small pains to keep up my resolution; which perhaps I had never been able to form, had not Mr. Markland been obliged that morning to go abroad with his father.

The time at length came; but, to my great disappointment, I was followed in by a country neighbour of her Ladyship's, who immediately desired to speak with her alone.

I was accordingly dismissed, and not recalled till the arrival of more company; upon whose appearance the first Lady took her leave. My purpose was equally disappointed; four visitors had taken the place of one.

One of the Ladies observed, that she who was gone away, looked very melancholy. 'Had you been mistress to the king, or his prime minister,' added she, 'I should have thought you had just refused a petition.'

'The most ridiculous woman,' said my Lady, 'surely, that ever was born! What do you think is the subject of her affliction?' Here her Ladyship laughed so violently, that she could not immediately answer their enquiry; tho' they all expressed great curiosity to know what it was.

'Would you believe,' continued Lady Markland, 'that all the excess of grief you see painted on the poor woman's countenance, proceeds from having discovered that her son, a young man of about three-and-twenty, keeps a mistress; and she came to communicate her sorrows to me, hoping that from my friendship she should receive some compassion?' Here they all joined in such peals of laughter, as Comus's crew[28] can scarcely equal.

'And pray,' asked one of the Ladies, 'what consolation did your Ladyship give her?' 'Consolation!' replied my Lady; 'I asked the woman, if she expected her son to be a Joseph?[29] That no man of spirit was without intrigues: It was a male privilege.'

Is this the person, said I to myself, to whom I meant to apply for refuge against her son's gallantry, and my own passion!

'A male privilege, indeed!' answered one of the Ladies. 'We may see the men not only made laws, but customs. They have carved themselves out pretty lives. They the primrose path of dalliance tread, while they would confine us to the thorny way.'[30]

'Do not be so severe upon them,' said another. 'You forget, that if none of our sex were in the path, it would not appear so flowery: They cannot exclude us.'

'That,' interrupted my Lady, 'is an advantage to women of an inferior rank; but people of fashion cannot well make use of it. If Spencer's Sir Calidore[31] had but been a real character, and the blatant beast, Slander, in fact killed, the case might have been different.'

'If it is not killed,' interrupted another Lady, 'it has barked so long, that nobody regards it; for really women are now under almost as few restraints as the men. But, pray, what is the woman this *unfortunate* Lady's son has pitched upon? Perhaps somebody very expensive; and that may have its inconveniencies.'

'No,' replied Lady Markland; 'the young man has been humble enough; he has contented himself with one of *Mamma*'s maids.'

Here again the Ladies were highly entertained: But one of them observed, that 'she thought the lowness of his taste might be mortifying to an affectionate parent: There was a want of spirit and proper pride in it.'

In this manner the conversation was kept up, till two gentlemen arrived. My office being ended, I withdrew.

I heard with surprize so many women of character, who were so much my superiors in age and experience, and consequently I thought in wisdom, treat that as a privilege, which I had looked upon as the greatest misfortune that could befal me; and against which I wanted a defence, that I might better rely upon than my own resolution. What Mr. Markland had said to me on that subject, had less power over my judgment, than my affection gave him over my heart. His arguments came from a suspected quarter; his interest was visible, and therefore they had less weight; but when Ladies, who had no such inducements, confirmed his doctrine, how could I avoid suspecting myself of those ill-grounded prejudices of which he so often accused me! My heart took advantage of this opportunity; and, with the assistance of such strong authorities, silenced my reason and my principles.

Full of these thoughts, I retired to my chamber, where I found Mr. Markland waiting for me. He received me with a transport beyond what so short a separation could make me expect. The joy so visible in his countenance, communicated itself to my heart; and I, who two hours before wanted to find a means of avoiding him for ever, was charmed at seeing him again. He told me, 'that, no longer able to live without me, he had left his father at a chocolate-house, and returned home with the utmost impatience.' Fatal impatience!

CHAP. V.

WE had now been in London above four months. I had continued corresponding with my sister; tho' not daring to communicate the thoughts that were uppermost in my mind, my style grew so constrained, and my letters so short, that she took notice of it; and, more grieved than offended, expressed fears for my health, attributing to some defect in that, the alteration in my manner; for it wore the appearance of melancholy. But if shame for the weakness I felt in my heart made writing to her so difficult to me, it is not strange, if, when guilt took its place, I was no longer able to write at all. I feared her advice, which was now the severest reproach to me; looked on myself as unworthy to address her; so much did I reverence a conduct, which I had not been able to imitate. From this time my correspondence with her ceased. As it had slackened so much before, she did not immediately observe it; but when a letter of hers had remained above a month unanswered, I received another from her, filled with the kindest anxiety and most alarming apprehensions.

They did not now appear without foundation, for my health was impaired: I grew pale and thin; my chearfulness was changed into tears and self-reproaches: For the little colour I retained, I was obliged to my blushes, which every eye that gazed on me, raised in my cheeks.

My Lady and Sir George observed the change, and very obligingly enquired into the nature of my complaints. I could by no means answer them with sincerity; but invented such disorders, as I thought they could not easily disprove.

The kind letter I have mentioned receiving from my sister, having remained unanswered, was followed by another, which informed me that she was soon coming to town; that the milaner with whom she was, had a daughter now grown capable of managing the business; and therefore she had got from her a recommendation to one of the same trade in London; and as soon as the terms were settled, she should come there with great satisfaction, as it would bring her near me.

This news filled me with distress. How could I, who was not able to take courage to write to her, bear her sight, who would so circumstantially examine me about every particular of my situation and conduct; and whose eyes would no less exactly observe my person, which I had reason to believe would soon appear as visibly altered as my face?

I could not conceal my uneasiness from Mr. Markland, who was both the cause and the consolation of all my sufferings. He told me, it only confirmed him in a purpose which he intended to propose to me; which was, to place me in a house, where I might live free from the continual apprehensions I now was in, and enjoy the ease and affluence I so well deserved; that it was but reasonable, that she who possessed his whole heart, should at least share his fortune. To see me so settled, would render him very happy, as he could then enjoy my conversation without restraint and interruption; and he flattered himself, that he should see less melancholy mixed with my tenderness, which was now an abatement to his felicity. He added, that he had considered of the impossibility of my attending his mother into the country; since a few months must affect my shape so as to render it apparent to her; and therefore he had intended to desire me to find some excuse for giving her notice that I should leave her, before the true cause could be perceived: and he was glad, that while he was gratifying himself in withdrawing from a state of servitude the woman, who in all eyes but those of the priests, must be looked upon as his wife (for as such he should ever esteem me in the tenderest sense), he should remove me from a sister, whose prejudices might be the occasion of much trouble to me.

This proposal was indeed a great relief to my spirits: I longed to be removed from the eyes I feared; but could find no good excuse for leaving my Lady. However, as the best I could invent, I took the first opportunity of informing her, that a relation in the country, whom I durst not disoblige, insisted on my coming to live with her.

Lady Markland suspected the truth of what I said; and told me, she wished it was not another kind of invitation that carried me away. 'But, girl,' added she, 'depend upon this; All your beauty will not keep one lover, tho' it may gain you a thousand. After a short possession, a woman not half so handsome will appear preferable, and you will be left on the common.'

Tho' I had no reason to suppose her Ladyship inspired with any spirit but that of experience, I could not help being shocked at so dreadful a prophecy. Scarcely capable of answering her, and utterly unable to insist on the lye I had made, I with much difficulty, and with tears starting from my eyes, said, I hoped my behaviour had not given her Ladyship grounds for such a suspicion.

'No, no,' replied my Lady: 'I have no fault to find with your conduct. You seem mighty sober and modest; but I never in my life knew a very demure girl come to any good.'

I was glad to come off with so general a reflection; for I was not without apprehensions from what she had said, that she suspected part of the truth. As for the fears she had excited, as soon as I told them to Mr. Markland, he dispelled them all, by the kindest assurances of constancy and unalterable love: Professions, which, contrary to all experience, will, I fancy, be believed, while love and folly exist.

Lady Markland having soon another servant recommended to her, I obtained liberty to depart before my sister came to town, and was guided by Mr. Markland's servant to my new house, which was very pretty, and furnished in the neatest manner imaginable, tho' not expensively. Mr. Markland was there to receive me, and was delighted with seeing me so well pleased with it, and with perceiving it was so much beyond my expectation; for Vanity had not yet found its way into my heart; Love too entirely filled it all.

I was desirous of putting my lover to as little expence as possible, therefore took but one servant; and endeavoured, by the regularity of my *menage*, to persuade the neighbourhood, that I was his wife, but obliged to conceal that circumstance during Sir George's life.

This opinion Mr. Markland gave all the colour to that he conveniently could; and indeed might safely do so; for whatever comfort my inexperience might draw from it, thinking I thereby avoided slander, he must well know that such indulgences to women in my situation are so common, that they find credit with none but the very lowest people; and that, instead of making a mistress pass for a wife, they often occasion one who is really a wife, to be taken for a mistress.

Sir George and Lady Markland did not stay long in town after I left them. Their son excused himself from going into the country with them, and by various pretences prolonged his stay.

He was now always with me, and always equally a lover. His tenderness continued unabated; tho' my frequent indispositions cast a languor over my countenance, and deadened my complexion. Whenever I was tolerably well, he carried me to some of the places of public diversion most frequented during the summer season. They were entirely new to me. His conversation would have rendered any place pleasing. It is not strange then that I was delighted with places so calculated to entertain. He thought the satisfaction I shewed in them a sufficient reward for the trouble of attending me; for he had been so long accustomed to them, that they had in great measure lost their charms to him.

Mr. Markland was extremely pleased at seeing me attract the notice of the company; and would, with particular satisfaction, make me observe the admiration that was paid; which was entirely overlooked by me, so wholly was my attention fixed on him. At first I was pleased with being admired, as I thought the approbation of others might recommend me the more to him; but at last I liked it for its own sake. Vanity, which had so long lurked unseen in my heart, began to grow perceptible; and the pleasure of being admired, made the greatest charm of a public place.

Mr. Markland was sometimes obliged to go down to his father for about a week; but short retirement urges sweet return. He always left me with regret, and returned with impatience. These little absences were great afflictions to me; from having been so long habituated to his company, I knew not how to live a day without him; a week was an age; and I became almost as insensible as a statue, till again cheared by his presence. I every moment regretted the loss of him; and sometimes, I confess, lamented that I was deprived of admiration; for when he was away, I never went abroad, unless some family business carried me: So that I not only lost the pleasure of my heart, but the delight of my vanity.

Towards the end of autumn, during one of these short excursions, I walked out to make some small purchaces. In my way, I went thro' a street which I had not been in before; and going by a milaner's shop, I stepped in for some little thing I wanted; when the first person who offered to serve me, proved to be my sister. We were both so affected, that we became motionless for some time. My sister recovering herself the soonest, ran to me to embrace me; when casting down her eyes, she perceived the alteration in my shape; and instead of coming up to me, sunk down into a chair, where a flood of tears relieved her.

I stood in no less want of relief, but could find none. I was almost suffocated with the struggle in my breast, between the various passions that affected me. My sister, seeing the condition I was in, cried out, 'Oh! my poor Emily!' And leading me into a parlour behind the shop, called for some hartshorn;[33] and when she had brought me to myself, 'Oh! my dear child,' said she, 'what can I say to you! How can I bear to see you in the condition you appear in! And yet, how dare I say what I would, when I fear that even the sight of me may have done your constitution irreparable mischief! I would not increase the shock I have given you; and yet can I, with any degree of propriety, see you again? The account I received at Lady Markland's door, when I went with the most tender and anxious impatience to enquire after you, is but too well confirmed. O thou fallen Angel![34] how can my fond heart support the sight of thee, thus involved both in present and future misery!'

I could answer only with my tears. I threw myself on my knees, and catching hold of hers, my streaming eyes begged for pardon, but my words could find no utterance, till at last I got power enough just to say, 'Forgive me, my dearest sister! My parent, best of friends, forgive me!'

'My dearest sister,' said she, 'ask not forgiveness of me: Ask it of Him whom you have most offended, and who not only can pardon the past, but preserve you from all future crimes.'

My sister thus continued her exhortations for some time, till she asked me, 'If I would quit the way of life wherein I was engaged, and never see the man who led me into a state of ruin and destruction; promising, that if I consented to this, she would take all possible care of me, and provide me with every convenience:

For tho' she was then going to be married to a young man, who was a very advantageous match for her, and whom she sincerely loved; yet if he, disapproving of her conduct in this particular, should attempt to restrain it, she would for ever forego all her expectations, and should think herself greatly rewarded by saving me from eternal ruin.'

What could I say, when I could not resolve to accept of so kind, so generous an offer! 'I begged her not to oppress me with her goodness: That I was not deserving of her care; and would never suffer her affection for me to prevent her happy establishment: Wished heaven might shower down all its blessings on her; but that as for myself, the die was cast; I was too far engaged to retreat.' She again pressed her offer: I told her, 'I could not deprive the child I went with of a parent; nor was it possible for me to forsake a man whose whole happiness was centered in me, and who deserved every thing from me, having no aim but to promote my felicity.'

When my sister found me unalterable in this respect, 'Then,' said she, 'my dear Emily, I will not urge what I might properly say, because I fear to hurt your health: I will not now endeavour at what I see your passions would render ineffectual to any purpose, but that of making you uneasy, when ease of mind will be most necessary to your recovery: I can only pray that your life may be spared till you are fitter for another world; and that He who alone can turn the heart, will take compassion on yours: But it is impossible for me to see you any more; it would only be increasing my wretchedness and creating yours. The thought of the situation you are in will embitter my most prosperous days; but it is my duty not to suffer it to disgrace them.'

I cried out, in an agony which no words can express, 'My dearest sister, do not despise me, do not hate me: Your hatred or your contempt would break my heart.'

'No, my dearest Emily,' replied my sister; 'be assured I can never hate or despise you: I shall pity, grieve, and pray for you; but, with all your faults, must love you; love you with a tenderness none but a parent can know; for such I have always felt myself for you: And whenever you will love yourself as truly as I love you, shall with joy receive you, forget the past, hope for the future, endeavour to relieve your griefs, and confirm your happiness.'

With many tears and embraces, we took leave of each other. A chair was called; for I was not able to walk; my body felt so strongly the effects of the agitation of my mind.

I never was so sensible of the sacrifice I had made Mr. Markland, as when I returned home, and reflected how true, how amiable a friend I had given up for him. When I considered my sister's whole conduct, how little did I appear in my own eyes! I do not know how I could have supported the view of my own meanness, had not Mr. Markland arrived in town, and restored me to my vanity; for nothing but vanity could preserve me from my own contempt; for I think I may properly give that name to an opinion that exceeds what we deserve.

A young woman called at my door, to inquire after my health, for two or three days successively, after this interview with my sister, who I judged was sent by her, in kind anxiety, lest the great flutter of my spirits should have impaired my constitution. After that, I heard nothing of her; nor durst I make any inquiries at that time.

CHAP. VI.

> The world's a scene of changes; and to be
> Constant, in nature were inconstancy:
> For 'twere to break the laws herself has made:
> Our substances themselves do fleet and fade:
> The most fix'd being still does move and fly,
> Swift as the wings of time 'tis measur'd by.
> T'imagine then that love should never cease;
> Love, which is but the ornament of these;
> Were quite as senseless, as to wonder why
> Beauty and colour stay not when we die.
>
> COWLEY.[35]

NO change happened in my way of life, 'till I was brought to bed of a very fine boy: Nor did this make any alteration, but my temporary illness, and the addition of this lovely child to our family; which was an increase of happiness. Our fondness for it was equal; and instead of our affection's being lessened, by having a third to share it with us, each seemed to look on the other's being parent to this little darling, as a new merit, which caused, if possible, an increase of fondness.

The winter altered, not lessened, our attendance on public amusements; but we were obliged to go in a more private manner, as there was a greater chance of meeting with some of Mr. Markland's graver acquaintance. This caution, if I had not been lost to shame, must have shocked me; but the violence of my passion, the extreme tenderness of Mr. Markland's behaviour, and the care he took to furnish me with books, that should in his absence keep alive my infatuation, made me regardless of every thing else; and no one was ever disposed to say more cordially from her heart,

Fame, Wealth, and Honour, what are you to Love![36]

A second year passed away in this madness of the mind; but at the beginning of the third, I thought I discovered an alteration in Mr. Markland: He endeavoured to appear the same; but the tenderness of his behaviour, instead of being the free emanation of his heart, seemed forced and constrained. The impediments to his coming to me were multiplied: One would have thought that people were now making themselves reparation for having lost so much of his company, and were determined to engross him entirely. Even his child grew less dear to him, tho' every day more engaging.

At first I endured this change in silence, and in tears I may add; for weeping was now my principal employ in his absence; and I believe nothing could have prevented its being constantly so, but the fear of rendering myself odious in the eyes of him, to whom it was too grievous to be looked upon even with indifference. At last, I gently hinted my apprehensions; but I found I gave offence, because I saw too clearly; and to avoid any thing that might make me lose the little of his company which I now enjoyed, I determined hereafter to bear all in silence. But it is not in the power of language to describe the anguish of my heart, nor the difficulty I found in concealing it.

In this wretched state I continued for three months; a state which seldom changes for a better, unless when it creates indifference in us, which, to some women, is almost as difficult as to conquer that of their lovers; and to add to my misfortunes, I was one of those, who, obstinately fond, can

Doubt, yet doat; despair, yet fondly love.[37]

Cruel as I thought my situation, yet I found there was a state of distraction beyond it; for into such I was thrown by a letter brought me from Mr. Markland, wherein he acquainted me, that he was then at his first stage towards Harwich,[38] where he was going, in order to embark for a foreign port, having accepted an employment under one of our ambassadors.

The distress of my mind was now beyond what any one can comprehend, who has not sacrificed all she did or ought to hold dear, to one man, whose tenderness seemed for some time to recompense her for all she had relinquished, whose love constituted all her happiness, and who at last, by the most cruel inconstancy, threw her from the airy height of bliss to which he had exalted her, into the lowest abyss of misery.

Before the receipt of this cruel letter, I thought my grief could not admit of increase: To lose Mr. Markland's affection, appeared to me the heaviest misfortune: I did not then understand how soon a woman, who cannot possess a man's esteem, loses all his regard when he ceases to love her. But to be left with such indifference! a child abandoned without one parting kiss! was a shock too great for my constitution to bear. My weak understanding was so shaken, that for two days I was quite out of my senses: To this a fever succeeded, which was violent, but not tedious.

As soon as my shattered brain grew a little composed, anxiety for my child made me desirous to preserve a life which seemed to promise me nothing but misery: But what would I not have undergone, rather than leave that dear babe friendless and defenceless, in a world which now was very low in my estimation! For it is the way of us all, if one person uses us ungratefully, to quarrel with the whole human race: Never sensible of universal faults, till we suffer by those of some individual.

Care for my child rendered me obedient to all the orders of my physician, who told me, I must not hope for recovery, without I could compose my mind to some degree of resignation. This argument made me use every means to change the natural current of my thoughts.

My little boy, as the only object now of my affections, (and the only inducement for my endeavouring to raise myself out of that state of despair) I would have always with me; but how often did that increase my grief, by reminding me of his father! If he smiled on me, I thought I saw his father's sweetness, which had charmed my soul: An endearing action brought to my remembrance his father's tenderness: If he was diverting, I said to myself, 'How would these once have delighted his father!' If he looked pale, how would this air of sickness have alarmed his father's fondness!

In spite of grief, my fever left me; and I found it necessary to resolve on some means for my child's and my own support. Mr. Markland had left no provision for us; but, as if he justly thought that after the loss of his affection, every thing else was insignificant, he was as regardless of lesser particulars for me, as he might imagine I should be for myself.

While Mr. Markland loved, he was generous; and as I was a good œconomist, I had near a hundred pounds by me; and having some cloaths, which were better than would be required in the way of life into which I intended to enter, I converted them into money; and turned the parlour, with little expence or alteration, into a haberdasher's shop, laying out all my money in stock. I sent my landlord warning that I would quit his house after the necessary notice, intending to take myself a cheaper habitation.

The execution of this purpose was of service to me: It employed my attention, and gave me a subject to think of; which, tho' productive of no pleasure, yet gave me no pain. I had not ease of mind sufficient to be anxious about my success; every thing appeared too trifling to move me much. As for my child, I wept over him, instead of rejoicing in him. I had now no affection but what gave me uneasiness: What I fancied was the source of sublime happiness, I found was productive of the greatest misery. But my sorrows were grown quiet; I was composedly wretched.

CHAP. VII.

I Did not succeed ill in my business; the humbled air, which grief gave me, I believe softened the rigid virtue of my neighbours; and as I sold rather cheaper than most people in the same way of trade, in order to incite them to deal with me, I seemed well established in about two months after I had furnished my little shop.

But great was my surprize, when one morning two men entered my house, who immediately arrested me, and seized my goods.

I was more amazed at this insolence, than frighted; for I was sure I had incurred no debts, and therefore told them they must have mistaken the house and person. Of which I had no doubt; but greatly was I shocked, when they informed me, that they were employed by my landlord, who had never received any rent from the time Mr. Markland took the house, nor payment for the furniture, with which, being an upholsterer and cabinet-maker, he had furnished him; and that he could easily prove that whatever I had belonged to Mr. Markland.

All the horrors of a prison now presented themselves to my imagination: I easily perceived my stock could not discharge this debt; and with little ceremony was told by these men, that nothing else could save me from a gaol, and that I must go with them. What now to do with my child I knew not: To expose it to the colds and damps of so nauseous a place, shocked my nature: As for myself, had no other depended on me, I should have been less anxious: I had resigned myself to misery, and which way it was brought upon me seemed of little consequence. One relief I immediately felt from this misfortune; the love which I had till now borne to Mr. Markland, whose inconstancy I almost forgave, as a weakness in his nature, was entirely obliterated, by so mean and cruel an action as leaving me exposed to such infinite distress; for he could not but know that his absence would determine the landlord to take care of his own interest: And probably I should not have been left so long in quiet possession of the house, but that he might the more certainly get all I had, when my shop was furnished in the best manner I was able.

I now despised the man I could not hate, and no longer felt the pangs of slighted love; but the terrors of my approaching fate took their place: I was weeping over my child, who, frighted at my agonies, was more clamorous in his grief, hung round my neck, and screamed, he knew not why, only he perceived the men were the cause of my affliction: And as they, provoked at the noise he made, began to swear at him, he grew more terrified; and with the assistance of the lamentations my maid uttered, who thought the degree of grief was to be measured by clamour, the uproar was great enough to bring in an old Lady, who came to hire a house at the next door to me.

She had been to see it the day before, and had taken notice of my child, with whom I was standing at the door, and asked me some questions about the neighbourhood, more, in appearance, for the sake of conversation than curiosity.

This Lady, as I said, was attracted by the clamour she heard in my house, and came in to ask the cause of it.

The bailiffs were the most able to speak, and gave her a surly answer; but one which was so much to the purpose, that in a few words they made her comprehend the whole matter.

She came up to me, and enquired if the balance against me was great. I told her I could not tell how that might be, as I knew not what difference would be made in the valuation of the goods, when they came to be appraised, from what they had been sold at; but that it ought not to be considerable, for the damage was small, they having been always used and kept with great care: That except this difference, the balance on either side could be but trifling, for my stock would answer the rent; but that to one who had nothing, a debt of thirty pounds was as bad as one of three hundred, and must render me equally insolvent.

She then asked the men what they designed should become of me till the affair was settled: They replied, I must either go home with them, or to goal.

'Have you no-body,' said she to me, 'to be bail for you?' 'No one,' answered I; for my sister was the only person to whom I could apply, and I would not harbour a thought of making her a greater sufferer by my ill conduct than she already had been, or of running the least hazard of causing any difference between her and her husband; for long before this time I imagined she was married. I was sensible that if she knew my distress, she would be anxious to relieve it; and as her husband might not chuse to give his money to one so unworthy, disputes and disgust might arise on the subject.

'It is hard,' said the old Lady, 'you should know no-body who will perform such an act of humanity. Tho' I am not fond of having any thing to do where the law is concerned, yet I cannot withhold my assistance from one who is in so very distressful a situation, and who seems born to suffer from the cruelty of mankind

I will bail this young woman, and will take upon myself the settling her affairs:' [Turning to the bailiffs.]

I was all gratitude: A thousand blessings and a thousand thanks I gave her. But the men were not so ready to accept her offer; they said they must first enquire into her character and substance, and know whether she was responsible.

'If you have any doubts of that kind,' said she, 'let the goods be appraised directly: The day is long enough for settling the whole affair.'

This proposal was agreed to; my landlord was sent for; my stock in trade was valued by the bills of what I had paid for it, and appraisers determined the value of the furniture.

My benefactress had left me before my landlord came; and as evening drew on, I grew under great apprehensions lest prudence should get the better of charity, and prevent her return: But before the whole was entirely settled, she came; the balance was drawn, and I remained debtor but about 20 pounds. She paid the money, and said she would require no consideration of me but a note of hand, in case I ever should be able to pay her; and as I was at a loss where to go that night, offered to carry me home with her.

This additional kindness charmed me: My heart was inexpressibly relieved by such generosity: For the present I forgot the destitute condition I was in; I was delivered from immediate distress, and Mr. Markland's baseness had relieved my heart from the tenderness which till then oppressed it; so that I think, entirely pennyless as I was, these were much the happiest hours I had enjoyed from the time that Mr. Markland's affections began visibly to alter.

My benefactress took me and my little boy into the coach, and we soon arrived at her house. She told me, that as my spirits had undergone a great deal of fatigue, and she was to have some company that evening, it might perhaps be more agreeable to me to retire to my own room; to which she led me, and ordered a servant to see that I had every thing I wanted; and then, taking her leave of me, wished me good night; saying, she feared she should not be able to get to me again that evening.

I repeated all the acknowlegements my gratitude could suggest, and wished her a rest equally refreshing to the infinite relief she had given to my despairing mind.

CHAP. VIII.

Prospects at distance please, but when they're near,
We find but desart rocks and fleeting air:
From stratagem to stratagem we run;
And he knows most who latest is undone.

GARTH.[40]

WHEN I was left alone, and began to reflect on the various events of that day, it seemed a general scene of confusion; they had pass'd in such quick succession, that the recollection made me giddy.

The variety of thoughts which all these things suggested to my mind, would have engrossed my attention a long time, had not my little boy interrupted me; the bustle of the day had wearied him. I put him to bed, and that being done, I began to observe the furniture of my room.

The furniture was old and tattered, and every thing very dirty; but had once been handsome. I was surprized at the condition it was in, as I imagined the mistress of the house to be a woman of fortune, from the generosity she had shewn towards me; and from her age I expected such a degree of œconomy, as would prevent so much dirt and rags. I wondered, therefore, what could occasion this appearance, and flattered myself I might be of some use in doing my best to repair the destruction, which seemed less owing to the ravages of time than to want of care.

A servant, not much more cleanly than my chamber, came to ask me what I chose for supper: I told her any thing the family had; I begged I might give no additional trouble. 'My mistress,' said she, 'thought you might be tired, and want to go to bed before their supper time, so ordered me to enquire.'

'At what time do they sup then?' I asked. 'It is quite uncertain,' answered the servant; 'sometimes it is vastly late, but never before eleven.'

I had been used to late hours at Lady Markland's, so was not surprized: I thought I had got again into the house of a fine Lady; but, since that was the case, desired a piece of bread and butter, which would be a sufficient supper for me.

My request was not soon complied with; but as I heard many raps at the door, I easily guessed the servants were either busied by the arrival of so much company, or it had made them forget me. It was near eleven o'clock before any one appeared again in my apartment, and then the same maid brought me part of a fowl, some punch and wine, telling me, that as she had found the company came earlier than common, she thought she had better stay till she could offer me a more comfortable supper than what I had ordered.

I asked her if they had often so much company; to which she answered in the affirmative; and added, with an air of pride and satisfaction, 'she did not believe there was a house in town that had more.'

I had observed while I lived at Sir George Markland's, that my Lady and many others piqued themselves on having a great concourse of people at their houses, and that, to acquire the more honour, they would often stretch the truth as to the numbers that had been there the night before; but I was diverted to find this pride descend to a servant, who, by her appearance, must be in the very lowest place in the house; and wondered what advantage she could find in her Lady's drums being more frequent or more crouded than other people's.

Being heartily tired, I went to bed as soon as I had supped; but had not been long asleep before I was startled with a variety of noises: some seemed laughing, others scolding, others at romps. I was terrified with the clamour; the first effect of my fear was jumping out of bed and bolting the door, and then I could attend to it with a little more composure, but not without a thousand apprehensions, which, tho' the house grew pretty quiet about four o'clock in the morning, would not suffer me to get any sleep.

I rose early, but found the family were making themselves amends for the time they had stolen from the night, for nobody came into my room till near ten o'clock, nor had I courage to go out of it, to see if any one was up: The same servant whom I had seen the night before, then made her appearance: I asked her if any disaster had happened, which occasioned so much noise at so late an hour? 'Nothing particular,' she answered. 'Is your company always so loud?' said I. 'Not always,' replied she, 'but sometimes still more so.' 'Indeed!' cried I; 'And pray how often may you have company?' 'Oh! every night,' answered the girl, 'whatever house may be empty, ours is always full.'

My apprehensions had encreased during this whole dialogue, and now they were almost risen to their greatest height: But to remove all doubt, I asked her, whether their company consisted mostly of gentlemen or ladies?

The girl laughed at the foolishness of my question, and told me, 'they had few Ladies come there; not but a Gentleman might, if he pleased, bring a Lady, and they would be very genteely accommodated; but they seldom chose it, as all her young Ladies were so handsome, it would not be easy to find any equal to them.'

I was indeed now past any doubt: Uncertainty, however anxious, would have been a blessing to this certainty: I thought I should have fainted; and indeed I believe nothing could have recalled my senses, which were just fled, but the screams of the servant, who was so used to clamour, that she did not think any moderate noise could be sufficiently expressive of fear, and set up her pipes with such a violence at seeing me sink, pale and breathless, into a chair that stood by me, that she not only called back my departing spirits, but brought two or three of the young *Ladies*, whose beauty she had been boasting, into my room.

As my colour had not returned with my senses, I still looked more like a corpse than one alive. The girl was asked the occasion of this disorder, but could give little account of it: She told them, 'the young gentlewoman had been asking her questions but the minute before, and she could not imagine what was the matter.' My poor little boy, frighted to see his mamma look so pale, ran to me, and, by his tender and amiable caresses, did more to recover me than all the attention of the young *Ladies*, who held salts to my nose, rubbed my temples, and did all they thought requisite for my relief; but their appearances counteracted their care, by terrifying me more than the other could revive me.

> *Uncomb'd their locks, and squalid their attire,*
> *Unlike the trim of love or gay desire.*[41]

The dirty rags in which they were cloathed, shewed their wretchedness. Their faces, which in the evening were to shine with borrowed charms, were now the emblems of decay and sickness; swoln excess, riotous intemperance, and foul misrule, were imprinted on each countenance.

I do not believe I could have quite recovered myself while they were in my sight, but, fortunately for me, they were called to breakfast, from which my indisposition excused me, and I was indulged with a dish of tea in my own room.

When I was left alone the distraction of my mind found some vent, by tears and lamentations. I now felt a degree of distress beyond what I had yet experienced, or ever feared. How severely did I arraign myself of folly, in having conceived no suspicion of this wretched woman; and quarrelled with my heart for having seen her action in no such very strange light, as to suppose it must arise from any thing but generosity. I thought that, in the same situation, I should have done like her; and therefore was grateful, but not surprized: so far was my candour in thus judging of her from administring any comfort to me, that I wished my temper more suspicious, tho' rendered so by defects in my own heart, from which it was now free: indeed, in this case, the most common prudence might have preserved me; but I was rendered so senseless by the terrors of my situation, that I was blind to every other danger.

I shall not tire you with endeavouring to describe the agitation of my mind, which was far beyond all power of description; but shall only say, that the prison I had so much feared, now appeared to me an eligible asylum; and all my hopes were, that if I was found refractory to the purposes of the person who had thus bought me of myself, resentment might tempt her to throw me into the gaol from whence she had so cruelly relieved me.

After breakfast was over, the woman, who the night before I had beheld with reverence and gratitude as my noble benefactress, came into my room; and taking hold of my hand with a fawning affectation of kindness, told me, 'she was sorry to find I had been so ill; she supposed it was occasioned by what I had suffered the day before; but she did not doubt but I should soon recover, as my mind would forget all past disasters in her house, which was a temple dedicated to pleasure;' and continued in such intelligible terms, that no further explanation was necessary.

To sit and hear the profession of such abandoned sentiments, was an additional shock: Criminal as I had been, my detestation to this way of life was as great as if I had been more consistently virtuous. I informed her, that 'she was disappointed in her views; but offered, if she would forbear all attempts to induce me to comply, that I would with pleasure submit to the lowest offices in her house, or rather what she esteemed the lowest, and perform the part of her menial servant, till she herself should acknowlege that I had amply paid my debt.'

She told me, 'that every word I spoke, more fully proved my folly; for I must be extremely silly indeed, to think she would be contented with my saving her three or four pounds a year, when she did not despair of my gaining her as many hundreds, for the first year at least; and after that, by paint and dress, I might make a very attracting figure amongst the rest of her girls.'

All that prayers and intreaties could do, I tried without success; and when that failed, I endeavoured to provoke her to send me to prison; but all to no other purpose, than, as she said, to shew my folly, in supposing she had not taught every passion, as well as every principle, to be subservient to her interest.

All I uttered had no other effect than to make her give orders that I should not be suffered to stir out of the house.

While I opposed her, she set me at defiance, and threatened me with immediate revenge; which she was too well able to execute, having every one at her command, and I no one to defend me. I therefore tried to delay what I could not repel; and by promising to endeavour to get the better of my reluctance, prevailed upon her to allow me time to learn to command my behaviour, which, in my present disposition, might disgust those she chose I should please.

CHAP. IX.

UNDER this pretence, I obtained liberty to live entirely in my own chamber for a whole month, hoping still that some fortunate accident might relieve me; but all in vain: At the end of that time, she assured me she would be fooled no longer, and made me dress myself with more than usual care, in a gown and ornaments which she provided for me; and told me, that she would absolutely bring a gentleman to see me that evening, whose generosity she so much extolled, that I had some hopes I might find him generous indeed; not in lavishing money on a bawd, but in relieving the distressed. I found I had been promised to him, which proved that he paid high; but this was but a poor dependance for my expectations.

This wretched woman kept her word with a diabolical exactness. She introduced the gentleman pretty early in the evening, for expectation had made him come sooner than her visitors usually did: She retired. I was sorry to see how much this man was struck with my appearance; it in a great degree damped my hopes; but despair encouraged me to proceed, and I began to attack his compassion in the strongest manner I could, by uttering all the sentiments of my soul. I kneeled at his feet, used tears and prayers to soften him, and did my utmost to excite his generosity.

At first he seemed to think all this was mere hypocrisy, with a design to raise the value of his conquest; but he soon found I was perfectly sincere, and with joy I perceived him affected. This animated me still more, and I pursued my intreaties till he granted them, and told me he would desire no more of me than that I would inform him how, in such a disposition, I could come into that house.

I then related to him the whole affair, suppressing only the manner in which I had lived with Mr. Markland, whom I called my husband: not, I think, out of pride: I was too much humbled to attempt to conceal even my crimes; but I feared, if he knew this circumstance, he would have less regard to my petition; and think my having offended with one man, gave every other a right to expect I should be the same to them.

When I had ended my story, the gentleman told me I might judge of his compassion from the mortification he inflicted on himself; for that, tho' he was much attached to the sex in general, and had always been so, he had never seen a woman he thought half so lovely as myself; that she who had the disposing of me was sufficiently sensible of my charms, as appeared by the price she set upon me; which, however, he was much more willing to lose, than to give up his title to me; but to shew me he could be generous to virtue as well as to vice, he would relinquish both, and at my desire, pretend himself better satisfied with my conduct than he had reason to be; for I had begged he would not betray me to the woman, whom I now beheld with as much horror, as I had once done with gratitude.

That he might be the better credited, he sat with me near two hours after he had made me this promise. I wished he would have secured me from persons less generous than himself, by redeeming me from this horrid place, but durst not hint my desire, for fear of offending him; and he stifled my hopes, by observing to me, how impossible it was for me to escape out of it, for that the money which she had laid down for me, would be but a small part of my debt; she would charge so much for my board, and the cloaths I had then on, that would run it up to a much more considerable sum.

After having represented all this to me, and the impossibility of my prevailing with other men as I had done with him, he endeavoured to persuade me to submit patiently to my lot, and not to grant to one less generous, what I denied to him; promising that I should share his bounty, whereas it commonly was dispensed only to the person who claimed the power of selling us.

He bore my refusal of this proposal as generously as he had done the first, and took his leave of me in the politest manner, and, if I may be allowed to form any judgment from his appearance, with real concern for me.

As soon as the gentleman was gone from the house, the old woman, and some of the young ones who were disengaged, came to me, and carried me down into a small room to supper, where none but ourselves were admitted; not so much to indulge me as a reward for my good behaviour, as because I was thought too valuable while new, to be exposed to common eyes.

My odious companions were all in very good humour, and I was so delighted with, and encouraged by, my success, that I had never before appeared so easy. I flattered myself I should continue as fortunate as I began, and the effect this hope had upon me, gave room for a supposition that I was grown better reconciled to my way of life.

I was not to continue long in doubt, whether my arguments would be always equally prevalent; the next day brought fresh occasion for my rhetoric. The appearance of the man was less encouraging; he wanted the politeness of manner and good-natured countenance, which was remarkable in the other; however, I was not turned from my purpose by my fears of failing in it; on the contrary, I was animated by despair more than before by hope, and by my tears and aversion, extinguished all thoughts of pleasure or of love in his rugged breast; but leaving me with curses, he went to the old woman, and bestowing some oaths on her, made her refund the money she had received from him.

This threw her into a violent rage, and not being able to vent it on him, I must necessarily fall the victim. She brought up with her into my room three of her young women, who, angry that I should by my conduct shew a disapprobation of theirs, were fit to assist her in executing her wrath on me; accordingly they fell on me with the utmost fury, and beat me in the most merciless manner, till one of them hit me such a blow on my temples as struck me senseless to the ground.

As murder was a crime which was not professed in this infamous house, they were alarmed lest they had killed me; and fearing the consequences of their rage, put me to bed, and took all possible care to bring me to myself.

As soon as they had done so, I found my person was one general bruise. I was so sore, I knew not how to lie or move; but my greatest pain was in my eye, near which the last blow was given. It was soon so swelled up, I could not see; and as defacing me did not at all answer the wretches purpose, they omitted no care to remedy the ill they had done, plaistering me up in the manner they thought most likely to hasten my recovery.

I was in hopes they had put out my eye; shocking as the thought was, it appeared in a desirable light to me, as I might reasonably expect from it a total dismission from that house, where I could be of no value when so disfigured. I had suffered too much by my beauty to be anxious for the preservation of it, and one eye might guide me to a more comfortable livelihood, than I was likely to gain in the house where I then was.

These thoughts made me take off the things they applied to my eye whenever I was alone, if possible, to prevent my cure; but, in spight of my endeavours, the swelling abated, and I found my sight had received no hurt; but the blood settling round it, I had such a black eye, as rendered me too rueful a spectacle to be produced.

This accident obliged me to be concealed for above a month; for it was thought imprudent to shew me till I was in full beauty.

This delay was precious, and I would have endured another beating for the like benefit; but they had suffered too severely already for this exertion of their power, therefore they resolved upon a method less detrimental to my person.

CHAP. X.

A S soon as I was thought to look tolerably well, the infernal woman told me that all my resistance would be in vain; that my ingratitude had quite disgusted her, and she was resolved no longer to shew me any indulgence, but would expose me to the addresses of people too low and brutal to regard my tears, till I was broke of my niceness; and would send my child to the officers of the parish where it belonged, for she should no longer gratify me with its company, when I shewed so little consideration for her.

These menaces were dreadful indeed; and to talk of exposing my little darling to the cruelty of parish-officers and nurses, was too much to bear. Enraged at such a monster, I replied, 'The law would grant me some redress against such inhumanity.'

'The law! thou idiot,' answered she, 'Dost thou take lawyers for knights-errant, who have nothing to do but to deliver distressed damsels? Know, that money only can obtain justice; those who cannot buy, must go without it; the redress of the law is out of the reach of poverty; content yourself, there is no law for you. But I shall not give myself the trouble of saying any more to you; I give you till tomorrow to chuse; either determine to conquer your squeamishness, or I send your brat away, and deliver you up to the first man who will disregard all your tears and intreaties. Your will shall make no other difference in the case, than in the degree of your lovers, and your brat's fate.'

With these words she left me to consider the alternative. The dear babe understood something of being sent from me, and running to me, hung round my neck, crying he would not go away without me, and begging me not to let that woman take him.

Alas! dear Innocent, I did not mean it: I could much sooner have parted with my life. The wretch had now found the means of subduing my resolution. Delicacy, for by that name, not by the sacred one of virtue, I must call my resistance, after a conduct so criminal as mine: Delicacy, I say, gave way to maternal love: Nor could the latter boast any great triumph; for I had no prospect of gaining any advantage by my further perseverance; on the contrary, I was only likely to be exposed to the greater insults.

The declaration of my resolution was received the next day with great satisfaction; I was flattered and caressed, and my child fondled; but I could not be sensible to kind treatment so obtained.

In this detestable house I had remained about a month after this, when the old woman was taken ill of a violent fever, occasioned by having eat and drank immoderately for some nights successively. This illness put a stop to her trade; and three days carried her into a world, where one cannot think of her without horror.

As soon as she was dead, a relation came to look into her effects, who had been ashamed to own any connexion with her infamy; but at her death was willing to receive the profits arising from her crimes.

By this accident we were all set at liberty; what became of the rest I know not; I was too glad to get clear of them all to make any inquiries; but for my own part, my joy at this release was beyond expression.

The best cloaths which were worn by us were sold; but those of less value were given amongst us; and the notes of hand,[44] and such other obligations as had been used as means of getting us into her power, were cancelled, the purpose of them being too well known to her relation.

I was quite destitute of money, for our pockets were searched every morning, so that what presents any gentleman made us were sure to be taken away; therefore I sold the best gown which had fallen to my share, in order to support me till I had found some means of gaining a subsistence.

Sensible that I should find great difficulty in maintaining myself and child, I took the cheapest lodging I could find, only mending it by cleanliness. I then enquired for plain work; but received every where for answer, that they could not trust their things to a stranger; they were acquainted with people enough who wanted such employment; they need not give it to one they knew nothing of.

This was a melancholy answer. I now thought I would try to get a place; but when I offered myself, one said, 'I was too handsome;' another, 'that I appeared too genteel for such a place as I offered for,' (not daring to attempt any high one, as having no hopes to get it) and, 'there must be something very bad in my conduct, or I could not be reduced to such low services.' Those who were not deterred by my appearance, asked, What recommendation I had? Who would give me a character? In this manner I was repulsed from every door, and found that one who can do no work but what great numbers of others do as well, may be reduced to want employment. I now wished I had learnt of my sister a variety of works, some of which might have afforded me a support; for people are less nice in those they employ, for things they cannot easily get done elsewhere.[45]

I was now reduced to manifest danger of starving. I would have attempted the most laborious work, but no one would try me in what I am afraid I should have acquitted myself but ill, tho' I offered my labour at half price; but even my industry was made an argument against me, 'I must be very bad to be reduced to that, and they supposed I intended to steal the other half of my wages.'

In this deplorable condition I determined to apply to my sister. I did not now live in actual sin, and therefore could do it with the more courage. By enquiring at the milaner's where I had seen her, I learnt her abode, and thither I went. Variety of misfortunes had altered me extremely. My sister was in her shop, and rejoiced to see me, hoping, by my venturing to her again, that I had reformed my conduct; but my changed countenance shocked her, and rendered her reception of me more melancholy, but not less kind. Before we had had time to interchange many words, her husband came in, who guessing at me by the description she had given him, very abruptly told me, 'I was not fit company for his wife, and desired I would not frequent his house; for all the ties of kindred were broken by my infamy.'

My spirits were lowered by distress, and I may say by hunger, for I had tasted nothing for above twenty-four hours; this cruel reproach, so ill timed, struck me to the heart: I was not able to make any answer; but to avoid encreasing his anger, which seemed falling on his wife for having received me, I withdrew, almost drowned in tears, and scarcely able to support the weight of my afflicted body.

A good woman passed by me as I was dragging myself along, and sobbing as if my heart would break, and being moved at my distress, put her hand in her pocket, and pulling out a shilling, asked me, 'If that would do me any good?'

It is easy to be imagined that I received it with joy and gratitude; in my distressed condition a less sum would have been a great relief. She seemed happy in the good she had done, and said, 'She wished she had more for me:' I bless'd her for that she had given me, and we parted.

I stopped in my way to buy some food for myself and child with this timely supply, and was there overtaken by a young woman, who told me she belonged to my sister, who having given her a wink after I went out of the shop, she guessed it was designed as a command to find out where I lived, and therefore had followed me.

I soon satisfied her curiosity, and then enquiring into the temper of my brother-in-law, which alarmed me for my sister's happiness; she told me, 'she had never seen him so out of humour before. That it was easy to see he was of a very jealous disposition; but her mistress's conduct was so extremely prudent, that he had never had an opportunity of taking offence; and the entire confidence he had in her, and his sincere affection for her, got the better of a warmth natural to him; so that by the excellence of her behaviour, and the sweetness of her disposition, no married people lived more happily together; and she attributed his treatment of me to a sort of jealousy, which made him dislike my having any intercourse with his wife, as he imagined me not so prudent.'

I could not from my heart blame him, but said, I hoped my future conduct would plead my excuse; and expressed the fears I really felt, lest my going there should occasion any uneasiness between him and my sister, or make her unhappy by awakening her affection for me.

'Oh! Madam,' said the young woman, 'it would admit of no awakening; for my mistress is continually talking of you, and weeping over your remembrance, whenever my master is not present; for he does not like to hear her mention you. Some time ago she sent me into the street where you did live, to enquire after you, but the account I received was such as increased her affliction.'

'What was told you?' said I.

'I do not know how to answer you,' replied she, 'but I was informed you was gone to a bad house.'

'I was indeed,' said I; 'but not knowingly: However blameable I have been, there I am sure I deserved compassion; and whoever knows all I have suffered, if they are not strangers to pity, will forgive me my faults, in consideration of the punishments they have brought with them.'

The good-natured girl could not forbear joining her tears with mine; and perhaps curiosity would have detained her longer, could she have hoped to have learnt any particulars; but she must see I was not in a condition to talk much, and I was in haste to return to my child, and carry him some food; tho' he stood not in the same need as myself, for I had had a little bread left, which I gave him that morning, and that sufficed for a tolerable meal.

CHAP. XI.

THE same young woman came to my lodging the next day: tho' it was a wretched hole, it pleased her by its cleanness. My poor little boy she admired extremely, but I could not help feeling distressed, at having reason to be ashamed of a child, of which so many great families would be vain; but his charms could not wipe off the infamy of his birth; an infamy, which, in justice, belongs only to the parents.

As soon as we were seated, she delivered me a letter from my sister, wherein she acquainted me, 'That she could no longer find any comfort in plenty, since she might not impart it to me. That as all her stock in trade belonged to her husband, she could not, without being guilty of a criminal injustice, attempt to appropriate to herself any thing out of what she sold; and that as her expences had always, by choice, been very small, it was but little she should be able to assist me with at present, as her husband would be watchful; but that she hoped in a month or two he might have me less in his thoughts, and then she should find the means of supplying me more suitably to her own inclinations.'

This was mixed with expressions infinitely kind, and very valuable, as coming from the sincerest of hearts. She had, I found, never been used to ask him for any money; when she bought any thing, the bill was brought him, and he paid it, and would have done so with pleasure, if it had been a much greater sum. If she had any immediate call, she took it out of the produce of the shop, and, in settling the account, told him what it was for. There was such entire harmony between them, that this became her custom, as the easiest way; but now she regretted it extremely, and yet knew not how to break through it.

I saw her difficulty plainly; it was insurmountable, and I had nothing left me but to intreat her to run no hazards for me, for that nothing could recompense me for causing the least uneasiness between her and her husband.

She desired me not to write, lest the letter should fall into his hands, and told me she should venture at nothing more than a verbal message, till she had brought him into a better disposition towards me: so in compliance, my answer was only by word of mouth.

Few questions were requisite to inform my sister's messenger of my great poverty, so she staid not long.

From time to time she visited me, bringing such little relief as my sister could secretly bestow, but what scarcely sufficed to pay for my lodging. However, this was a great consolation to me; for, little as the expence might sound, it was a heavy burden on me, who neither had any thing, nor the means of gaining it; and my landlady's provident spirit made her require to have a week's pay in hand, not chusing to give so short a credit. Nor could I blame the woman; for where they are forced to let their rooms to such indigent persons as I was, if they were not to be rigidly exact, they would never receive their rent.

My sister's situation being now added to the other impediments which prevented me from obtaining any support, I was reduced below hope: Willing and able to work, and yet to starve for want of employment, seemed a hard fate, but touched no heart but my own. In this extremity, the humanity shewn me by a stranger in the street, determined me to try if casual charity would afford me any relief; and in the bitterness of my soul, I set out with my child to ask the charitable benefactions of passengers.

But here my success was small: I found that beggars had a society amongst them; that the town was divided into so many shares, and to every one was appointed their particular district, from whence they drove every interloper, by means too formidable for me to contend with, who feared almost equally their oaths and their more forcible methods. Thus I had no places left me, but such as were so little frequented, they were not thought worth their notice. Like the first planters in a colony, they divided amongst themselves all but the barren lands.

Among the few who passed where I durst attempt to beg, I seldom obtained any thing but reproaches for my idleness, in begging at an age when I was so capable of working. It was to no purpose that I told them I desired nothing so much as work, and intreated them to try me, by giving me any employment. They would answer, 'That they saw I was newly entered upon that trade, and it would be a shame to encourage me in it, as then I should never leave it off.'

Sometimes I should be so fortunate as to obtain a few half-pence from people whose compassion got the better of their reason, and who durst not give me an absolute refusal, for fear I was indeed as near starving as I said I was. But these small and uncertain benefactions would not preserve two persons alive, tho' used in the most sparing manner. Sometimes for two or three days I should not procure a farthing.

One time, when I was thus reduced to the last extremity, myself almost starved, and my child in the same condition, and piercing my heart with his cries; as the last effort, I dressed myself neatly, and went out to try if I should have any better success, as a higher degree of beggar; and left my poor boy with an old woman in the same house, who used to take care of him in my absence, tho' she was too poor to relieve his necessities.

I attacked many of my own sex, who told me they never gave to begging gentlewomen: I then addressed myself to the other, and received a refusal from the first; the second told me if I would go with him to the next tavern, I should be satisfied with his generosity.

I answered him, that he mistook my purpose; the smallest alms would content me, but that I could not leave that street. This occasioned some altercation; each kept to their resolution, till at last he produced five shillings to my view to strengthen his arguments. A sum, then, in my estimation, so considerable, at length prevailed.

I returned home to my famished child, as soon as possible, carrying food with me, that I might receive some reward for money so ill gotten; and I confess my recompence was great, in seeing the dear babe, almost at the gates of death, revive as he eat, and the smiles of joy by degrees take place of the anguish which the pains of hunger had imprinted on his lovely face.

I preferred the trade of begging so much to the making a traffic of my person, that I endeavoured by pursuing it to make this little fund hold out; but without success. I was at last attacked by the beadles, who receiving no gratuities from me, declared they would execute the rigors of their office if they saw me there again. Thus the little liberty I before had in this occupation was much restrained, and my gains sunk to almost nothing.

The only consolation I had, was the hope that my sister would be suffered to countenance me so far, that by her recommendation I might obtain some employ; but every time her messenger came, disappointment accompanied her. But still I hoped on, and was often led by it to the utmost extremity of famine, till, no longer able to support it, I resolved to try the means which had once succeeded, when I did not aim at it. How often, shocked at the odiousness of my purpose, have I turned back, determined to suffer myself to die, rather than preserve my life in such a manner! But when I returned home, and saw the distress of my poor child, every other evil appeared light in comparison of his sufferings; and I again fled from the anguish I felt at the sight of him.

I seldom had far to go before I met with some gentleman, who, tho' hardhearted to my distress, would be indulgent to his own vice. I often thought the cleanly simplicity of my dress, (for I had no ornaments) pleased more than the tawdry decorations of the women who generally follow that course; for while a man courts our vice, his reason hates our impudence.

I was sensible that, by entering into a society of prostitutes, I might gain a settled subsistence; but I could not think of engaging in a way of life I detested: I still hoped some means would at last relieve my necessities, and that I should not always be reduced to a prostitution, to which I could not bring myself to consent, till the severe pains of hunger, and the still sharper pangs I endured from those my heart's darling felt, got the better of the little delicacy I still had remaining. There could not be a more sparing manager than I was of what I gained, as, while it lasted, I was freed from a course most odious to me.

CHAP. XII.

Want is a bitter and a hateful good,
Because its virtues are not understood:
Prudence at once, and fortitude it gives;
And, if in patience taken, mends our lives.
For ev'n that indigence that brings me low,
Makes me myself, and Him above, to know:
A good which none would challenge, few would choose,
A fair possession, which mankind refuse.

DRYDEN.[47]

IN this manner I lived for near three months; the sobriety of my behaviour at home giving no suspicion to the people where I lodged, who were not used to be over-curious in prying into the lives of their lodgers, which perhaps would seldom bear a strict scrutiny. I concealed it equally from my sister; sensible, that if she knew it, the desire of bringing me out of such infamy and suffering would drive her to any extremities, to the hazard of all her conjugal happiness. The vexation I had given, and still gave her, was one of my strongest afflictions; therefore I could not, for any consideration, make her a greater sufferer.

One day, when I was reduced so low that I had not sufficient to purchase a supper for myself and child, my landlady came up to my room, and invited us to drink tea and sup with her, it being her birth-day. Never did a royal birth-day give such joy to the vainest lady. I doubt whether the birth of a child ever was more welcome to the person most anxious for an heir, than this good woman's anniversary rejoicing was to me. We readily obeyed her invitation; and I was too well pleased with the entertainment, to criticize the conversation of my company.

A little before supper, a man entered, who said he was just come from the new *Hospital*, so he called it, and that every thing was now completely finished; but he fancied it would be a long time before it was full.

'Do not talk of it,' said my virtuous landlady: 'I have no patience with the gentlemen who give encouragement to such wicked wretches: Starving is too good for them.'

I, who knew so well what starving was, thought this was almost too cruel a sentence for any crime; and begged to know who the wretches were she spoke of.

I was answered with all imaginable plainness; and felt, that coarse as the name was, I had too good a right to it; and therefore was enough concerned in the conversation to enquire what gave my landlady's virtue such offence.

I then first heard of this blessed charity: I made all necessary enquiries about it; and could scarcely contain the joy I felt, at the smallest hopes of being one of the objects that should be relieved by it.

Sorrow had robbed me of many nights rest; joy had a good title to a tribute I had so seldom paid it: I could not shut my eyes that night; and the next morning, as soon as I thought the Secretary's Office would be open, I went thither; not without fears that my child would be a bar to my admission;[48] for I had heard of no provision being made for children.

My good fortune was without allay: I was not only accepted, but was told I might come the day but one after, and my child should be taken care of.

To form an adequate notion of the rapture I felt, a person should have been reduced to the same excess of misery. My soul overflowed with gratitude, and my countenance shone with joy. It is true, I found I must part with my child; but then I could have no doubt but he would be far better taken care of than I could ever expect he should be while he depended on me. For his sake, I could part with him; and should find a constant consolation for the loss of him, in thinking how well he would be educated and provided for.

The satisfaction of my heart was so visible, that at my return home, my landlady enquired what had made so great an alteration in me, for she had before often taken notice of my melancholy; and used to tell me, she wondered what could make one so young, and so pretty, look so dismal. I once told her very frankly, that being so young and so pretty were the very things that made me so: But this I found was a riddle to her, which I did not chuse to explain; nor did I now think proper to acquaint her with the real reason for the alteration she observed; but informed her, that within two days I was to go to a good place, which I had obtained that morning.

I wrote a letter to my sister, acquainting her where I had applied for an asylum, and of the success my application had met with; and added, that I hoped a course of regularity would so far wash out the infamy from my reputation, that her husband might in time suffer me to see her; which would always be necessary to my happiness, but could never contribute to it, till she was at liberty to act in that respect according to the dictates of her own heart, without the least chance of giving offence to the man on whom her happiness then depended.

This letter I gave to my landlady, the morning I left the house; desiring her to deliver it to the young woman who used to come from my sister, the next time she called there. And then I delivered my child where I was ordered; which I confess cost me many tears; for the tenderness of the mother got the better of true maternal love, which should have made me rejoice in this separation. That severe pang being over, I came hither, and was received with a degree of humanity beyond my expectation. I expected relief; but I found from this good matron tenderness and pity, of which I was then the only object; but a very short time increased the society, and rendered her humanity more extensive.

Thus you see, in compliance with your desire, I have exposed all my crimes and follies; and given a strong proof how much evil one bad action draws along with it. Nor was I sensible of my wickedness when I applied to be received into this place: I sought it as a refuge from distress and misery; my heart grieved, but did not repent till I came hither, where I was shewn my sins in their black colours; and, awakened to repentance by a sense of guilt, was taught to apply for pardon to Him who came on earth to save sinners.

The society returned their thanks to Emily, for indulging their curiosity. She told them they could in no way so agreeably acknowlege it, as by following her example: which being readily promised, it was agreed that they should proceed in the order in which they arrived at the House. A good expedient to avoid ceremony. How often have we seen some such method necessary to adjust the ceremonial between people who have no title to place or precedency, nor can pretend to claim any so good as a priority of reformation!

CHAP. XIII.

Should some brave Turk, who walks among
His twenty lasses, bright and young,
And beckons to the willing dame,
Preferr'd to quench his present flame,
Behold as many gallants here,
With modest guise, and silent fear,
All to one female idol bend,
Whilst her high pride does scarce descend
To mark their follies; he would swear,
That these her guard of eunuchs were;
And that a more majestic queen,
Or humbler slaves, he had not seen.

WALLER.[49]

THE person who, according to the regulation agreed upon, was to have the precedency in talking of herself; a valuable privilege! was about three-and-twenty; tall and genteel; her complexion was brown, but her features good, and her countenance animated with a pair of the finest black eyes imaginable, which shone with a vivacity that distress could not extinguish. She began as follows.

My father was a very rich trader in a country town; and known to be so substantial, that it rendered him one of the principal people in it; an advantage of which I partook: For a tradesman's daughter is as much raised above others who are included in the same class, by a little superiority in wealth, as a lady of quality is by the priority of her ancestors admission among the nobility. I had two brothers; and a sister a few years older than myself, who had but one eye, and was besides lame of a leg. She had sense enough to see she was not made to be admired in public, and therefore placed her ambition in shining in domestic life. Like most girls, she had been taught to think marriage the ultimate end of her creation; and that woman was made for man, in a more humble sense still than our first mother, who had the person for whom she was designed, ready to receive her as soon as created.[50] My sister looked on this as the peculiar privilege of the first of the species; and that all her female descendants were to wait till that superior sex should please to accept them; which might never happen at all.

As she was sensible she must not expect their passions to be her friends, she placed all her battery against their prudence; and by her œconomic virtues, hoped to conquer that entirely. The fortress she attacked was not strong; but unfortunately, when taken, the town was little nearer surrendering than before.[51]

When my sister observed the preference my person procured me, she comforted herself with considering that it might gain me many lovers, but perhaps not one husband; and paid so great a compliment to male reason, as to believe that one eye, which was always directed to some wise employ, must, by a man who thought of marriage, be held in higher estimation, than a pair of the brightest eyes wandering in search of admiration; and that one leg, which hobbled constantly in the road of œconomy and notability, was preferable to any two that were ever gadding abroad to places where flattery abounded.

For my own part, my prudence was less, and my conceit greater. I could not suppose, that so admirable a being, as I then thought myself, was made for any secondary purpose: But I did not trouble my head much whether I was made for man; I was sure lovers were made for me; and when once, by reducing them to assume that character, I had deprived them of all pretence to superiority, I concerned myself little what high ideas those which were indifferent retained of themselves: I left them to find charms in my sister's humility and good housewifery; and did nothing but carry myself to places where I might be seen; which appeared to me the ultimate end of my being.

The first beauty in a country town would be rather envied than despised by many fine ladies, if they were acquainted with all the gratifications her vanity receives.[52] To be universally acknowleged as the prettiest woman in the place, preferred by all the men in it, and addressed by every stranger who happens to arrive there, is a very flattering circumstance: And as I make no doubt but many of my sex have as much vanity as Cæsar had ambition,[53] if they knew the life of a country beauty, they would sooner choose to be the first woman in a small town, than the second in the most populous metropolis. Divided sway never yields entire gratification: When a woman has a rival in admiration, she is subject to many mortifications, and is kept in some degree of order by the fear of being supplanted: She is forced to controul her insolence, and stifle a thousand caprices, which, to one who is under the extremest intoxication of vanity, afford much gratification.

This was my way of thinking at that time, when vanity, unrepressed and unmortified, possessed my whole soul. I had no competitor, and felt myself of as great consequence, and with as much reason, as she who with conscious dignity struts about Bedlam[54] with a straw scepter and paper crown, convinced that she is the sovereign of that place. Where-ever I went I was attended by all the idle young men of the town; for every rank and every place affords a great number of those who are such by nature, or are easily made so by the first pretty woman, who, hanging out the colours of a professed beauty, shews them where they may repair, and be sure of an obliging reception: For such an one values her charms in proportion to the number, not the merit, of her followers.

But what greatly increased my train, was the situation of the town I lived in, which was but a very few miles from one of the Universities:[55] This seminary of learning, as it is generally called, is much more certainly a nursery of danglers. The boys will travel some miles to see a pretty woman, if the town wherein they are situated is not well supplied. Their vacant minds and unemployed eyes want amusement; and they find more in gazing at a girl who has ever so few charms to boast, than in searching in Homer for a full description of Helen's beauty. While they are young, no labour is too great that is spent in pursuit of a woman, whom their imagination has dignified with various attractions; and when they grow old, tho' they are become less volatile, they are not less danglers: But the time which before was spent in hunting a beauty, is now passed in a more lazy admiration, the scene of which is the fair one's shop.[56]

By the advantages of this situation, no lady of the first rank, both in birth and charms, ever had a larger train of admirers; and perhaps few have made a greater progress in the arts of coquetry. The first part of the business of every day was adorning my person; for a beauty will not, any more than a Persian monarch, appear without the outward circumstances which add to her lustre.

> *For beauty, like supreme dominion,*
> *Is best supported by opinion.*[57]

And she who would maintain the character of her charms, must endeavour to render them at all times, and to all people, equally resplendent. The task is laborious; the heroine who rants her hour upon the stage,[58] finds some consolation in descending to common life; and she who more humbly personates the pert chambermaid, after the curtain is let down, may return to social and serious converse. The theatrical statesman is not confined to a life of politics, nor the stage coquet to an endless repartee. But those who on the greater theatre of the world assume any character, even tho' of a trifling sort (for I cannot exalt very highly those of a wit or a beauty) have condemned themselves to never-ceasing labour. She who will always dazle with the charms of her person, or surprize by the force of her genius, without allowing the least indulgence to sickness, indolence, or stupidity, is a slave to that vanity which she thinks exalts her to a kind of empire. Even the sun does not shine with unabated lustre; clouds will often eclipse his glory, and sometimes very nearly extinguish it; what then can reasonably expect to dazle with uninterrupted resplendency!

No one has more reason to know the fatigues of being a beauty, for no one laboured more industriously in the calling, than myself; and I have returned home so entirely weary of the labour that I had gone through, in exhibiting all my charms; sometimes confining my spirits, that, by conversing gravely, I might wear an awful dignity on my countenance; at others, in spite of a depression on my spirits, affecting vivacity and mirth, to shew the brightness of my eyes, and the various dimples in my cheeks; I have, I say, returned home so tired with acting a part quite contradictory to the turn of my mind at that time, that I do not know whether I should not have given up my profession, and, laying aside the beauty, have turned a rational woman, if my sister had not, when she fancied, by my gravity, that I had met with some disappointment, been always ready to pique my pride, by telling me, that

> *Beauty soon grows familiar to the lover;*
> *Fades in his eye, and palls upon his sense;*[59]

With every thing else to the same purpose with which her reading could furnish her. Nor was she always content with quoting all she could find in poetic authors suitable to her desires, but would borrow from divine writ; and when I had got the better of all her verses by an inundation of lines that contradicted hers (for which I could not be at a loss, as poets have generally been of my side of the question), then she would confute me by Solomon's authority, and tell me 'that favour is deceitful, and beauty is vain:'[60] Nor could I silence her by observing, that, vain as it was, it got the better of Solomon's wisdom: Self-love fixed her opinion so firmly, it was not in my power to bring her over to mine.

This sort of opposition would revive my wearied spirits; and to shew her the power of beauty was not of so very short duration, I would again commence my labours, to renew its triumph.

However, intoxicated as I was with the worst fever of the brain, that of vanity, I was sensible I had no great share of beauty to boast. I knew how much obliged I was to my situation, which placed me near so many young men, who were ever seeking for something to admire, and satisfied with small success; and that I was not a little indebted to nature, in having been most niggardly in dispensing charms among the rest of the young women in the neighbourhood.

I saw many old gentlewomen, who convinced me, that had I been born a generation earlier, I should scarcely have been looked at: But all this I kept secret within my own bosom; for I plainly perceived, that the imposing air of a beauty goes a great way towards causing a person to be esteemed such: The world is so obliging, or so indolent, it seldom disputes our title to what we seem confident we are in possession of.

CHAP. XIV.

IN this giddy round of vanity I passed near three years, without, in any degree, disproving my sister's opinion; for tho' I was flattered by thousands, addressed by hundreds, was sighed to by great numbers, pestered with verses by all the small wits of the University, and attacked in sober prose by many who could not coin a rhime, or had not poetry enough in them to fill up a *bouts-rimés*;[62] yet I had not one who offered to venture into wedlock with me: Nor could I wonder at it, for I had not vanity enough to think my appearance promised much conjugal felicity. But at last, a young gentleman of the University made more serious addresses to me.

This gentleman, by name Mr. Monkerton, was agreeable in person and understanding; but what particularly distinguished him, was an easiness and gentility of air and manner, which is so seldom found in very young persons at those places. He seemed to have studied the present age more than the past; and tho' he might give less satisfaction to his tutor, than many of a more bookish turn, he was much properer to please a woman, as he could render his conversation agreeable by other means than that of flattery; the only merit to which most of my admirers could pretend.

Nor was Mr. Monkerton much less qualified to please by fortune; he had a good estate, and no father; that insurmountable obstacle to a young girl's marrying to advantage, who has no dower but her personal charms. He was indeed yet under the power of guardians, being a minor; but as he was above nineteen years of age, their authority could not last long; and his allowance was very ample.[63]

I had reason to believe Mr. Monkerton's views were not at first so serious. He was in reality captivated; I could perceive that he did not follow me merely from idleness or fashion, but because he could not bear my absence. He was as constant as my shadow, and as near me too; for he always took care to be next me, whatever number at his first approach he found in his way.

His knowlege of the world made him think that a vain girl of my rank was attainable on easy terms by a man of his fortune: This gave him that degree of assurance which seldom turns to a man's disadvantage with our sex; who are too apt to be less charmed with modesty, than with a freedom of manner, which gives them better opportunity either to signalize their own good behaviour, or to furnish them with an excuse to lay it aside.

I confess myself one who was pleased with Mr. Monkerton, for being void of that aukward bashfulness which I saw in most of his age. He soon perceived he was preferred to all his rivals, and did not intend to leave what he thought so promising a circumstance uncultivated. After having performed the duties of a public courtship as long as he imagined my vanity could require, he began to sollicit for private interviews. I soon penetrated his meaning; which made his sollicitations for some time prove fruitless. I had virtue, and its necessary companion decorum; both of which were offended with the thoughts of an assignation: But he pressed it so long, and with such earnestness, that my pride was piqued; I could not bear he should think a private meeting was of so much consequence; he shewed he thought me very frail; and I was apprehensive, that, by the obstinacy of my refusal, I seemed to have as low an opinion of my virtue as himself.

From this motive I resolved to endeavour to lessen his importance, and raise myself in his opinion; and accordingly gave him leave to come and see me one day, when I knew my father and sister were engaged at some miles distance. To have granted him a meeting at any other place, would have been an impropriety of conduct, which might have argued too great a levity, however prudently I had behaved when I was there.

I see you all tremble at this step of mine, and think my pride is going to humble me; but not at all: My lover found this interview was not worth so much solicitation. He lost much rhetoric, swore many oaths in vain, and found all Love's artillery of sighs, tears, and vows, was not sufficient to answer his expectation.

When evening came, he was obliged to leave me, without obtaining, as he thought, any other advantage from his visit, than the satisfaction of having entertained me some hours uninterrupted, with all that his passion could dictate; but, in reality, he had much increased mine: His tenderness infected me; I had not half loved before; I knew not till then the pleasure of being beloved; my vanity had been more engaged than my heart.

To the impression Mr. Monkerton had made on my affections, was owing my not discarding a lover, whose views I so plainly saw through. I had fansied myself of too much importance to be thoroughly sensible of the superiority which rank and fortune gave him over me: This imagined equality increased the offence; but my heart pleaded for the offender; nor was my vanity quite silent: I was not without hope, that when he saw how much he was mistaken, his passion might conquer all his reasons against matrimony. I plainly perceived how much the advantages in such an alliance would be on my side; tho' I thought it no more than what I was intitled to by nature.

He obtained leave to make me so many tête à tête visits, as served to convince him that there was no chance for succeeding in his views; and at the same time to increase his passion as well as mine. He grew melancholy, and kept at College for a week, without coming to see me.

This touched me extremely; but pride came to my aid, and enabled me to give him a worse reception, for what he thought might have induced me, by additional kindness, to recover a conquest which I seemed in danger of losing.

This was too painful a piece of self-denial for him to practise it again, when it had proved so useless; and therefore, after professing his esteem to be equal to his passion, and declaring himself charmed with a virtue which had baffled all his hopes, he assured me he could find nothing in an everlasting union with me, that would not be the most ardent wish of his heart, if it was in his power to proclaim me for his wife; but that he was left so much in the disposal of his guardians, that he could not marry publicly without their consent;[64] but that, if I would agree to a private marriage, when he came of age, I should see how much it would be his care to recompense me for my condescension.

I was not a little pleased with hearing Mr. Monkerton propose wedlock to me, tho' I did not like the terms. I endeavoured to persuade him that a year would soon pass away,[65] and that he would then be at liberty to do what he chose, without any restraints: I offered to discard every other lover; to change my way of life; to be always at home; and always happy to receive him, as there could be no doubt but my father, proud of the honour he intended him, would be glad to make so short a delay as little irksome as possible.[66]

He exclaimed at my cruelty, in calling a year a short delay, to a passion so ardent as his; and, to say the truth, I had belied my own heart in that expression; therefore was the more ready to suppose it insupportable to him. But a private marriage had an odious sound:[67] I valued the reputation of virtue, as highly as the inward satisfaction arising from it; and knew not how to sacrifice it, even for a year. I was sensible how difficult it was to wipe off a blemish from any thing so tender; it is scarcely possible but some stain will remain behind. All this I represented in the strongest light, but met with no answer, but accusations of want of love: He represented, that he relinquished all prospect of increase of fortune, and of great alliances, for my sake, and that I would not endure one year's obscurity for him. My reputation, he added, by marriage became his;[68] it could receive no blemish that would not be reflected on him; and it would be as much his interest as his duty to make my virtue conspicuous; which, like the sun, might be a little overshadowed, but could never be totally eclipsed.

But the most prevailing of all the things Mr. Monkerton could urge to bring me to consent to a private marriage, was a declaration, that if I persisted in my refusal, he would go abroad; for he could better bear to be separated from me, than to drag on life thro' a tedious year of expectation.

The best arguments reason could have suggested, had it all been on his side, would not have availed him so much as this menace. My heart could not bear to part with him; nor could my vanity support the thought of losing a marriage so much to my advantage. I had scarcely any principles of action left, but love and vanity; how then could I resist, when both were on the side of my adversary!

And yet the conditions were hard; for Mr. Monkerton required I should go off with him, without informing any of my family of the true state of the case; because, he said, their pride would hint our marriage to so many, if they did not publicly proclaim it, that it would come to his guardians knowlege. Many assurances of the strong proofs of our union, which he would give to my relations, as well as to all the world, as soon as he should be of age; with the most flattering prospect of the splendor in which he would then bring me to visit them; were requisite to make me consent to such mortifying terms; nor would I leave my father's house, but on condition that he should give me the strongest contract imaginable, till we were married;[69] and that we should set out so very early, that we might arrive at London, where the ceremony was to be performed, before the canonical hour was past.[70]

CHAP. XV.

Hail, wedded love! Mysterious law! True source
Of human offspring! Sole propriety
In Paradise; of all things common else.
MILTON.[71]

EVERY thing being at last agreed upon, I stole out of my father's house very early, with trembling steps, and a more trembling heart, and went to the inn, where I was to meet Mr. Monkerton; who was not so cold a lover but he was there before me, and had got a chaise ready, which carried us out of the town directly, and proceeded with great speed to London.

I could not leave the place where I had so long lived, and which contained most of my relations and friends, without many tears. Mr. Monkerton said all that love could dictate, to make me easy; not without success: I loved him too well not to find great pleasure in the happiness which every word and every look expressed; and at last I grew happy too; but it was rather a tender than a lively joy; some melancholy would remain, but such as gave me an appearance of more softness, not of less love, than before I had taken this rash step.

We were carried directly to the Fleet:[72] I was an entire stranger to London, and knew not what bad repute this place was in; but it did not seem a fit resort for happiness: However, to avoid all delay was so necessary a point to me (after having put myself thus into the hands of a young man, whose honour I had reason to believe arose only from having found it necessary for the success of his passion), that I made no objections: We were married there; after which, I gave up my contract, as being of no farther use; and we drove to the other end of the town in search of lodgings, and were soon accommodated.

My heart began now to be a little at peace; I was married to a man much my superior, from whom I might in a short time expect to have my reputation restored, and to be placed in a rank far above my birth; in the mean time, might hope that mutual love would yield me more happiness. If all brides were so reasonable as to depend on love for their felicity only for one year, fewer disappointments might arise from marriage. But, I am afraid, I was not so very moderate in my expectation as my expressions would signify; for my hopes of reciprocal affection extended to as great a length of time as those of the most

61

unreasonable of my sex; but for the first year it was all the satisfaction I could expect from my new state.

When my fate was once fixed, I endeavoured to see it only on the brightest side. My spirits were by nature remarkably good, and I had never met with any affliction to weaken them. This disposition enabled me to chace from my thoughts too great anxiety for my reputation; and, instead of it, to dwell on the joy I should receive from clearing it up to the world, at once vindicating my virtue, and doing honour to my charms.

Mr. Monkerton's fondness for me filled up my time; for when he was not with me, I wanted no employ, but to recollect every tender assurance he had given me of his love; and mine, thus indulged, increased daily. But, tho' every hour seemed productive of happiness, yet I could not forbear wishing to hasten the steps of tardy-footed time,[73] in order to get to the end of my year of obscurity and shame, tho' it never sat heavy on my mind, except when Mr. Monkerton was obliged to go to College; which he sometimes thought it necessary to do, as a blind to his guardians: But these absences were very short; and it was necessary they should be so, for my days hung very heavy on my hands when he was away. I could not bear to go abroad, because I knew I must be looked upon as his mistress.

This change of life, from a desire to produce myself 'where most might wonder at nature's workmanship,'[74] to be afraid of shewing myself to any eyes but Mr. Monkerton's, could be rescued from extreme dullness by nothing but love. When he was away, my spirits would sometimes sink, from reflecting on the great alteration in my mind; that I, who used never to be seen without being admired, could not now stir out of my house without being covered with shame: But my consolation was, that every day brought me nearer the end of this distressful circumstance.

Mr. Monkerton often endeavoured to prevail on me to go abroad with him; and was the more urgent, as my confinement in some degree impaired my health: But herein he was unsuccessful; all he could obtain, was, that after it was dark, I would often walk round a neighbouring square with him for an hour or two.

The house we lived in was very elegant, and my cloaths expensive; for Mr. Monkerton was lavish in his presents, and took great pleasure in adorning me: In every particular our appearance was genteel, but few were witnesses of it. I could not have kept any company, which I should have thought suitable to me; and I would accept of no other; nor would I be put on the footing of a mistress to his acquaintance; and therefore he admitted few to his house. Two or three gentlemen, who were his more intimate friends, he introduced to me; and these were often with us, which served to enliven the conversation, tho' it did not render it always more agreeable; for people who love much, are apt to be more desirous of avoiding other company than in prudence they should be; since interruption, if mortifying, serves to render each other's conversation more delightful, by giving them an impatience to be at liberty to enjoy it.

At last the time came which delivered Mr. Monkerton from all tuition; that so much wished for year of twenty-one, which sets a man of fortune free from all restraints, at an age when the passions are generally the strongest, and consequently least under the guidance of reason. But so the law ordains; and when a man is most unfit to govern himself, he is set at liberty from every governor. Nor did I want to lengthen the term, having impatiently longed for the end of Mr. Monkerton's minority.

I did not fail to remind him of his promises the day after that which declared him major; but he put me off with pretences of difficulties in settling accounts with his guardians, which would engross all his leisure for a little time, and make it impossible for him to declare his marriage with so much eclat as he could wish; but as soon as that was over, assured me he would do every thing I desired.

It was now winter; Mr. Monkerton's guardians were in town; and as every time he was absent, he said he was with them, I had reason to hope, however intricate their affairs were, so unwearied an application must soon clear them up: But new difficulties I was assured were continually arising; and Mr. Monkerton told me, that it was very disagreeable to him to be so frequently pressed on a subject with which he could not at that time comply; and gave him reason to believe that I either doubted his honour or his truth; and he should take it as a favour if I would say no more till he was able to keep his word, having often given me sufficient reasons why he could not do it then.

It is true that the intricacy of his affairs was often alleged to me, but as no immediate hopes were given me of their being settled, I could not be free from apprehensions that this was a mere pretence. I had endeavoured to persuade him to lay aside the thoughts of the eclat with which he talked of proclaiming me as his wife; desiring it might be done only in such a manner as the business he was engaged in would permit, and to leave to time its being generally believed. I was willing to resign all the gratifications of vanity, and desired only to be rescued from shame and infamy. But these petitions, which justice would have allowed me to ask with less humility, were become offensive; and Mr. Monkerton told me, with great indignation, that my pride would conquer his affection, and that my great haste to be acknowleged a wife, would make me lose a husband.

These were grievous menaces to a woman who asked as a favour, what she might demand as her due; and who valued nothing so highly as her reputation, except the man to whom she had made a temporary sacrifice of it. I was awed into silence, and waited with apparent complacency, tho' with inward impatience, for two months longer, without once urging my request: But hearing nothing on the subject in all that time, I broke thro' the restraint I had laid on myself, tho' not without fear, and expressed my desire of knowing how his affairs went on, in the mildest terms.

I was heard with good humour, and thanked for having avoided the subject so long; and an intimation was given me, that to this was owing my being now listened to with civility: I was assured, 'that the most difficult points were settled; and that I might depend on his diligence for determining the whole as soon as possible, tho' not so soon as he wished, for the nature of the dispute made it tedious; but that my prudent silence would facilitate the dispatch, as teazing him rendered his mind wholly unfit for business; and he hoped I would shew my confidence in him, by being quite easy and passive in that particular; for nothing was so great an incentive to generosity, as being generously treated;[75] therefore I could not doubt, by such behaviour, of securing to myself what from him was only justice.'

In this manner I was partly intimidated, and partly wheedled into silence, till three months more were elapsed. The town grew empty, and my suspicions increased daily. When I considered that Mr. Monkerton had been brought to marry me only from finding all his hopes frustrated of gaining me on easier terms, I had reason to fear that he might design to keep clear of the incumbrances of marriage as far as he was able.

CHAP. XVI.

ONE evening, as I was sitting with Mr. Senwill,[77] one of Mr. Monkerton's friends, who was waiting for his return home, and who seldom seemed dissatisfied with my company, I was so absorbed in my melancholy apprehensions, that the conversation flagged extremely; and he, walking about the room, took up some letters, which had come by the post for Mr. Monkerton; and looking at them, asked me, if I ever saw a worse hand than Mr. —'s, shewing one of them to me. This Mr. — was the chief of Mr. Monkerton's guardians. I answered, that the hand was indeed a vile one; but it could not be that gentleman's, for it came by the post; and shewed him the mark of York upon it; whereas he was in London.

Mr. Senwill told me, I must be mistaken in that particular; for Mr. — had been at his country seat near two months.

This startled me extremely; but I persisted in my assertion, that I had very lately heard Mr. Monkerton mention having just parted with him, and three other gentlemen, whom I named, and who were Mr. Monkerton's other guardians.

'I have been in doubt,' said Mr. Senwill, 'for an hour past, whether you were not asleep; but I am now convinced of it, for I find you dream. One of the gentlemen you mention has not been in town this year; another came only to deliver up his trust to Mr. Monkerton, and returned directly into the country; and the others, upon my honour, have long ago left London.'

Struck to the heart with this information, I started up, and said, with great emotion, 'I have indeed been long asleep, and dreadful is such an awaking!' and walked about the room in an agony that astonished Mr. Senwill, who knew not the importance of what he had said.

He came up to me, and taking hold of my hand with tender concern, asked me what he had said or done, that could have so cruel an effect upon me? And upon my refusal to explain myself, he omitted no intreaties to prevail upon me to satisfy his curiosity, which, he assured me, 'did not arise from impertinence, as I might easily imagine from the silence he had always preserved concerning some puzzling appearances in my connexions with Mr. Monkerton, which he had never attempted to pry into; but that he saw himself so much the cause of the emotion I was in, that he should be wretched till he knew how he had been so unfortunate as to give pain to one, whose peace and happiness were dearer to him than any thing on earth.'

I persisted in my refusal; but told him, if he would make me any amends for the uneasiness he had given me, he must tell me where the gentlemen we had been talking of lived in London.

Mr. Senwill 'wished he knew the reason of that request; but since nothing but implicit obedience was allowed him, he would shew, by his readiness to obey me, how sincerely he was attached to my service, if I would but accept his most faithful endeavours to remove the disquiet he had innocently occasioned.' He told me, that only two of the gentlemen had houses in town, to which he gave me a particular direction; but the other's stay was so short, he knew not where he was during that little time.

Tho' I spoke but little, yet, in the agony of my mind, I uttered something that shewed resentment against Mr. Monkerton; from which Mr. Senwill suspected that jealousy was the occasion of my uneasiness, tho' he could not perceive how it should be excited by any thing he had said; and very generously told me, 'he believed I suspected his friend of some inconstancy; and that he thought himself obliged, in justice to him, and compassion to me, to assure me, that he could answer for my having no rivals.' Much to this purpose he urged to little effect, as my suspicions were levelled more at his honour than his love: But at last I told Mr. Senwill, that I should take it as a favour to be left alone, and should be glad to see him when I was more fit for company. With unaffected concern he left me: My heart thanked him for his pity, of which I felt myself a true object.

I had no reason to doubt the truth of what Mr. Senwill had said: I had suspected him of a stronger attachment to me than was consistent with his friendship for Mr. Monkerton, tho' till this night he had never said any thing to give me room to form that opinion: But he was ignorant of the use which had been made of those gentlemens names; and if he had known it, the man who could generously endeavour to remove the jealousy he suspected me of, would not have made a bad use of it.

I was sensible of the impropriety of shewing a bad opinion of my husband to any man, but especially to one who I thought did not look on me with indifference; therefore I chose to send him away, and venture alone to the houses where he had directed me, tho' it was now dark. Accordingly I went to each, with all the haste that anger, impatience, and a whole army of passions could inspire me with; and there had the account which Mr. Senwill gave me, confirmed.

I returned home, filled with resentment, despair, and contempt for the man who had stooped so low to deceive me; and found him there, full of surprize at my being abroad. It was so strange a circumstance, that he knew not how to take it, and was prepared to be angry; but in so small a degree, when compared with the indignation which actuated me, that it soon subsided, till it was turned to another subject.

I told him, without much circumlocution, the discovery I had made of his meanness, and how basely he had drawn me into a sort of acquiescence with his delay of owning me for his wife.

Mr. Monkerton at first endeavoured to soothe me into forgiveness; but finding it all in vain, and that I now insisted highly on the justice he had so long evaded; he asked me, in a surly manner, 'If I would have him own me for what I was not?'

'That,' I told him, 'he had too long done; therefore I expected he should now own me for what I was, and publicly acknowlege me his wife.' He replied, 'that I, who was so much offended at a breach of truth, could not require him to publish such a falshood.'

This manner of treating me almost turned my brain. I asked him, 'What he could mean by it? He could not deny me to be his wife!' 'Indeed,' replied Mr. Monkerton, with an affected coldness, 'thanks to the law, I am not married; therefore can have no wife!'

I could not forbear exclaiming at this speech, 'When, by all laws divine and human, we are married, what law can set you free?'

'The Marriage Act, my dear,' answered the monster; for such he now appeared to me: 'We were neither of us of age; and therefore no marriage between us could be valid, without the consent of our friends.'[78]

It is impossible to describe what I felt on this occasion: I was a prey to almost every passion that can afflict the human breast: Despair alone would have been a state of bliss, compared to what I endured: The tumultuousness of my passions increased my anguish: I had heard the Marriage Act talked of, but had never attended to the purport of it; nor did I believe it could affect the validity of our marriage.[79]

Mr. Monkerton did not think my company inviting, nor chuse to trouble himself with fruitless endeavours to make me credit what I was obstinately bent to disbelieve: So telling me, 'that he should pass the night where he could hope for quieter rest,' he left me; and about a quarter of an hour after, his servant brought the Marriage Act, with his master's compliments, and that he had sent it for me to peruse, for the clearing up of my doubts.

The cold insolence of this message almost rendered me incapable of examining into the truth of what Mr. Monkerton had asserted; but at length I composed my spirits enough to read it, and there found the fatal truth too certainly confirmed.

Had virtue only actuated me, the integrity of my own heart would have given some degree of composure to my despair: I might then, in silent tears, have wept my fate; and, from principles of truth and justice, despised, and calmly hated, the wretch who had thus betrayed me into shame and infamy. But pride and vanity had too great a share in my heart, and turned despair into desperation. I passed the night in ravings and exclamations, more like a frantic than an afflicted woman; and could not be prevailed upon to go to bed; nor durst my maid leave me,[80] fearing my distraction might lead me to some desperate course.

CHAP. XVII.

O honour! frail as life, thy fellow flow'r;
Cherish'd, and watch'd, and hum'rously esteem'd;
Then worn, for short adornment of an hour;
And is, when lost, no more to be redeem'd!

D'AV.[81]

THE agitation of my mind at length exhausted my spirits; and, like children, I cried myself to sleep, on a sofa where I had laid me down, without expecting any such interruption of my sorrows; for I cannot call it a refreshment; having, after about two hours rest, waked only with greater power to grieve. Nature had gathered strength by that little cessation, and lavished it, like an unthrifty fool,[82] as soon as obtained.

In this condition I passed three days, alternately a prey to despair, to rage, and grief: But by the fourth, my body was grown so weak, with the agonies of my mind, and want of food (for I had not been able to eat any thing), that a languor seized me, which not only affected my outward frame, but deadened my mental faculties. This was a real relief; tho' my melancholy was extreme, yet by this means it became quiet, and I was less violently afflicted for knowing better why I was so.

I looked on my ruin as irretrievable: Tho' I could not accuse myself of want of chastity, yet I was not free from just cause of self-reproach. I now saw that I had been as regardless of my happiness as of my duty to my father, when I had been prevailed upon to transact an affair of so much importance without his advice; and that it was great imprudence to suppose I could receive any detriment from the person, who, of all the world, must naturally be most anxious for my welfare.[83]

When I first married, I wrote a letter to my father, requesting his pardon, and telling him, that in a short time I hoped to appear less criminal in his eyes.

To this I received no answer; but comforted myself in thinking that my great exaltation would procure my forgiveness. This expectation was now over; and I could not support the thought of carrying my infamy amongst all who loved or envied me. Tho' I had no guilt to reproach myself with, but that of disobedience (a heavy burden indeed to a delicate conscience; but yet does not bear that badge of infamy which is stamped on other crimes), I could not expect such lenity from the world, as to have my innocence allowed without any other proof than my word. Many people are ready to believe any ill of one person, if that belief does not tend to the justification of another; but when it does, they become charitable and good-natured, and will credit but half the evil, that they may lay the remainder on the other party, and so humanely blame two instead of one. This I take to have given rise to the declaration, by which many think they shew a candid and impartial humanity, that there must be faults on both sides. As Mr. Monkerton's extreme villainy in a great degree made my excuse, I had all reason to expect that most people would believe that no man could be so great a villain.

Shame is often very inconsistent with itself, and makes us do what we ought to be most ashamed of. The only prudent step I could have taken, was, to have gone home to my father, and endeavoured every means of prevailing on him to receive me; but shame, as I have said, prevented me: And tho' prudence is oftener looked upon as a branch of wisdom than of virtue, yet she who offends against the one, is in great danger of swerving from the other.

I had as strong a sense of virtue as pride can give: I felt it so necessary to my happiness, that the mere imputation of vice made me give myself up for lost to the world, and to myself; since I was lost to reputation. I saw no glimmering of hope to be rescued from infamy; but, with a dramatic poet, agreed, that when a woman has once sacrificed her fame,

> *In vain with tears the loss she may deplore;*
> *In vain look back to what she was before:*
> *She sets like stars, that fall to rise no more.*[84]

I did not perceive the difference between virtue and reputation; and that I might preserve the one, tho' I could not regain the other; but felt myself totally deprived of every comfort, and my passions all subsided into a settled despair.

Mr. Monkerton and Mr. Senwill had both often called on me, when I was not capable of bearing the sight of the one, or conversing with the other; but after some days repeated refusals, the former prevailed on my maid to admit him. His appearance rouzed me out of my lethargy of grief; my passions began to rise; and he found I had more resentment remaining than he imagined I was then capable of, from the account he had received of me.

The design of Mr. Monkerton's visit was to prevail with me to become what I had so long appeared, and live with him as his mistress, which he represented as the only part that remained for me to act; called what he had done excess of love, and promised every indulgence that could make me happy.

To presume thus on the love he imagined I must still entertain for him, and on the deplorableness of my situation, was a fresh insult, which he found I was capable of resenting. I from my heart detested him for his baseness; and, with truth, told him, that beggary and famine would be more eligible to me, than any further intercourse with him.

The only satisfaction I had received from the moment of the fatal discovery of Mr. Monkerton's treachery, was from seeing him really touched at my resolution. However, he flattered himself, that as my anger subsided, this might alter; and he well knew that my pride allowed me no resource, after so mortifying a circumstance; and therefore renewed his solicitations, both by letter and by speech, whenever he could obtain admittance, but to little purpose; my hatred was founded on my strongest principle, pride; and therefore was unconquerable.

When he saw the power it had over me, he was extremely afflicted; he wept, beseeched, used every means to move my compassion; and I never saw a greater wretch than he appeared when he found me inexorable: Upon which, deprived of all hopes, he determined to go abroad; and actually did so, as soon as he could equip himself for his journey.

Mr. Senwill had likewise obtained permission to see me as soon as I was able to bear conversation; and from his I found some relief, for it was filled with all the tokens of compassion; he wept with me when I wept; he joined in my rage against Mr. Monkerton, with unaffected detestation of his proceedings; and I found had dropped his acquaintance, from the time that he learnt his treatment of me.

The tenderness of a friend is always pleasing, but never so much as when distress deprives us of all other comfort. Mr. Senwill's principles appeared such as merited my esteem, and his attachment engaged my gratitude. With him I could lament over all the horrors of my situation, and ask his advice about the means of rescuing me from them.

In this point alone his friendship failed me; for he did not assist me in any expedients, but constantly offered his fortune to my acceptance, with an air of such disinterested generosity, as gave me pleasure, tho' it could not procure my acceptance. He all the time professed only the tenderest friendship, avoiding every expression of a passion, with which he had reason to think I was in no very good humour.

When Mr. Monkerton took leave of me, the day before he set out for Dover, from whence he was to proceed to France, he offered me the continuance of such part of his income as would enable me to live as I had done since I belonged to him, if I would gratify him with the acceptance of it, which he had the better hopes of, as his image was not stamped on his money. This offer I totally rejected: Destitute as I was of support, I could not accept it from one who had so grievously injured me.

The money I had by me served for my maintenance for about three months; during which time I lived upon it, irresolute in what way to fix the future part of my life; but when it was almost spent, I found it necessary to take a speedy resolution, and consulted Mr. Senwill on every scheme which offered itself to my mind, tho' I had little reason to expect much assistance from him; for, as I have already said, he always appeared more at a loss than myself: But the distressed and the irresolute oftener consult a friend in order to gain a good excuse for talking of their grievances, than from a desire or expectation of receiving much benefit from their advice.

Mr. Senwill had done little more than increase the difficulties which presented themselves to my view, on every thing I thought of undertaking, till he found my circumstances required some immediate determination. He then began to profess a passion, which, he said, he long had stifled, and would have still concealed, rather than have run a hazard of my thinking him too self-interested, if he could have prevailed on me to suffer him to supply me with an income suitable to the way of life I had been used to; but since a too delicate generosity made me obstinately reject his offers, he would shew me how to render him under eternal obligations to me, and at the same time free myself from all my difficulties.

He assured me he would do all that was in his power to raise my blasted reputation, by treating me as his wife, and consenting to my assuming his name. All this he urged with a sincerity of love, which affected me, who was full of esteem for him; and, by having continually drawn his compassion into a comparison with Mr. Monkerton's cruel treachery, had conceived a high opinion of him. But I could not listen to such a proposal without very humiliating reflections, at seeing how much I was sunk in the world, to have them made me with so little ceremony.

These drew tears from my eyes, which Mr. Senwill wiped off, with an air which spoke the softest tenderness and pity; and had, I believe, delicacy enough to guess from whence they sprung, for he avoided asking me the cause; but allowing something to the last struggles of that pride which I called virtue, he mixed some tears with mine, and, from partaking of my melancholy, made himself a pretence for becoming more tenderly familiar.

Tho' I was mortified at Mr. Senwill's presuming to make me this offer, yet I could not be offended. Innocent as I had been, I could not expect he should think of marrying a woman who had nothing but infamy to bring him; and if he had been so generous, or so weak, which-ever you please to call it, as to have harboured such a design, he had a father, who would have been a sufficient impediment to his putting it in practice: And I have often thought since, that as he knew all the workings of my mind, he must see that pride, which now was robbed of all opportunity of taking the shape of virtue, would lead me into vice.

When a woman receives such proposals without anger, compliance is seldom far off. I saw a means of avoiding all the difficulties which had occurred in my various schemes; and that only by contributing to the happiness of the man who seemed so interested in mine; whom, tho' I did not love with all the heights of romantic passion, yet I esteemed with a tenderness which was more rational, and likely to be not less satisfactory. Virtue and reputation were to me synonymous terms; I therefore looked upon myself as much lost to them as I ever could be; and like, I believe, many of my sex, thought, that after being once entered into that way of life, it was impossible to go back, as if a point of honour had obliged me to fulfil the expectations which my former conduct might naturally have raised.

A lover is not in danger of having a very tedious cause to plead, when his mistress strengthens his arguments by such reasons of her own. Mr. Senwill was not many days in obtaining my consent to all he had offered, and I became in reality what I before had only appeared; and, what was odd enough, seemed now to some, among whose faults incredulity could not be numbered, to be what I before thought myself, A wife.

CHAP. XVIII.

OTWAY.[85]

MR. Senwill's behaviour won my whole heart, which did not pique itself upon being incapable of ever admitting a second object of its affections;[86] and as I was grown desperate in the point of reputation, I no longer made myself a prisoner, but kept such company as I could, and went to public places in a moderate degree, tho' with less satisfaction, as Mr. Senwill could not venture often to accompany me there.

One night that I was peculiarly happy in Mr. Senwill's being with me in the gallery at the play (for we went into that part of the house, in order to avoid being seen), I heard somebody come in with more than ordinary bustle, and sit down behind me; which tempted me to turn round, and my sister proved the person. I started with surprize; but much greater was her emotion, filled with horror, as she said, to think she was near so shameless a wretch; and gladly would she have fled, for fear of contagion; but the rows behind her had filled so fast, that she could not get away.

I saw no one with her but a youth, who was 'prentice to my father when I left him, and could not be out of his time.[87] This excited my curiosity; and I expressed my surprize at seeing a person of her great prudence without any other companion.

'Surely,' replied she, 'a woman cannot be in better company than with her husband: I wish you were in any so creditable.' 'Your husband!' said I; 'How can that be? I am sure my father could never consent to such a match.'

'Well,' answered my sister, 'if he did not consent, I have, however, done no harm; for marriage is holy and honourable too: I wish no one of his family had done worse.'[88]

Mr. Senwill pitied my situation, and told her, he would not dispute the merits of her husband; but he confessed he rather took it ill, that she should imagine he did not make her sister as good an one; for he thought it his duty to make his wife happy, and had done all that lay in his power for that purpose.

Tho' my sister had so much feared to be contaminated by sitting near me, her situation began now to be rendered more uneasy by envy, than it was before by her virtuous apprehensions; and she could not bring herself to speak to me afterwards: While she thought she had the advantage of matrimony over me, she could bear the superiority of my appearance; but when she believed us on an equality in that particular, it became insupportable.

As I could not engage her in conversation, I got Mr. Senwill to put such questions to my new brother-in-law, as should gratify my curiosity; and he, young enough to be vain that a woman of discretion had fallen in love with him, was more communicative; and we learnt, that she ran away with him, that they were just married, and were endeavouring to obtain my father's forgiveness, and to be received by him.

It would have been cruel not to have pardoned the consequence of so high a value for his sex, and a despair of meeting with a reward for so much prudence, whose recompence had been long enough delayed to alarm her apprehensions with a possibility that it might never arrive.

I lived with Mr. Senwill in great tranquility, full of confidence in his love, his generosity, and his honour. He possessed a delicacy of mind, and a gentleness of manners, which rendered him peculiarly amiable. He suffered for every mortification I received, and was delighted with every incident that gave me pleasure. I had, I believe, less passion for him than I had felt for Mr. Monkerton, but much more tenderness. The one had captivated my fancy, and amused my mind; he had charms enough to over-balance the faults or follies I saw in him, but still I perceived them. But my judgment applauded all my sentiments for Mr. Senwill; without intoxicating my fancy, he gained my whole soul; my attachment to him was of a more serious sort; it gave a gravity mixed with tenderness to the whole turn of my mind, and rendered it more suitable to his; which, free from the flights of youth, was steadily fixed in the paths of honour; and except his frailty in regard to myself (and this, instead of then appearing a crime in my eyes, was, if not his first, yet his most endearing merit), I believe he never performed an action, which was not directed by honour and virtue. This testimony is due to an integrity by which I suffered; but suffered without repining, acknowledging the justice of my fate, and esteeming the cause of my uneasiness still the more for having inflicted it upon me.

In Mr. Senwill's society I enjoyed such a sober uninterrupted happiness, as deadened in me the sense of reputation; and I almost ceased to regret what I considered as irrecoverable.

My servants seemed to believe me really married; they saw nothing in my behaviour or manner of life to make them doubt it: I was not too indulgent, in order to blind their eyes to my failings, nor mean enough to wish to make them feel their inferiority, by adding weight to the burden of servitude: I made them neither my companions nor my slaves; but enabled, by the happy composure of my mind, to preserve a just medium, I treated them as persons to whose happiness it was my duty to contribute, without putting them out of their sphere. I imagine nothing was more conducive to my gaining their good opinion than this behaviour; for women who are casually placed in a station superior to their expectations, and in which they are supported only by vice, are apt to be 'vain of a little brief authority;'[89] and for fear they should not be known to have persons under their sway, they become their tyrants.

I had a few acquaintance, indeed as many as I desired; they were people fit for the companions of a tradesman's daughter, but not for Mr. Senwill's wife. People of condition were not so easily imposed upon; therefore I could not expect to be admitted into their society; and I was content without it.

In this manner about a year had passed, when Mr. Senwill began to appear melancholy and uneasy; a change which much alarmed me. I often enquired into the cause, but for some time without success; till, no longer able to resist my importunity, he acquainted me, that my brother-in-law, at his return into the country (upon the strength of what he had said in answer to my sister's insolence, which he could not bear, considering himself as the subject of her reproaches), had spread the report of our marriage so universally, that it had reached his father's ears; who enquiring narrowly into our way of life, was equally disturbed with the fear that we were really married, or that his son had entered into engagements, which he looked upon in a light more serious than the rest of the world.

I could not but be very uneasy at finding Mr. Senwill's father was apprised of our connexions: I knew how much his son respected him, his high sense of the duty owing to a parent, and the more particular reverence which his peculiar virtues demanded; and therefore was sensible that while the father was offended or uneasy, the son could not be happy.

Old Mr. Senwill is a man of uncommon integrity; of manners as gentle as his son's; tenderly affectionate, wisely indulgent to his children, mild to their frailties, but rigid to their vices; a man of great sincerity, and strictly religious. His paternal affection, which prevented his ever being angry with his children, rendered him liable to be extremely afflicted with any fault in their behaviour: He was much interested in their temporal welfare, but inexpressibly anxious for their future happiness.

This amiable disposition could not fail of meeting with a most affectionate return from such a son, who feared nothing so much as giving his father pain. He knew that caprice or ill humour had no share in the direction of his father's actions; tender paternal love was the sole motive of every thing he said or did; and his son repaid him by every thing that filial affection could dictate.

Sincerely as Mr. Senwill loved me, I do not believe he would ever have ventured to enter into any connexions with me, if he had thought there was much danger of its coming to his father's knowledge, who had for some years retired into the country; and was brought to London only by the report of his son's marriage with a woman of ill fame, which had disturbed the peace of his retirement.

I knew not what to expect from this event: I had no doubt of Mr. Senwill's love, and knew that he thought his honour in some measure engaged to me, and was sensible of the sincerity of my attachment to him: These were strong ties; but could scarcely be more potent than his obedience and affection to his father. Which would get the better, I knew not; nor was it of great consequence; for I saw that if I was conqueror, still he would never be happy, while he thought he was acting contrary to duty and gratitude.[90] It was almost as great a misfortune to me to see him uneasy, as to see myself forsaken: Every way I had nothing but unhappiness in view.

Mr. Senwill's tenderness seemed to increase with his melancholy; his love was never more apparent, but always accompanied with a visible distress of mind; and every token of affection from me, which used to give him so much pleasure, now put him into agonies of despair. I often begged him to give vent to all his thoughts, which I knew not how to interpret; but he as often told me he could not express his sensations, nor communicate all his afflictions. By these expressions I learnt to fear evils beyond what I already suffered.

CHAP. XIX.

OTWAY.[91]

I PASSED some months in this state of suspense, suffering much, and fearing more; but was at last cleared of all my doubts, by a visit from one of Mr. Senwill's friends, deputed by him with a message, which he could neither write nor speak to me himself.

This gentleman acquainted me, that about two years before, a match had been negotiated between Mr. Senwill and a young Lady of large fortune, whose person and disposition were perfectly amiable; and her regard for Mr. Senwill so visible, tho' veiled under great natural modesty, that every body expected it should much endear her to him. In consequence of this disposition in his favour, her father had proposed the match, tho' her fortune was superior to what Mr. Senwill could possibly expect. His father had been greatly pleased with it, and accepted it readily, not supposing it possible his son should be averse to an union with a woman so infinitely desirable.

The young gentleman was sent for down, and told, that every thing was agreed upon; his father having often heard him speak of her with the greatest esteem, and having some time before fansied he saw a partiality in him towards her. And thus far he judged rightly; while Mr. Senwill had no other attachment, he liked no one so well; but tho' she had pleased his reason, she had not enslaved his fancy, which was reserved for one less deserving.

He received his father's summons after his passion for me commenced, tho' he had then no expectation of meeting with a return, or any thought of declaring it; with-held by a sense of honour, while he looked on my affections as the property of his friend. But yet he could not think of marrying another woman; especially one who, he was conscious, deserved the whole possession of a heart, which he had not to dispose of.

It was difficult for a man of Mr. Senwill's politeness and humanity to decline an affair so far advanced, especially when he was not ignorant of the regard the young Lady had for him; but he was too firmly determined, not to effect it; and his father's indulgence would not suffer him to insist on what he had engaged in, tho' his honour and his inclination strongly interested him in it.

When the old gentleman found his son's attachment to me was so strong, and had inquired enough into my past life to have even a worse opinion of me than I deserved (for he neither knew the whole of my case, nor had any partiality to plead in the behalf of my faults); he was fully bent on dividing us. He met with more opposition from his son than he imagined him capable of giving to any thing he so much desired. He knew the strength of his son's reason and dutiful affection so well, that he did not suppose it possible they should be conquered by passion. But he found it easier to make him wretched than passive; he saw him miserable; but he discovered that he still visited me, and despaired of preventing it, unless he could bring his honour and humanity on his side. To effect this, he intreated him to consent to his renewing the negotiation with the young Lady, whom he had before refused.

To this Mr. Senwill was more averse than ever; and it was his father's continual solicitations which had occasioned the extreme distress he had appeared in. But at last the old gentleman making this the only means of giving him any ease of mind, or of gaining his pardon for his son's offences, and representing to him the melancholy effects which the love of him had had on the young Lady whom he rejected, who ever since had been in a decline of health and spirits, which deserved the more compassion from him, as she had been led into liking him by an appearance of his partiality for her; these arguments, continually urged to him, at length determined Mr. Senwill to sacrifice his own inclination to the will of a father, whom he thought he could never sufficiently obey. And by this gentleman he sent me this intelligence; tho' he could not part with me without one last farewel, but knew he should not have courage to tell me it was to be for ever.

This circumstantial detail was, in part, designed to break my misfortune to me the more gently; and to render, it supportable, was concluded with assurances of Mr. Senwill's everlasting esteem and gratitude, which no change of circumstances could extinguish; and with a promise, that he would wait on me the next day.

The shock was great to part with a man whom I loved with reverence (for such was my affection for Mr. Senwill), and to be left again without support or comfort. But I was prepared by the expectation of some great evil, and was so wretched at seeing his distress, that nothing but such an event could render me more so. My passions, which had once been so outrageous, were now softened by previous sorrow; besides, I had nothing to move my anger; and grief, unaccompanied by any other passion, will not cause impatience.

I perceived what I had to expect, before the gentleman had advanced far in his story, and tears came to my relief: As he proceeded, the torrent increased, and they calmed my soul; and perhaps my sorrow was more easily confined within the bounds of patience, from the fear I had of losing some part of the narration.

I found this gentleman had been desired to use every argument of consolation: He urged all he could think of; but what a cold heart utters with indifference, can have little effect on one which is tormented with the most poignant grief. When he found the small success of all he said, and that I gave as little ear to his philosophy as Romeo does to the Friars, which he holds entirely unavailing, as it cannot make a Juliet;[92] he left me, without receiving the acknowlegements due for the trouble he had taken; but those who are 'With themselves at war, neglect the shews of love to others.'[93]

I found I grieved more from the fear of losing Mr. Senwill's affection, than for the loss of his society, or his fortune. To see him, was necessary to my happiness; but to be loved by him, seemed requisite to my existence. Herein I received some consolation the next day.

With what impatience did I wait for the hour, when I might expect to see Mr. Senwill! Impatience mixed with fear; a joy, as it approached, blended with sorrow. My mind was a complication of contradictions. He came as he had promised, 'But, Oh! that meeting was not like the former!'[94] With steps as hasty and unequal as the beating of my fluttering heart, he came up-stairs; but when he entered, and saw me like a spectre, with scarcely life or motion, he threw himself on a couch, in such an agony of grief, as rouzed me from the state I was in; and, neglectful of my own sorrow, I sunk on my knees at the side of the couch by him, endeavouring to soothe his affliction. But this attempt only served to increase it; and above two hours passed before either of us was capable of any utterance, but sighs and tears: I continuing in my posture, weeping over him; while, with his arms round me, he clasped me to his bosom.

The desire of lessening his sufferings, by concealing part of my own, enabled me to be the first who broke thro' this scene of silent woe: I begged him to compose himself, intreated him not to grieve for me, who, I imagined, was the chief object of his affliction; for I could never be wretched if he was happy; which I trusted he must be, with a woman so much worthier than myself, and with the satisfaction arising from a consciousness of his obedience to the best of fathers.

But while I was telling him, that the contemplation of his felicity should be my consolation, my look and manner so contradicted my words, that my despair and grief were never more strongly painted; and little amendment appeared in us the whole day (for he spent it all with me), except that we grew able to express our wretchedness.

He sent an excuse to his father, who expected him in the evening; for he was very unfit to be seen by any one, and utterly incapable of conversation. But in all our discourse, nothing afflicted him more sensibly, than my obstinately rejecting a settlement from him: He had brought one ready drawn up, and intreated my acceptance, with such earnestness, as the only consolation he could receive, and the only means of his enjoying a moment's peace of mind, that nothing could have made me capable of a refusal which appeared so cruel, but consideration for his happiness.

I was too well acquainted with his generosity, not to foresee this circumstance; and therefore had reflected upon it, when he had not, by his importunity, the means of rendering me incapable of judging. I was afraid, that if such a thing came to be known, as in a length of time it in all probability must, it would give cause of discontent to his wife, who would not easily be persuaded that he had never seen me after his marriage; and I could better support any distress, than a thought of occasioning the least uneasiness between him and his wife.

No consideration of less consequence could have enabled me to resist. He assured me that the sum was no greater than he might with justice dispose of; for he should restrain his own particular expences within such bounds, that his share of their fortune could not be thought above his due, tho' his wife would bring the greater part of it; and that he should lose all esteem for her, if he thought she would desire him to behave otherwise to a woman who merited so much from him; or, if she could wish to deny that one gratification, to a man who sacrificed all the happiness of his life to her.

Tho' I was unconquerable in my resolution in this particular, I could not refuse to promise that I would accept what money he had by him; which he insisted on sending me, when he had no hopes of prevailing in his other request.

He informed me, that he was to be married the day but one following; for he had been desirous of having a day to recover himself, after taking leave of me, that he might be the better able to go thro' the solemn ceremony, which would oblige him never to see me more; at least, till age should have robbed us of our passions, and of the charms which excited them. This opened to us a prospect, which we then seized as our sole consolation, and promised a constant remembrance of, and esteem for, each other; and that, when that happy period should come (for such it then appeared to us, as we thought that age could take nothing from us, which would not be far more than compensated by the restoration of each other's society), we then might meet again, and converse as free from guilt as from scandal.

But tho' this seemed some consolation, yet it could not enable us to take so long a farewel without an agony of grief, which greatly prolonged it. Many times we said, Adieu! before we could think we had taken absolute leave of each other; and whenever we had, we found the suffering so great, we agreed to defer it one quarter of an hour: By these delays the night was far advanced, before Mr. Senwill could prevail on himself to go; and when he did, he was obliged to the assistance of his servant, or he could not have got into his chair.

CHAP. XX.

Our life is short, but to extend that span
To vast Eternity, is virtue's work.
SHAKESP.[95]

AS for myself, my situation was beyond the power of description; pardon the tears which the recollection draws from me: My grief was intense, but not bitter: I admired the man who had inflicted it, if possible, still more than ever; I loved him better for being thus forsaken by him; and I had one satisfaction which accompanied every thought, that he still loved me to excess. Tho' I had lost his conversation, I preserved his affection: This was a resource, in which my heart found relief from despair, tho' not from regret.

I had desired Mr. Senwill not to send me the money he insisted on my accepting, till the day after his marriage; that I might have an opportunity of enquiring how he had supported his spirits. Accordingly on the appointed day, the friend, who had before been with me, came and delivered me a pocket book, wherein he said the sum was inclosed.

My thoughts were so much more employed on the giver than on the gift, that, instead of opening it, I enquired after Mr. Senwill's health; and learnt from his friend, that he was not able, till the evening of the day after he was with me, to wait either on his father or his mistress; that the former excused it, knowing the struggle in his heart, and was sufficiently thankful to him for conquering his inclinations at all: The latter knew not the cause of this seeming neglect, which he attributed to illness,[96] and with great truth, for the body cannot be well when the mind is so ill at ease. She had, during the whole negotiation, perceived a melancholy in Mr. Senwill, which had given her some apprehensions: she thought him but little of a lover; but the affection which made her feel it the more sensibly, inclined her to over-look it, and rather to seem ignorant of it, than run the hazard of an explanation, which might be worse than doubt. She plainly saw, that he beheld their approaching marriage with coldness; but she trusted to his honour and humanity for being well used, and thought his generosity would not return indifference to the love he would perceive she had for him, and to her constant endeavours to please him. With most men this would have been but a frail dependance; but with Mr. Senwill it was infallible.

They were married, as had been agreed upon; and the gentleman, who brought me this intelligence, accompanied Mr. Senwill, from the time he rose, to the end of the day; and was one of their attendants at church.[97] He told me his friend got up with such a depression of spirits, and so fixed a melancholy in his countenance, that he was alarmed, lest he either should not have resolution enough to go thro' the ceremony, or that his appearance would cast a damp on every heart. But that, after conversing together about two hours, and summoning every argument to his aid, he assumed an air, which persons inclined to look on the side most agreeable to themselves, might think rather solemn than melancholy. He had endeavoured by dress to give a chearfulness to his general appearance; and thus fortified, with all the resolution he could summon to his assistance, they went together to the bride; whom they found elegantly beautiful; her dress not gaudy, and her countenance not devoid of fear, which Mr. Senwill's coldness had raised.

They soon proceeded to church, and there, as well as the whole day, his friend behaved with as much chearfulness as he could expect, tho' he saw frequently such struggles in his mind to keep up any tolerable degree of it, as filled him with apprehensions, lest he should at last lose all command of himself; and with compassion for the lady, who he feared might see thro' it, as he plainly perceived old Mr. Senwill did, whose parental tenderness shone in his countenance; where pity for what his son suffered was blended with joy, in the prospect of happiness, which he flattered himself was opening before him, when his first melancholy was worn off.

Tho' every particular of this narration went to my soul, yet I listened greedily after it; and never votary put up a more ardent prayer than I did for the happiness of this marriage; for what I wanted in devotion towards the Being I prayed to, was made up by love to him I prayed for.

This gentleman left me a direction to him, begging, that if ever it was in his power to serve me, I would without scruple apply to him. This, he said, he owed to Mr. Senwill's friendship, who had desired him to grant me any protection or assistance I should find requisite; but that, independent of such a request, the esteem which, from my behaviour and his friend's good opinion of me, he had conceived for me; his sincere compassion for what he had seen me suffer; and the title nature had given me to every regard from his sex, would have made him ardent in offers of his services, as nothing could yield him greater pleasure than to be so employed.

I promised, if ever I saw occasion, he should hear from me; and after he was gone, and I grew composed, I opened the pocket-book he had brought me, and, to my surprize, found it contained bills to the value of 600*l.* but what was to me of much more worth, with them was a letter from Mr. Senwill.

I could not forgive my want of curiosity, which had so long delayed my receiving this blessing. I felt new life flow into my heart at the sight of his hand, and opened it with rapture and impatience: It contained all that words can express of kind, generous, and noble, with such deep distress, that I forgot I was a sufferer to grieve for him; but I was called off to some attention to myself by the latter part of it, wherein he told me, 'That the only thing which could have prevailed on him to leave me, was having his conscience convinced that we lived in sin; and that all the alleviations custom had taught him to allege, were fatal deceptions. That this afflicted him more for me than for himself; for he was not able to bear the reproaches both of his conscience and his love; for having drawn in, to be partner of his guilt, the person whose welfare was dearer to him than any thing on earth. That he could not mention this circumstance in his message, nor when he saw me, fearing I should look upon it as a reproach for my past conduct, which in him would have been highly unjust; since he was conscious that the crime was all his own: that I was in nothing to blame, but for my too partial opinion of his honour and integrity, two qualities to which he could no longer pretend any title, since they had not prevented him, who found me innocent, tho' unhappy, from taking advantage of my distress; and, because I was exposed to shame, leading me into guilt; which would be an eternal cause of sorrow and repentance to him.'

He then told me all the arguments his father had used to convince him of his crime; pointed out every text of scripture which declared the guilt and punishment attending it; wondering how he, who had in other things entirely acquiesced in its authority, could have been blinded in these particulars, by such poor evasions as the world makes use of to excuse the irregularities of which they are guilty: and added, that, had not this consideration far out-weighed his filial duty, his father could never have had his compliance to boast of; but he could not support the thought of bringing everlasting misery on her, whose smallest pain gave him inexpressible uneasiness.

He ended his letter with all the tenderest wishes, and the most ardent prayers, that a love, which was anxious both for the present and the eternal happiness of its object, could dictate: And intreated me not to restrain myself in any expenses that could give me the least satisfaction; for I might depend on having so constant a supply, that I should never find any deficiency.

Mr. Senwill's friend had hinted something to this effect; and I now saw plainly, that, altho' I would not accept of a stipulated sum, fixed even out of the power of the giver of it, and secured beyond his life, yet he was determined to bestow that as a present, which I would not receive as my due: But this I was resolved to prevent.

The part I have mentioned so particularly in Mr. Senwill's letter, made a very strong impression on me. My nature must have been very perverse, if he, who had led me into error, could not guide me to truth. I read, I examined the Scriptures as he recommended, and, above all, I continually perused his letter, where the arguments were so strong and clear, that, had my disposition been worse than it was, I could not have withstood conviction; which was facilitated by my having then no inducement to disbelieve truths so evident; for I am inclined to think our incredulity is oftener caused by an unwillingness to comply with the doctrine, than from a want of sufficient light to see the force of it.

The fears which were thus awakened in me for my soul, withdrew my thoughts, more than any thing else could, from Mr. Senwill; tho' I am afraid he was so interwoven with every consideration, that, even in my repentance, I was in some measure actuated by a desire of extenuating his guilt, by making him the means of my conversion.

CHAP. XXI.

I PASSED a week in this manner, and settled the plan of my future life conformably to it. I determined to convert the 600*l*. Mr. Senwill had so generously given me into an annuity; to settle in some cheap part of England, where I should be known only by my future conduct; and there to live in the exercise of Christian duties, to repent of my own sins, pray for him who had been a partner in them, and to endeavour, by all the means in my power, to contribute to the present ease and future felicity of all on whom I could have any influence.

The money I had by me, and the produce of some things which I intended to sell, as foreign to the purpose of my future life, the presents which the vanity of Mr. Monkerton, or the fondness of Mr. Senwill, had made me, I designed should maintain me, while I was seeking out for a proper place for my abode, and purchase me what conveniences I might want there: For this purpose it was more than sufficient, and would, in all probability, allow me a small sum to keep by me in case of exigence.

I had made no secret of my intention to my maid, tho' I did not intend to take her with me, as I would not have one about me who had my reputation in her power.

As I was at a loss for a place to fix on, and knew no good means of enquiring, I thought I would take advantage of the offer Mr. Senwill's friend had made me, and ask his assistance in the choice of one; and, perhaps, I was not sorry that Mr. Senwill should know a resolution, which I imagined would give him pleasure.

In pursuance of this determination, I sent my maid with a letter to him, and felt some impatience for her return, as I wanted to begin the course I had resolved on, and was not less desirous of an opportunity of inquiring after Mr. Senwill, which I flattered myself I should have, as I made no doubt but his friend would come to me on this occasion. But dinner was brought up, and my maid was not returned; I thought, perhaps, the gentleman was in company, and had made her wait for his answer. This supposition lasted a little time; but night came on, and still no news of her. I had made such frequent inquiries, that a less circumstance would have alarmed my under-maid, than seeing that all her things but one great box were gone, as she perceived was the case, on going into her room for something she wanted. The girl ran to me in a fright, and told me this particular. Tho' I had never conceived the least suspicion of her honesty, this account startled me; I asked if any people of ill appearance had been with her lately. The girl said, that, the night before, a man had called after it was dark, to whom she had given a box, saying, it was a carpenter who was to mend it, for it was broken; and as she was to move soon, it would be necessary to put all her things in repair.

Upon this I went into my room, to see if my things were safe. My trinkets, and such little things as I designed to sell, had been put off my toilette, out of her great care, as she pretended, from the time that I received notice of Mr. Senwill's design of leaving me, as no longer of use to me, who had then no temptation to dress with any care, beyond what cleanliness required. I went to the drawer where she had laid them, and found it empty. I now was prepared for the worst. I opened my bureau, and could find neither the notes for the 600*l.* nor the money I had by me, which I kept in the same place.

I no longer remained in doubt. I saw I was robbed, and knew not any means of recovering what I had lost. I was shocked at this circumstance, but had suffered too many sharper afflictions to be much grieved.

Here again I thought to have recourse to Mr. Senwill's friend, for his advice how to pursue the woman, and sent my only remaining servant to his house, to beg he would call on me; but she brought back word, that he was gone into the country for a fortnight.

To be deprived of all hopes of assistance from Mr. Senwill's friend was a mortifying circumstance: I knew no other person from whom to expect much help. I would not, on any consideration, have applied to Mr. Senwill; and when I reflected on the consequences which would probably have followed my acquainting his friend with my distress, I was no longer sorry that he was abroad, as it would, in all likelihood, have led Mr. Senwill into an expence, very inconvenient to him at that time; for he would have been desirous of reimbursing me.

I consulted one or two of the most sensible tradesmen with whom I dealt; but what they advised, took up the greatest part of the little money which I happened to have in my pocket, without bringing me any intelligence of what I had lost. I had therefore nothing left me, but to find out some means of providing for myself; the little plan, in the execution of which I had formed hopes of some remaining comfort, being now entirely overthrown.

The only thing that offered itself to my thoughts was service. I attempted several places which I heard of; but the want of recommendation procured me a constant refusal. I could not even venture to refer them to any of my neighbours, since my late situation was too well known to them.

When I found I had no chance for being received as a servant, I tried if I could maintain myself by plain work; but, by enquiry, I understood that my employment this way must be very precarious, so many seeking the same; and, by experience, I knew myself to be so very slow a worker, that, had I been always provided with employment, I should scarcely have been able to have procured myself the poorest sustenance.

Sincere repentance had humbled me; my pride was subdued by religion, which, in every particular but one, Mr. Senwill had been ever instilling into my mind, while we lived together; therefore I was the better prepared to receive all the truths of it. Having now no chance for a support, I wrote to my father, tho' I blushed to think of appearing before one I had so much offended, till I considered, that I had ventured to apply to the General Parent, against whom I had sinned more grievously: Thus encouraged, I wrote my father the most affecting letter which real distress could dictate; but it availed me little; I received for answer, that he disclaimed so shameless a daughter, and would never see me more.[99]

I had conceived great hopes of being accepted by him: To be thus rejected, therefore, afflicted me most sensibly: but I could not blame the severity which wounded me so deeply; I was conscious of my own unworthiness, and that in his eyes I must appear still worse than I was.

Deprived of every hope, I knew not what course to take; till I recollected having heard Mr. Senwill speak, with great praise, of this blessed asylum, for such wretches as myself. Here then I determined to apply, and the hand of pity received me, moved, like its Maker, by my penitence.

The day before I entered here I wrote a letter to Mr. Senwill; telling him, that he had compensated for perverting of me, by having wrought my repentance, and given me a sense of religion; which, without him, I might never have had; and that nothing should have made me trouble his peace, but my desire to give the ease to his mind, which I hoped it would receive from this information. I added, that I was going into a quiet and pious retreat, where he would share in all my prayers, and be for ever remembered by me.

This letter I carried to his friend's house; and, having found him at home, informed him of the robbery my maid had committed; of my unsuccessful endeavours to provide for myself; and of my last determination. He intreated me not to put this in execution; but I told him nothing could alter my resolution; and accordingly came the next day: and have enjoyed so much content since I entered these doors, that I cannot repine at my maid's dishonesty, especially as she left me Mr. Senwill's picture, which I contemplate hourly with a melancholy, but I hope an innocent, satisfaction.

You may remember, that in the first week after I was admitted, a gentleman came to speak to me; but not gaining admittance, a letter was brought me, which, as in duty bound, I shewed to the matron. The gentleman was Mr. Sen-will's friend, whom he had sent to prevail with me to suffer him to repair my loss; but that failing, he wrote to me for that purpose; intreating me, with the most tender and affecting earnestness, to comply with his request; for that he could not bear to think I should be reduced to live on charity, while he was supported in affluence. He added, that he pleaded herein for his own happiness; and therefore did not think I would deny him. In short, he omitted nothing that could give him a chance for prevailing: but my resolution was unalterable, with which I acquainted him in such positive terms, as should put an end to all further solicitations; and since that I have heard no more from him; but flatter myself he is contented with thinking me happy; and that all circumstances concur to render him so.

CHAP. XXII.

All born alike; from virtue first began
The diff'rence that distinguish'd man from man:
He claim'd no title from descent of blood;
But that which made him noble, made him good.
DRYDEN.[100]

GREAT pains have been taken by philosophers, to discover from whence proceeds the pleasure we receive by having our pity excited: Some have attributed it to the tenderness, others to the cruelty, of our natures; but neither have confirmed their hypothesis by unanswerable reasons: so that we still pity, and still are ignorant why we do so.[101] But while we participate with the distressed in their affliction, and grieve for their sorrows, we think ourselves free from all imputation of inhumanity, tho' we feel pleasure in our grief, and sometimes delight so much in it, that the observation of one, whose wit seldom spared the frailties of mankind, 'that every one can bear the misfortunes of others, perfectly like a Christian,'[102] falls so short of the truth, that they might be said, by one sect of the philosophers I have mentioned, to support them like Barbarians.

But I am not inclined to subscribe to their opinion, nor think that so tender a sensation arises from cruelty or pride; but whatever was the source, the society, whose biographer I am become, had listened both with compassion and pleasure, and thought the person who had thus entertained them, deserved their thanks.

If pride had any share in their pity, it led them not to exult over the failings they commiserated, by comparing them with their own superior merits; the only way it had to exert itself was in rejoiceing, not that they were unlike that Pharisee, but that the Pharisee[103] was like themselves.

It is easy to imagine, that, amongst persons whose lives have born some resemblance, many reflections must arise on every incident related; but as reflections are not the taste of the times, and are indeed too apt to want both spirit and novelty, one of which is at least requisite to make them entertaining, and to have no other property of easy writing, but that they are what any one may very easily write, as it has been defined, therefore I shall not trouble my readers with them, but proceed to the history of the rest, with more expedition than the curiosity of the hearers required.

The next who was called upon, was a very young girl, very pretty, but very little; with so strong an air of simplicity and innocence in her countenance, that it could not be effaced,[104] even by the loss of the virtues which originally had been the cause of it. Her cheeks were often dyed with so beautiful a vermillion, as shewed that nature had bestowed on her the finest complexion imaginable, with so resplendent a bloom, as eclipsed all the efforts of art; but tho' she was still extremely young, yet her constitution was so impaired, that her complexion had shared in the decay, tho' it would occasionally revive. Obedient to the first summons, she proceeded without ceremony, as follows:

My misfortunes began very early. When I was eight years old, I was told, by the person whom I had till then taken for my mother, that I was no child of hers, but that my real parent was of a rank far superior, and gave me this account of my birth, which I might not so well have remembered, had it not been repeated to me several times afterwards.

A lady came down to a neighbouring village, and took lodgings at a cottage, where, after some short stay, she was brought to bed of me. She went by the name of Tent, and was very lavish of her money, rewarding highly all those about her. She was very young and extremely melancholy; and generally found in tears if any one went into her room; watching impatiently for the post, but often disappointed of the letters she expected.

Before she was able to travel, she inquired for a sober good woman, with whom she might entrust me; and the person I took for my mother, the wife of a poor labourer, was recommended to her, to whose care she gave me, with all the charges which maternal tenderness could dictate; and agreed to remit her a very large allowance for my maintenance. She parted from me with the greatest agonies of grief and despair; and, from all appearances, I might have expected to receive every proof of a mother's fondness.

For four years the promised allowance was regularly remitted, accompanied with such cloaths as were suitable only to a child of the first rank. But after that time, notice was sent to my nurse, that my mother was dead, and she must abate of the price that was paid her for me.

As I had been hitherto their chief support, this was melancholy news; however, they were obliged to acquiesce; but had soon reason to think that the making such a bargain was entirely unnecessary, for they received no pay at all, nor knew where to apply for any.

However, these humane people let me suffer as little as possible by this omission. They fed me and cloathed me like their own children; but as they had a great number, and only one person's labour to support us all, it was in the poorest manner. The only difference they made between me and their own offspring, was in treating me with a little more distinction.

The place we lived in was extremely lonely; the people simple and ignorant to an excess: Our employment was spinning,[105] and the only thing we were taught. In this situation I remained a sharer in the poverty and content of those I lived with, till I was thirteen years old, when I had the misfortune to lose the only one whom I could look on as a mother. I lamented her as a parent; for I really loved her as such. Her husband had been in a sickly state of health some time, and was now unable to support his family, without the assistance of the parish; who not chusing to do works of supererogation, sent me to that wherein I was born, and whose business it was to provide for me.

As my qualifications were so few, I was a heavy burden to the parish,[106] which was therefore glad to get rid of me on the easiest terms; and having found an old gentlewoman willing to take me, I was consigned over to her. My cloaths and food were thought a sufficient reward for my merits, and indeed I believe were entirely so; but it was a reward I did not enjoy.

My mistress was an ancient virgin, who had what was called a competence to live on; that is, she had enough to maintain her, provided she half starved herself, and quite starved her servant.

She was, by birth, of a gentleman's family, worn thread-bare by that length of its existence which constituted the sum and substance of all her pride. The little she had, was spent in keeping up the appearance of gentility. She afforded herself a neat lodging, decent cloaths; and would not live without something by way of servant, tho' she could not afford to maintain one. She dressed me tolerably, that she might not be disgraced by what she meant should render her appearance more genteel; but, to gratify this pride, she scarcely allowed herself a sufficient share of sustenance, tho' of the meanest sort. As for myself, I could truly say, that I lived in the practice of that abstinence, which is recommended to those who would preserve their digestions in good order. I always rose from my meals hungry. To eat till I was able to eat no more, was a piece of gluttony with which no one could reproach me. I had just food enough to keep me always hungry;[107] a greater degree of fasting, would have damped my appetite: I, properly speaking, eat to live; for any abatement in my meals must have had mortal consequences.

My business was not well proportioned to my feeding, for of that I had an ample quantity. My mistress piqued herself on the utmost excess of cleanliness; tho' she was too neat to dirty her rooms, yet they were always cleaning; besides which, I washed all her linen; but that scarcely took up so much time as the daily folding it; for by pinching, plaiting, and stroking, it lasted a long time clean; and by wiping and brushing, her cloaths were as well preserved.

She was tall and thin, upright to a great degree of stiffness, which her well starched linen, its excessive cleanness, and the prim manner in which it was put on, greatly increased. Whenever I was not employed at home, she sent me about to retale her civilities in the town; no one was so constant in their inquiries into their neighbours health: If her humanity had been measured by her messages, she would have stood foremost in the rank of the benevolent.

By all this care she kept up a sort of respect, and had the satisfaction of being called Madam Selton, for that was her name, and esteemed one of the *top* people in the town where she lived. A sufficient reward, in her estimation, for greater labours. Then she had the honour of being the standard for fine work,[108] having wrought herself chairs, filled promiscuously with men, beasts, and flowers, in such an admirable degree of perfection, that no small ingenuity was required to know the animal from the vegetable part of her creation. She was the first in the place who exhibited any new sort of work, and had distinguished herself in every way of wasting time and materials that had been invented during the course of a long life.

No part of my business pleased me so well, as that which her civility gave me; for, as she was known to keep no profuse table, people would sometimes take pity on me, and invite me to partake of the superfluities of the house they lived in.

As curiosity runs thro' all stations, the story of my birth became pretty well known; and indeed my mistress was not backward in publishing it, having various inducements; first of all it gave her an opportunity of animadverting on the supposed imprudence of my mother, and the consequences of man's deceit, woman's folly, and the wickedness of both; blessing herself, all the time, that she had preserved herself from female frailty and male art; then there was enough of the marvellous in it, to make it no unentertaining part of conversation; and what perhaps pleased her the most of all, was, that it gave an air of distinction to her servant, which her imagination reflected back on herself.[109] Tho' the virtue of my parents appeared but in a suspicious light, yet their gentility seemed apparent; and she always observed, that it was her principal reason for taking me, 'as she thought it was the duty of people of fashion to do what they could for young persons of birth, as that might be an objection to many, who do not love to have those about them that are better born than themselves; and besides, there was a nobler way of thinking in *people* who had *good blood in their veins*, than in *the vulgar*, whose ideas were as mean as their birth.'

End of the FIRST VOLUME.

THE

HISTORIES

Of Some of the

PENITENTS

IN THE

MAGDALEN-HOUSE,

AS

Supposed to be related by Themselves.

In TWO VOLUMES

In the corrupted Currents of this World,
Offence's gilded Hand may shove by Justice:
And oft 'tis seen, the wicked Prize itself
Buys out the Law: But 'tis not so Above;
THERE is no shuffling; THERE the Action lies
In his true Nature; and we ourselves compell'd,
Ev'n to the Teeth and Forehead of our Faults,
To give in Evidence. What then? What rests?
Try what REPENTANCE can: What can it not?

SHAKESP.

VOL. II.

LONDON:

Printed for JOHN RIVINGTON in *St. Paul's
Church-yard*, and J. DODSLEY in *Pall-mall*.

M.DCC.LX.

THE

HISTORIES

Of Some of the

PENITENTS

IN THE

MAGDALEN-HOUSE

CHAP. I.

None knew, till guilt created fear,
What darts or poison'd arrows were.
ROSCOMMON.[110]

ALL my young acquaintance were continually advising me to leave my mistress, and go to London, where I might find out my mother; or, if I failed in that, could not be nearer starving than where I was. They had so little notion of the size of this metropolis, and the numbers it contains, that they persuaded me it could be no very difficult matter to find out Madam Tent; who seemed to them, by the accounts of her, to be such a very fine lady, that there could not be many such, even in London.

My ignorance was not likely to be less than theirs; since I had scarcely ever heard the name of the town but from them: and the advice so many *good friends* gave me, joined with my dislike of my place, and the desire of finding myself the daughter of a great Lady, determined me to execute this scheme, after I had lived near two years with my mistress.

I was not quite fifteen[111] when I set out, without any money in my pocket, but just what was necessary to pay for my passage in the waggon, and my maintenance on the road; for part of which I was obliged to some visitors to my mistress at Christmas; and the remainder was the contribution of those who advised me to this step; to whom I was to make a grateful return, when I was settled with my *Mamma*. I had so little fear of not finding her, that I was not at all disturbed by the emptiness of my pocket.

97

The waggon arrived in London about noon.[112] My possessions went into so small a compass, that I carried them with ease under my arm; and, as soon as I alighted, went the way which chance directed me, inquiring of every body where Madam Tent lived.[113] Some laughed, others answered me surlily; but as I knew no way of accounting for this behaviour, I did not attribute it to any absurdity in my question. I strayed in this manner a long time, hoping every good house I saw was Madam Tent's; but the frequent disappointments I met with began to discourage me.

At last, having put the same question to a man who stood at a shop-door, to my great joy he told me he knew such an one well enough; but asked, what Madam Tent I meant? 'My mother, an't please your Honour,' replied I, who took him for a very fine gentleman, never having seen even the 'Squire of our parish with so much lace on his waistcoat.

'Oh!' answered he, 'then it is the same: she lives in the next street: it must be her; for she is mother to a great many.'

'If she has so many children,' said I, 'it may be she will not be glad to have any more.'

'Never fear,' answered the man; 'she will hardly refuse such a daughter as you are: no, if there were an hundred like you, they would be all welcome: she is mighty good-humoured; an excellent kind mother you will find her.'

'Alack, Sir!' I replied, 'I am proud to hear it.' And being particularly directed, I went to the house; where knocking with much impatience, I soon brought a woman to the door, who asked me, with no very smiling countenance, what I wanted? I told her, 'Madam Tent.' The girl looked very hard at me; and then bidding me come along with her, carried me in to her mistress.

Madam Tent might sooner claim an air of dignity than of gentility. She was fat, red-faced, and dirty; her cloaths half off, for want of pinning; and, in short, so intirely the reverse of my late mistress, that I found a charm in what would have disgusted any one else. I was so much awed by the presence of so great a Lady, as I fancied her, that I stood dropping my little country court'sies at the door, as fast as could be, without attempting to speak.

The *good* Lady, seeing there was no end of my civility, or my silence, came up to me, and taking my hand, and smiling with wonderful affability, asked me if I wanted her? She exhorted me many times not to be ashamed of telling her what brought me there, before I could get courage to inform her, that, 'if I might be so bold, I believed she was my mother.' 'Very likely,' replied she, 'my pretty dear; or if I am not already, I am willing to be so: but tell me, my love, how I came to be your mother.'

Encouraged by her kind expressions, I gave her the best account I could of my birth, and of the resolution I had taken to find out my mother, and how long I had walked about the town before any one would tell me where she lived.

I saw my supposed mother give a significant look at a young woman, who was in the room, which I imagined implied her approbation of my courage in seeking her out; and then expressing great joy at finding her lost daughter, embraced and kissed me, and told me, that she would introduce me to a great many sisters. Accordingly several young women were called down, who all received me very kindly, and asked me many questions. I saw they were diverted at my answers; which I did not wonder at, as I was sensible I must appear very odd and aukward to such fine ladies.

I need not tell you, that this supposed mother of mine was an old bawd,[114] whose name being the same of that I was inquiring for, it was not strange I fell into her hands. But to render the motives for her proceedings better understood, I shall tell you her views as I go on in my story, tho' I did not know them till some time afterwards.

As soon as she saw me, my extreme youth, my fresh complexion, and the great innocence and simplicity of my appearance,[115] made her think me no small acquisition. When she heard what brought me there, she readily acquiesced in the claim I laid to her; and resolved neither to undeceive me, nor to suffer me to be broke of my innocent aukwardness, which she thought would be a great charm to many men; and tho' often imitated, yet could never be equalled by any art. For this purpose she charged all her young women to avoid every thing that could lessen my ignorance in any particular; and began to consider how to turn her young savage to the best account.

She kept me out of the way of her company, telling me I must not appear till she had got me cloaths fit for her daughter; and a mantua-maker was employed to fit some she had by her to my person. The hopes she had of turning me to her advantage, put her in such good humour, that to appear fond of me was no hard task; and I was delighted to find the man's account of her good-nature so true.

As I perceived an aukwardness in my manner and expression, I was desirous of correcting it, and begged my mother and sisters would assist me in polishing myself; but my mother charged me to avoid making the least alteration in either; for she should not love me half so well, if I was without those peculiarities; and assured me they would be looked upon by every one as so many graces; for nothing was so attracting as novelty. This made me lay aside my design, and consequently grow inattentive to differences, which had before struck me so much; and I indulged my rusticity without controul.

As soon as I was perfectly equipped, I was suffered to drink tea in the parlour with the gentlemen who came to the house; but was always directed to retire to my room very soon afterwards. Various reasons were given me why I should not stay; which passed upon me for the true ones, not having the least notion that I was then only shewing to different people, that Mrs. Tent might know who would bid the highest for me.

After this manner of proceeding for a few days, my supposed mother told me, that Mr. Mastin, one of the gentlemen who had drank tea with us two or three times, had desired to come that afternoon to see me, without going into so much company; and therefore I should receive him in my own room.

I expressed my surprise at his preferring the conversation of such an ignorant unbred girl as myself to that of my sisters, who were so much more genteel and agreeable. She told me my ignorance was my charm; that he was delighted with my innocence, and declared he never saw so inchanting a young creature. 'He is vast good,' replied I, 'to excuse my aukwardness.' As this led us into some discourse about my rusticity, I ventured to ask her 'If my sisters were not a little bold; for seemingly to me they were sometimes a little bold and forward.' 'O child,' answered my mother, 'it is natural you should think so, having been educated amongst vulgar people; but their behaviour is that of persons of fashion: all such conduct themselves in the same manner.' I begged pardon for my vulgarity; and our conversation was interrupted by the arrival of Mr. Mastin.

Soon after Mr. Mastin came, my mother was called out of the room, and we remained *tête à tête*.

Whether he had any doubt about the reality of my simplicity, or only an inclination to be convinced of it from my own mouth, I know not; but he by questions drew from me an account of my whole life, from the first of my remembrance: which indeed was no difficult matter; for I was qualified to talk on so few subjects, that I was very well inclined to make myself the topic of my discourse.

Mr. Mastin shewed so much compassion at any incidents in my relation which implied distress, and interrupted me by so many compliments and tender expressions, as pleased me much. There is great pleasure in being loved and pitied. They were both almost new to me; and I felt myself much obliged to a gentleman, who, tho' so late an acquaintance, seemed so fond of me.

Mrs. Tent had sold this interview at a pretty good price, tho' Mr. Mastin had engaged to forbear shocking my vulgar notions, as she expressed herself, all at once; and accordingly, when the stipulated time was expired, she returned to us, and not long after he took his leave, having obtained permission to wait on me the next day.

As soon as Mr. Mastin went away, my *mother* asked me how I liked him; and I replied 'Desperate well: he has the winningest ways with him, surely, that ever gentleman had: so humble, that, would you believe it, he kiss'd my hand I dare say forty times, and seemed to love me as well as if I had been his own daughter. He called me the sweetest names! you cannot think how desperate engaging he was.'

'Good gentleman!' cried Mrs. Tent, 'he is indeed mighty sweet-tempered and obliging, and I believe loves you much.' But she could not so well compose her countenance, as not to let a tendency to smile appear on it; which alarming my simple pride, as I thought she laugh'd at my folly, I asked what excited it? 'Only, my dear,' replied she, 'to think that your simplicity should have won the heart of a man, that so many ladies have been aiming at in vain.'

This answer pleased my vanity too well to leave me any doubt of its being the true reason of a smile, for which I was inclined to account in a manner less civil to myself.

CHAP. II.

> For what one likes, if others like as well,
> What serves one will, when many wills rebel?
>   POPE.[116]

MR. Mastin came the next day, and was brought up into my room. As the liberty he had purchased was more extensive than the day before, he soon surprised me by his familiarity; and at last I threatened him, that if he did not behave better I would tell my *mother*. He desired I would, and I should learn from her, that there was no impropriety in his behaviour.

Ashamed of the complaints I had to make, I did not immediately keep my word; but finding I could not make him desist, I told him, that 'if he did not mend his manners, I would go and tell all to my mother.' He declared I should not leave him; but was very willing that I should ring the bell, and send for her.

I did accordingly; and when she came, I acquainted her with 'what a horrid rude man Mr. Mastin was; and that he was so desperate bold and impudent, I would stay with him no longer; and desired she would scold him.'

'What for, child?' said she, with a very discontented countenance, having flattered herself that the great prejudice I had expressed in his favour would have secured him an easier conquest; and that the shame I should feel for what I had done, and my desire of concealing it from her, would have been an additional proof of my simplicity, and greatly enhanced my charms. But finding her hopes frustrated, she had another resource. 'What should I scold Mr. Mastin for, child?' said she: 'May not a man take what liberties he will with his wife?'

'With his wife!' interrupted I. 'But how am I his wife? I never was so much as in the same church with him in all my life.'

'What is that to the purpose?' replied Mrs. Tent: 'None but low country people make all that fuss about marriage. No other ceremony is required among people of fashion,[117] but for a gentleman to tell a lady that he will marry her daughter; and then, if she consents, they become man and wife.'

'I do not know how that may be,' said I; 'but I am sure 'Squire Scrimshell's daughter was married at our church; and yet she was as fine a lady as hands and pins could make her; and he was a desperate fine gentleman too.'

'Very likely,' replied my *mother*: 'Country 'Squires keep to old fashions; but people of quality have left off making such a bustle about it.'

'I am sure,' added I, 'that I remember poor Susan Stokes was made to stand in a white sheet in our parish,[118] because she had a child by a man to whom she had never been married in the church; and they had been asked-out too, which is more than I and Mr. Mastin have been; and she was called a sad wicked creature by all our neighbours for it. This I am certain of.'

'Very likely,' answered Mrs. Tent; 'but then I warrant you will find the man she had her child by had never agreed it with her mother.'

'No indeed, I believe not,' replied I, 'for her mother was sad and angry about it, and desperate grieved too, and said she should break her heart.'

'Well, you see the difference then,' said Mrs. Tent. 'If I had not given my consent, you could not be Mr. Mastin's wife; that is the very thing which makes you two be married. You may take my word surely; for you see by your Susan's mother what an affliction it is to a parent to have a daughter too free with a man she is not married to.'

'That is true, indeed,' said I: 'but are we then truly and certainly married?'

'Most certainly,' answered Mrs. Tent. 'Can you think I would tell you a lie? I desire you will learn to respect your mother more: your duty is to believe every thing I say, and do every thing I bid you, or I shall disclaim you for my child: I will harbour no undutiful children.'

'Dear mother, do not be angry,' said I, half crying; 'I will be very dutiful: but how should I know we were married? You did not tell me.'

'I was wrong there, to be sure,' replied she; 'but I forgot to acquaint you with it, or indeed thought Mr. Mastin would tell you.'

'Would you believe,' said I, 'that he never said so much as one word about it; but howsomdever, if he had, I do not think I should have believed him.'

My scruples being satisfied, Mrs. Tent left us; and I received Mr. Mastin's visits regularly, seldom seeing any one else; for I since learnt, that he had made my being kept out of all the company that came to the house one of the articles of his agreement.

This confinement was rather dull; and I told my supposed husband, 'I wondered he would not take me home, for that I thought a wife was always to go to her husband's house; that I was sure Miss Scrimshell went with her husband the very day they were married.'

Mr. Mastin told me, that our *mother* had insisted on our making a pretty long stay with her; and would not consent to our marriage on any other terms: for she said, she could not so soon part with a daughter she had so lately found.

I felt myself obliged to my *mother* for her love; but had so great a notion of the pleasure of having a house and a coach of my own, that I could have excused her that proof of fondness.

The weather growing fine, Mr. Mastin carried me out of town for a few days, to a place about twenty miles from London; and by such little excursions reconciled me the better to staying at my *mother*'s: But business called him to his country house, where he did not think proper to carry me; and after many charges to my *mother*, to take care of his wife, which were strengthened by many private instructions, he left me, with excuses which, tho' he thought plausible, did not prevent my resenting his not suffering me to accompany him.

When Mr. Mastin had been gone about a week, Mrs. Tent brought up a gentleman to see me; and, after we had drank tea, left us. He soon grew very familiar and impertinent, and gave me great offence. I was sure I could not now be married again without my knowlege, as I had a husband already; so I expressed my anger very freely; and Mrs. Tent, who had gone no farther than the next room, came in to pacify me: and upon my complaining that he had attempted to be as familiar as if he was my husband, she told me there was nothing in that: ladies of fashion never scrupled such things; and that if Mr. Mastin had had any dislike to my admitting the courtship of others, to be sure he would not have left me behind him, when it was quite unnecessary to do so. She added, that I exposed my ill breeding and ignorance by not following the customs of the world, and doing like other people; and she was ashamed of such a vulgar-minded daughter; but she saw my low education had quite spoiled me; that none of my sisters would have made any such foolish objections.

I was indifferent as to the customs of people of fashion in this particular, having no sort of inclination to take advantage of it; for I found no temptation to imitate them. To have done so, I must have been intirely actuated by a desire to be genteel; which was not so strong in me,[119] but that I opposed compliance from choice as strongly as I could have done from duty; and did not attempt to dispute the propriety with my *mother*, whose assertion I could not easily credit.

My visitor, at last, tired with my obstinacy, left me; but renewed his visits daily; and his sollicitations were always assisted by my *mother*'s importunities, which much lessened my regard for her: but neither prevailing, she brought him up one night after I was in bed and asleep. Tho' I had little sense either of virtue or duty, conscience was not silent: I felt in my heart, that all my *mother* urged was false reasoning, tho' I was too ignorant and too silly to refute her. My tears shewed how far I was from being convinced by her; but she had learn'd to behold sorrow without feeling the least compassion, therefore was not to be moved by seeing me weep.

The first beginning of a crime is always the most grievous. Mr. Mastin did not return till near a week after; and this gentleman continued his visits during that time. I was extremely vexed at this circumstance, tho' not so wretched as at first. Virtue seems to act a little like a coward, and fly precipitately from those who commit one act of hostility against her.

Mr. Mastin's arrival was rendered the more agreeable to me for putting an end to the other gentleman's visits. Tho' my *mother* was lavish in her assurances of the perfect retirement in which I had lived during his absence, and, as I afterwards learn'd, had protested I had not beheld the face of a man from the day he left me; yet Mr. Mastin was not intirely freed from the apprehensions which had possessed him, from the knowledge of her mercenary disposition, and thought he might better depend on my word than hers; therefore he asked me how far what she said was true.

The morning that Mr. Mastin returned, Mrs. Tent cautioned me against acquainting him with any thing that had passed, and added menaces to her prohibition; and enumerated all the ill consequences that might arise from my disobeying her in this particular.

This was a sufficient proof of the false light in which she had represented the inconstancy of which she had persuaded me to be guilty. I was not so very silly as to overlook this circumstance, and it had shocked me much: for tho' she had not quite convinced my very weak reason before, yet she had confounded it: but now truth broke thro' the cloud of falsehood which had overshadowed it, and shewed me my guilt in its strong colours. But it had not the effect she expected: for instead of forcing me to conceal what had passed, it made the sense of it so heavy a burden, that my heart was glad Mr. Mastin's inquiries gave me an opportunity of unloading it. I answered all Mr. Mastin's questions with a frankness and simplicity, which pleaded my excuse better than all the force of rhetoric; but it exasperated him the more against Mrs. Tent. I never saw a man more agitated or distressed than he was. He was for some time quite outrageous; and left me to vent his anger on my *mother*; till, being tired with such expence of spirits, rather than really pacified, he returned to me much more composed, and able to enter into farther conversation, tho' it was still on the same subject.

After having heard all I had to say, he told me, that, grievously as the thought of what had passed tormented him, yet he must confess he deserved it; 'for, my dear Fanny,' continued he, 'if I had not given into the deceit practised upon you, and indeed become a principal party in it, I see by your frankness I should not have had any inconstancy to lay to your charge.' He then gave me a full account of the occupation of her whom I took to be my mother, of the reason of her so readily assuming the appearance of such, of her views in preserving the innocence and simplicity which I had brought with me to her house, of the falsity of her and his assurances of our being married; and informed me fully of my true situation.

I cried sadly, to hear I had neither husband nor mother; not so much out of any affection I retained for Mrs. Tent, whose vile conduct, thus fully displayed, extinguished all regard towards her, as, like Prince Prettiman,[120] from a fear of being no-body's child at all; and I found at the same time I was no man's wife.

To lose two such supports at one instant was a very melancholy circumstance. I sobbed out, that 'I was afraid I had been very wicked.' Mr. Mastin removed that apprehension with all the fallacious arguments with which he had long blinded his own reason and conscience; tho' they are too poor to appear even specious to a person of sense and thought, if passion was not the supreme judge, to whose sentence they appeal. They might perhaps have imposed a little time on my folly, had I been less prejudiced; but it was so much my present and most apparent interest to believe all he urged, that I gave him full credit.

Mr. Mastin quieted my mind almost as easily as he had done my conscience; for by promising me an everlasting constancy, and a more than matrimonial love, as he expressed himself, I began to be less concerned that I was not married, and pretty easy whether I was any-body's daughter at all, as he engaged to take me from that house, and place me in one of my own. His passion was rather increased by absence than abated; and he was resolved to leave me no longer in the hands of a woman, who had so manifestly broke the trust reposed in her. That she did so, surely is less strange, than that a man of sense, who knew she lived by a constant practice of breaking thro' all the laws of religion or humanity, should expect she would scruple violating her word to one individual.

CHAP. III.

Love is not sin, but where 'tis sinful love:
There is a flame so holy and so clear,
That the white taper *leaves* no soot behind.
DRYDEN.[121]

THE next morning, as soon as Mrs. Tent was up, Mr. Mastin told her he was resolved to take me away; which she obstinately refusing to consent to, with all the rage of a mercenary wretch, who fears being deprived of what she esteems the most valuable property she has; he, by threatning to have her brought to punishment, and her house suppressed, and by an offer of some money in case of a quiet acquiescence, at last prevailed, and carried me off.

I was now placed in a very pretty lodging, surrounded with every convenience of life, and introduced into diversions which gave me both pleasure and surprize. Mr. Mastin kept me out of all infamous acquaintance; but got his tradesmen's wives to visit me; and they were so much more genteel than myself, that I could not wish for higher company; and their conversation wore off some of my rusticity, which ceased to please, when it was no longer a proof of my innocence; that great attraction, which very unnaturally charms those most, who are most desirous of destroying it.

I lived in this manner a year and a half, about which time Mr. Mastin fell in love with another woman, perhaps more engaging, but certainly more new than myself. However, he was too good-humoured to tell me this; but complaining our connexion was grown too like matrimony,[122] to which he had a mortal aversion, he fairly acknowleged his resolution to break it off; but as he would not suffer me to be reduced to any distress, because his passion for me was extinguished, he offered to recommend me to his sister, who wanted a servant to attend on her person; for which office I was grown genteel enough.

I had perceived the decay of Mr. Mastin's affection with some uneasiness, tho' without the bitter pangs which those feel at a lover's inconstancy, who are passionately in love with him. I had never conceived a passion for Mr. Mastin: his person and manner were agreeable; his age about forty; he had a great deal of complaisance and good nature, was generous, and fond of me; but had none of the tender delicacies of mind or behaviour which charm even the coldest heart.

106

I might more properly be said to be pleased with him, than to love him; I was grateful, but not affectionate; my heart was a stranger to passion.

Tho' I had suffered but moderately at seeing an abatement in Mr. Mastin's love, yet I was shocked to think of parting with him; wherein perhaps the thought of relinquishing the pleasure and affluence in which I lived, and returning to a state of servitude, had not the smallest share. But as a disposition must be extremely selfish and interested that feels very poignant pangs when only convenience is concerned, I was consoleable; and had not so intirely forget my former condition, as not to think myself much exalted by that Mr. Mastin proposed to me.

After some expressions of concern, and more tears, I accepted his proposal without reproaches: for which he acknowleged himself obliged; promised to be always my friend; to contribute, as far as his convenience would permit, to the advancing of my fortune in any way that should offer; and assured me it would be a great satisfaction to him to have me placed where he should often see me.

Mr. Mastin recommended me in such a manner the next day to his sister, as secured me a favourable reception from her, who knew less of her brother's private vices than of his apparent good humour; for he was a man, who was by constitution free from every vice but one; and tho' without any fixed principle, was decent by inclination: this procured him the reputation of a generous, good-humoured, amiable man; and as such he was highly esteemed by Mrs. Lafew[123] his sister, who was of a very different character.

Mrs. Lafew had an understanding superior to her brother's. She was bred up by an aunt, who had been fixed in the country for many years, whose life was spent in the exercise of every Christian virtue: she was the reliever of the poor, the comforter of the afflicted, a nurse to the sick, a prudent and faithful adviser to her neighbours, a guide to the young, a support to the aged, and an instructor of the ignorant. The character of Job in his prosperity had been the model on which she had formed her conduct;[124] and she had copied it exactly. Every eye that saw her blessed her; and the ear that heard her witnessed to her.

Under the care of such a person, it is not strange if Mrs. Lafew, who was naturally of an happy disposition, acquired an uncommon degree of merit; especially as her aunt had always looked on the education of a niece, who was likely to enter into the world in a rank, where, by precept and example, she might be of extensive service, as one of her most useful employments.

Mrs. Lafew was naturally of a gentle disposition, which, by her aunt's example, was improved into the most engaging sweetness: she was modest and humble, sincere and open, and had found the art of being polite without falshood. She had every moral virtue heightened by religion into every Christian grace. Her person was elegant, and her face handsome, and exactly corresponded with the delicacy of her mind.

Mr. Lafew made his addresses to her at a time that her aunt was sensible her dissolution was approaching; and therefore was particularly glad to marry her niece to a man of sense and character, who was passionately in love with her; and was the only man she had ever seen her niece listen to with complacency on that subject.

Mrs. Lafew had too much sincerity, and too just a sense of the intire confidence she ought to repose in her aunt, to conceal from her that she was disposed in Mr. Lafew's favour. The good old lady had the satisfaction of seeing them united before she died, and giving her blessing to a marriage, which promised much happiness to both parties.

This couple had been married about six years when I went to live with Mrs. Lafew. They had four children, who were so many additions to their felicity, being in every respect such as might be expected from the most amiable of parents.

Mr. Lafew is, I think, the handsomest man I ever saw; graceful in every motion, and polite and elegant in all his expressions. His heart is susceptible of the tenderest impressions, and every look expresses his sentiments in the strongest manner. When he married Miss Mastin, he loved her with all the passion she was so well formed to inspire; and what time had abated in the warmth of his affection, was compensated by the addition it had made to his esteem. If her person charmed less for being grown familiar, her virtues endeared her to him the more the longer he experienced them; and every day discovered some new excellence, or made those he was before acquainted with shine with brighter lustre.

I do not imagine greater happiness can be enjoyed in the marriage state, than subsisted between this amiable couple when I entered their family; the pleasures of mutual love being increased by the joy they took in their lovely offspring, which they beheld with equal tenderness. My evidence in this case is not suspicious; for were it possible, I would think otherwise. This circumstance, by increasing my guilt, adds infinite weight to the burden of my conscience; which reproaches me hourly for being, like the serpent,[125] the destroyer of happiness, and the cause of the fall of innocence; a crime which repentance can never expiate. But what bounds can be set to infinite mercy! That is the Foundation of all my hopes of pardon; and on what could I so properly rely?

Mrs. Lafew's sweetness of temper secured a favourable acceptance of every attempt to serve her; and I found no difficulty in my place, but in answering such questions as she asked me in a manner consistent with the account Mr. Mastin had given of me, and the reasons for his interesting himself in my welfare. As he had invented a melancholy story of the death of my parents, decorated with many distressful circumstances, I found no other means to avoid betraying myself, but to appear so much affected with the recollection of my misfortunes, as rendered her humanity a bar to her examining me very narrowly about them. It was not difficult for me to seem distressed; for whenever any part of this imaginary story was mentioned, I was so terrified with the fear of discovering the truth, that the agitation of my mind required but a small addition of art to excite the compassion of Mrs. Lafew.

Nor was Mr. Lafew devoid of pity. He seemed greatly touched with my distress; which he observed must, thro' so quick a sensibility as appeared in me on these occasions, be always great, tho' I generally had a sufficient command over myself to conceal it.

I am naturally fond of children; and none could be more engaging than Mrs. Lafew's; which attracted me much into the nursery. My mistress saw with pleasure my attachment to them; as every person receives gratification in finding others love those, for whom they feel great tenderness: and she likewise expressed her approbation at my chusing, young as I was, to be with the children rather than with the servants; to many of whom, it might naturally be supposed, my company would not be unacceptable.

By living so much in the nursery, I saw a great deal more of my master and mistress than I should otherwise have done: and as their good opinion of me rendered them particularly obliging, I felt both gratitude and love towards them. The children likewise were excessively fond of me, as all my leisure was dedicated to their amusement.

CHAP. IV.

Shiv'ring death crept cold along his veins;
A gloomy night o'erwhelm'd his dying eyes.
BLACK.[126]

MR. Mastin often came to see his sister; and behaved with such easy natural humanity and regard towards me, as would have dispelled suspicion, if any had been conceived: but none of the family harboured a thought to my disadvantage, tho' I had not Mr. Mastin's command of countenance: but the effect his presence had on me was attributed to bashful gratitude, not to the shame of guilt; and my mistress sometimes seemed apprehensive that the obligations she imagined I and my family had to her brother, might have awakened rather too tender a sensibility in my heart: but this excited her compassion, and not her anger. The safety of my situation, and her great opinion of Mr. Mastin's honour and integrity, prevented her conceiving any fear of the consequences, which, with more opportunity, might arise from the prepossession she imagined I had in her brother's favour.

Mrs. Lafew's behaviour excited my gratitude and affection: but I confess I was still more sensibly affected both by my master's conduct and his perfections. Nature had endowed him with very uncommon charms; and they made a strong impression on my heart, which was till then a stranger to love; indeed so ignorant about it, that I knew not the nature of my sensations. I had not imagined a possibility of my being in love with him; and therefore supposed every one, who knew him as well as I did, must be equally attached to him. I found I loved my mistress more because she belonged to him, than for her own merits; and, charming as their children were, nothing endeared them so much to me, as the consideration that they were his. Every proof they gave of their affection to him was a new charm to me: but I did not receive the same pleasure from his fondness for them: I envied their title to his tenderness, and the great share they enjoyed of it; and could not forbear lamenting that I stood in none of those near and dear relations to him. But still I would not believe myself in love: want of hope stifled my passion in such a manner, that it might have deceived a person less ignorant of the human heart than myself.

I had lived near a year in this family, distinguished by the favour of my master and mistress, when the latter was seized with a scarlet fever, which immediately filled us all with fears for her valuable life. Her physician thought her in great danger; and my master seldom left the room, watching her with the utmost tenderness.

As soon as she was taken ill, she endeavoured to procure the nurse who used to take care of her in her lyings-in; but she being engaged, Mrs. Lafew expressed so great a dislike of having one about her whom she knew nothing of, that I undertook to nurse her. She and Mr. Lafew were both afraid that I had not strength to go thro' so much fatigue; but were well inclined to be persuaded out of that fear, as it removed her apprehensions of a stranger.

In consequence of the office I had undertaken, I sat up every night with my mistress, and never left her but for two or three hours in the day time, when my master would insist on my retiring to rest: but I allowed myself as little of this refreshment as possible, finding nothing recruit my spirits so much as being in her room in the day, as my master was then almost always there; and would often converse with me, and greatly recompense all my fatigue, by the strongest expressions of his gratitude for my care of his wife, and of the high esteem I had thereby given him for me.

If the smallest ray of hope had ever awakened in me an expectation of being regarded for my own sake, I might perhaps have felt more uneasiness than pleasure in thus gaining consideration only thro' the love Mr. Lafew bore another; but it was great gratification to me to obtain it by any means; and I increased it by my unaffected grief, when my mistress was pronounced to be in the utmost danger. My concern was real, but the cause mistaken; for I confess I felt my master's extreme affliction more sensibly than her danger. While he grieved, I was inconsoleable; and he was charmed with such a proof of my affection for the great object of his.

The next day afforded us some comfort by her amendment, and her fever gradually abated; but she remained so weak, that her recovery was likely to be very slow.

Several of the servants caught the infection, and were extremely ill; which gave my master an opportunity of shewing his humanity; for he was frequent in his inquiries after them, and visited them daily, to see that proper care was taken of them. He, as well as myself, was in constant expectation of falling sick, and only sollicitous to escape the ill effects we had reason to fear from our attendance, till Mrs. Lafew was sufficiently recovered not to suffer by our absence.

Our wishes in this respect were gratified: but as we grew easier on her account, we were alarmed from another quarter. Their eldest daughter, who was near four years old, tho' she had, as well as the rest of the children, been kept out of her mother's room for fear of infection, was taken ill, and the scarlet irruption soon after appeared. At first the physician had good hopes of her; but the fifth day the irruption disappeared; she was as cold, and almost as stiff, as marble; and the doctor, who was immediately sent for, thought her in the agonies of death.

Mr. Lafew, who, from the time she was taken ill, had divided his time and care between her and her mother, and had wished me to do the same, having great confidence in my attachment to her, was shocked to the last degree, and knew not how to appear with any tolerable chearfulness before his wife; who hearing more movement in the house than common, and her husband being absent, was apprehensive he was taken ill; and so agitated with this notion, that I was obliged to go into the nursery, to desire he would repair to her, and quiet her apprehensions; the only motive which could at that time have prevailed on him to leave his little daughter's bed-side.

The physician was then declaring the little hope he had of the child's recovery; but turning to the nursery-maid, told her, that if any thing could restore it, it would be going to bed to it, which by warmth might bring out the irruption again. The maid perceived that he applied to her for this purpose; but not chusing the office, which was attended with some danger, observed, that no-body could be expected to run such hazard of their lives; for there would be little chance of escaping the distemper in that case: And how dangerous it was no one could doubt, at a time that one of her fellow-servants lay dead of it, and another was dying.

My apprehensions were less, as my desire to save the child, and oblige the parents, was greater. I told the doctor I was very ready to try the experiment. He begged then it might be done immediately; and left the room for me to go to bed; which I did directly, and took the child in my arms, laying her close to my bosom.

The doctor returned into the room, waiting the event of this experiment. In this situation Mr. Lafew found us, as soon as he could get clear from his wife without giving her any suspicions, and indulge his anxious impatience to know whether there was any alteration in his child. The physician acquainted him with what had passed, and the readiness with which I had undertaken to try this last and only thing he could think of for his little patient's relief. Mr. Lafew was excessively affected with this action; so much, as to shed tears of gratitude and affection at this proof of my generous humanity, as he called it. His words did not express less than his tears: His acknowlegements were unbounded, and his praises of me so exalted, as shewed the great value he had set on the life I endeavoured to save. How nobly was I rewarded! the deadly coldness of the poor babe had chilled me; but the inexpressible joy I felt from seeing him so much obliged, and hearing myself placed so very high in his estimation, warmed my heart, and renewed the vital heat, which was so much suppressed by having almost a corpse in my arms.

In about half an hour, the child, whose eyes were fixed, began to shew some signs of life; the stagnated blood seemed to flow again, and the doctor conceived hopes from his prescription. As for my master, he was almost distracted with joy; he threw himself on his knees at the bed-side, and catching hold of one of my hands, embraced it; called me 'the preserver of his child, his best, his kindest friend:' In short, every thing that an unbounded transport could dictate.

Charmed as I was in being thus addressed, I was not free from fear lest the event should not answer the favourable symptoms which had thrown the tender parent into such ecstasies. But my apprehensions were vain; for the child revived more and more; and in a few hours the irruption began to appear again, which confirmed all our hopes.

The physician was so well pleased with his success, that he intimated a wish, that I would not leave the child for some time; and accordingly I continued in bed with it for two nights and days, tho' Mr. Lafew opposed it, expressing his fears of my catching the infection, and that he should at last lose his great benefactress, her who had bestowed the greatest blessing on him; and lose her by that infinite generosity to which he owed his darling child.

My mistress was so little used to my absence, that she soon inquired after me; and being told I was taken ill, and put to bed, she intimated her concern with great humanity, as fearing my illness was the consequence of my attendance on her: But as soon as I was released from the child, I waited on her again.

I had the satisfaction of seeing Miss Lafew in a fair way of recovery, and of believing myself in great measure the occasion of it. But my joy was soon troubled by Mr. Lafew's being seized with this cruel fever; which became so epidemical, that very few in the family escaped it.

CHAP. V.

MY mistress was greatly to be pitied. It was impossible to conceal my master's illness from her, tho' we did not acquaint her how violent his fever was. She was so weak, she could not walk alone; and we were so continually alarmed with fresh appearances of the irruption, that the physician, apprehending a relapse would be the consequence of the least cold, would not permit her to be carried out of her room; which however we could not have prevented, if we had not pretended that my master declared himself so sensible of the danger she would incur by moving, that nothing would be so hurtful to him as her attempting it.

We were reduced to urge this in the strongest manner, and to invent a thousand messages from him, when he was incapable of sending any; for he soon became delirious; a circumstance which, if known to her, might have proved fatal; therefore we were obliged to pretend he was as well as the nature of the distemper would permit; the doctor thinking it adviseable to deceive her as long as was possible, in hopes Mr. Lafew might recover; and not let her suffer by her fears of an event, which, in her weak state, he thought her unable to support. His fever was indeed excessively violent; but the natural strength and goodness of his constitution gave his physician hopes that he might struggle thro' it.

The whole family was in affliction; but no one in it surely more to be pitied than myself; who, tho' overwhelmed with grief, was obliged to go often to my mistress with a chearful countenance, and rack my imagination, which was tormented with a thousand dreadful phantoms, for pretended messages, and every other invention that might serve to persuade her he was in a better way. I do not think I could have supported so hard a task, if my mistress had not required me to be as much as possible in my master's room, from the great opinion she had of my care and good nursing; and therefore drove me from her presence as soon as ever I had made my report to her.

Mr. Lafew continued in this condition three days; the greatest part of which was spent by me in tears. He was seized at last with great sickness and fainting fits;

and after lying a little time in appearance senseless, and quite without motion, while I was on my knees by his bed-side, weeping with an excess of agony, he opened his eyes, and his senses returning, after looking steadily at me for about a minute, asked me, with a broken voice, what was the matter; and, by calling me by my name, shewed me he had, at least in some degree, recovered his senses, and thereby gave me immediate consolation.

I thought there was a sort of presumption in having so strong an affection for one so much above me; therefore I could not prevail on myself to answer my master's question with entire veracity; yet I accounted so poorly for my grief, that he could not long doubt the cause. He inquired how long he had been ill; and found that he had been delirious. I could not give him a detail of his illness without fresh tears, which sufficiently explained the former. 'My dearest Fanny,' said he, 'my guardian angel, how can I ever reward such goodness?' Laying his hand on mine, which, without knowing what I did, I pressed to my lips, and wept over it. 'Tenderest, most enchanting creature!' cried Mr. Lafew, with a faint voice; and, taking my hand, returned the kiss, I had in a manner involuntarily given his.

This first exchange of caresses between us at once opened my eyes; the appearance of tenderness in him rendered me sensible how much I was in love. This sense made me retire from his bed-side; and, like our first parents, I was taught shame by want of innocence.

Mr. Lafew called me back, to ask me after the healths of his wife and children; and when his mind was made easy about them, he fell asleep, and did not wake till the doctor came; who was agreeably surprised to find his senses returned, and his fever much abated. We informed my mistress of his amendment; but still without letting her know how ill he had been. He kept his bed a considerable time longer, before his fever would leave him; and my attendance continued; but without the pain which had at first accompanied it; for I saw him recover every day; and every hour brought me some proof of his regard and affection for me. But even this, great as the pleasure was, could not prevent me from beginning to sink under the fatigue of body, and anxiety of mind, which I had undergone: But while it was possible to keep up, I could not give way to what must deprive me of the sight of my master; and so great power had this consideration, that I continued the duties of my place till he was able to go into my mistress's apartment: For tho' he was the last of the two that was taken sick, he was well much before her.

When I was no longer able to conceal my illness, no doubt was made but that it was the consequence of the infection, and I was put to bed; where I continued four days without any appearance of irruption; and grew so much better, that my disorder was judged only the effect of fatigue; which was really the case, and rest soon recovered me.

When I was first taken ill, no one could think it strange my master came to see me, as he made it his custom to visit every servant that was sick, when my mistress was not able to do it. To them he was humane; but to me he was tender. He appeared wretched, as he expressed himself, with the supposition, that after having so long escaped the infection, I should at last catch it of him. He would sit by my bed-side for an hour at a time, lamenting his ill fortune, and accompanying his words with the tenderest caresses. It was in vain that I assured him my disorder was only the consequence of fatigue, and that I felt no symptoms of the fever which had been so general: I could not quiet his apprehensions; which would have given me more concern, if I had not owed to them the pleasure of knowing that gratitude had begot a softer passion, and that I was tenderly beloved.

Tho' Mr. Lafew had made so strong an impression on my heart, yet I am convinced the affection would never have become reciprocal without this unhappy illness; wherein I had so many opportunities of recommending myself to him, and of making myself an interest in his heart, by exciting his gratitude.

No other means, I am well persuaded, could have overcome his fondness for his wife. It is true, she had some claim too on the side of gratitude, for a series of actions arising from the most entire affection, and every proof of the most solid merit: But one circumstance made an essential difference; the virtues of a woman, whose person has been long in a man's possession, will excite his esteem; and, in Mr. Lafew's case, I might almost say his veneration; but the merit of a pretty woman, whom he has never possessed, gives rise to warmer passions. In one case, gratitude is the foundation of regard; in the other, of love.

Perhaps I might, with a great deal of truth, state the difference between myself and Mrs. Lafew more to her advantage, and attribute the rise of Mr. Lafew's passion for me as much to a persuasion of my frailty, as gratitude for the obligations he was pleased to think I had conferred on him. Had he been influenced only by the latter, his affection would never have led him beyond the bounds of virtue; but after esteeming me for actions which he thought the result of generosity and humanity, the knowlege of my love for him, which was too apparent, extinguished his esteem, while it excited his tenderness; and the affection which was founded on my apparent virtues, increased on the appearance of a weakness, which probably would change them all into vice. By falling lower in his opinion, I rose in his love: A change which should have mortified my pride, while it soothed my passion. But there is some degree of virtue in that pride which rises from an esteem for virtue; and I had none of either; for

> *She must be humble, who will please:*
> *And she must suffer, who will love.*[128]

Tho' sickness gave rise to all tenderness of intercourse between Mr. Lafew and myself, instead of ceasing with it, it increased daily; and continued undiscovered till I proved with child.

My mistress was of so open and generous a nature, that even love could not render her suspicious; and our intercourse remained for some time a secret to her; till the nursery maid, who had never forgiven my shewing more affection for Miss Lafew than she had done, having discovered a private correspondence between us, imparted it to my mistress, who resented the calumny, as she called it, to the malicious girl; appeared very angry with her insolence, in daring to hint that her master was guilty of any fault; and reproved her, for throwing aspersions on a servant, who deserved so much from her and Mr. Lafew, that no distinction they could either of them shew her was equal to her merits.

The girl, piqued with so different a reception from what her meanness had made her expect, replied, 'She did not know, indeed, how great Mrs. Fanny's merits might be; but she was sure she was with child.'

This assertion startled my mistress, who at first really hoped all the girl said arose from envy; but she had herself observed an alteration in my complexion and countenance, and recollected some of my complaints, which bore a resemblance to those of a breeding woman; but she shewed no emotion before her informer, except that of anger at her insolence, and commanded her to leave the room.

When Mrs. Lafew was left alone, she revolved over all the circumstances that occurred to her remembrance. Suspicion was now awakened, and she found sufficient reason to believe the account she had received was true. The attachment which Mr. Lafew had to me was so visible, that it had not passed unobserved by my mistress; but the generous confidence she had in his affection and integrity, led her to attribute it all to gratitude; and she admired him the more for that proof of his sensibility.

To attempt to describe what she felt on this occasion, as I learned it afterwards, would be too painful a task to me, who must all the time be filled with the most severe self-reproaches; but it may be in some measure conceived, by whoever considers that her happiness consisted in her husband's affection for her; that from the tenderness and constancy of his love, she had enjoyed for some years the most perfect bliss this world can afford; a degree of felicity too great to be lasting here; and that at once she saw herself deprived of it. Nor had she the usual relief of anger; for he had behaved so well to her, even since his affection was placed on a new object, that she felt herself indebted to his humanity, and was sensible that a great degree of virtue was requisite to preserve him from a temptation which attacked him on the side of gratitude and generosity.

As soon as Mrs. Lafew could sufficiently compose her agitated mind, she made a pretence for calling me. While I remained employed in what she had set me to do, she asked me several questions, which she thought might tend to the satisfying her doubts: Nor was she mistaken; for they appeared to me the result of suspicion; wherein I was confirmed, by an air of distress and inward agony, which overspread those features that used to express nothing but tranquil happiness and grateful love. This apprehension threw me into a confusion apparent in every thing I said; and I got out of her presence as soon as I possibly could: Nor did she wish to detain me; for I had so confirmed her doubts, that she was no less desirous of my absence, in order to have free liberty to indulge her grief.

The first time I saw Mr. Lafew afterwards, I communicated my apprehensions to him; but he assured me they were ill grounded; for he had just left his wife, whom he never saw more placid and affectionate, tho' much indisposed. This, I replied, was no confutation; for she was not of a disposition to break forth into rage and reproaches. He allowed the truth of what I said; but thought it impossible for a woman of her frank and tender temper to conceal any thing that much affected her; besides, that, gentle as she was, she could not in such a case be so void of resentment, as to treat him with her usual affection.

I was glad to be persuaded out of my apprehensions, and helped to deceive myself. However, Mr. Lafew observed, that as the consequence of our mutual love could not long remain undiscovered, it was necessary I should leave the house; and he thought I could have no pretence so good as the declining state of my health.

This being agreed upon, the first time I could get courage to do it, I told my mistress that my health grew so bad, that, with the utmost concern, I saw it necessary to leave the best of mistresses, being no longer able to perform the duties of my place.

Mrs. Lafew distressed me, by replying, that I should not leave her on that account; for she thought herself too much obliged to me to require any service from me; and would take a servant, that I might live there without having any thing to attend to but my health; which should receive all the assistance the best advice and tenderest care could give it.

This would have been her real wish, had she believed me sincere; and her generous mind, unwilling to condemn me entirely, imagined infinite pleasure from my accepting this offer, as it would have removed her suspicions, and gratified her generosity.

I knew not what to say: Such goodness in one, from whom I so ill deserved it, increased my confusion; and for some time I could make no reply. A tear of compunction stole down my cheeks, but not unobserved, nor unaccompanied; for my mistress's eyes followed the example of mine, and overflowed with a mixture of grief and compassion for what she saw I suffered. At last, I stammered out, that I hoped change of air might do me good; and therefore, with her leave, would go to my friends in the country, for a time at least.

At this instant my master entered the room. My mistress informed him of what had passed: He pretended to agree with her in the offer she had made me; but with so ill a grace, and in so faint a manner affected to press me to stay with them, that a child must have seen thro' it. However, his wife pretended to think him in earnest; and when he said, that 'since I was resolved to try change of air, he hoped that, if I recovered my health by it, or found it of no use, in either case I would return to them, and afford them the gratification of contributing all in their power to the ease and welfare of one, to whom they owed the life of their child, and in great measure their own.' The close of this sentence was pronounced with such warmth, and so lively an expression in his eyes, that had all he said been accompanied with the same air, his wife would almost have thought him sincere: But the change in his manner only served to shew her that he was so sensibly affected by those circumstances, that the mention of them entirely got the better of his confusion.

CHAP. VI.

AS soon as Mrs. Lafew had got another servant, I took a place in the stage-coach which went nearest the place I had said I was going to; and having taken leave of my mistress the night before, and promised to return to her as soon as was consistent with my health, I went out in the morning at the proper hour; but, instead of going to the coach, hastened to a house which Mr. Lafew had taken for me. It was very small, but clean and neat; and he had placed a servant there ready to attend me.

I could not be so insensible to my mistress's goodness, as not to feel some remorse for having thus stepped in between her and felicity; and should have grown melancholy with the reflection, had not Mr. Lafew relieved me from it pretty soon, by coming to inquire how I liked my habitation; which he was impatient to know, as well as to shew me the necessity of the restraint he laid himself under some days before I left his house, fearing that I might attribute his caution to coldness.

As I now enjoyed a great deal more of his company, and that without alarms or apprehensions of discovery, I grew still fonder of him, and happier in my situation; consequently, thought less of the injury I had done his wife; for when our own hearts are at ease, we are apt to attend too little to the sufferings of others.

A very beautiful boy was added to our society, and compleated my happiness. I am afraid I must not apply that word to us both: Mr. Lafew was too sensible of his ingratitude to the best and most lovely of wives, to be satisfied with the part he acted. When he seemed most delighted with me, he would utter a self-reproaching sigh; and often told me, that tho' he still retained for his wife the strongest affection that the most perfect esteem could give, yet he should be glad never to see her; for he could no longer behold her without the greatest uneasiness, knowing how little he deserved her goodness. I am afraid it is not uncommon for people to attempt to make themselves easy by removing the sense of their guilt, rather than by relinquishing their crime; and the only consequence of their concern for having done an injury to another, is their adding farther injuries to that which the recollection of gives them pain.

Mr. Lafew flattered himself, that his lady was ignorant of his connexions with me; and it was not my interest to express my suspicion of the contrary, any more than it was for my peace to believe it; since I could not reflect on the probability of it without great uneasiness. Mr. Lafew often spoke with concern of the bad state of her health, and the effect it had on her spirits; but as she never hinted at any apparent decay in his affections, nor at any suspicions of his inconstancy, or ever appeared the least out of temper; but when he had been the longest absent from her, received him with the greatest tenderness and complacency; he thought it impossible but she must be intirely ignorant of the whole transaction.

I wished to be as well convinced of the truth of Mr. Lafew's opinion, as he was: But tho' I was sensible such a degree of patience was far above me, yet I had so high a veneration for Mrs. Lafew, that I could not think her incapable of it; and therefore had some painful doubts and fears on the subject; which, however, I concealed from Mr. Lafew, lest his affection for his wife, if it had compassion on its side, might get the better of his passion for me.

I had lived above a year in this manner with Mr. Lafew, when he was obliged to go into Cumberland, to look after an estate he had there, his steward being just dead. This separation gave me great concern, tho' I received all possible alleviation from a constant and frequent correspondence by letters. But before he had been gone a month, I was seized with a fever.

When I found myself extremely ill, I sent for the physician who attended Mr. Lafew's family while I nurs'd them; he being the only one of the faculty of whom I had any knowlege, and his conduct had given me a confidence in his skill. Of his behaviour to myself I was not long a judge; for the fever affected my head so much, that I became delirious the second day of his attendance, and remained so for above a week; when, recovering my senses, the first object I beheld was Mrs. Lafew at my bed-side.

There was not perhaps a sight in the world which could have shocked me so much; for what is so painful, as to look on those whom we have injured! I hid my head from her benign countenance, and was ready to die with shame and remorse. It threw me into an agitation of mind and body, which alarmed her, as well as those who attended me; tho' no one but herself guessed the reason of it. She endeavoured to compose my mind, by every soothing expression and kind attention the most perfect humanity could dictate; which drawing a flood of tears from my eyes, quieted my spirits; and a day or two made great amendment in me.

I then began to enquire of Mrs. Lafew to what I owed her charitable visits; and received the following account in answer.

One of Mrs. Lafew's children was, at the time I fell ill, under the care of the physician I sent for; and he went there directly from me the second day of his attendance. In the course of the conversation he had with Mrs. Lafew, he told her, that he had just left the young woman, who had so carefully and tenderly nursed her and her family, when they were so severely afflicted with a scarlet fever; adding, that my behaviour then had given him such a regard for me, that he was shocked at my being in so bad a way.

Mrs. Lafew hereupon inquired particulars; and found he thought me in the utmost danger. She asked him, whom I had about me; to which he replied, nobody but a very young girl, and a very ordinary servant, who let him in: He added, that he wished he knew where my relations lived; for better attendance was necessary, and he must be obliged to seek out for a nurse for me himself, tho' he much disliked the office, if he could meet with no one else who would take that care.

Mrs. Lafew, after a little pause, said, she would save him that trouble; assuring him she would go directly to my house; for she was much care in my debt. After informing her of the place of my abode, he left her, and she came to me, whom she found intirely delirious, and as ill attended as my doctor had represented.

My little boy was just beginning to walk, and was then going round the room with the assistance of the chairs, taking hold of each as a support in his little progress; but at the sight of a stranger, tottered to me, as to one by whom he expected to be defended from all danger; for a new person was a very formidable sight to him, being naturally of a shy disposition, and that increased by not seeing any variety of people; which the retired life I led prevented.

Mrs. Lafew was variously affected with the sight of my child; she could not behold a descendant from Mr. Lafew, and one too who resembled him extremely, without tenderness: but when she considered him as a proof of her husband's attachment to another woman, and his inconstancy to her, it shocked her severely; however, her tender sentiments prevailed, and the distress the poor babe appeared in, at meeting with a total disregard from *her* whose great pleasure it had been continually to fondle him, moved Mrs. Lafew's compassion. I was then so void of sense, as not to know even my dear child, tho' I had preserved that knowledge after all other had left me.

Mrs. Lafew endeavoured to prevail on the poor boy to come to her, and by all the bribery of sugar-plums and sweet-meats, prevailed in her next visit. She engaged her own nurse to attend me, and never failed coming every morning and evening to see that all possible care was taken; and would often sit a considerable time by me, before I recovered sense enough to know her.

She saw two letters on the table, which came by different posts after my delirium began: She perceiving by the hand they were from Mr. Lafew, but unopened, gave them to my maid, to keep till I asked for them, and then to deliver them.

I had not long recovered my senses before I enquired if there were no letters for me; and those which were hereupon given me were my best cordials; tho' the last expressed an uneasiness at not hearing from me, which put me under a great difficulty; and the next post increased it, by bringing me much more to the same purpose. I was so weak, that to hold a pen was an utter impossibility; my maid could not write; my doctor, or my nurse, I could not trust, as they might inform Mrs. Lafew of my request. This really distressed me greatly: I could not tell how to support the vexation of prolonging the extreme anxiety which Mr. Lafew, by his letters, appeared to feel; nor could I suspect the truth of his expressions; and yet I was incapable of removing them.

From this dilemma I was delivered by the last person from whom I expected such a service. Mrs. Lafew having privately inquired, whether I had asked for my letters, and being answered in the affirmative, and that I had received another by that day's post; she told me, that she understood I had had my letters, which she ordered to be put safely by for me, till I was able to read them.

This implying an intimation that she had seen her husband's letters, and so generously left them untouched, filled me with confusion, and painful remorse, which drew some tears from me. Mrs. Lafew, who meant to comfort rather than afflict me, and thought me then able to bear the subject, with the greatest gentleness, and even an air of tenderness, desired me not to be shocked at what she had said; for she meant not to reproach me; on the contrary, her design was to relieve me. She had been reflecting on the uneasiness Mr. Lafew must be under at not hearing from me, as she plainly saw, by the frequency of his letters, how constant our correspondence was; and she could not support the notion of his suffering any pain, tho' perhaps she did not seem the person to whose pity he was best intitled; but that, whatever she endured, she could not let him feel an uneasiness, from which it was in her power to relieve him.

The last part of this sentence was uttered with many tears, which affected me beyond expression; and I was so unable to guess her meaning, that I could make no answer.

Mrs. Lafew then asked me, if Mr. Lafew expressed no apprehensions at having been so long without hearing from me; and finding me unwilling to reply, she intreated me to tell her plainly; and, to encourage me to do so, took hold of my hand, assuming a smiling countenance, and an air of affection, while her eyes ran over with tears.

I should have thought myself unpardonably ungrateful to a goodness I had already too much offended, if I had any longer resisted her intreaties; and frankly confessed, that Mr. Lafew expressed more anxiety on my account, than such a wretch as I was could deserve from any one. Nor did I herein affect humility; Mrs. Lafew's superior conduct had so truly humbled me, that I saw myself the vilest and most despicable of the creation.

Mrs. Lafew replied, that she knew the strength and tenderness of his affections too well to doubt of it; and, as I was incapable of writing, she would, if I chose it, disguise her hand in such a manner, that he should not discover it, rather than Mr. Lafew should continue to suffer by his anxiety, or that I should expose his failings by employing any other person to write for me.

This offer surprized me extremely. How few women are there, who would not have thought with pleasure on the pain their husband suffered from his love for another? Nor are there many more, whose delicacy, in regard to their husband's honour, would have induced them to undertake such an office. It is easy to imagine I was not backward at accepting an offer which gave so much relief to my mind, in affording me a means of abating Mr. Lafew's uneasiness; and I was under no apprehensions of his discovering the hand I employed, as no resemblance of his wife's could possibly persuade him that it was really hers.

Mrs. Lafew desired me to dictate to her. When I had such a secretary, my expressions could not fail of being much constrained: I could not ask her to transmit any tender sentiments from me to her husband; therefore I gave her no very tedious task; only desiring her to thank him for his kind anxiety; to let him know the occasion of it, and of the great amendment of my health; excusing the conciseness of my letter, on being obliged to the assistance of a friend, for the power of giving him that short information about me. This, I hoped, would account for the cold answer I returned to three most affectionate letters, which, because of the tenderness of their contents, I did not shew to Mrs. Lafew; nor did she hint at a desire to see them. I believe she was too prudent to wish it; for her sensibility on that subject appeared plainly in the tears which trickled down her cheeks all the time she was writing for me; for all her endeavours could not conceal them. But notwithstanding the pain it gave her, she repeated it every post-day, till I was able to hold my pen.

CHAP. VII.

— Heav'n has but
Our sorrow for our sins, and then delights
To pardon erring man: Sweet mercy seems
Its darling attribute, which limits justice;
As if there were degrees in Infinite;
And Infinite would rather want perfection,
Than punish to extent.

DRYDEN.[130]

I Several times asked Mrs. Lafew, how it was possible for her to forgive the injury I had done her, as she seemed to do; and not to hate, instead of pitying me for any thing I suffered. She declined answering me, till I was much recovered; and then, on my repeating the question, replied, 'I will not pretend to say, that if I had seen you in no other light than the object of my husband's tenderest affections, and the cause of his inconstancy, I could have thought you more worthy of my compassion than of my resentment; but as gratitude had taught me to love you enough to be sincerely interested in your welfare, my own misfortune did not engross all my thoughts. I considered what I suffered was but for a time. You indeed seemed to have a present advantage over me; but how dreadful were the threatened consequences! The short triumph of a few years must, if unrepented of, be succeeded by eternal misery. The heart must be very hard, which, in such a situation, could be void of compassion for one, who possibly might be on the brink of the most dreadful eternity, but from whom, at least, it could not be far distant; for the longest life is short while passing, and still shorter in reflection.'

'I acknowlege,' continued she, 'that Mr. Lafew was the more immediate object of my concern, as he was most dear to me; and so great have been my apprehensions for him, that I can with truth say, I have suffered much more on his account than on my own. All my worldly happiness is indeed come to its period; but death promises me certain relief; it may for some years delay its healing balm; but at last it will not fail of yielding me a certain cure. But this unavoidable event opens to the adulterer an horrid scene; and he, whose conscience has inflicted already frequent pains, will find, that small is the part which guilt has thus anticipated, in comparison of those to which he will then be awakened.'

This last sentence was interrupted by many tears: She fell into such extreme agonies of mind, that it was long before she could grow sufficiently composed to resume the subject; nor was I capable of solliciting her to continue it; for her words had filled me with a horror I had never before felt. However, as soon as Mrs. Lafew was able, she thus proceeded.

'Tho' you had had but a small share in my thoughts before, and I hoped for some mercy for you on account of the greatness of the temptation (for I was convinced no common share of religion and virtue could resist Mr. Lafew's superior power to charm); yet, when I heard that you were on the brink of appearing before HIM, whose most sacred laws you had violated, I perceived, that what I had called hopes in your favour, arose only from my indifference to you, which the nearness of the danger removed; and my compassion for you was strongly excited by your condition. Every moment threatened you with a dreadful change; a removal from a state of worldly pleasure to an eternity of endless pains. How great an object of pity was the person now become, whom I had sometimes been tempted to envy, till I reflected on the greater eligibility of my own situation, with mortified affections, disappointed love, but a clear conscience, than that of one, whose pleasures must be embittered with self-reproaches here, and punished with unspeakable torments hereafter!

'Who could forbear to compassionate a person in your deplorable condition? Certainly not one who had experienced the good effects of your humanity. I immediately resolved to see that all possible care was taken of you, and to attend you assiduously, tho' I could do little more than pray for your recovery and repentance. Without the latter, the first could be no benefit to you; it would be adding only a greater weight of guilt to your past crimes. But that I must leave to HIM, who alone can change the heart: My business was to see that all human means were tried to preserve your life, and thereby give you time to expiate your offences by penitence.'

Tho' I had never heard the actions I had been guilty of represented in so serious a light, yet conscience, now for the first time seriously awakened, bore witness to the truth of all Mrs. Lafew asserted. It is not easy to imagine how much I was affected with what she had said. I was too much agitated to pursue the subject; but the next day I asked her, If she was not peculiarly serious in her way of treating what I had hitherto heard called by no worse name than that of gallantry.

Mrs. Lafew, upon my putting this question, told me, 'that, whatever names might be given to our actions here, they would not be judged hereafter by fallacious appellations appropriated to them in this world: That the bible was given us as the rule of our faith, and guide of our actions, by Him who would judge us according to our conformity to it; and therefore from it we must learn the true nature of them.'

She then began with a summary account of the Christian revelation, and instructed me in all the fundamentals of religion, of which I had before but a scanty knowlege. From this time she passed every day with me; and read, and, where my ignorance rendered it necessary, explained, the Scriptures to me. In them I did indeed find my own condemnation; and was so terrified at my situation, that Mrs. Lafew feared she had brought me to despair, rather than to repentance. She referred me for hope to the same book which had deprived me of it; and, by producing to me all the passages which promised forgiveness to repenting sinners, she convinced me, from the whole tenor of the New Testament, that I was within the reach of mercy.

I stood too much in need of it to slight the call, and determined no longer to continue my course of life. Apprehensions of the consequences of my love for Mr. Lafew abated my passion; and my affection led me to be as desirous of his reformation as of my own. Could I have overcome the sense of my guilt as an adultress, I felt myself so greatly indebted to Mrs. Lafew, for her care both of my temporal and eternal welfare, that I could not have continued in a conduct which must render her unhappy.

My resolution was firmly fixed; but I considered Mr. Lafew was absent; I feared the sight of him might again awaken all my frailty; and therefore wished to put a relapse out of my power. For this reason I rejected all Mrs. Lafew's offers of settling me in a state of ease and plenty at a distance from any abode of theirs. I feared myself; and was apprehensive that Mr. Lafew might be displeased with his wife, if he thought she was privy to my concealment; and might think me grown rather indifferent than penitent, and more prevailed upon by the temptation of ease, than by a sense of my crime.

As I was no enemy to employment, and wished for a society which should confirm me in my resolutions, I determined to enter into this Asylum; Mrs. Lafew engaging to take care of my boy, and to bring him often to see me.[131]

My letters had from the first of this alteration in my mind, borne the signs of it. Melancholy took the place of the passionate expressions with which they used to be filled; and I frequently intimated my compunction for our past way of life. When I had settled my plan, I wrote an account of all that had passed, and the effect it had had upon me; intreating him not to grieve for the loss of me, but for the danger in which his eternal welfare had been involved with mine. I expatiated on the great obligations we both had to Mrs. Lafew; informed him of the perfect knowlege she had had of our intercourse, almost during the whole course of it; and was not silent on the great merit of her behaviour on the occasion. I added, that I had committed our dear child to her care, and was resolved to devote the rest of my life to penitence.

This letter, as soon as finished, I dispatched to him. With what money I had, I defrayed my lodgings, and paid off my servants; and, after taking what I hoped would prove but a short farewell of my darling infant and Mrs. Lafew, I came hither, and was most charitably accepted.

This lady is the person who has been twice to visit me; and the boy which came with her is the object of my tenderest love, tho' the offspring of my crime. Mr. Lafew had been in town above a fortnight before she last came; and from her I had the pleasure of learning that my letter had affected him as I wished; that he had begged her pardon for his past injurious conduct, in the most frank and affectionate manner; and tho' he spoke of me with unaffected kindness and regard, yet was so far from asking to what place I had retired, that he desired her not to inform him, lest in some weak moment he might endeavour to see me.

To complete my satisfaction, she assured me, that she had never known him more affectionate in his behaviour to her than since his return out of the north; only it was mixed with a degree of veneration and respect, which gave her pain to receive from a husband whom she so tenderly loved, and whose past lapses she so cordially forgave. The excellent lady added, that my child was beloved by both, and treated, in every respect, as their other children.

What more can be wanting to my felicity! My temporal concerns are all supplied in the most perfect manner; and I have every means of providing for my future welfare. I may appear blameable for taking advantage of this charity, when I had the means of subsisting what may be called better without it; but I hope I am not so bad a worker, but that I shall rather be a benefit than an expence to the society;[132] and if not, I trust in their boundless humanity for pardoning my having recourse to it for preserving me from a failure in virtue, as readily as if my motive had been to obtain relief from necessities of a still less pernicious nature, the want of subsistence.

Whatever censurers Fanny may meet with, she was in no danger of being blamed by her companions; who had all been greatly edified by her industry and piety, since she came into the house, and were so pleased with the mildness and sweetness of her behaviour, that they could not blame any motive which brought her thither; where, perhaps, she was the only one who was induced to apply to that asylum merely from penitence, unaccompanied with any distress of circumstances; tho' many, who were led by other motives, have, when instructed in the true nature of their crimes, become as penitent.

CHAP. VIII.

THE next person called upon to communicate the particulars of her *eventful* life, was a woman of above thirty years of age, in whose face appeared beauty in decay. Her features were extremely fine; but her eyes, which had been naturally languishing, were now become languid;[134] and her complexion shewed the ill effects of time and irregularity, and of the pernicious arts made use of to restore a fictitious bloom, when the true one is passed.[135] Her person was less impaired; she still preserved a genteel air, accompanied with some degree of dignity, which her manner and behaviour did not contradict. It is generally allowed, that vanity requires more sollicitation than diffidence: It is no wonder then if this society, who had much to humble them, and nothing whereof they could be vain, did not resist the general agreement and desire. They might indeed plead a title to honour, wherein few in more respected ranks of life can rival them, the merit of being sensible of their errors, and penitent for them: But such real desert can be no subject for vanity; on the contrary, it is both the consequence and the cause of the truest humility.

The person I have been describing, as the next who was to be her own biographer, was ready to obey the desire of her companions, as soon as they intimated it, and proceeded in the following terms.

My father was a country gentleman, who had impaired his fortune in his youth; but prudence came to his relief before his ruin was completed; and having married a woman with a tolerable fortune, and a great deal of economy, he settled intirely at his country seat.

My mother's extreme good housewifery might have restored his estate to its former bulk, had she not frustrated all her care by being extremely prolific; insomuch that breeding and saving went hand in hand, in such due proportion, that all we could expect from our parents was mere subsistence.

There were so many of us, that my mother had sufficient employment in the necessary care of our bodies; nor could my father afford more time for the cultivation of our minds than was requisite to teach us to read and write, and that to no great degree of perfection.

We had several neighbours, with whom we lived on good and equal terms; tho' the charges of so large a family rendered us unequal to them in opulence. One of these was a gentleman, who had two sons; the eldest was on his travels when I was first admitted into company, which was in my sixteenth year; for my mother very prudently kept us in the nursery till that age, to lessen the expence of our cloaths; which, if we had appeared to visitors, must have been more genteel than otherwise was necessary.

This neighbour, whose name was Turnham, had his second son at home; a youth little more than two years older than myself. His person was agreeable, and his manner very insinuating. His father had designed him for the study of the law; but soon perceived it was too laborious a profession for so volatile a genius.

The young gentleman had been guilty of some juvenile excesses; and when he found his school-master intended to punish him, he ran away from school; and his father could not prevail on him to come home, but on a promise of never sending him thither again. This indulgent parent then put him under the tuition of the curate of his parish; but found it impossible to fix him to any sort of study, and that his head ran entirely on the army.

When Mr. Turnham found that it was impossible to make his son apply to any thing serious, he thought it most prudent to gratify his wish, and bought him a commission.

Young Turnham had just acquired the title of captain, and a red coat, when I first knew him; two distinguishing circumstances, which made me look on him as a very fine gentleman; and I being then very young, and in the full bloom of youth, attracted his notice, of which I soon became sensible, by his assiduities where-ever I met him; and as he was idle both by profession and inclination, he had nothing to do but to visit his neighbours; and contrived to know our motions so well, that he generally met us where-ever we went, pretendedly by chance; but he took care I should be better informed of the cause, to which I owed a circumstance highly agreeable to me.

Captain Turnham's vivacity and natural good breeding made him much caressed. His conversation enlivened every company he came into; and the young women were all my rivals, each endeavouring to attract the man, who appeared to them the most agreeable in the country: But I had the satisfaction of seeing they were all unsuccessful; and found my vanity most pleasingly flattered, in being preferred to so many, who omitted no means of gaining the heart which voluntarily gave itself to me.

Captain Turnham took all opportunities of drawing me aside from the company; nor was I backward in complying with his inclination in this request,[136] since the short conversations thus obtained yielded much greater satisfaction than mixed company could give. On these occasions his vivacity was changed into tenderness, and he became more pleasing to me, by the thing that would have rendered him less entertaining to others.

As I had more sincerity than art, he was not long a stranger to the return my heart made to his affection. From this knowlege arose a correspondence by letters, which was very diligently carried on by us both, wherein we communicated our tenderest sentiments; and I never failed giving him information of every opportunity of meeting me; nor did he ever neglect the summons.

But the most pleasing of all our interviews, were a few stolen meetings in a neighbouring wood, whither he generally went every morning by five o'clock, and staid till seven; and whenever I could possibly get clear of the rest of my family any part of those two hours, I went to him, and staid as long as I durst venture to be absent from home.

I paid dearly for this pleasure, by the constant perturbation of my mind, which was ever anxious for fear of disappointment, and grievously mortified when I was prevented from meeting him, which was frequently the case; for we judged it necessary to be extremely secret in our mutual passion, tho' our actions and our views were wholly innocent; but we were both so entirely dependent on our parents, and so destitute of fortune, that we could hope for the liberty of seeing each other only from their ignorance of the strength of our mutual attachment. In this wood we interchanged a thousand vows of eternal love, with all that profuseness wherewith they are lavished by boys and girls, who neither know the nature of their own hearts, nor of the passion they profess. Here we formed various schemes for our future union, all founded on the hopes of my lover's preferment, which our wishes represented to us as not far distant.

I had no confidante at home: I had two sisters and three brothers older than myself, and two brothers and one sister younger; but my elder sisters were so much older, that they tyrannized over me as a child, and my younger sister was an infant. Most of my brothers were placed where youth may be commendably and commodiously boarded, lodged, taught, &c. for the moderate sum of ten pounds a year; and those who had outgrown the age for these cheap seminaries, were apprenticed to such businesses as they were designed to follow, except my eldest brother; and it being thought proper that the heir of the family should be able to write and read, and have a gentleman's education, he was sent to a school where learning was not sold so great a pennyworth, and afterwards to the University, where he was during the time Captain Turnham made his addresses to me.

I believe the air of intrigue adds a pleasure to courtship: Ours had this recommendation in a supreme degree; and perhaps, had we received permission from our parents, it might have diminished our passion. We were of an age for romance, and were delighted with every circumstance that bore the air of it. An allowed affection, like an established religion, is apt to turn the warmth, which in one case is called passion, in the other zeal, into lukewarmness. In most cases opposition is as necessary to preserve mental fire in its full blaze, as air is for the more material kind; and I have seen that love, which, while approved by all, has burnt faintly, like smothered embers, blown into such a flame by unexpected opposition, that it has almost consumed every principle, and turned the whole mind into a general conflagration.

The attachment between Captain Turnham and myself was not wholly unobserved; but it was looked upon only as a coquetry on both sides; for as there was no apparent advantage on either, our parents were not very ready to take alarm; and we found so much pleasure in secresy, that we took great care to preserve it; whilst we continually complained of the constraint we were under as the heaviest misfortune, and of the distant prospect of our marriage, which we really felt very severely, in the language of despairing lovers, who did not find that every vow, which passion or suspicion ever invented, never to marry any other person or not to prove false to their professions, was a sufficient gratification.

CHAP. IX.

IF the necessity of concealment helped to raise our passion to so great an height, what addition did it not receive from the open opposition which broke out in the second year of its existence!

The cause of this event was a gentleman, who came to make a visit to one of our neighbours. His name was Merton: He confessed but fifty years of age, tho' he appeared in every respect above threescore. Whether he thought proper to sink a considerable number of his years, or whether the debauched life he had led gave him the infirmities and appearance of a more advanced age, I cannot pretend to say; but, by chusing rather to have the latter believed, he rendered those defects nauseous, which otherwise one should only have pitied.

Mr. Merton, in short, was a battered rake, whose body was worn out, but his mind unreformed. While his person exhibited all the imperfections of old age, he affected the dissolute manner and loose conversation of a thoughtless boyish rake; whereby, instead of inspiring that respect which we feel at seeing a man full of age and honour, who, like the ruins of a noble edifice, is rendered more respectable by time, and receives new charms from his decay, Mr. Merton was the most contemptible, as well as most nauseous, of mankind.

This gentleman my ill fortune gave me for a lover; and so combustible was his heart, at an age least proper, that it took fire the first time he saw me, and burnt with such violence, that he could not rest out of my presence. The gentleman whose visitor he was, happened to be a great friend of my father; and thinking it would be happy for him to dispose of a daughter to a man of so large a fortune as Mr. Merton was possessed of, he encouraged him in his passion.

Mr. Merton was sufficiently sensible of his own infirmities, to think a nurse a necessary appendix; and tho' he had been well acquainted with our sex, was weak enough to fancy a girl of seventeen a proper person for a wife. This consideration, joined with the passion he had conceived for me, soon determined him to make his addresses.[138]

This was the only circumstance which could have rendered him more odious to me than he was before. My mind was the very essence of romance; could fansy a state of perfect bliss in more barren plains than those of Arcadia with my Strephon;[139] could even imagine scenes of happiness in wilds and desarts; and with sincerity have addressed him as Belvidere does Jaffier; and have promised not to forsake him, tho'

> *the bare earth should be our resting place;*
> *Its roots our food; some cliff our habitation;*

that I would

> *Have made my arm a pillow for his head,*
> *And watch'd him till the morning.*[140]

Such was then the extravagance of my notions; the most unfit state for the contrary madness, which, as ignorant of the power of riches as I was of that of love, fansies that wealth, however encumbered, must give happiness.

It would, in the disposition I have been representing, have been very difficult to have persuaded me that Mr. Merton could confer any benefit on me by becoming my husband; and he found I listened to him with so little complacency, that he thought he should find a shorter way of arriving at the completion of his wishes by applying to my father; and accordingly changed his addresses from me to him.

Mr. Merton, in this change of his measures, certainly judged well. My father received his proposal with pleasure, and my mother with joy: For an offer to take a daughter off their hands, without requiring any fortune with her, was an irresistible argument for their consent; and however distasteful he might be to me, such a lover was sure to have many charms for them.

Mr. Merton in nothing shewed so true a knowlege of himself, as in being sensible that the part of a lover was not the best suited to him; and would have been much in the right to have put as speedy an end to it as possible, had he found any other means than that still more improper one of converting the lover into the husband. He pressed for a speedy marriage, and my parents were not desirous to delay it; therefore an early day was fixed for the ceremony.

All I could urge against this determination was of no effect. My tears and my intreaties excited only anger in those whose compassion I attempted to raise. I suffered all, that hatred for the man I was going to marry, and love for him from whom I was to be thus cruelly torn, could inflict; and my expressions were adequate to my distress, but they were all unavailing. I confessed my love for Captain Turnham, and his for me, hoping that might plead for me; but, on the contrary, it convinced them the more of the necessity of marrying me, to prevent me from becoming the wife of one as poor as myself. It had likewise another disagreeable consequence; it made them watch me so narrowly, that I could not get one moment's interview with Captain Turnham; if he came to the house, I was locked up in my chamber till his departure. I got the means of writing him word of my situation, intreating him, if he loved me, to deliver me from it; offering to fly with him where-ever he pleased: But I had no opportunity of knowing whether he was too wise to accept my proposal, which I am apt to believe was the case; for all possibility of further intercourse was stopped between us; so very circumspect were my parents; and the day of my marriage found me still exposed and defenceless, to be the victim of their prudence.

I was led, much more dead than alive, up to the altar, where my tottering knees could not support me; but my mother on one side, and my eldest sister on the other, did that office: But before the end of the ceremony, even their assistance was not sufficient; for I fainted away, which only delayed it; and as soon as I appeared come to myself, it was concluded; tho' I was no more capable of joining in it, either by thought or speech, than when I was in that state of temporary death.

An unprejudiced spectator would have drawn melancholy prognostics for Mr. Merton's future happiness from my conduct; but he seemed unalarmed, appeared all joy, without one sigh of pity either for me or himself;[141] admired my virgin modesty; wished to dissipate my diffidence; but did not once suspect that aversion alone produced all the effects which he attributed to such various causes.

After staying a few days at my father's, Mr. Merton carried me to his country seat, where all was magnificent, and indeed beautiful; but *he* was there; and that was sufficient to change the nature of every thing about me. While he was present, nothing could please. The house was elegant, but *he* inhabited it: The park was fine, but *he* always accompanied me there: The prospect would have been charming, if he had not made part of it: But while he was always at my elbow, my situation appeared to me no better than a gaudy prison.

Mr. Merton had expected to see me delighted with all the magnificence around me; my insensibility therefore could not fail of being very disagreeable to him. I took no pains to conceal it: My romantic imagination found a melancholy pleasure in shewing my discontent. I formed my conduct on some of the romances I had read; and fansied I acted a noble part, while I was indulging a passion now become criminal, and endeavouring to render a situation, which must be allowed an unhappy one, still more wretched than was necessary. Like most lovers, while their passion remains unabated, I valued *constancy* highly; and therefore placed much merit in sacrificing all the little satisfaction I might have enjoyed, to what I called the delicacy of my affection for Captain Turnham. The

Princess of Cleves[142] was so much my favourite heroine, that had Mr. Merton treated my melancholy with indulgence and good-nature, I have no doubt but I should have made him the confidante of my passion; but as my ill-judged conduct rendered him morose, I thought her highness's example therein, not quite expedient.

All the people of fashion in the neighbourhood came to visit us, as soon as they thought it proper to intrude on the leisure of a new-married couple. The reluctance with which I had accepted this splendid slavery[143] was by some means known in the country; and my appearance shewed how little I was reconciled to it. An old man, who marries a girl whose youth and person prejudice beholders in her favour, has but little chance of being treated with much candour. The cause of pity on one side is obvious; on the other, indeed, it is very probable: But then so it might have been to the husband himself, before he became such; and if he shut his eyes on the danger into which he was running, while it was not too late to avoid it, people do not very readily give him leave to open them afterwards.

A young woman, who marries an old man, brings her virtue into some danger, and her reputation into more. Young men look upon the wife of an old one as part of their property: They may be disappointed of their conquest, but they generally make the trial. This exposes a woman to frequent temptation. Age is seldom unaccompanied with peevishness; and the retrospection of a man's own folly, which every contrariety in taste or temper represents in glaring colours to him, is not likely to let it lie dormant. Thus he, who can have no merit to a young girl but indulgence, becomes harsh and ill-tempered; while every younger man is polite, attentive, assiduous, and tender. The contrast is dangerous; but virtue founded on religion (for no other foundation is firm enough to bear so strong a virtue as that must be which has every passion to conquer) may lead a woman thro' this ordeal unhurt; yet even that cannot always secure her character: Probability, built on human frailty, is against her; as in most cases there is an apparent want of principle[144] in a woman's promising love to a man to whom she knows she cannot give it, and entering into a state, whose bonds should be mutual affection, with one who has nothing to render him agreeable to her but money: Every opinion is prejudiced against her, and people are apt to imagine, that she who violates truth, for the indulgence of vanity or avarice, may break the most solemn vows for the gratification of another passion. And thus mankind will always think, because it flatters their hopes; tho' experience continually shews them how very far the argument is from being conclusive, by the very good behaviour of many women, who have reduced themselves into this situation, and who suffer with virtue, tho' with sorrow, during the most valuable part of their lives, for this fatal vanity.

Another circumstance which is apt to hurt a woman's reputation in this situation, is the desire most people have, that the folly of an old man in this respect should not be unpunished; and because they wish it, they are sure to believe it on the smallest evidence.

Pity was visible in every eye that beheld me; which convinced me the more of my own misery. How great must it be, if those who knew only half my sufferings, and who were void of all regard for me, could yet not see me without compassion! Thus I argued, and thus endeavoured to increase my discontent.

One of our visitors told us she was going to Tunbridge;[145] upon which Mr. Merton, to my great surprize, informed her, that we should meet her there. He had never hinted this intention to me; I suppose, because he imagined it might give me pleasure: Nor did I much blame him, as it could not do so but for reasons very far from flattering to him; and my behaviour did not give me a title to expect a very disinterested regard for my satisfaction, as his vanity, together with ignorance of some of my sentiments, must prevent his knowing that I deserved his pity, at least as much as his anger.

Tunbridge had no charms for me, but the chance it seemed to offer me of having less of Mr. Merton's company, and much fewer *tête à tête's*, which were very dreadful, his fondness or his anger being equally odious; and of a reasonable medium between them I saw no hope. Instead of looking on Tunbridge as a place of gaiety and diversion, I proposed no satisfaction from it, but more frequent opportunities of indulging my melancholy, and retiring from every eye.

CHAP. X.

And doubts and fears to jealousies will turn;
The hottest hell in which a heart can burn.
          CONG.[146]

BEFORE the second month of my wedlock was quite expired, we went to Tunbridge; a place where Mr. Merton resorted yearly, to patch up his tattered constitution. The season was then very full; but as I had few acquaintance, and wanted spirits to make new ones, it appeared very dull to me; yet it answered my hopes; for Mr. Merton was always engaged abroad; and at first I enjoyed a retirement which the country did not afford me. But the lady I mentioned, by whose means I first learnt Mr. Merton's intention of going thither, was inclined, by the sociableness of her own nature, both to pity the solitude I lived in, and to end the misfortune, by makeing me come abroad. She would call upon me both morning and evening, and not depart till she prevailed on me to accompany her. I was as void of spirits to resist her importunities, as to enjoy the diversions into which she carried me.

As Mr. Merton had ornamented his victim with many family jewels and fine cloaths, (an expence he had taken on himself) I made too resplendent a figure to pass unnoticed. I soon found I had no occasion to put myself to any trouble for acquaintance; it would have been a greater labour to avoid them. The old ladies were moved by my youth and melancholy to pity me, which gave a pleasing softness to their civility: The young ones forgave me my superior finery, and any advantages of person, when they looked on the doleful consequences of the latter; and when they placed all that vanity could render desirable in me in one account, and the mighty sum of all Mr. Merton's disagreableness in the other, they could not suppose the balance of happiness was sufficient to excite one grain of envy.

Thus I became a favourite with my own sex; and I have already given reasons why the other was not likely to be less disposed in my favour. I soon became the determined idol of the men: Some perhaps addressed me from real liking; others, from the hopes my situation inspired; and still more, for the pleasure of making an old man jealous, or to obtain the honour of being thought to have sown dissention between a new-married couple.

I was so indifferent to the opinion of all the people in the place, that I do not believe I should soon have found out this general admiration of the men, if Mr. Merton had not opened my eyes. As soon as they began to shew the least attention to me, he grew jealous; and as he was a plain speaker, I was not long ignorant of it. I wondered at his whim; and set it down to his account as another of his faults: It made no great addition to the number; for I had collected a large catalogue in my mind, and could make none to my dislike, for it was past increase.

I did not consider how natural jealousy is to a man who knows he is not beloved. My countenance and air sufficiently shewed me capable of love; and he was sure not to be the object. In such a situation, jealousy was pardonable; but I was too young to reason deeply; and had no prepossession in his favour to help me to excuse him. Because I was intirely indifferent to all the men in the place, I thought he injured me grievously; and resented it accordingly. If I let the men talk to me, it was because I was too indolent to go from them; and was so absorbed in my own thoughts, that I scarcely heard one sentence in ten of all they addressed to me.

The indifference I shewed to all, gained me much praise from the old ladies; and the young ones complimented my behaviour, and caressed me extremely, in order to get into the circle of the gentlemen who commonly attended me; and to whom they hoped to recommend themselves by that vivacity which I so much wanted; not doubting to get away every admirer from a woman, whose coldness of manner, and languid mind, scarcely afforded them an answer.

The approbation my conduct received from every other person, made me more highly resent Mr. Merton's suspicions; which soon grew as brutal as they were unjust. I saw no means of avoiding them, but by shutting myself up intirely; which was impossible, unless I had told the reason; and I had sense enough to see that I could not take a more imprudent step. Nor do I imagine any care could have quieted a passion grown to such a rage as Mr. Merton's jealousy, and which undoubtedly was without the least colour of reason from any misconduct of mine: But the sequel seemed to justify him; his imagination did but anticipate the cause; and with him suspicion was prophetic.

Tho' the addresses of many lovers, and the extravagant rage of my husband, could not bring me out of my lethargy of grief (for my spirits were so intirely sunk, that it could be called by no other name), yet a circumstance happened which effected it at once.

I went out one evening, more languid than ever, wearied with flattery in the morning while I was abroad, and with abuse at noon, when dinner brought a *tête à tête* between my husband and myself at home. I was scarcely able to sit up; so much did the extreme depression of my spirits affect my whole frame; and was more inclined to vent some of my melancholy in tears, than to go into company: But a lady came to see me, who would take no denial; I must either go to the rooms with her as usual; or, if I was not well enough (for that was the turn I had given to my refusal), she would spend the evening with me.

In my state of dejection, nothing was so distressing as to be obliged to support a conversation with so little assistance; therefore, as the less grievous of so disagreable an alternative, I consented to go to the public room with her. She had a great deal of good-nature, and therefore was sincerely glad she had prevailed; convinced that dissipation would be of service to one, whose disorder she plainly saw was on her spirits: But her satisfaction was soon checked, and turned into a fear of having done me harm; for we had not got above half up the room, when I fainted away.

This accident drew numbers round me; all the smelling bottles in the room were collected about me; when I came to myself, water and drops were presented me, and every thing offered that promised relief. The lady, who brought me out, immediately asked assistance to carry me home again; but I, who came abroad so unwillingly, now insisted on staying where I was.

A change which so much surprized my companion, was occasioned by the sight of Captain Turnham; which affected my depressed spirits to so violent a degree, as occasioned the disorder that had raised so great an alarm. When I came a little to myself, all the volatiles presented me did less towards reviving me than the appearance of Captain Turnham; who in the croud was attending; tho' with a countenance which expressed real concern, while those of others only spoke the language of civility.

The captain was so prudent as to address me only like a common acquaintance, while we had so many spectators. I took the hint, and answered him in the same manner; but endeavoured as soon as possible to dissipate the croud, and could with a good grace assure them I was quite well; for my joy had proved to me such a cordial, that all agreed they had never seen me look so well.

Captain Turnham watched the opportunity, and we got half an hour's uninterrupted conversation; wherein, after lamenting our hard fate, he informed me, that had it not been for his father's sickness, and then his death, of which I had heard, he should have set out for Tunbridge the moment he knew we were gone thither; and that he could not persuade himself to remain in the country an hour after he had performed the most necessary duties. He was in doubt whether it might be proper to come to my house; therefore dressed himself as soon as he arrived, and repaired to the public room, where he hoped to find me; and after having walked round it, and convinced himself that I was not there, he placed himself near the door, that he might not fail of seeing me as I entered.

I thought myself lucky in having that half hour allowed me; and I found I was not to expect its continuance; for I perceived some of my acquaintance coming up to me, at which I could not forbear expressing my vexation. Captain Turnham just hinted the necessity of appearing country acquaintance, which might excuse our intimacy. Accordingly I asked many questions about my family, and my former neighbours, who had indeed borne no share in our conversation till then; and this was repeated in every new set of company, both that evening and the next day.

As Captain Turnham had made some acquaintance with Mr. Merton, when he first came into our neighbourhood, and learnt from me that my relations had been prudent enough to conceal the share my love had in my reluctance to the marriage, he went up to the card table where he was playing, carried him the compliments of my family, and of his friend, and of many others who had never sent them; for he had not declared his intention of going to Tunbridge.

Tho' Mr. Merton was not then mightily delighted with the consequences of his visit in that county, yet, as he had received great civilities there, he enquired after them with pleasure, and gave the captain a general invitation to his house, and a particular one for the next day, which was sure to be accepted.

An intimacy between me and one with whom I was supposed to have been acquainted from my childhood, appeared so natural, that people were not quick at taking offence at it; and Mr. Merton, who boiled over with rage if I did but speak to, or look at, any other man, appeared free from all suspicion of Captain Turnham; tho' the change in me was so very apparent, as might have been observable to one less jealous. My eyes became animated; my complexion glowed; I spoke with ease; and my whole air was changed: But this was all attributed to the waters, which I drank from the time I first came there; and I was quoted as the greatest cure they had performed that season, by all but Mr. Merton, who imagined the alteration proceeded only from the pleasure I took in being admired; and if I looked particularly blooming, or more animated than common, it would throw him into such outrageous passions, that Captain Turnham's presence could not restrain, who thereby often became the witness of his brutality: which gave me less uneasiness, when I knew I was tenderly pitied by the object of all my affections: Nor indeed could I well have been angry; for tho' Mr. Merton had nothing particular to lay to my charge, but only supposed, that as I did not love him, I must like some of those whose assiduities he observed, tho' my behaviour gave not the least reason for his suspicion, yet I was conscious that he had in reality sufficient cause, though he knew it not.

Captain Turnham was extremely cautious in his conduct to me; and by that means taught me a care, which, infatuated as I was, I should probably not otherwise have taken: But as this laid him under a great restraint, he thought he deserved to be rewarded by some private interviews, wherein he might have liberty to speak his passion, without being obliged to guard every look, to prevent spectators from knowing the subject of our conversation.

To this my fears of a discovery made some objection; nor was I without apprehensions from the imprudence of his passion, which I feared my own was too violent to be able to repress. I saw that a lover, who knew he was too much beloved to give any real offence, must be a very dangerous person. Tho' Mr. Merton had no share of my affections, I was determined to keep what I called my conjugal fidelity. '*He comes too near, who comes to be denied*,'[147] has been truly said. My behaviour gave Captain Turnham sufficient encouragement to be very importunate in his solicitations for a private meeting, and the weakness he presumed upon was his friend; for at last he prevailed; and as it was not very difficult to contrive it at such a place as Tunbridge, he took care that I should not have leisure to retract, and the meeting immediately followed my consent.[148]

CHAP. XI.

Anger, in hasty words and blows,
Itself discharges on its foes:
Our sorrow too finds some relief,
In tears, that wait upon our grief.
Thus every passion, but fond love,
Unto its own redress does move:
But that alone the wretch inclines
To what prevents her own designs;
To acts that render her despis'd,
Where she endeavours to be priz'd.
                              WALLER.[149]

A Woman seldom stops at the first imprudence. I had been with difficulty prevailed upon to consent to the first private interview with Captain Turnham; but after that was once granted, I made no scruple of another meeting; and then of another still; and so on, till they came almost daily. The respect with which he at first behaved, encouraged me to trust him again. The danger vanished from my thoughts; and I did not see why I should deny myself and my lover so great a pleasure as we received from the liberty of professing our mutual love, and lamenting the cruelty of fortune and parents, which had divided us, when this indulgence might be granted without an infringement of virtue; for I did not perceive that my husband had a right to require me to be prudent as well as to be chaste; and that encouraging the passion of another man, or indulging my own for him, was an offence against virtue, within whatever bounds I restrained my actions.

A woman who hopes to preserve her virtue after she has laid aside decorum, is as foolish as a man would be, who should expect to defend a town, whose fortifications and outworks are destroyed, against a powerful enemy; especially if there is treachery within, which I am afraid is the case when a woman's affections are strongly engaged.[150]

I could not so easily deceive Captain Turnham as I did myself: He knew the consequence of all my actions, and how long respect was necessary to deprive me of all fear; the only enemy he had: And virtue followed my prudence,[151] as is generally the case with her who parts with the latter.

These private meetings enabled us the better to constrain ourselves in public; and we had the satisfaction of continuing our course unsuspected, till one night that my housekeeper passed by just as I came out of Captain Turnham's lodging with him, and visibly observed me. I that instant anticipated the punishment of my crime; the immediate consequence occurring at once to me. My fright was excessive; I could not support myself; and was forced to return with the Captain into his lodging, till I was enough recovered to walk.

This housekeeper was one, who, as I learned from the lady I have mentioned as my neighbour, had, during the continuance of her youth, lived with Mr. Merton in another capacity; nor had her office quite ceased till he married me: But as her bloom was past, corpulency had impaired her beauty, and possession had long rendered Mr. Merton tired of her. He informed her, that she could no longer serve him in the same character; but, as a reward, he constituted her housekeeper.

As this woman looked on me as the cause of her being degraded into a servant, and an interloper on her rights, it is no wonder she hated me; and she soon made me sensible of it by her insolence; which was so great, that I had several times expressed to Mr. Merton my inclination to part with her; thinking it a necessary piece of complaisance to him, as she had been his servant before she was mine.

At first, he mildly desired me to try her longer; telling me, good servants would take upon them: But I could not perceive her such; for I saw she was extravagant, wasteful, and idle; and at each fresh instance of her insolence, urged her other faults, as reasons why I should not be exposed to her insults: But as Mr. Merton's temper grew worse, he began to receive such complaints with much ill humour, and to tell me plainly, that she should not be turned away; that the housekeeper was as much his servant as mine; and he would not lose a good one by my perverseness.

As this woman knew by whose interest she kept her place, and saw therein a sufficient proof of the little power I had, she lost all respect, and behaved to me with continual insolence, and scarcely suffered any other servant in the house to obey me. This would have been a very mortifying circumstance to one, whose thoughts had not been so entirely engrossed by other vexations, as to receive little additional uneasiness from lesser griefs. It had indeed increased my contempt for, and aversion to Mr. Merton; but it never appeared to me in the light of an affliction till now, that I saw all possible use would be made by such a woman of the discovery she had in her power; and if any addition or exaggeration was necessary I did not doubt but she would supply the defect.

In this situation I knew not how to return home; nor could the Captain offer me any consolation; for he was almost as wretched as myself. The only expedient he could offer to save me from the brutal rage of my husband, was, that I should fly with him: But I could not resolve to give up my character, fortune and friends, and live the object of contempt and scorn. I had but little reason to expect any favour from a man whom I had so cruelly injured, when I had experienced the greatest brutality imaginable from him without the least cause. But I thought it scarcely possible for him to treat me worse than he already had done, without my giving any occasion for it. He had not proof sufficient for a divorce; therefore I hoped to avoid public shame: For had it been told that I was seen coming out of the Captain's lodging, my reputation was on so good a footing, that it would only have been treated as an ambiguous circumstance.

With these considerations I encouraged myself as much as possible. I had gone into the public room as soon as I left the Captain, and could not prevail on myself to go home till most of the company was departed. At my return to my lodging, I soon found Mr. Merton had been long enough at home, and the time had been made so good use of by the housekeeper, that he was acquainted with the place where she had seen me; for I was received with such an air of rage and fury, that I was really afraid for my life.

I had not been able to invent a very good excuse for my being in those lodgings; and what I had framed, might with some examination perhaps have been proved to be false; as I designed to pretend that I had made visits to ladies, who possibly were in the public room: But some such thing was necessary to account for my time, and for my passing by the Captain's. As I was so poorly provided with an apology, it was no part of my misfortune that Mr. Merton would not give me an opportunity to defend myself.

His abuse descended to every infamous appellative; and I was forbid to appear in his presence, put into the custody of my accuser, and ordered to be locked up in a garret.

This command was punctually obeyed, and I was rudely dragged to the dirtiest garret in the house, which stunk with filth and damp. In that consisted my sole consolation; for my jailor did not chuse to stay in so noisome a place; therefore I was delivered from her insults: But she was resolved I should receive as little relief as possible from her absence; for she took the candle with her, leaving me in the midst of all this dirt without light to enable me to avoid it.

I had not strength to go feeling about for a seat, but sunk upon the ground; and there I remained, a prey to despair, remorse, and resentment, till the morning's dawn tempted me to rise from the filth with which I was encompassed, and turned some of my thoughts to the loathsomeness of the place where I was confined. I soon perceived it must have been long uninhabited, and intirely converted into a lumber-room, which no living creature occupied, but spiders, beetles, and much other and more offensive vermin: As there was neither chair nor bed in it, I could hope for no rest, but on scraps of old boxes and such lumber.

The day made no other alteration in my sufferings, than in subjecting me to the cruellest insults from the infamous wretch by whose brutality I was committed. I begged earnestly to see Mr. Merton, and to have leave to defend myself. I asserted, that tho' the circumstances against me gave room for suspicion, yet they were not sufficient cause for such treatment. But all I could urge was in vain: I addressed unwilling ears; and on such there is little chance to make much impression.

Grief and watching rendered me extremely dry; but it was with difficulty I obtained a little tea: For the cruel wretch, from whom I asked it, said, she did not know whether she should not be false to her trust if she gave me any, being only ordered to provide me with necessary sustenance; but she thought tea was an indulgence, and therefore out of her instructions: However, finding I could eat nothing, she let me have some twice in the day, provided I would eat some bread with it; for she thought it so easy to be starved, even by a short abstinence, that I believe she was afraid of losing a power wherein she took so much satisfaction, and that death should rob her of her victim.

I asked, if I was never to go to bed, any more, since no such piece of furniture seemed to be thought necessary.[152] She told me, I might do very well without for some time longer: Some mortification was proper after too much indulgence. I then begged for a chair, and that one of the servants might be suffered to sweep and dust the room. She answered, 'that if I had been as nice in my behaviour as about my habitation, I should never have been there.' Tho' the reproach was insolent from her, yet it was just; my conscience assented, and I was silent.

In this way the day passed; and it is scarcely possible to imagine a greater agony of despair than I was in. Towards the evening I heard a footstep at my door, and a rustling: The oddness of the noise made me look round, and I saw a paper was pushed under the door. I made all the haste to snatch it that I was able; and as soon as opened, I perceived it was Captain Turnham's hand. Joy would hardly suffer me to read it directly; and when I began, the fear of being caught in the perusal, and that my confusion in hiding it should cause suspicion, and occasion a second search (for my pockets had undergone one before, less to the satisfaction of my persecutor than to my own), agitated me so much, that I was with difficulty able to go thro' it,[153] especially as it was pretty long.

Captain Turnham told me in it, that he had not been able to rest all the past night, from his apprehensions for me; which were greatly increased, by neither Mr. Merton nor myself having made our appearance in the morning. He was afraid of coming to our lodging to make any inquiry; and could not bear to return to his own, as he had there little chance of getting any information. About noon a rumour began to be spread, that Mr. Merton had discovered a criminal correspondence between him and me, and had confined me to my room, till he determined what further was to be done. He had observed a whisper run round the room, and every eye turned towards him; and a friend gave him that account of the occasion of it. This, he continued, increased his apprehensions: He understood by this that the housekeeper had not been silent, and feared the first effects of Mr. Merton's rage; but the circumstance was so short of proof of any thing criminal, that he did not imagine it possible for him to be guilty of any lasting outrage in consequence of it; but, to be the better assured of all particulars, he went home, and sent his footman to our lodging, to inquire of our servants the occasion of some strange reports which were spread about me. He waited in his apartment for his man's return, who brought him a full detail of all that had passed; which by no means lost in the repetition; the servants being disposed in my favour, having always found me better tempered than their master or his housekeeper.

The captain added, that the account of the brutality with which I had been treated, almost distracted him; and in the most tender and importunate manner beseeched me to suffer him to deliver me from this horrid tyranny; which he proposed to do, by fixing a high ladder to my window, the night but one after I received this letter. He said he had viewed it, and found it practicable; that he would come up it, and guide my trembling steps, and have a post-chaise ready to carry us directly to London. He proposed delaying it till the time mentioned, that he might get a chaise from thence, to prevent our being discovered immediately; for if we hired one at Tunbridge, we should be too easily traced.

That most eloquent metal gold had prevailed on one of Mr. Merton's servants to deliver this letter; but as there was no means of answering it, he informed me he should proceed in the plan he had mentioned to me without delay; and trusted, that if I had any value for my life or his, I should not be backward in complying with his proposal; for my reputation was as much lost as if I had taken the most public steps to destroy it. Every tender sentiment, which he thought could afford me the least consolation, was added to the letter; and I confess it proved a great cordial to me.

The assurances of his love, the hopes of a deliverance from what I suffered, and the strength of my own passion, left me no scruples about complying with his proposal: And tho' the time appeared too distant, yet expectation gave me such a recruit of spirits, as enabled me to bear it.

CHAP. XII.

MY greatest fear now was, that my jailor should relent, and place me in a more comfortable room; as it seemed scarcely possible that she should leave me three nights without the power of going to bed, or even of putting myself into an easy posture: But my apprehensions were vain; her malice preserved its full force, and her insults continued: Nor did I then endeavour to pacify her; but received her, when she entered, either with sulleness or resentment, lest her anger should flag.

I could indeed have wished she would have granted me a candle, that I might enliven the tedious length of the night with the perusal of Captain Turnham's letter; as I should then have enjoyed it with more liberty, freed from the apprehensions of her coming into the room: But herein I could not prevail; so had nothing but my imagination and expectation to console me.

This enabled me to support life till the appointed night came. I longed to shed poppies over all the family, to send them early to their rest;[155] and was impatient at their sitting up so long. But when I had my wish, and the house seemed as quiet as the grave, instead of the joy I expected to feel on the occasion, I was full of tremors: I trembled if my own gown rustled; the striking of a clock alarmed me; and if a dog barked, I fell into agonies.

My imagination suggested a thousand noises; and every one was more dreadful to me than the execution bell of a poor criminal. When it grew dark, I had placed myself just by the window: I now opened and shut it continually, not knowing well why I did either; but after two hours expectation, which in the anxious agitation of my mind appeared an age, in one of the periods that the window remained open, I heard a little noise, and immediately the voice of my love whispered my name.

The beating of my heart rendered me almost unable to answer him; but if I had been more loquacious, he would not have waited for my indulging it. He was so impatient to get me out of my prison, that he intreated me to make no

"

delay; telling me at the same time, that the highest ladder he could get was not quite long enough;[156] but he had found some broken places in the wall, which giving a rest to his feet, had supplied that deficiency, and he hoped he should convey me down as successfully as he had mounted.

This particular was very dreadful to me, who had looked with horror on the great height I had to descend, from the time I first received Captain Turnham's letter; But he allowed me little time for reflection; catching me up in his arms, and lifting me out of the window, ready to expire with fright. The second step he made, he revived me, by saying, 'Now we are safe enough'. He had then reached the ladder, which afforded him firmer footing; and it was not long before we were quite down it.

He hurried me to the chaise, while his men carried the ladder away; and I had now recovered the power of speech; and, according to a design I had framed, begged he would let his servant guide me to what place he thought proper, and that he would remain at Tunbridge a few days longer, to remove in some degree the suspicion from himself; and to contrive to have it given out, that I had made my escape in the night, only in order to fly from the brutal usage I had received, and without any male companion in my flight.

Captain Turnham was not well inclined to comply with my request; but as it was much the most prudent proceeding, I prevailed upon him to grant it, and was put under the care of his servant.

We travelled with great expedition; and, tho' the night was extremely dark, arrived in London soon after break of day. According to the Captain's direction, I was placed in a convenient lodging in the city; the busiest place being judged the fittest for concealment. Idleness renders people curious: Those who have little business themselves employ their time in observing others; and a vacant mind, empty of ideas, is always searching abroad for things foreign to itself, to fill the void; while the sons of care and industry, and votaries of riches, are too good œconomists, even of their thoughts, to throw them away where they can hope for no return of profit: They are so used to traffic, that they look on their attention as one of their commodities, which should not be expended without considerable advantage.

I had reason to think the choice of my situation was well made. The people, with whom I lodged, beheld me in no other light, than as one who was to pay them a stipulated sum weekly; and if they saw no reason to doubt my payment, nothing else in me could merit their attention. I came indeed at an unusual hour; was very fine, and very dirty; having passed three days and nights in the same dress: But this was my business and not theirs; so they paid no regard to it.

I was void of all necessaries, and longed for the refreshment of clean linen; and fortunately had sufficient in my pocket to purchase it. For this I was obliged to a piece of carelessness, for which I must have been angry with myself, if the consequences had not excused it. I had given my maid a bank bill for thirty pounds,[157] to get converted into cash; wherein not having succeeded, she gave it me just as I stepped out of the door. I was then going to Captain Turnham's lodgings; a proceeding which I was sensible was so wrong, that I could never do it without great flutter of spirits. In this hurry, I put it loose into my pocket; having only just precaution enough to stuff it into my little pocket within my large one, made originally for my snuff-box. When the housekeeper searched me, she took my pocket-book and purse, and whatever else she liked, esteeming it a lawful capture; but happily this little scrap of paper remained unfelt, and so became no part of the prize.

This was a great resource to me; for tho' the Captain had ordered his servant to provide me with every thing I wanted, yet it would have been painful to me to have made such immediate use of that liberty, as I knew his circumstances were but narrow.

I purchased change of linen, and a gown less rich and gaudy, ready made; and tho' I still was in a situation which would a week before have appeared dreadful to me; yet, when compared to the misery I had suffered the three preceding days, it seemed tolerable, and I soon became able to take food and rest; for I stood in great want of such refreshment.

The next day brought me a letter from Captain Turnham, filled with expressions of his impatience to come to me; but yet he acknowleged my commands were prudent. He informed me, that knowing me in safety, free from my brutal tyrants, gave him spirits enough to be one of the earliest abroad; and, with a composure, and ease of countenance and manner, which assisted the deception we intended, he applied to the servant he had before bribed, to know what passed in Mr. Merton's family; and from him learnt, that my escape was not discovered till near ten o'clock the next morning, the housekeeper not finding leisure to go before into the room.

Upon seeing the window open, and her prisoner missing, she raised a great clamour, which brought up Mr. Merton: Then all the servants were called and examined; but no one being able to give any account of an event they all rejoiced in, it was immediately determined I was run away with Captain Turnham. This news was soon brought to the walks by a Lady, who had received it from her servant. The fact was denied by the person to whom she related it, and who assured her she had but just left the Captain in the public room.

Upon this, many confused stories were raised; in none of which there was any truth, except that I was gone. Mr. Merton went to the inns, but could not hear of any equipage or horses that had come there or gone from thence that night. He sent to Tunbridge town,[158] with as little success.

Intirely at a loss what to think, he carried proper officers, when the Captain was abroad, and searched his lodgings. After having thus persuaded himself that

I could not be gone from that place, he fansied I had got no farther than my legs could carry me, and sent his servants different ways, to search all the roads and fields as far as he thought it possible for me to stray. The servants agreed on an alehouse for their rendezvous, where they ended their perquisition; and were drinking success to my escape, while their master imagined they were assiduously endeavouring to trace it. The housekeeper was the only one who did her office; she had also undertaken the search, and walked more that day than she had done for three years before. Animated by rage, she went on till she was so spent, that she was scarcely able to get home again, and remained very ill with her fatigue.

The reports she gave of her little success, and the unavailing labours of the rest of the servants, which they set forth in strong colours, having had sufficient leisure to settle their several marches, recommended them much to their master's favour, but gave him little satisfaction. He had no hope left, but that in a few days necessity must bring me out of my concealment.

This search after me was known to the whole place; and curiosity made all the company as eager to learn the event, as the person most concerned. There was not one who did not go to the back part of the house, though the road to it was very rugged, to see the window from whence I had made my escape. Some of them, surprised that Captain Turnham had not had the curiosity to look at it, carried him to see what a dreadful height it was.

No one appeared so anxious as he: 'He had the regard,' he said, 'of an old acquaintance and neighbour for me, and was sincerely interested in my fate; but should be very miserable, if he thought the treatment I had received could bear any reference to him; which he thought impossible, as every one must see there was no air of gallantry between us.' Many agreed with him; others were convinced that jealousy could not be without some cause. Thus the whole place was engaged in disputes, which they were not likely to determine.

Mr. Merton easily conceived the window was too high for me to get out of without a ladder. He therefore went to every place where he supposed any were kept, to inquire if theirs had been used that night; but the Captain had bribed a man to get it out of his neighbour's yard; and lest he should have an opportunity of telling, bought his absence from the place for a fortnight.

When the Captain heard Mr. Merton had searched his lodging, he thought it not consistent with his character to suffer such an outrage patiently; therefore he went to Mr. Merton, and inquired what reason he had for such insolence. Mr. Merton was too wise to chuse to venture his life, for which he had no small regard, because he had lost a wife he did not love; and, with due meekness and civility, begged his pardon, if he had done what was not proper: But desired him to consider his case deserved some allowance; for few men could bear to have a wife run away, without being turned a little beyond the bounds of reason and good manners.

'Very likely,' replied the Captain; 'but why was I to be the person on whom this was to fall?' Mr. Merton then told him, that he thought he had just reason to suspect a criminal correspondence between me and him, and mentioned the cause of his suspicion.

The Captain acknowleged the fact, and accounted for it, by 'having met me in a visit, from whence he offered to wait on me to the public room; but in my way I fell down, and hurt my ankle so much, that I could not immediately walk; and being near his lodgings, he helped me in there, and left me to rub it with lavendar water, which I had in my pocket, till I was sufficiently relieved to be able to proceed: That he would have sent for a chair for me; but it being only a step to the walks, I chose, with leaning on him, to go there on foot.'

Mr. Merton did not think the Captain's word a sufficient confutation of his suspicions; but judged it more proper to appear satisfied, than to resent. The extreme bustle that arose from this incident had confounded the fact; every body supposing the action must be very flagrant, which was followed by such consequences. Thus the truth was dropped, and the various reports were so contradictory, that at last it became doubtful whether there was any foundation for all that had been done against me. Every man acquitted me in his own opinion; for each knowing me to have been reserved to *him*, thought it impossible I should not be so to all; for whose charms could be superior?

CHAP. XIII.

THO' I could no longer pretend to virtue, I was not so lost to shame, but that I wished to preserve what reputation I had remaining: It could be but little; for every spot on a woman's fame is indelible. But there is a great difference in the situation of one whose character is ambiguous, and of her who has put it beyond all doubt.

I flattered myself, that if my parents would espouse my cause, I might still be preserved from infamy, and obtain a separate maintenance: Which, however small, would have contented me.

As soon, therefore, as rest had sufficiently refreshed me, I wrote my father an account of the whole of Mr. Merton's treatment of me, and of his outrageous jealousy of Captain Turnham, so highly and so suddenly conceived; omitting no circumstance which I hoped might plead in my favour; intreating his countenance and intercession towards procuring a separation, which would not brand me with infamy, and bring shame on my family, as well as ruin on myself. I desired him to direct his letter to one who was a friend of Captain Turnham's servant, from whence he could fetch it; for I was not sure enough of success, to trust my father with the knowlege of my abode.

Captain Turnham remained above a week at Tunbridge; from whence I heard from him regularly; and found, that as every day rendered the contradictions and absurdities in the stories relating to me more palpable, it was still possible that I might be acquitted by the generality of the world. This made me very impatient for my father's answer, on which it intirely depended; for without Mr. Merton could be brought to consent to a separation, and some allowance,[160] I could not venture to shew myself to any one; but must skulk in corners like a criminal, for fear of falling again into the cruel hands from which I had escaped.

I had strongly represented to my father the dreadful consequences of his refusal; and hoped the honour of his family, if no other consideration availed, would obtain his concurrence: But when his answer came, I found I was mistaken. He wrote me word, that 'had Mr. Merton been jealous of any other man than Captain Turnham, he would not have determined against me without examining the case; but the knowlege he had of my violent passion for him, and his having followed me to Tunbridge, together with my aversion to my husband, convinced him so fully of my guilt, that no other proof was wanting: That the honour of the family, for which I pleaded, forbad his shewing any countenance to her who would disgrace it; and that on that account, as well as for a necessary example to the rest of his children, he disclaimed me for ever.'

This letter shocked me beyond description. I valued my reputation highly, and now saw it lost for ever. I was become the outcast of the world; Captain Turnham alone was willing to receive me; but I dreaded a dependence on a man whose esteem could not equal his love; and how soon might general contempt extinguish his passion! All this I saw when it was too late.

In the bitterness of my soul I answered my father's letter; and represented to him, with all the anguish that I felt it, how he had totally effected my ruin, first by sacrificing me forcibly to a wretch I hated, and must despise; and then by refusing me a protection, which might have made me some recompence for his past cruelty. I then represented the inevitable infamy to which he consigned me; I laid my vice and shame to his charge, and pressed it home upon his conscience.

I had just disburthened my heart of some of its anguish, when Captain Turnham arrived, and revived me so much by his presence, that I almost forgot my sorrows. I had now given up all hopes of assistance from my family, and consequently of preserving my reputation; therefore endeavoured, as far as I was able, to banish all thoughts of it; and my lover, in order to contribute to my ease of mind, assisted me in this attempt; whereby all the principle I had left was totally overthrown. While we keep a regard for the opinion of others, we have some remains of virtue; but she who consigns herself over not only to vice, but to shame, never fails of becomeing abandoned: She is reduced to it in her own defence; for by no other means can she obtain a moment's ease of mind, if that indolence of temper, which is the best state such an one can arrive at, can be called by the name of ease. When every virtuous principle we have reproaches us, we are apt to employ all endeavours to extirpate them; and to deliver ourselves from the pain our guilt inflicts, by becoming more guilty. We fansy it will be a less labour to lose the sense of virtue, than to learn the practice of it: A great and fatal error! For we can never intirely fear our consciences; and there are times when the most hardened severely suffer for all the pleasures their crimes have yielded them.

I experienced this truth in its full force. Tho' Captain Turnham's passion for me was unabated, and I loved him to distraction, yet I was not happy. But as few people can bear the melancholy of others, I concealed it as much as possible from him; and endeavoured to please him, by a chearfulness which was often a stranger to my heart. As his income was small, I knew I must be a heavy burden on his purse; and found I was likely to become still more so. I therefore applied myself as much as possible to œconomy, as some relief to my pride, which suffered at the thought of being maintained at his expence.

We had lived together above half a year, without Mr. Merton's having been able to find out where we were, when Captain Turnham was ordered to quarters at Reading.[161] This was a melancholy circumstance to us, tho' no more than we had reason to expect sooner. It affected us doubly: The expence of living separate was more than could easily be afforded by the Captain's income; and we still loved too well to bear to be asunder, especially when my situation rendered it more grievous, being then big with child; but it was too dangerous for me to venture to his quarters, as I might there be so easily found out.

We were obliged then to part, tho' with the utmost regret; and as he was not able to get leave of absence for more than a day at a time, while I could travel, we used to meet half-way; and, after the consolation of a few hours of each other's company, returned to our respective homes. This was an expensive indulgence; but when seeing each other was in question, all œconomy was forgot.

When I lay-in, Captain Turnham pressed for leave of absence with such importunity, that he obtained permission for a whole week; during which his company enabled me to bear my sickness with more content than health could give me in his absence. He made me another visit before my confinement was over;[162] which, tho' but for a day, was a great cordial to my spirits.

The child I brought into the world was a boy, and my only pleasure in his father's absence, who seemed to look on him as an additional tie of affection to me. But he promised me much care and anxiety, being a weakly child.

When I had intirely recovered my lying-in, the Captain being taken ill, tho' of but a slight fever, intimated a great desire to see me; upon which I went to Reading directly, and after staying a week there, left him quite well; and we engaged to continue the practice of meeting half-way: In which short journeys I flattered myself our little boy might safely accompany me, as the sight of him would be an additional pleasure to his father.

I returned in the stage-coach; wherein all my fellow travellers were women. My heart had been heavy at parting with Captain Turnham; but as I drew nearer London, the expectation of seeing my little boy afforded me consolation, tho' the thought of his sickly frame mixed a little anxiety with it, not being free from fears that I might find him still worse than when I had last heard of him.

When we were within two miles of London, the coach was stopped by some men, who rode up to us. We prepared for being robbed; and part of the company was excessively frighted: My purse was near empty; and my apprehensions were small, till I perceived, amongst those I took for highwaymen, a servant of Mr. Merton's. This sight threw me into the utmost terror; and it was immediately completed by the approach of his coach, wherein I saw my husband, and my bitter enemy his housekeeper.

The coach-door was opened; and the servants, whose countenances expressed more compassion than suited their office, took hold of me to lift me out of the stage into Mr. Merton's. I gave a loud scream, and immediately fell into fits. My companions, terrified with such a scene, screamed too, with such unwearied cries, that they were not over when I came to myself.

The servants, alarmed at the effect their attempt had on me, desisted; but as I recovered, I heard Mr. Merton cursing them for minding a woman's fits, and ordering them to take me as I was. They obeyed, and put me into the coach to him: On which my fits returned, and I was not sensible[163] for many minutes at a time that day; which was therefore happier than many that succeeded it.

At night we arrived at an inn, where I was put to bed directly. I found the housekeeper was to lie in the room; but for the present she was content with locking me in, and went downstairs, not chusing so irksome an employment as attending me in my fits, nor concerning herself what became of me in them.

I was sensible of one more attack; but am inclined to think that was all; for I burst into a violent flood of tears, which relieved me; and my terrors were a little abated by finding myself alone.

Excessive terror, like excessive pain, brings itself some relief, by depriving us for a time of sense. Tho' my fear was not so extreme, my misery was now greater; since I had acquired the power of feeling it, by the recovery of my senses. I had every thing to dread for myself from the hands into which I was fallen. When I considered the cruelty wherewith I had been treated on a bare suspicion, what might I not expect when my offence was great and palpable! But this was not my only affliction; I was torn from the man I loved, Heaven knows! much better than myself: He would remain ignorant of what was become of me; perhaps think that the woman who had broke sacred vows for him, had now violated those solemn vows she had so often made to him, and left him for some new lover: Or, if his heart still did me justice, he would not be able to deliver me from this new slavery; for I could not doubt but entire care would be taken for the future to prevent a possibility of escape.

My child was another addition to my misfortunes: He wanted the tender care of a mother, to watch his infant weakness. I feared no one would well supply this place, now I was torn from him; nor knew I how to support life in an entire ignorance of his existence, which hung by so weak a thread.

How miserable is that wretch, who in her misfortunes cannot pray to the only Being who has power to alleviate her distress! who, when the world appears armed against her, cannot have the consolation of thinking she has a friend in superior mansions! and need not fear man, who can only kill her body, when she knows there is One who will preserve her soul; and if she is thrust with violence from this land of wretchedness, will receive her into everlasting habitations, where the wicked cease to trouble, and all tears are wiped from the eyes!

How far was I from this situation! I had offended as grievously against the laws of God, as against human institutions; and if I considered him as a Being who beholds the works of the children of men, I must see myself the object of his wrath. I had therefore learned to think He regarded us but little; which had lessened my terrors, but deprived me of all hope of relief from Him. And what could I expect from a sorrow, which would not have been for my sins, but for their consequences: I could not give up the object of my affections; greater faith, and much divine grace, were requisite to enable me to make such a sacrifice; therefore my thoughts durst not wander beyond this world, where my prospect was most wretched, without a glimmering of hope to chear me in the dreary road of affliction that lay open before me; and which I was conscious I deserved from the person who inflicted it.

CHAP. XIV.

I have been in such a dismal place,
Where joy ne'er enters, which the sun ne'er chears;
Bound in with darkness, overspread with damps!
                                        DRYDEN.[164]

MY gaoler required a great deal of refreshment after the wearisome day she had past; which prevented her coming to bed very early, and gave me leisure to weep myself almost into a state of stupefaction. This was the most desirable condition I could be in. My persecutor looked into my close-drawn bed-curtains, and vented some reproaches; but feeing me scarcely sensible, she would not throw away such precious words, and went to her rest.

As day began to break, I fell into more lively terrors, fearing I should again be exposed to see, and be seen by, Mr. Merton; which was the most dreadful circumstance imaginable to me, as it occasioned both the greatest apprehensions and self-reproaches.

When my gaoler awaked, she called to me to rise. I was hardly able to obey her; so much was I spent with the violence of my fits the day before: But she quickened my feeble motions with the harshest expressions; and fear restored part of the strength of which it had deprived me. After frequent efforts, she found it was impossible for me to get down-stairs without help; but not condescending to assist me, she called two of the footmen, who supported me to the coach, and lifted me into it; for the fear of seeing Mr. Merton there, as I approached it, deprived me entirely of the little strength I had remaining.

Surely all mental sufferings put together cannot make so great a sum of misery as a mixture of anxiety and fear, such as I at that moment felt. I verily think, if Mr. Merton had then appeared, nature must have been totally overcome with the shock; but the shutting of the door after the housekeeper got into the coach to me, gave me breath. I took it as an indication that we were to perform the rest of our journey without him; but durst not ask if my hopes were well grounded.

Tho' I had been long exposed to shame, yet, in the midst of all my apprehensions, I was not insensible of seeing myself a spectacle to every person in the inn, or belonging to it. They were all standing in the yard to see me, with such faces of eager curiosity, as expressed too little compassion for a wretch, who, however blameable, was now surely a melancholy object.

The silence I kept was an example not followed by my fellow-traveller; she soon began to descant on my wickedness, and on my ingratitude to one who had taken me without a farthing, and made me mistress of so many fine things. The charge against me was not put in terms most likely to affect me; but I had sufficient cause for tears, and wept without uttering a syllable the whole day; great part of which she passed in exercising on me her talent of abuse: But sleep was sometimes my friend; for tho' it would not close my eyelids, it did her's, and stopped the almost perpetual motion of her tongue.

I was so ignorant of the roads, that I did not know whether we were travelling that which led to Mr. Merton's seat; but judged, by the distance it was at from London, that if we were bending our course that way, we must arrive there before night: On the contrary, as it grew dusk, we entered into another inn. I began to wonder where they were carrying me: I asked the servant who helped me out of the coach, what town that was? But the answer only served to shew me we were certainly not in the road to the place I most feared.

My gaoler guessed the reason of my question; and thinking I should be more vexed at knowing the truth, than I was by my perplexity, she satisfied my curiosity, as soon as we got into the inn, by telling me, 'we were going to an old house of Mr. Merton's; a proper place to be turned into a prison for such a creature as I was; but that indeed she should not stay in such a doleful hole any longer than till a proper person was found to take care and keep me in order, till law had procured a divorce, and left me to starve,[165] or to lead such shameful courses as I had begun.'

The only part of this information which was not some relief to my spirits, was the last article. Sunk as I was in the world, I shuddered at the thought of being publicly branded with infamy by the law, and made the subject of all the ribaldry used on such occasions: But this was at some distance; and to learn that I should not be again exposed to the sight of Mr. Merton, nor long be the sport of this woman's cruelty, was a present satisfaction, and enabled me the better to perform the remainder of my journey, which ended the next day.

Before it was dark we descended a very steep hill; at the foot of it stood rather a ruin than a house, to which we drove. 'Here,' said my gaoler, 'you may remain to old age, if the walls do not release you from your captivity by falling down, and knocking your brains out.' The alternative did not sound very comfortable; but life appeared at that time of too little value, for me to view, with any great uneasiness, the tottering building which was become my habitation. In an happier state it would have filled me with horrors; for half of it was already fallen, and much of the rest supported with props, which did not appear adequate to the weight they were to sustain.[166]

The inside of the house was not less ruinous. The wainscot was rotted to pieces, and the wall, which appeared thro' the large holes decay had made in it, damp had covered with mould so thick, that each spot seemed a little wood; whereon the spiders, having taken advantage of the convenience it offered, had spread numberless webs. The floors were as decayed as the wainscot, and so full of holes, that one could not walk but at the peril of one's limbs; and in many places the grass had grown up to a tolerable height, and weeds flourished most luxuriantly.

The ground round the house had once been a moat, but was now become a bog, wherein large families of frogs had fixed their abode, and kept a never-ceasing croaking; which made a proper base to the pert chirp of the crickets, who inhabited the chimnies. To the music of these was added the whooting of two owls, who lived in an old yew-tree, just under my window, and contended with a neighbouring screech-owl which should most constantly serenade me.

All these animals, as if desirous of entertaining the stranger who was just come amongst them, were particularly sonorous the first night; and to complete the whole, the house-dog, unused to be disturbed by the arrival of equipages and horses, was put into such agitation, that he could not recompose his spirits, but howled without ceasing till morning.[167]

One would imagine, that a person, whose whole soul was so filled with inward agony, was incapable of being affected by outward circumstances: But I experienced the contrary; for these I have mentioned turned grief into horror, and I could scarcely preserve myself from distraction.

The inhabitants of this falling mansion were an old steward and his wife, and their only child, a young woman about nineteen years old, whose countenance expressed the simplicity of her country breeding, added to that of her youth and innocence, and at the same time indicated so much good nature, that I thought, if I might have been allowed her company, it would have proved some little alleviation to my melancholy: But of this I had little hope; for my gaoler would suffer no one to be in the room alone with me, tho' she continually complained of the slavery of attending of me: Not with a great deal of reason; for she never came into the room but at the necessary times of bringing me food; so that I was always obliged to sit in the dark till supper, and the evenings were then grown pretty long, as it was in the beginning of November. Nor was I better provided with fire; for tho' I had little to do but to take care of it, yet it was with great difficulty I could keep it in; for she would not let any coals be left in the room, nor any to be brought me but at the time I have mentioned. Depression of spirits makes one cold, and the season was sharp for the time of year; so that I was almost perished: And the dampness of my room gave me a very violent cold, which I could never get free from while I was there.

My windows had been nailed up before I came; but the closeness which might have been feared, was remedied by the great winds which came in, the casements being very old, and the cases of them much shattered. Indeed, the crevices round the whole room were numerous; from all which I received most refreshing breezes.

Great endeavours were used to render my food a means of mortification; for the little that was given me was of the very worst sort, and designedly dirty, which disturbed me most; for as I had no appetite, it was very difficult for me to eat enough to keep me alive.

But none of these outward circumstances, nor my tattered bed, which did not defend me from the air, nor the feather bed, which by damp was all clotted into great lumps, as hard as so many tennis-balls,[168] and made my whole body sore and almost black and blue, nor a thousand other things, which would have appeared grievous to a mind at ease, gave me any pain, in comparison of my anxious desire to see Captain Turnham and my child, or at least to know how they did, particularly the latter, whom my dreams, in the short periods of sleep I could obtain, represented continually to me as dead or dying; nor was my imagination, when awake, much less cruel.

Perhaps, had I been permitted to take either air or exercise, or had any indulgence been allowed me which could have proved of a little service to my health, or relief to my mind, I might have been better able to bear my sorrows; but every thing round me was as dismal as my own thoughts; and what refreshment could I expect from sleep, when my lullaby was a serenade of all the animals I have mentioned.

My despair was risen to such a pitch, that I was in continual fear of losing my senses. I was almost blind with crying and want of sleep; and both my health and appearance were so affected, that I had reason to hope life would not long hold out against so severe a distress; but death, which seemed so desirable to one in my condition, was rendered more dreadful by the thought of dying without a friend to close my eyes, with no one whose compassion would endeavour to relieve my agonies, or whose affection would abate the sense of pain; and if I considered death as a passage into another world, the reflexion was still more horrible.

CHAP. XV.

—Tho' he posted e'er so fast,
His fear was greater than his haste.
For Fear, tho' fleeter than the wind,
Believes 'tis always left behind.
                                    Hud.[169]

IN this situation I continued above three weeks, without any alteration, except an increase of ill humour in my gaoler, who became every day more weary of her employment. Even the gratification of her spite and cruelty could not recompense her for the mortification she received from the dullness of the place. She had indeed provided as well as she could for herself. The steward had repaired the corner of the house which he inhabited; and she got a room in that part; indulged herself in a very plentiful table, and in every gratification the place could allow her: But still it was too wretched a spot to be rendered tolerable by the brightest human invention.

I found, by what she said, that Mr. Merton had promised to relieve her from her post before that time, by sending some other person to take care of me: But whether he had not been able to find a fit successor (no easy task, I am sure), or whether he was glad to get rid of us both at once, I cannot tell; but certain it is, she received no intelligence of a substitute; which increased her ill-humour so much, that she was still more lavish of her abuse, and was more in the room with me for that purpose. The case was hard; for, however the law might esteem Mr. Merton and I one,[170] no two people certainly were ever more divided in fact; therefore I had little title to the whole sum of fury, of which we were then become pretty equal objects.

Fretting, and the dampness of the place, at last proved my friends; for my gaoler was taken with a fever, which, as she was never negligent in care of herself, confined her to her room for some time. She transmitted the care of me to the steward's wife, who was a quiet woman, and often deputed her daughter to give me what she thought necessary attendance.

My situation now began to mend: They were not only civil to me, but much more attentive to my convenience; and I became better accommodated in every respect: But the girl, whose name was Sally, desired me not to mention to Madam, that they did not strictly follow her example, as she had commanded them.[171]

I conceived hopes, if not of effecting an escape, at least of giving Captain Turnham some account of my situation, by Sally's assistance: I therefore took every occasion of talking with her, and pressed her to give me as much of her company as she could. The good-natured girl was so affected by the melancholy life I led, and by finding me always crying, that she very readily complied. Her mother soon began to be alarmed, fearing, by the bad account she had had of me, that I might corrupt her daughter; but Sally assured her I must be the best lady in the world; for she never received so much good advice from any body.

This might well be true; no one is so capable of warning a young person against the errors into which youth and passion may lead them, as she who has experienced all the distress which is the usual consequence. Whenever I had an opportunity, humanity led me to advise her to shun the rock on which all my happiness had been shipwrecked; and one of the subjects of my lectures was a mercenary marriage, as I looked upon that as my first step to ruin, tho' not a voluntary one.

In pursuance of the design I had on this young girl,[172] I examined into what degree of dependence they had on Mr. Merton, and found it was pretty considerable. All they possessed was got in his service; and that not being equal to what a steward's profits often are, they still wished a continuance of their employment, that they might increase the little fortune they had gained. This did not encourage my hopes; but as it was the only slender twig I could catch hold of, I was not willing easily to relinquish it.

I found Sally had a great curiosity to know my real history; which generosity of nature inclined her to think was more favourable to me than my persecutor represented it. As I hoped for some advantage from her pity, I was not unwilling to satisfy her. I could not pretend to conceal my guilt; but endeavoured, as much as possible, to suppress such circumstances as were most atrocious. I did not attempt to defend my actions; but the heavy sufferings they had brought upon me, made them excite more compassion than censure. And the tears, which flowed during my narration, washed them pure in the eyes of the good-natured Sally. She wept with me, and appeared so touched at every circumstance I mentioned, that I saw plainly her heart was not free. The tenderest heart could not melt so feelingly for the pangs of a lover, if it had not been softened by love.

I then drew her in to give me an account of the state of her affections; and, by being her confidant, became a sharer in them. I learned from her, that she was not insensible to the addresses of a young farmer, who lived near ten miles off; but his fortune not being so good as her father and mother thought she might expect, they made some opposition to their marriage, tho' not enough to discourage their hopes.

I took the first opportunity of setting before the eyes of Sally's mother the danger of disappointing a young woman's affections, when there was no great impropriety in the indulgence of them: This my own misfortunes made a natural subject; and I could therefore do it without seeming to dictate to her. I was so earnest in the cause, that it would have been hard if my arguments had been quite unavailing. I had the satisfaction of finding they made some impression; and it ingratiated me so much with Sally, that I ventured to open my intentions to her, which were no less than to get her lover to assist me in my escape. The proposal was bold; but I understood that my persecutor was so near recovered, that I had little time to effect it in.

Sally was startled at the thought of such an attempt: She knew her father's interest, and was unwilling her lover should incur his displeasure. It was difficult to obviate her objections, which were too just: However, I could not easily relinquish my hopes; and told her, that the distance he lived at would prevent his being suspected; and that if he would bring a couple of horses, one for me, and another for himself, I was a good rider, and the nights were long enough to allow us time to get a great way from home before day-light. My room was on the ground floor; and I thought it would not be impracticable to break the case of the casements, which was extremely old; and by her account I found there was only a common lock to the door of the yard into which my window opened, and that he might easily take off.

My part could not be done without a good deal of noise; for old as the window was, it would require a great deal of force to break it: But the part of the house which was inhabited was so far from my room, that there was no great danger of being heard. To strengthen the attack I made on Sally's humanity, I promised to give her lover ten guineas,[173] if he would grant me the assistance I asked. This I had the power of performing; for Captain Turnham had paid me twenty pounds[174] the night before I left him; and, for fear of being robbed of a sum I could not conveniently spare, I sowed it within the lining of my stays, where it remained till I had this means offered me of laying it out for my liberty.

After many prayers and persuasions, I prevailed on Sally to write her lover the proposal I had made her; to intimate that she was desirous he should comply; and to let him know it must be effected the next night, as I should have the power of making some progress in breaking down my window before the family went to rest; which could not be done, if my gaoler was able to come into my room; for she examined every place most circumspectly before she went to bed.

Sally had a favourable answer to her letter: The young farmer consented to an enterprize, which so well suited a lover, and was agreeable to his mistress.

I found the task I had undertaken was more difficult than I expected; old as the wall was, it made great resistance; and I had no instrument but a poker. After having fatigued myself almost to death, I began to despair of success; and saw myself in danger of still worse treatment from the discovery of my design. My disappointment was a sufficient affliction; but this was an additional distress, and animated me to continue my attempt, till I lost all strength in my hands, and was reduced to sit down in an agony of despair, which almost distracted me.

But my new knight-errant having waited at the door, from whence he had taken the lock, till he began to fear there was some mistake, came into the yard, and past my window, which was open enough for him to hear me uttering part of my distress. Hereupon he endeavoured to assist me; and so successfully, that he made a breach large enough for me to get out of it, tho' not without tearing both my cloaths and flesh.

When this was once effected, we soon got on our horses, and proceeded with the expedition of persons who had every thing at stake. To avoid discovery, we took a cross road, part of which was extremely bad; but the night was too dark for us to see danger, and my joy too great to suffer me to fear any; and my guide was used to all sorts of roads. Our having taken this course made it longer before we came to a town; and I was not inclined to hire a chaise at the first we arrived at, as I thought, that, by avoiding to do so, I might escape my pursuers knowledge; for if they could hear nothing of me there, they would scarcely inquire farther on the same road.

Thus I lengthened my ride, and increased my fatigue; but it had the effect I desired. When we got to the second town, I gave my guide his reward, with a thousand thanks, and many kind messages to the good-natured Sally, whose love's success I heartily wished; and made the young man promise to inform me of it, whenever their marriage was completed. I have had the satisfaction of hearing from him, that they attained their wishes, and were happy in the possession of each other, and the enjoyment of easy circumstances; both which he attributed, in great measure, to the money I had given him; a sum he then had particular occasion for, to enable him to buy some stock that was offered him for less than half the usual price.

This circumstance has led me to digress a little from myself, as it is an incident which gave me more satisfaction than most things that have befallen me.

CHAP. XVI.

THO' I was much tired with my ride, having been so long out of practice, yet I would not venture to allow myself any rest till the night following, by which time I was not half a day's journey from London. I was unwilling to stop when I had got within that distance; but was so excessively weary, that even the earnestness of my inclination could not enable me to go on.

The next day by noon I arrived in London; and going to the house where I had lodged with a beating heart, from my anxious expectation of seeing my child, if it was alive, I was told that Captain Turnham had sent for it to Reading, and discharged the lodging. I did not think it adviseable to stay in a place where I had been so long, and probably might have been discovered. I took another lodging, and wrote directly to Captain Turnham to inform him of all that had happened to me, and of my impatience to see him and my child; yet intimated my fear of coming to Reading, where all my wishes would carry me, lest I might be as unfortunate in another visit, as in the last.

Captain Turnham, on receiving my letter, was so impatient to see me, that, without waiting for permission, he ordered his servant to give out that he was too ill to stir out of his room, and came post to London, where he was received by me with the sincerest joy; but his seemed greatly troubled, by observing me so emaciated and altered, as shocked him excessively.

It was great pleasure to me, to find the Captain really glad of my return: I feared the inconvenience of being incumbered with me might incline him to wish to be quit of one, who could now have none of the charms of novelty. He was obliged to return to quarters the next day; but appointed to meet me at our usual place of rendezvous, where he would bring his boy, and deliver him up to me.

This was performed; and I had again the pleasure of indulging a mother's fondness over my helpless infant, whose health was improved under his father's care.

Nothing new happened in our situation, till I was again near lying-in of my third child; and then the regiment Captain Turnham was in, received orders to march into the most northern part of Scotland, where quarters were appointed them.

Mr. Merton had just brought his cause to a conclusion; and a divorce was decreed him, sufficient proof being brought of my having had a child after I left him: But Captain Turnham's prudent care prevented Mr. Merton's being able to bring witnesses to accuse him; and tho' no one doubted of the person, yet the law could not charge him. I had made no defence, nor appeared at all in it; all the pains Mr. Merton took could not discover where I was: But the proofs were too strong to require my confession; therefore the cause was finished without my presence; which gave me liberty of living where I pleased, no one now having any power over me.[176]

This freedom was very acceptable, as it enabled me to accompany Captain Turnham to his quarters; tho' the condition I was in rendered the thought of such a journey very formidable; and I knew not whether the place where I was going would afford me tolerable assistance. But these considerations could have no great weight with one, to whom there was no other being existent but Captain Turnham. I felt myself the outcast of the world: He was the only one I could expect should look on me without contempt; and to have staid in London, when he was so far off, would have appeared to me little less solitary than to have been placed in a desert. Besides, I felt the pains of dependance so sensibly, that I would have willingly endured much inconvenience, to lessen the expence I was to Captain Turnham.

We had been but a little time settled in Scotland before I was brought-to-bed of another boy. I rejoiced in the sex of my children, as it saved me from all fears of their becoming as forlorn and wretched beings as their mother.

I had one comfort in this lying-in superior to the others; and which more than compensated the thousand inconveniencies we were subject to in the place we then lived; Captain Turnham and I inhabited the same house, whereby I had much more of his company.

This, tho' a circumstance then highly agreeable to me, was, upon the whole, I believe an evil. Most men are soon tired by possession: Captain Turnham, endowed with more than common constancy, was proof against this general cure for above three years; and perhaps might have continued so much longer, had there remained any difficulties, or necessary concealments, in our commerce: but now it bore all the appearance of matrimony; we were established in a settled menage; and as we were unknown in Scotland, we assumed the same name; and interchanged the appellations of husband and wife as freely, as if the matrimonial service had given us a title to them.

Our life was more domestic than is usual in that state; the place afforded no company to interrupt us; nor had either of us business to occasion those short absences, which are so well rewarded by the pleasures of meeting. Captain Turnham was not fond of rural sports; we were neither of us accustomed to read, so that we lived a constant *tête à tête*. Our children made our only variety; and, when they became capable of instruction, the teaching them afforded a little employment.

Love requires to be treated with great delicacy: Long separations, or a constant course of various dissipations, starve it; and being always together, without interruption, or additional amusement, is as apt to surfeit it. The right medium which should be preserved in these cases, is seldom learnt but by the experience we gain from having fallen into one of the errors, and felt its fatal effects.

I have heard of a lady, who, jealous that the gentleman she loved preferred another woman, contrived to shut them up for some time together, convinced indifference must be the consequence; and she thereby have room to hope for a return to her passion, when her lover's prepossession in favour of another was cured. I never heard a certain account of her success; but am persuaded it would seldom fail.

We are all so full of faults and follies, that we could no otherwise become the objects of a violent passion, but from the ignorance of those who conceive it. They see us, when nature and art combine to shew us to the best advantage. The rugged temper can assume a smile of gentleness, and for a time wear as smooth a brow as if no storm could ruffle it; the mercenary will appear disinterested; the avaricious put on the mask of generosity: In short, there is no part a person cannot act for a season, if they have but intermediate spaces, during which they can indulge their natural disposition.

Thus, therefore, while we borrow the smiles and graces to render our persons attractive, and assume the semblance of every virtue to confirm the charm, we are beloved equal to what we appear; and as we hide our imperfections, we lead captive every affection of the soul. But when, by being seen every hour, our follies and our frailties become conspicuous, the love which was founded on a supposition we were free from them, must decay; and when we show ourselves subject to all the failings of mortality, we must expect to be loved with only a mortal passion, in which eternal constancy can have no share.

Of this I was very sensible; but yet I could not avoid being greatly affected, when I saw Captain Turnham's fondness abate. I was always at work; his vivacity could not for ever be proof against a dismal situation, and a total want of company. Conversation would flag, and even playing with his children would often become tedious. *Ennui*, that great destroyer of the happiness of those who have no misfortunes to distress them, reached even our solitude, and oppressed Captain Turnham's spirits. I had no particular reason to complain; for he grew as weary of every thing about him, as of me; but the difference was, I only was sensible of it, and that to a great degree. His affection was the only thing in the world that could afford me any satisfaction; I had no treasure but that, no friend but him, no one else to receive me, to support me, or even to afford me the least countenance.

I had placed my affections on him from my earliest youth; for him I had given up all the comforts affluence can bestow; and, what was much more, to him I had sacrificed my conscience, my fortune, and my fame. For all these blessings his love had appeared to me a sufficient exchange; how much then must I have valued it! And in proportion, you will easily imagine, my grief must be, at losing it; for 'if I lost his love, I lost my all.'[177] This I could say with more propriety than it is generally applied, having, in reality, nothing in this world beside to enable me to endure my existence.

CHAP. XVII.

IF I had been able to reflect seriously on Captain Turnham's behaviour, I ought
to have thought myself fortunate in having so long enjoyed his affections: Few
men shew so much constancy; but the fate of others seldom prepares us for our
own.

Tho' I had cause to grieve, I had none to complain; for the Captain's indifference, which came by degrees, was only the common weakness of human nature:
But he always behaved to me with regard and civility; and continued humane,
tho' he ceased to be tender.

This was more conducive to his honour than to my peace; for my affection
was unabated; and mere humanity is but an unsatisfactory return for extreme
love. But I did not from this receive more pain than from my pride, which now
felt I was supported by his charity: While he was attached to me, he was insensible to the diminution of his fortune; but when it continued to lessen, without
yielding him any gratification, he could not but be uneasy at it.

For a long time I appeared blind to this alteration, fearing to turn indifference into dislike, and that my company, which was now only dull to him, should
become irksome; but at last, when I saw he grew alarmed at the decrease of his
fortune, I could not help offering to deliver him from so great a burden, assuring
him, that I had rather venture any distress, than bring him into difficulties.

Captain Turnham, with an appearance of real regard and generosity, intreated me never to mention such a thought any more; for that he would always
share his fortune with me; and felt too much gratitude for the attachment I had
shewn him, ever to let me suffer by it, in any respect from which he could save
me; and that if time had cooled his passion, nothing should ever extinguish his
generosity.

I could not deny there being a great deal in his proceeding; but the most delicate generosity is known by few. A person may give much, and yet have little of
it. Vanity, a sense of duty, or several other motives, may occasion donations; but

the truly generous will wish to conceal their bounty from the objects of it, and pretend some gratification to themselves, in every thing they do for the good of another; they know that poverty gives pangs less sharp than the humiliating benefactions of indelicate persons. Nor ought an extreme sensibility, in this respect, to be called pride in the indigent; for to be without it would be meanness. The casual gifts of the rich may be received without suffering; but none can endure a settled state of dependance, that has a possibility of avoiding it, who has not a groveling mind.

What friendship bestows, we receive with pleasure; it proves the affection which we cherish; and while we feel the benefit of the effect, we rejoice more in reflecting on the cause. Those who love,

— In owing, owe not,
And are at once indebted and discharg'd.[179]

Had Captain Turnham attributed his behaviour to friendship, which had succeeded to love, and which his conduct would well have warranted, I should have more contentedly accepted his good offices; but when it was made the gift of generosity, one only consideration could make me continue the dependant on his bounty; and that was our children: I could not leave them; nor could he consent to part with them. Indeed if he had, it was impossible for me to support them and myself.

My love for them was accompanied with no alloy; for they returned it in the tenderest manner; and made it impossible for me to leave them to the care of those, who would feel none of a mother's fondness. This tie I fansied was all; but I have since learned, that my affection for Captain Turnham was still so great, that tho' beheld by him with indifference, his absence would have appeared still a heavier misfortune.

We lived in our solitary situation four years, when we were rather removed than relieved; Captain Turnham, with the rest of the regiment, being ordered to Gibraltar.[180] There likewise I accompanied him.

This place, tho' not agreeable to the Captain, was less dismal than that we left; but more so to me in one respect: For as we there met more who knew him, and my history, I no longer appeared his wife; but was known for what I really was.

This shut me out of the company of all the women of any consideration; and had another effect more disagreable to me; for, in the dejected state of my mind, I was not very fit for company. The gentlemen soon perceived, or naturally apprehended, that the Captain's love for me must be worn out: And whether women were scarce or ugly there I know not; but several were willing to deliver him of a mistress, who they thought must be grown too much an incumbrance, for any addresses they could make to her, to be taken as an offence by him.

Amongst the number who thought that the woman, whose frailty had rendered her the mistress of one man, would not refuse to be so to others, the most assiduous was a person of great distinction there. He offered me affluence and love, two blessings of which I sensibly felt the want; but the latter appeared to me desirable only from one person; and I could not think of obtaining the other by prostitution.

I had some reason to believe Captain Turnham would not have been sorry, if I had proved more complying; but he seemed to honour my constancy, and respect the perseverance with which I refused all that gentleman's proposals. This was a great gratification to me: I flattered myself I had acquired his good opinion; this strengthened me in my resistance; for there was nothing I could not have suffered to fix his esteem, which, after my conduct, appeared so difficult for me to obtain: But a man's vanity pleads in excuse of the faults we commit for him; and his great idea of his own charms makes him think us less blameable, than if any other had been the occasion of our frailty.

In the third year of our abode at Gibraltar, the Captain was seized with a fever; it was not violent, but tedious; and, after suffering a long time, he was at last as sensible as those about him, that his death approached. I had nursed him with the utmost assiduity; and the near prospect of parting with me, and his children, rekindled his affection for me, and still increased his for them. He lamented in the most pathetic terms, that he should leave us destitute of any provision; tho' he had the satisfaction of reflecting, that this did not proceed from extravagance, but from the necessary expences of our family, which exceeded the income of his small commission, and by degrees had consumed his whole fortune.

He asked my pardon for the indifference he had shown to me for several years past; and thanked me for my constant attachment to him, with so much tenderness as made me forget all his former coldness, and feel as much distraction at the approach of his dissolution, as if his life was a certain source of happiness.

It is scarcely possible to suffer a sharper affliction than I did for his death; which was increased by the sensibility of my children, who were old enough to feel great grief for their father, tho' they were not apprized of the full extent of their loss: Nor indeed were they capable of understanding it; for our affections generally come earlier than our prudence.

Upon examining the state of the Captain's affairs, I found that his fortune was entirely spent; and there remained by us scarcely enough to discharge the expences of his funeral.

This could not but be an additional grief to the mother of three children, which began now to require education, and yet were far from being able to contribute towards their support, the eldest being but nine years old. He had gone to school from the time we came to Gibraltar; but he was now little likely to continue there.

As soon as Captain Turnham was dead, some of the persons, who before had addressed me, renewed their proposals; but they were accompanied with such expressions of satisfaction in the decease of their favoured rival, that they turned my indifference into detestation, and I rejected them all; shewing that the bare remembrance of a man so much more justly esteemed by me, was sufficient to frustrate all their hopes. In this I felt great satisfaction, as an exercise of my fidelity to him; which was my first wish, tho' I had no prospect of a support but from a continuance in the way of life to which I had been so long accustomed; but to persevere in it for pecuniary motives, was very irksome to me. To my romantic disposition, love had given a sort of sanction to my actions; and tho' they were vicious, yet they appeared to me less mean, than those of a mercenary prostitute.

With this turn of mind, it is easy to imagine, that I could not determine on a course so odious to me, while I could subsist without it. Accordingly I sold the little effects we had, and raised a small sum, on which I lived with the utmost frugality for some time, waiting an opportunity of returning to England.

CHAP. XVIII.

I Thought myself very fortunate, when I heard that a Captain, with whom I had some acquaintance, was ordered to sail for England. I had not seen him from the time of Captain Turnham's death; but on this occasion I applied to him. I was able to pay but little for my passage; and therefore addressed him with some fears of not succeeding; but was more fortunate than I could have hoped.

The Captain received me with the greatest civility; and very politely assured me, that my company would render his voyage much more agreeable than he had expected to find it.

I thought it necessary to intimate, that I was very sorry it was not in my power to make the return for the favour I asked which I could wish; but should be glad to know what would be required for my passage and my childrens.

To this the Captain very generously answered, He should think himself over-paid by our company; for that he always found it very irksome to be shut up with no other conversation than that of his ship's crew, which was not generally the most agreeable. Tho' I pressed his agreeing to accept what little I could pay, yet he continued the same assertion, and would not hear of any thing I could say against it.

This generosity was so seasonable a relief, as it afforded me a support for some time, without taking from me the little remaining money I had, that I should have accepted it without hesitation, had it not been for the peculiarity of my situation. I feared the Captain's bounty was not quite disinterested; and therefore could not take the benefit of it with so little ceremony as I should otherwise have done; but was not sorry that he persisted in his offer of conveying me at no expence to England, tho' I thought it proper to contend with him upon the subject.

Before we set out I had my suspicions strengthened: His attentions to me were beyond what common politeness dictates; and he shewed a fondness for my children, which I could not suppose he felt. However, I was not in a situation to stand on great delicacies; therefore I did not alter my purpose, which must have been attended with the greatest inconveniencies.

After we put out to sea, the Captain became more explicit in his addresses; and told me, that he had loved me during Mr. Turnham's life; but respected my attachment to him, and my great constancy, too much to attempt to obtain my favour: That my conduct to that gentleman had made his esteem correspond so well with his love, that it had fixed all his affections on me; and if he might be so happy as to succeed Mr. Turnham in my heart, I should find that his gratitude and constancy were equal to my wishes, and he would look on my children as his own.

As this was a subject he often began, he communicated to me the views he had in favour of my children; which were so much to their advantage, and at the same time so practicable, that I had great reason to expect they must succeed. He promised me likewise, that if I would grant his suit, he would make a settlement on me as soon as we came on shore; and such a provision for my children as should secure plenty both to me and them, if death took him out of the world first.

This was greater good fortune than I could by any means have expected; and there was such a visible sincerity in the Captain's manner, that I could not doubt his fulfilling his promise. This delivered me from all the solicitude to which I was before a prey, when I looked on my helpless children; and my heart felt a degree of composure, that I welcomed as a long absent friend. But I was to be brought to true happiness by the road of disappointment and sorrow.

One day in the afternoon, as we were sitting in the Captain's cabbin, and playing with my children, of whom the Captain seemed as fond as if they were his own, we were alarmed with a cry, that a French man of war[182] was coming towards us. The Captain immediately ran upon deck, and found it true. He prepared every thing for an attack; and had but just leisure to step down to me, and beg I would support my spirits as well as I could, during a scene which must be shocking to one of my sex; assuring me that he did not doubt giving a good account of the French ship (that was his phrase); for his was a good one, and his men brave fellows.

The attack began soon after he left me; and was so very terrible, that I was scarcely in my senses. I kept my three children embraced the whole time, determined, if possible, that we would go together; for I imagined it probable a ball might reach us; but I was so stunned with the thunder of the guns, and so heartily frighted, that I was incapable of any farther thought.

But at once I was roused by the Captain's being brought into the cabbin pale and bloody. They laid him down on the bed, and left him there. The spectacle filled me with horror and grief. My children screamed with terrors, which added to mine; and the first moments were passed in distraction: But a recollection that there might be a possibility of assisting him, brought me to my reason: I went to him, but found him without sense or motion: However, hoping it might be only the consequences of the great effusion of blood, I tore my apron and handkerchief, to tie up his wounds. Before I had performed it, the surgeon came, who took my office out of my hands; but told me, that there was no hopes; for he believed one of the wounds was thro' his heart.

The surgeon was too right in his judgment; for the poor Captain never shewed any signs of life, tho' every thing was tried to revive him. This shock took from me all thought about the success of the fight, and of any dangers to which I was exposed, till loud huzzas made us sensible that our ship had obtained the victory; but, upon inquiry, it was too much shattered, and all were in such confusion from the Captain's death, that they thought it not proper to pursue the enemy far.

A resolution I much approved; for the sea was now become terrible to me; and my grief for the Captain was very sincere; which will be easily believed, as my interest was so much concerned; for his death robbed me of the hopes on which I had so firmly depended, both for myself and children: But all my affliction was not only on this account; for I had so great an esteem for his generosity, and so much gratitude for his humane intentions for me and my children, that I sincerely regretted the loss of so worthy a man.

The wind was fair; and it was not long before we got into port. The person who had been appointed administrator[183] in case of the Captain's death, before he went abroad, when he made up the Captain's accounts, demanded of me the usual price of a passenger; and as I had no proof of the Captain's generous intentions, I could not defend myself. The unexpectedness of his death had prevented his giving me any security in this respect, or of making any disposition in my favour.

The demand upon me was greater than I had money to acquit. What I had, I offered; but the administrator would not believe it was my whole stock, and threatened me with imprisonment, if I did not advance the remainder. This was a dreadful situation: I had no redress in my power; and thought the hazard was too great to wait the event; so took the first opportunity of going on shore; and as we were then come to Deptford, a very short time carried me and my children to London.

I wrote him word from thence that I had left the ship, not out of a desire of depriving him of what money I had, but to save myself from being imprisoned for the payment of what I had not. I asserted the promise the Captain had given me of taking nothing for my passage; but at the same time offered to pay him all I possessed, if he insisted on it; and informed him where to direct a letter, to acquaint me with his resolution; intending to take care that he should not by that means find out where I was.

The administrator now began to fear, that by too obstinately requiring all he might demand, he should lose what he might get. He therefore dispatched a letter to me directly, and offered me an acquittance on the terms I proposed.

Thus the dispute was settled, and I left without a shilling for the support of myself and children. All the consolation I had, was the liberty I had feared to lose, and which now I began to think was more dreadful than imprisonment, as that would have obliged the person who put me there, to maintain me.[184] Certainly those must have a great love for freedom, who think it a recompence for the want of a subsistance; and indeed what liberty can a person in the utmost want boast of possessing? Necessity is the worst bondage; it forces our wills, and enslaves our bodies; it obliges us to do things most contrary to our choice.

CHAP. XIX.

DESTITUTE of money and of hope, I was in the utmost distress of mind and body. My children, who had hitherto been a consolation under all my misfortunes, were now my heaviest grievance, as I felt their wants more sensibly than my own; and had no hope of being able to gain a support for so many. This thought almost discouraged me from doing what I might, because I knew it would not be sufficient. However, pressed by necessity, as much as by despair, I applied to my landlady to procure me some needlework; the only thing I was capable of doing. My landlady, who kept a little shop, told me, she had a good customer, from whom she fansied I might receive employment; and went directly to ask for some, and accordingly brought me a little.

I dispatched this work with the utmost haste a starving person could make, to procure food for herself, and those who were still dearer to her, and prepared to carry it home; whereupon my landlady hinted, that at my return she should expect to receive what was paid me, in part of my week's lodging, which was then due.

This was a great damp on the joy I felt in going to claim the trifle I had gained; which was so little, as sufficiently proved the impossibility of maintaining, with my own hands, myself and family. I had not long to indulge my reflections; and they were too melancholy for me to wish their continuance; for the house, to which I was to carry my work, was very near.

I was led in to the mistress of it, whose appearance, as well as that of every thing about her, left me in no doubt of her occupation. She inquired into my circumstances; which I told, with that readiness wherewith the unhappy always relate their sufferings.

She asked me, if I thought it possible to maintain so many by my plain-work. I acknowleged I was sensible I could not; but could as yet think of no other means of livelihood. She then expatiated much on the advantages I might receive from a person remarkably engaging; an expression you must attribute to flattery, because there is now little appearance of it remaining; so great are the ravages made between that time and this, by a course of life, which destroyed my health, and tormented my mind; a period so odious to my remembrance, that I shall pass over the relation as concisely as possible.

I shall therefore omit the arguments this woman used, and those still stronger which were urged by necessity, to prevail on me to add other means for my support to those I had already begun. My children were too great an incumbrance for her to wish to have me in her house: Her offers were more advantageous, as she left me at my liberty; and only claimed half of what was given me. Upon the strength of this agreement, she was sure to procure a considerable price for me; and tho' the bloom of youth was past, yet she composed so fine a romance for me, as gave a dignity to my appearance; which answered her purpose entirely, and consequently was equally profitable to me.

I had now a sufficient maintenance; but the vileness of the means whereby I gained it, rendered me miserable. I despised myself, and detested every one I conversed with; for I was excluded from the society of any but the most profligate and abandoned. They indeed thought my situation worthy their envy; because I enjoyed my liberty, as they called it, and had a great share in the products of my vice; whereas they were only maintained as slaves; and had as little the command of themselves, as if they were such. But I was too wretched to perceive this preference; and was no less unhappy than they were, tho' perhaps with less apparent reason.

The extreme melancholy which this course of life brought upon me, agreed very well with the romance the old bawd invented for me, and gave it an air of truth; and a distinction to me, which set me much above the rest. As disagreeable as the sight of the wretched is to most people, yet there was something so new and surprising, to see a woman, oppressed with melancholy, among a crew, where the most dissolute wantonness, the most frantic mirth, and abandoned licentiousness of manners reigned, that it had a great charm for many, and made them suppose there must be something very peculiar in the fate of a woman, who could cloath profligacy in the garb of modesty and afflicted virtue.

During this time, my eldest son died, and the second's health daily declined, and filled me with continual alarms. I had kept both of them at school from the time I was able to afford it. Their master was a man of very rigid piety, and a good scholar. The forward genius's of both these children charmed him: They learned so fast, that he thought they deserved his particular attention, and took more than common pains with them.

As he conceived it of still more consequence to instill religious principles into their tender minds, than to fill them with learning, his greatest care was employed in instructing them in their religion; he taught them both the faith and practice of christianity; and was delighted to see with what attention his little pupils listened to him, and how well they remembered all his doctrine.

The effect was greatly exemplified in the death of the eldest, who, with uncommon sagacity, perceived his end approaching, and bore it with amazing composure. Seeing me in the deepest affliction, he endeavoured to offer me all the consolation his principles could dictate. He begged me not to grieve for him; for 'he hoped he was going to a better world: That I had often told them how destitute their condition was; but that he was now hastening to a place, where all his wants would be supplied: That he was sorry to leave so affectionate a mother; but received great comfort from thinking he was going to a merciful and indulgent father; to Him, *who had so loved the world that he gave his only begotten Son, to the end we might not perish, but have everlasting life;*[186] and hoped to be received by that Son, the God of mercy and love.'

He then gave his brother much good advice, intreating him 'since he might not, like himself, have the blessing of being taken so early out of a wicked world, to guard against all the temptations of it; to bear afflictions, pain, and distress of every kind; to endure all that man can inflict, rather than offend his Maker and Redeemer.' He represented, 'how dreadful it must be for those to fall into the hands of the living God, who have nothing but wrath to expect.'

A long time, like one inspired, did he expatiate on this subject, intending to warn his brother from the evil he might fall into; but how much more did his words affect me! His brother received his advice with satisfaction; had nothing to repent of; and resolved to regulate his conduct by it; but it filled me with horror and remorse. I felt, that they were my sins which deprived me of such an angel, before he knew the deplorable wickedness of his mother; which, to his divine disposition, must have been far worse than death.

After he had said all that he thought could be useful to me, or his brother, he begg'd the latter to request his school-master's presence; and that, as an additional obligation to all he had conferred upon him, he would come and pray by him.

The good man complied, and came directly. My son asked his pardon for giving him that trouble; but told him, 'he thought he should pray with more satisfaction, and freedom of spirit, if he assisted him, than if any other performed that office; and had reason to believe his humanity would readily grant that favour to one whom he had blessed with so much of his care, and so many admirable instructions.'

The good man burst into tears at so affecting a scene, and assured him, 'he looked upon the request, for which he apologized, as the highest obligation; and found his heart both warmed and edified by his behaviour.'

My son then told him, he had one thing to wish, if it was not improper. 'He should feel great joy, if he might receive the sacrament; but, if the Doctor judged him too young, as he feared he was, he begged he would not, to comply with that inclination, indulge him in any thing to which he thought it a presumption in him to pretend.'[187]

The Doctor replied, that 'tho' his age seemed unfit, yet his understanding was so perfect, and his principles so pure, that he had no objection; on the contrary, should receive great satisfaction from administring it to him; but feared too long a service might oppress him.'

The poor boy assured him, 'that, so far from it, he must beg he would read both the office for the dying, and the whole communion service; for it would refresh rather than fatigue him; and he wished death might find him at prayers, that he might die, as he would rise again, praising and adoring God.'

The good man desired to have every thing prepared directly, and, till his office began, indulged his tenderness, which made him grieve for my child as if he had been his own.

He turned to me, and told me 'he supposed I would partake of the communion with my son,' and began the service not waiting for my answer. I felt myself not fit for so solemn an act of devotion,[188] but knew not how to avoid it. I therefore conformed; but as the service proceeded, it awakened my conscience to so bitter a sense of my wickedness, that I fell into such an agony of horror at the thought of my iniquity, that I could not attempt to join in an act of worship with persons so unlike myself. I therefore, as obliged by the condition I was in, retired.

When the service was over, the old gentleman came to me: Supposing the agony which had seized me proceeded from my tenderness for my child, he meant to offer me some consolation. Accordingly he congratulated me 'on having a son whose exemplary piety, at an age when few think of religion, was so greatly edifying; and that when he considered his extreme youth he should be apt to believe him supernatural, if his brother was not as extraordinary for his years.' He endevoured to persuade me that his death did not come too soon, since it would lead him to a glorious and blessed eternity.

He then shewed me how happy it was to be taken out of the world before he was tainted with the vices of it; and represented the danger to which he would have been exposed had he lived to a maturer age, in colours which set my own crimes in so strong a light, that while he lessened my grief for my son, he increased my affliction for myself.

He was interrupted by being again called by the poor boy; who, finding himself fail very fast, begged him to pray again; and while he did so, he expired without a groan, with a smile of joy on his countenance, and hands lifted up in prayer.

I was now past listening to any consolation; so the good man left me, and went away, praying that all present might have as happy an end to this life, and as blessed a beginning of the next, as he made no doubt this youth had.

My conscience was too much awakened, to suffer me to continue my dissolute life: But I knew not by what means to subsist: However, as I had a trifle by me, I allowed myself time to reflect on all that offered itself to my thoughts.

I had heard of the institution of this Asylum; but my children appeared to me an insurmountable obstruction. I then fansied, that this good school-master was so excellent a man, that, perhaps, if I confessed all my crimes, and told him that my children only prevented me from taking refuge here, he might possibly assist me in getting them off my hands, rather than hazard my being tempted to continue in a way of life so pernicious both to soul and body; tho', when the one is concerned, the other does not deserve the least consideration.

This thought occurred to me, as I was attending my children in a walk a little way out of town, which I had begun to practise, in hopes the air might be of service to the poor boy, who was now become my eldest son.

As I was forming the plan on which I should pursue the scheme, which appeared the only one that offered me a means of reformation, I passed by some children playing. The neatness of their dress, and the orderly manner they appeared in, tempted me to inquire who they were, and was told, they were the offspring of penitents who had been, or were just going to be, received into the Magdalen-House;[189] some of their mothers being detained out of it by sickness.

This awakened a most pleasing hope in me. On inquiry, I found the most humane Institutors of this charity did not object to the additional charge of children, since it doubled the benefit they conferred. I could not forbear examining into the care that was taken of these helpless infants; and was charmed to find how plentifully all their necessities were supplied, and the still greater attention that was paid to the cultivation of their minds, that they might be instructed to avoid all the vices which had occasioned their parents destruction, and the great danger their children had incurred of being no less unfortunate.

I let slip no time in presenting myself to this Hospital: I attended the meeting the next day; and was soon received, and my children taken care of.

Here has all my misfortunes ended; and here I hope, by repentance, to wash out my sins. The hope of mercy is my consolation; and great as my offences are, I know Divine mercy is greater; and that can pardon what is too atrocious to be expiated by repentance; but my life shall pass in petitions for that grace, which, by asking for, we are assured we may obtain; and in praying for, and blessing, those who have offered me, and wretches like me, the power and means of reformation.

If, as we are told, those who save a soul shall shine like the stars in heaven,[190] how bright must be that glory, which is reserved for the Beneficent Institutors of this charity! They have found out a means for finite beings to do infinite benefit; since the good they have conferred on us will reach thro' all eternity; but their happiness therein exceeds ours, how great soever it may be, as much as it is *more blessed to give than to receive.*[191]

FINIS

ENDNOTES

1. *acknowleges itself to be a fiction*: The author's insistence that *The Histories* is a work of fiction, despite the fact that the 'incidents' it describes are 'not only probable, but such as must frequently have happened' (p. 3), is at odds with William Dodd's preface to his otherwise barely rewritten version of the first of *The Histories*' inset narratives, published as *The Magdalen, or History of the First Penitent Received into that Charitable Asylum* (London: W. Lane, 1783). Dodd, recalling Samuel Johnson's claims for the primacy of biography in *Rambler* no. 60 (13 October 1750), presents Emily's story as a true account, adding that 'THE reality of a tale of woe, and of the greatest distress, it must be owned affects us much more sensibly, than that which we know to be fictitious' (p. ix).
2. *Every man must stand or fall to his own master*: see Romans 14:4.
3. *He maketh his sun to shine on the just and on the unjust*: see Matthew 5:45.
4. *the sting of death is sin*: see 1 Corinthians 15:56.
5. *efface her guilt*: The question of whether or not the Magdalens' guilt could ever be effaced was widely debated by the charity's supporters and detractors. William Dodd, for example, devoted much of his *Sermon, Preached before the President, Vice-Presidents, Treasurer, and Governors of the Magdalen-House*, reprinted with *An Account of the Rise, Progress, and Present State of the Magdalen Charity* (London: W. Faden, 1761) to countering claims that 'the reformation of such [women] was impossible' by suggesting that they possessed an innate virtue, which could not be 'obliterated', even by a profession so 'contrary to the nature and condition of the female sex' (pp. ii–iii).
6. *no such shall enter into the kingdom of heaven*; 'Except ye be converted, and become as little children, ye shall not enter into the kingdom of heaven'; see Matthew 18:3.
7. *They have been eyes to the blind, and feet to the lame*: see Job 29:15.
8. *They have delivered ... it shall witness to them*: see Job 29:11–12 and 16.
9. *I was an hungred ... and ye visited me*: see Matthew 25:35–6.
10. *No person ... to save from eternal torments*: Proponents of the Magdalen House vehemently dissociated the charity from institutions such as the Lock Hospital (1746–1948), which treated patients suffering from venereal disease. According to the fourth edition of *The Rules and Regulations of the Magdalen-Charity* (London: W. Faden, 1769), any woman seeking to enter the institution but found to be suffering from 'the foul disease' had to be cured before her application would be reconsidered (p. 18). As Jonas Hanway pointed out, the charity had a higher end in view than the alleviation of physical ailments. Unlike the Magdalen House, the Lock offered only 'temporary expedients to *alleviate* misery' and was unable to 'render the objects *happy*, in *this* world, much less ... the *next*'. *Thoughts on the Plan for a Magdalen-House for Repentant Prostitutes* (London: James Waugh, 1758), p. 48.

11. *Amongst the greatest nation ... members of society*: The wording of this paragraph is strikingly similar to the following passage from William Dodd's *Sermon Preached before His Royal Highness the Duke of York* and reprinted with the 1761 *Account of the Rise, Progress, and Present State of the Magdalen Charity*: 'If *Rome* decreed a *Civic* crown, and public honours to him, who saved the life of a single citizen; of what honours may not they be thought worthy, who shall conduce not only to save so many lives, to their country; but also to rescue souls' (pp. 46–7).

12. *If Æsop could make birds and beasts teach by their actions*: Samuel Richardson's revision of Roger L'Estrange's version of *Æsop's Fables* was published in 1739 (dated 1740).

13. *Livy or Tacitus*: Livy, or Titus Livius (59 BC–AD 17), was the author of a 142-book *History of Rome* to 29 BC. Tacitus, or Publius (Gaius) Cornelius Tacitus (AD 56–120), was the writer of *Annals* and *Histories*, which document Rome's history between AD 14–68 and 69–96.

14. *Seven champions of Christendom*: the seven national saints of England, Ireland, Scotland, Wales, France, Spain and Italy. The saints' lives were commemorated in Richard Johnson's popular romance *The Famous Historie of the Seaven Champions of Christendome* (part I published 1596; part II published 1597).

15. *Guy Earl of Warwick*: a popular hero whose travels and exploits were celebrated in chapbooks and ballads throughout the seventeenth and eighteenth centuries. The origin of his story can be traced back to the thirteenth-century Anglo-Norman poem *Gui de Warewic*.

16. *whose thoughts never extend to the causes or the consequences*: The preface's rejection of romance and defence of the novel appear to be indebted to Samuel Johnson's *Rambler* no. 4 (31 March 1750). Johnson rejects romance, in which 'every transaction and sentiment [is] so remote from all that passes among men, that the reader [is] in very little danger of making any applications to himself', in favour of 'familiar histories', in which the 'adventurer is levelled with the rest of the world' so as to 'convey the Knowledge of Vice and Virtue with more Accuracy than Axioms and Definitions'. Samuel Johnson, *The Rambler* (6 vols, London: J. Payne and J. Bouquet, 1752), vol. 1, pp. 30–1.

17. *this performance may warn them against giving way to the emotions of vanity*: The author's concern that popular fiction commonly corrupts its female readers is explored further in the story of the fourth Magdalen, whose 'romantic imagination' is dangerously inflamed by 'some of the romances' she has read (p. 135).

18. *Let my tears thank you ... to vent such thoughts as mine.* DRYDEN: John Dryden, *Don Sebastian, King of Portugal* (1690), IV.ii.937–9.

19. *Each fair advance ... her own romance*: Richard Graves, 'The Heroines: or, Modern Memoirs' was first printed, in March 1751, in the *London Magazine*, 20, p. 134–5, the *Universal Magazine*, 8, p. 127 and the *General Advertiser*. The editors thank Mary Peace for alerting us to these last two sources. The poem is a satirical reflection on the fashion for scandalous memoirs, which singles out those most celebrated 'modern wh—res' Laetitia Pilkington, Constantia Phillips and Lady Frances Vane for particular condemnation. 'The Heroines' was reprinted, in revised form, in Graves's *Euphrosyne* (1776).

20. *after the work of the day was past*: The list of employments that appeared in the charity's 1759 *Rules* reads as follows: 'to make their own cloaths, both linnen [*sic*] and woollen; spinning the thread and making the cloth.—To knit their stockings from the raw materials.—To make bone-lace.—Black lace.—Artificial flowers.—Childrens [*sic*] toys.—Spinning fine thread; also woollen yarn.—Winding silk.—Embroidery.—All branches of millinary.—Making women and children's shoes, mantuas, stays, coats.—

Cauls for wigs, weaving hair for perukes.—Knitting hose and stockings.—Making leathern and silken gloves.—Making garters.—Drawing patterns.—Making soldiers [*sic*] cloaths and seamen's slops.—Making carpets after the *Turkey* manner, which may be easily suited to their strength and their abilities.—Or whatever employment their several abilities and genius lead to.' The additional tasks included the 'spinning of wool and flax, winding silk, making fine, and also slop shirts; making gloves, and embroidering the backs of them, and making all the houshold [*sic*] linnen, and all their own cloaths'. [Anon.], *The Rules, Orders and Regulations of the Magdalen House for the Reception of Penitent Prostitutes*, 2nd edn (London: n.p., 1759), p. 20.

21. *How happy ... enjoys them all.* ROSCOMMON: Wentworth Dillon, Earl of Roscommon, 'Part of the Fifth Scene of the Second Act in Guarini's Pastor Fido' (1685), ll. 21–8.

22. *100l. per annum*: equivalent to approximately £12,400 in 2005.

23. *Hottentots*: one of the two sub-races of the Khoisand, characterized by short stature, yellow-brown skin and tightly curled hair. Throughout the eighteenth century, this derogatory term was used to denote an uncivilized person (*OED*).

24. *Love gives esteem ... plains and levels all.* DRYDEN: A conflation of two pieces of dialogue from John Dryden's *Marriage à la Mode* (1673). The first line appears in II.i.284, the second in III.i.294–6. Both pieces of dialogue are spoken by Leonidas.

25. *to furnish out their weekly contributions*: That Methodist preachers resorted to various iniquitous schemes to extort contributions from their congregations was a commonplace in anti-Methodist discourse. See, for example, John Downes, *Methodism Examined and Exposed: or, the Clergy's Duty of Guarding their Flocks against False Teachers* (London: John Rivington, 1759).

26. *all the vows and oaths that ever lover broke*: In *A Midsummer Night's Dream* Hermia speaks of 'all the vows that ever men have broke' (I.i.175).

27. *Where more is meant than meets the ear.* MILTON: John Milton, *Il Penseroso* (1645), l. 120.

28. *Comus's crew*: the band of men led by Milton's sorcerer in *A Masque Presented at Ludlow-Castle, or Comus* (1637).

29. *expected her son to be a Joseph*: A reference to Potifar's efforts to seduce her husband's slave. Unlike Emily, who gives in to Markland, Joseph resists his mistress's advances and is imprisoned. See Genesis 39: 1–20.

30. *They the primrose path ... thorny way*: *Hamlet*, I.iii.48–51.

> *Ophelia*: Show me the steep and thorny way to heaven,
>   Whiles, like a puff'd and reckless libertine,
>   Himself the primrose path of dalliance treads,
>   And recks not his own rede.

31. *Spencer's Sir Calidore*: the knight of courtesy in Edmund Spenser's *The Faerie Queene* (1590–6).

32. *The friends thou hast ... hooks of steel.* SHAKESP: *Hamlet*, I.iii.62–3. The use of 'hooks' instead of 'hoops' is common in eighteenth-century editions of the play, although Edward Bysshe's *Art of English Poetry*, a principal source text for the novel, has 'hoops'. See *Art of English Poetry*, 8th edn (2 vols, London: F. Clay, J. Brotherton, J.R. and J. Hazard, W. Meadows, T. Astley, S. Austen, L. Gulliver & J. Clarke, C. Corbett and Tho. Payne, 1737), vol. 1, p. 199.

33. *hartshorn*: a solution of carbonate of ammonia (whether extracted from the antlers of the hart or not) used as smelling salts (*OED*).

34. *fallen Angel*: Satan in Milton's *Paradise Lost* (1667). A possible reference, also, to the heroine of Samuel Richardson's *Clarissa* (1747–8), who is referred to as a fallen angel by several characters in the novel even before her rape by Lovelace. See *Clarissa; or, The History of a Young Lady*, (7 vols, London: S. Richardson, 1748).

35. *The world's a scene of changes ... stay not when we die. COWLEY*: Abraham Cowley, 'Inconstancy' (1647), ll. 19–28.

36. *Fame, Wealth, and Honour, what are you to Love*: Alexander Pope, 'Eloisa to Abelard' (1717), l. 80.

37. *Doubt, yet doat; despair, yet fondly love*: misquoted from *Othello*, III.iii.172: 'Who dotes yet doubts; suspects, yet soundly loves!' Iago's words are quoted correctly when they are used again in the novel as the epigraph to vol. II, chap. V (p. 114).

38. *Harwich*: a port on the Essex coastline.

39. *I pass'd this very moment ... to seize all thy fortune. OTWAY*: Thomas Otway, *Venice Preserv'd, or a Plot Discover'd* (1682), I.232–6.

40. *Prospects at distance please ... who latest is undone. GARTH*: Samuel Garth, *The Dispensary* (1699), III.27–30.

41. *Uncomb'd their locks ... love or gay desire*: John Dryden, 'Palamon and Arcite', from *Fables Ancient and Modern* (1700), part I, ll. 539–40. In the original, in which the lines refer to the dishevelled appearance of the lovesick knight Arcite, 'their' reads 'his'. Emily, the first Magdalen's name, is also that of the heroine and love object in Dryden's reworking of Chaucer's *Knight's Tale*.

42. *Who can all sense ... in human shape. TATE*: Nahum Tate, 'The Fifteenth Satyr of Juvenal' (1693), ll. 185–6.

43. *Famine is in thy cheeks ... contempt and beggary hang on thy back. OTWAY*: Thomas Otway, *The History and Fall of Caius Marius. A Tragedy* (London: Tho. Flesher, 1680), p. 61. 'Famine is in thy cheeks' is, in turn, a quotation from *Romeo and Juliet* (V.i.59).

44. *notes of hand*: promissory notes.

45. *I now thought ... get done elsewhere*: This paragraph anticipates the work of later feminist writers who also targeted women's limited opportunities in the labour market as a leading cause of prostitution. At least one of these writers, Mary Ann Radcliffe, was aware of *Histories*, if only through its rewriting as William Dodd's *The Magdalen*. Radcliffe cites the novel in her attack upon the gendered division of labour in her *Female Advocate: or, an Attempt to Recover the Rights of Women from Male Usurpation* (London: Vernor and Hood, 1799), p. 91.

46. *Oh! that I had my innocence ... its native whiteness gain'd. WALL*: Edmund Waller, *The Maid's Tragedy Alter'd* (1690), I.23–6.

47. *Want is a bitter and a hateful good ... which mankind refuse. DRYDEN*: John Dryden, 'The Wife of Bath's Tale', from *Fables Ancient and Modern*, ll. 473–84.

48. *not without fears that my child would be a bar to my admission*: In fact, the *Rules* of the charity are silent on the issue of what might have happened to the inmates' children. See Introduction, p. xvii, n. 26.

49. *Should some brave Turk ... had not seen. WALLER*: Edmund Waller, 'Of Love', ll. 27–38, in *The Workes of Edmund Waller, Esquire, Lately a Member of the Honourable House of Common, in this Present Parliament* (London: Thomas Walkley, 1645).

50. *our first mother ... as soon as created*: see Genesis 2:20–4 for God's creation of Eve, so that Adam will not be the only animal without 'an help meet'.

51. *when taken, the town was little nearer surrendering than before*: This paragraph compares the ugly sister's approach to finding a husband with an army's efforts at raising a siege. By

implication, although the young men are 'taken' – that is, she has sex with them – they do not agree to marry her. This not only foreshadows the second Magdalen's relationship with Mr Monkerton, but also exposes the hypocrisy of stigmatizing only the women who are publicly known to be sexually active, rather than all those who indulge in extramarital intercourse. See note 150.

52. *The first beauty in a country town … her vanity receives*: This is also the heroine's situation in the inset story 'The History of Leonora, or the Unfortunate Jilt' in Henry Fielding's *Joseph Andrews* (1742). Leonora, who is engaged to the sincere Horatio, attracts the attention of a Francophile fop, Bellarmine, at a local assembly. Enamoured of Bellarmine's equipage and his manners, Leonora jilts Horatio; but her mercenary father refuses to give her a dowry, so Bellarmine regretfully bids her adieu. It has been suggested that Sarah Fielding in fact wrote an early letter from Leonora to Horatio, describing her enthusiasm for the match: see Linda Bree, *Sarah Fielding* (New York: Twayne Publishers; London: Prentice Hall International, 1996), p. 7, n. 13.

53. *Caesar had ambition*: In Shakespeare's *Julius Caesar*, Brutus justifies the conspiracy to murder Caesar by insisting 'as he was ambitious, I slew him' (III.ii.26–7). Mark Anthony, however, then dismisses this claim in his funeral oration for Caesar, repeatedly juxtaposing the assertions 'But Brutus says he was ambitious; / And Brutus is an honourable man' (III.ii.87–8) to cast doubt on Brutus's sincerity.

54. *Bedlam*: Bethlehem Royal Hospital. An asylum for the mentally ill since 1377, this hospital – originally attached to the Priory of St Mary Bethlehem – was bought by the Mayor and Corporation of the City of London from Henry VIII in 1547. By the eighteenth century it had moved from its original location in Bishopsgate to a new site at Moorfields, and like the Magdalen House it was a popular tourist destination. See Ben Weinreb and Christopher Hibbert, *The London Encyclopaedia* (London: Macmillan, 1983), p. 62.

55. *one of the Universities*: either Oxford or Cambridge. Oxford, however, seems more likely, as it is frequently associated with sexual misconduct in novels of the mid-century: in Samuel Richardson's *Pamela* (1740–1), Mr B seduces and impregnates Miss Sally Godfrey while he is a student there; and in Eliza Haywood's *History of Miss Betsy Thoughtless* (1751), an attempt is made upon Miss Betsy's chastity by one of the students while she is visiting the city.

56. *the fair one's shop*: For further discussion of the notoriously lubricious relationship between shopgirls and their customers, see Richard Steele, *The Spectator*, no. 155 (28 August 1711).

57. *For beauty … by opinion*: Jonathan Swift, 'Strephon and Chloe' (1734), ll. 223–4.

58. *the heroine who rants her hour upon the stage*: In her description of the beauty's eternally theatrical existence, the second Magdalen echoes Macbeth's response to Lady Macbeth's death: 'Life's but a walking shadow; a poor player, / That struts and frets his hour upon the stage, / And then is heard no more' (V.v.24–6).

59. *Beauty … his sense*: Joseph Addison, *Cato* (1713), I.iv.145–6.

60. *that favour is deceitful, and beauty is vain*: see Proverbs 31:30.

61. *Happy the innocent … from faults.* WALL: Edmund Waller, *The Maid's Tragedy Alter'd* (1690), ll. 69–70.

62. *bouts-rimés*: a fashionable poetic game. According to Joseph Addison, '*Bouts Rimez* … were a List of Words that rhyme to one another, drawn up by another Hand, and given to a poet, who was to make a Poem to the Rhymes in the same Order that they were placed upon the List': see *The Spectator*, no. 60 (9 May 1711).

63. *He was indeed yet under the power of guardians ... his allowance was very ample*: Until Mr Monkerton reaches the age of twenty-one, he is still a minor; as summarized by William Blackstone, 'full age in male or female, is twenty one years, which age is completed on the day preceding the anniversary of a person's birth; who till that time is an infant, and so stiled in law': see *Commentaries on the Laws of England* (3 vols, Dublin: John Exshaw, Henry Saunders, Samuel Watson and James Williams, 1766), vol. 1, p. 451. In the eyes of the law, Mr Monkerton is not an independent agent; rather, he is subject to parental authority. As his father is dead, Mr. Monkerton's guardians – the paternal replacements selected by his father – are responsible for him.

64. *he could not marry publicly without their consent*: This is not in fact true: according to the nuptial procedure established by the Act for the Better Preventing of Clandestine Marriages (26 Geo. II, c. 32), also known as the Marriage Act, parental consent is required for minors who wish to marry by licence, but not for those who wish to marry by banns. If a couple succeeded in having the banns called on three separate Sundays before the wedding, and their parents or guardians did not publicly oppose the match, they were entitled to marry.

65. *a year would soon pass away*: When the second Magdalen introduces Mr Monkerton, he is 'above nineteen years of age' (see p. 57). As he is presumably now twenty, this indicates that their courtship has lasted for an extended period, justifying her belief in the sincerity of his love.

66. *my father ... a delay as little irksome as possible*: The second Magdalen is here implying that her father would not have objected to an increased intimacy between his daughter and Mr Monkerton once their engagement was acknowledged; and this suggests that she might have indulged in premarital sex with him. However, in sentimental novels of the mid-century, any kind of sexual relationship, even between people whose union was imminent, was read as an indication of the prospective bride's essential promiscuity: see 'The History of Miss Selvyn' in Sarah Scott's *Millenium Hall* (1762) and Hugh Kelly's *Memoirs of a Magdalen* (1767).

67. *a private marriage had an odious sound*: With the second penitent's preference for a public rather than a clandestine wedding, the author of *The Histories* is participating in the debate over the Marriage Act of 1753, which required all marriages to take place in the couple's parish church. Opponents, like MP Robert Nugent, claimed that 'the proclamation of banns and a public marriage is against the genius and nature of the people: it shocks the modesty of a young girl to have it proclaimed through the parish, that she is going to be married': see William Cobbett, *The Parliamentary History of England, from the Earliest Period to the Year 1803*, ed. John Wright (36 vols, London: Longman & Co., 1812–20), vol. 15, p. 19. Supporters, however, maintained that it was ridiculous to argue that women 'would rather go Virgins to their Graves, than expose themselves to Notice and Remarks, by being married in Parish Churches': see the anonymous pamphlet, *A Letter to the Public: Containing the Substance of What Hath Been Offered in the Late Debates upon the Subject of the Act of Parliament, for the Better Preventing of Clandestine Marriages* (London: Charles Marsh, 1753), p. 39.

68. *My reputation ... by marriage became his*: Similarly, in Samuel Richardson's *Pamela: or, Virtue Rewarded* (London: n.p., 1741), Mr B. argues that the husband's quality determines his wife's: 'a Man ennobles the Woman he takes, be she *who* she will; and adopts her into his own Rank, be it *what* it will' (p. 541).

69. *he should give me the strongest contract imaginable, till we were married*: This demonstrates early on the second penitent's uncertain grasp of nuptial regulations: on the one hand,

she knows that Mr Monkerton's promise to marry her must be formalized; on the other, she does not realize that, according to the thirteenth clause of the Marriage Act, 'in no Case whatsoever, shall any Suit or Proceeding be had in any Ecclesiastical Court, in order to compel a Celebration of any Marriage *in facie Ecclesiae*, by reason of any Contract of Matrimony whatsoever'. This was an attempt to eliminate from British nuptial culture the pre-contract, a conditional agreement to marry which, according to the ecclesiastical courts, was as binding as a marriage that had been publicly solemnized: see Lawrence Stone, *Road to Divorce: England 1530–1987* (Oxford: Oxford University Press, 1990), pp. 51–96.

70. *before the canonical hour was past*: According to the Canons of 1604, all marriages had to take place between eight in the morning and noon.

71. *Hail, wedded love ... all things common else.* MILTON: John Milton, *Paradise Lost* (1667), IV.750–2.

72. *the Fleet*: The area immediately outside the Fleet Prison, known as the Rules, was notorious for 'marriage shops' in the late seventeenth and eighteenth centuries; for a fee, disreputable parsons, often inhabitants of the prison itself, would perform clandestine marriages, usually in the back rooms of taverns or nearby houses. The Marriage Act of 1753 nullified all such Fleet marriages: see Weinreb and Hibbert, pp. 291–2; and Miles Ogborn, 'This Most Lawless Space: The Geography of the Fleet and the Making of Lord Hardwicke's Marriage Act of 1753', *New Formations*, 37 (1999), pp. 11–32.

73. *tardy-footed time*: In *A Midsummer Night's Dream* (III.ii.200), Helena refers to the 'hasty-footed time'. This could be a misquotation, or a deliberate inversion.

74. *where most might wonder at nature's workmanship*: This is a misquotation from Milton's *Comus*, ll. 744–6. The original, from a speech by Comus on the necessity for beauties to distribute their favours, reads: 'Beautie is natures brag, and must be showne / In courts, at feasts, and high solemnities / Where most may wonder at the workmanship'. Sarah Fielding also uses this quotation in *The History of the Countess of Dellwyn* (2 vols, London: A. Millar, 1759), vol. 2, p. 228.

75. *nothing was so great an incentive to generosity, as being generously treated*: In Richardson's *Pamela*, Mr B. also uses this rakish logic in his attempt to make Pamela complicit in her own seduction. When he imprisons her in the Lincolnshire house, he writes, 'Can you place so much Confidence in me, as to *invite* me down? Assure yourself that your Generosity shall not be thrown away upon me' (p. 158).

76. *A generous fierceness ... allow'd some pride.* DRYDEN: John Dryden and Nathaniel Lee, *Oedipus* (1679), III.i.395–6.

77. *Mr. Senwill*: The inversion of the vowels conceals the fact that this character's name could be 'Sinwell', a morally dubious construct that he embodies through his companionate extra-marital relationship with the penitent.

78. *We were neither of us of age ... without the consent of our friends*: Mr Monkerton is referring to the eleventh clause of the Marriage Act: 'That all Marriages solemnized by Licence ... where either of the Parties ... shall be under the Age of Twenty-One Years, which shall be had without the Consent of the Father of such of the Parties, so under Age (if then living) first had and obtained, or if dead, of the Guardian or Guardians of the Person of the Party so under Age, lawfully appointed, or One of them; and in case there shall be no such Guardian or Guardians, then of the Mother (if living and unmarried) or if there shall be no Mother living and unmarried, then of a Guardian or Guardians of the Person appointed by the Court of Chancery, shall be absolutely null and void to all Intents and Purposes whatsoever.'

79. *I had heard the Marriage Act talked of ... it could affect the validity of our marriage*: The second penitent's experience and her ignorance of nuptial law embodies the anxiety expressed by opponents of the Marriage Act: as MP Charles Townshend opined, 'I am persuaded, that a few years hence many a young woman will be debauched under the pretence of a sham-marriage ... for though those of the present generation may remember something of the law, and be a little cautious, yet the young women of the next will be as ignorant and as regarless of it, as they are now of our laws against wearing cambrics': see Cobbett, *Parliamentary History,* vol. 15, p. 54.

80. *nor durst my maid leave me*: The presence of a lady's maid indicates the luxury in which the penitent and Mr Monkerton live.

81. *O honour! ... to be redeem'd! D'AV*: Sir William D'Avenant, *Gondibert: An Heroick Poem* (1651), canto 4, stanza 32.

82. *an unthrifty fool*: In Nicholas Rowe's *The Fair Penitent* (1703), Calista asks, 'wherefore did I play th'unthrifty Fool / And wasting all on others, leave my self, / Without one Thought of Joy to give me Comfort?' (II.i.90–2).

83. *my duty to my father ... most anxious for my welfare*: According to the model of spousal selection outlined by Attorney General Sir Dudley Ryder during the Marriage Act debate in the House of Commons, 'In this step the happiness both of the parents and children is so intimately concerned, that children ought never to make it without the approbation of their parents, and nor ought the parent to refuse his approbation, when the match proposed is not such as apparently tends to the dishonour of his family, or may probably bring about the ruin of his child. Yet we often find the passion called love triumphing over the duty of children to their parents, and on the other hand we sometime find the passion of pride or avarice triumphing over the duty of parents to their children.' Cobbett, *Parliamentary History*, vol. 15, p. 2.

84. *In vain ... no more*: Nicholas Rowe, *The Tragedy of Jane Shore* (1714), I.ii.191–3.

85. *Oh! When this tyrant ... any more. OTWAY*: Thomas Otway, *Don Carlos, Prince of Spain* (1676), IV.260–4. The first three lines should read:

> Still how this Tyrant Doubt torments my Breast!
> When shall I get th'Usurper dispossest?
> My thoughts like Birds when frighted from their rest...

86. *a second object of its affections*: Samuel Richardson would have heartily approved of the penitent's practical approach to falling in love: as he wrote to Hester Mulso, describing his third novel, *The History of Sir Charles Grandison* (1753–4), 'I want to have young people think, there is no such mighty business as they are apt to suppose (and so never struggle against a bias) in conquering a first love.' See *The Selected Letters of Samuel Richardson*, ed. John Carroll (Oxford: Clarendon Press, 1964), p. 218.

87. *a youth ... out of his time*: The apprenticeship traditionally was for seven years.

88. *if he did not consent ... had done worse*: The lack of parental consent casts a shadow of doubt over the legitimacy of the sister's marriage. Her age is not specified, so she may well have attained her majority; but her husband is a 'youth', implying that he is not yet twenty-one, in which case, without the consent of his parents, their marriage is null and void.

89. *vain of a little brief authority*: This is adapted from *Measure for Measure*, II.ii.118–19. The original reads, 'proud man / Dress'd in a little brief authority'.

90. *contrary to duty and gratitude*: Mr Senwill's reverence for his father demonstrates his filial piety, both an emotion and an obligation according to eighteenth-century notions of parent-child relations. As described by John Locke, '[God] has laid on the Children a

perpetual Obligation of *honouring their parents*, which containing in it an inward esteem and reverence to be shewn by all outward Expressions, ties up the Child from any thing that may ever injure or affront, disturb, or endanger the Happiness or Life of those, from whom he received his; and engages him in all actions of defence, relief, assistance and comfort of those, by whose means he entred into being, and has been made capable of any enjoyments of life.' See *Two Treatises of Government*, ed. Peter Laslett (Cambridge: Cambridge University Press, 1988), pp. 311–12.

91. *What have we gain'd ... to die.— OTWAY*: This has been misattributed; it is actually from John Dryden, *Troilus and Cressida, or Truth Found Too Late* (1679), IV.i.83–7.

> *Cress.*:   What have we gain'd by this one minute more?
> *Troil.*:   Only to wish another, and another
> A longer struggling with the pangs of death.
> *Cress.*:   O those who do not know what parting is
> Can never learn to dye!

92. *as little ear to his philosophy ... as it cannot make a Juliet*: In *Romeo and Juliet* (III.iii.57–60), Romeo exclaims to Friar Lawrence:

> Hang up philosophy.
> Unless philosophy can make a Juliet,
> Displant a town, reverse a Prince's doom,
> It helps not, it prevails not. Talk no more.

93. *With themselves at war ... to others*: *Julius Caesar*, I.i.46–7; Brutus accounts for neglecting his friends, explaining 'poor Brutus, with himself at war, / Forgets the shows of love to other men'.

94. *But, Oh! that meeting was not like the former*: Nicholas Rowe, *The Fair Penitent* (1703), I.i.167.

95. *Our life is short ... virtue's work. SHAKESP*: As with the epigraph to chapter XIX, this has been misattributed and is also from Dryden's *Troilus and Cressida*, V.i.94–5.

96. *which she attributed to illness*: Although Mr Senwill's fiancée is the subject of this sentence, the pronoun 'he' indicates that Mr Senwill himself has concocted this prevarication.

97. *They were married ... one of their attendants at church*: Of the three weddings mentioned in this narrative, this is the only one that takes place in a church, before witnesses, with paternal consent. The legitimacy of Mr Senwill's marriage is therefore unquestionable, and this sheds an even more unattractive light on the clandestine unions contracted by the penitent and her sister.

98. *An easy quiet ... his happiness. DRYD. & VIR*: Virgil, 'The Second Book of the Georgics', ll. 655–8, from *The Works of Virgil: Containing his Pastorals, Georgics, and Aeneis*, trans. John Dryden (London: Jacob Tonson, 1697).

99. *I wrote to my father ... never see me more*: This paternal coldness also features in one of the inset narratives told by the minister in William Dodd's *The Magdalen* (1783); in Dodd's version, however, the penitent's father ultimately forgives her, after she has been rehabilitated, leaves the Magdalen House and contracts a fatal illness.

100. *All born alike ... made him good. DRYDEN*: John Dryden, 'Sigismonda and Guiscardo from Boccace', from *Fables Ancient and Modern*, ll. 510–14.

101. *GREAT pains have been taken by philosophers ... still are ignorant why we do so*: A reference to the work of moral sense philosophers Anthony Ashley Cooper, Third Earl of Shaftesbury (1671–1713), Francis Hutcheson (1694–1746), David Hume (1711–76) and Adam Smith (1723–90), whose *Theory of Moral Sentiments* was published in

1759. Unlike Thomas Hobbes and Bernard Mandeville, who emphasized man's inherent competitiveness and pursuit of self-interest, these writers foregrounded sympathy as the basis of civil society. Although their accounts differed (particularly in their understanding of the relationship between reason, aesthetics and moral response), they were united, like the author of *The Histories*, in their condemnation of those 'UNNATURAL' and 'INHUMAN' individuals who view 'Distress, Calamity, Blood, Massacre and Destruction, with a peculiar Joy and Pleasure'. Anthony Ashley Cooper, Third Earl of Shaftesbury, *An Inquiry Concerning Virtue, or Merit*, ed. David Walford (Manchester: Manchester University Press, 1977), p. 101.

102. *that every one can bear the misfortunes of others, perfectly like a Christian*: Slightly misquoted from Jonathan Swift, *Thoughts on Various Subjects*, in *Miscellanies. The Second Volume* (London: Benjamin Motte, 1727), p. 357: 'I never knew any Man in my Life, who cou'd not bear anothers [*sic*] Misfortunes perfectly like Christian'.

103. *Pharisee*: Originally a member of a religious party within Judaism between the second century BC and New Testament time, that was distinguished by its rigorous interpretation and observance of Mosaic law. By the eighteenth century the term was used to denote a legalist, formalist or hypocrite (*OED*). That is to say, the women take pride in their recognition of shared failing rather than in exulting themselves above their fellow inmates, and thus can take pride in their lack of hypocrisy.

104. *could not be effaced*: see note 5 above.

105. *Our employment was spinning*: One of the iconographic images produced by the Magdalen House was an engraving of a solitary Magdalen kneeling at prayer by her spinning wheel, which appeared in the second volume of Jonas Hanway's *Reflections, Essays and Meditations on Life and Religion*, (2 vols, London: John Rivington and R. and J. Dodsley, [1761]). Spinning epitomizes, here, the charity's conception of virtuous industry.

106. *I was a heavy burden to the parish*: Fanny's experiences as a young girl, dependent on the parish for support, recall those of the young Moll Flanders in Defoe's 1722 novel.

107. *I had just food enough to keep me always hungry*: Before their sentimentalization in the mid-century, prostitutes were commonly associated with insatiable appetite. See, for example, Dodd's *The Sisters*, in which Lucy Sansom's relationship with her lover Leicart is described as a 'luxurious feast': *The Sisters; or the History of Lucy and Caroline Sanson* (2 vols, London: T. Waller, 1754), vol. 1, p. 156. The fact that Fanny eats only to survive, rather than to indulge her senses, challenges this association, but the novel does not entirely overwrite prior literary tradition. Fanny's hunger – she is given enough to keep her wanting more – rehearses the earlier association of libidinous and gustatory appetites. On the highly regulated diet of the real-life Magdalens, see Jonas Hanway, *A Plan for Establishing a Charity-house, or Charity-houses, for the Reception of Repenting Prostitutes* (London: n.p., 1758), pp. 23–7. Further possible allusions to *The Sisters* are documented in notes 117 and 122.

108. *fine work*: ornate or 'fancy' needlework, particularly embroidery. This leisured pursuit contrasts with the honest and industrious practice of spinning, in which Fanny is skilled.

109. *it gave an air of distinction to her servant, which her imagination reflected back on herself*: Here, Madam Selton resembles Mrs Colraine in Sarah Scott's *A Journey through Every Stage of Life* (1754), who remarks that 'The Attendants of a Woman of Fashion should be genteel, it does her Credit; it shews she is not reduced to be served by the Scum of the Earth'. *A Journey through Every Stage of Life*, ed. Gary Kelly, in *Bluestocking Feminism:*

Writings of the Bluestocking Circle, 1738–1785, ed. Gary Kelly, (6 vols, London: Pickering and Chatto, 1999), vol. 5, pp. 292–3.

110. *None knew ... What darts or poison'd arrows were. ROSCOMMON*: Wentworth Dillon, Earl of Roscommon, 'The Twenty Second Ode of the First Book of Horace' (1684), ll. 3–4. The editors thank Stuart Gillespie for his help in footnoting this quotation.

111. *not quite fifteen*: Fanny is almost exactly the same age as her namesake, Fanny Hill, whose 'ills' begin as she is 'entering on [her] fifteenth year'. John Cleland, *Memoirs of a Woman of Pleasure* (2 vols, London: G. Fenton, 1749), vol. 1, p. 7.

112. *The waggon arrived in London about noon*: This scene recalls plate 1 of William Hogarth's *Harlot's Progress* (1732), in which Moll Hackabout is approached by a bawd on arriving in London, as well as re-imagining in Cleland's *Memoirs of a Woman of Pleasure* (1748–9).

113. *Madam Tent*: Here, the author is playing on the double meaning of tent as something which protects and, in its more vulgar usage, something which probes. In the seventeenth century 'tent' was a vulgar term for a speculum (*OED*).

114. *I need not tell you, that this supposed mother ... was an old bawd*: An indication that the author anticipates that her readers will be aware of narrative paradigms of which her heroines are, tragically, ignorant.

115. *the great innocence and simplicity of my appearance*: The non-ironic use of terms such as simplicity and rusticity, descriptors used liberally and often satirically in *Memoirs of a Woman of Pleasure*, is another example of the novel's effort to rewrite prior literary representations of the prostitute.

116. *For what one likes ... when many wills rebel? POPE*: Alexander Pope, *Essay on Man* (1733–4), epistle III, ll. 274–5.

117. *No other ceremony is required among people of fashion*: Madam Tent's sentiments on marriage recall those of Lucy Sanson, one of the eponymous *Sisters* in William Dodd's 1754 novel, which relates the story of Lucy and Caroline's entrance into London society and subsequent downfall. Lucy's fate is sealed when she comments that '*love* alone', without a ceremony, 'can make marriage firm and acceptable in the sight of God'. Her villainous cousin Dookalb convinces her that by sleeping with her lover she will be married 'in private', the falsity of which she realizes only when her virtue has already been sacrificed (vol. 1, p. 30). Further possible allusions to *The Sisters* are documented in notes 107 and 122. On the 1753 Marriage Act see notes 64, 67, 69, 78, 79 and 83.

118. *made to stand in a white sheet in our parish*: A form of public penance under canon law for crimes including incest and adultery. Offenders were forced to appear in the parish church or a public marketplace wearing a white sheet 'to satisfy the Church for the Scandal given by an Evil Example'. See Thomas Wood, *An Institute of the Laws of England*, 8th edn ([London]: Henry Lintot, 1754), p. 533.

119. *a desire to be genteel; which was not so strong in me*: Parents' and daughters' aspirations to gentility were cited as principal causes of prostitution in several of the Magdalen House pamphlets. See, for example, Saunders Welch's *Proposal to Render Effectual a Plan, to Remove the Nuisance of Common Prostitutes from the Streets of this Metropolis* (London: C. Henderson, 1758): 'The maxim of the parents of these children is, to give them what they call a good education; and if Miss happens to be pretty, her vanity is indulged by dress, &c. in hopes that she may mend her fortune by captivating some rich gudgeon' (p. 4).

120. *Prince Prettiman*: the hero of *The Rehearsal* (1671), a satire on heroic drama by George Villiers, Second Duke of Buckingham.

121. *Love is not sin … That the white taper leaves no soot behind.* DRYDEN: John Dryden, *Don Sebastian* (1690), II.i.575–7.

122. *our connexion was grown too like matrimony*: Lucy Sansom, of Dodd's *The Sisters*, suffers similarly when her lover finds their relationship too nearly resembling that 'slavish miserable state matrimony' (vol. 1, p. 154). Further possible allusions to *The Sisters* are documented in notes 107 and 117.

123. *Mrs. Lafew*: Lord Lafew is a character in *All's Well that Ends Well*, noted for his judiciousness.

124. *Job in his prosperity*: After undergoing a series of trials at the hands of Satan, Job is made prosperous again by God and has his friends and family restored to him.

125. *like the serpent*: Throughout the narrative, Fanny presents herself as both tempter and tempted. Although she identifies herself with the serpent here, she later appears as Eve 'taught shame by want of innocence' (p. 115).

126. *Shiv'ring death crept cold … o'erwhelm'd his dying eyes.* BLACK: Sir Richard Blackmore, *Prince Arthur: An Heroic Poem in Ten Books* (1695), book viii, l. 356; book x, l. 344.

127. *For, oh! what damned minutes … yet strongly loves!* SHAKESP: *Othello*, III.171–2.

128. *She must be humble … who will love.* A misquotation of Matthew Prior, 'Cloe Jealous' (1718), ll. 19–20: 'She shou'd be humble, who wou'd please/ And She must suffer, who can love.'

129. *To threats the stubborn sinner oft is hard … He melts, and throws his cumb'rous cloak away.* DRYDEN: John Dryden, 'The Character of a Good Parson Imitated from Chaucer', from *Fables Ancient and Modern*, ll. 34–7.

130. *Heav'n has but … Than punish to extent.* DRYDEN: John Dryden, *All for Love* (1678), IV.537–43.

131. *Mrs. Lafew engaging to take care of my boy, and to bring him often to see me*: Mrs Lafew's decision to undertake the care of her husband's illegitimate child rehearses a plot device Sarah Fielding used in *The History of the Countess of Dellwyn*, in which the genteel but impoverished Mrs Bilson supports herself, her children, her wayward husband and his illegitimate child through her work as a milliner.

132. *I shall rather be a benefit than an expence to the society*: Fanny is, crucially, the only one of the four women who enters the Magdalen House by choice rather than necessity.

133. *Love is … madmen know.* DRYDEN: This is misattributed; it is in fact from Benjamin Hawkshaw, 'The Fever' (1693), ll. 14–16.

134. *languishing … languid*: By juxtaposing these similar terms, the author implies that the penitent's corrupt life has permanently impaired her: 'languishing' means 'an attack of languor or faintness, esp. such as proceeds from disease'; whereas 'languid' signifies 'not easily roused to emotion, exhibiting only faint interest or concern; spiritless, apathetic' (*OED*).

135. *her complexion … the true one is passed*: In the eighteenth century, the base ingredient of the 'paint' used to colour ladies' cheeks was often white lead; small amounts of verdigris or arsenic were sometimes included. It was thus a physically dangerous preparation, above and beyond the representation of its moral or aesthetic undesirability. See Neville Williams, *Powder and Paint: A History of the Englishwoman's Toilet* (London, New York and Toronto: Longmans, Green and Co., 1957), pp. 16–17, 67–8.

136. *Captain Turnham took all opportunities … this request*: The danger of a *tête à tête* to a woman's reputation is also expressed in Sarah Scott's *Millenium Hall* (London: J. Newberry, 1762): 'Lady Mary did not perceive she was left alone with Lord Robert, till the growing freedom of his address made her observe it; … Lord Robert, encouraged by her easiness on the occasion, declared himself so plainly, that she was no longer able to blind herself to his views, and with surprize found seduction to be his aim' (p. 170).

137. *Interest is ... an easy bent.* DRYDEN: John Dryden, 'The Hind and the Panther' (1687), ll. 394–9.
138. *to make his addresses*: A marriage between old age and youth features in both Scott's *Millenium Hall* – Miss Melvyn is forced into marriage with decrepit Mr Morgan – and in Sarah Fielding's *The History of the Countess of Dellwyn*, which opens with a wedding between the wheelchair-bound Lord Dellwyn, in his 'grand Climacteric' (vol. 1, p. 2), and seventeen-year-old Miss Lucum, who radiates a 'natural Glow and Freshness' (vol. 1, p. 4).
139. *with my Strephon*: The name 'Strephon' signifies a typical Arcadian lover.
140. *the bare earth ... till the morning*: Thomas Otway, *Venice Preserv'd* (1750), I.i.375–81:

> Tho' the Bare Earth be all our Resting-Place.
> Its Roots our Food, some Clift our Habitation,
> I'll make this Arm a Pillow for thine Head;
> As thou sighing ly'st, and swell'd with Sorrow.
> Creep to thy Bosom, pour the Balm of Love,
> Into thy Soul, and kiss thee to thy Reil;
> Then praise our God, and watch thee till the Morning.

141. *he seemed unalarmed ... for me or himself*: This description of the groom's delight and the bride's despair also occurs in Scott's *Millenium Hall*: '[Miss Melvyn's] distress was visible to all, even to Mr. Morgan, who was so little touched with it, that it proved no abatement to his joy; a symptom of such indelicacy of mind, as increased his bride's grief and apprehensions' (pp. 100–1).
142. *The Princess of Cleves*: the heroine of Madame de Lafayette's novel *La Princesse de Clèves* (1678)
143. *this splendid slavery*: Mary Wollstonecraft also mentions 'the slavery of marriage' in *A Vindication of the Rights of Woman; With Strictures on Political and Moral Subjects* (London: J. Johnson, 1792), p. 355.
144. *an apparent want of principle*: This is the same rationale that Harriet Byron uses in Richardson's *History of Sir Charles Grandison* (7 vols, London: S. Richardson, 1753–4) to reject numerous suitors after she has met and fallen in love with the exemplary Sir Charles. As she writes to Sir Rowland Meredith, 'my esteem for this noblest of men is of such a nature, that I cannot give my hand to any other: [you] would not wish me to give a hand without a heart' (vol. 4, p. 212).
145. *Tunbridge*: A spa town thirty miles southeast of London, Tunbridge Wells was a fashionable destination in the eighteenth century; it is used as a setting in both Scott's *Millenium Hall* and in Sarah Fielding's *The History of Ophelia* (2 vols, London: R. Baldwin, 1760).
146. *And doubts ... can burn.* CONG: William Congreve, 'To Cynthia, Weeping and Not Speaking' (1710), ll. 69–70. It should read:

> And Fears and Doubts to Jealousie will turn,
> The hottest Hell, in which a Heart can burn.'

147. *He comes too near ... to be denied*: from Lady Mary Wortley Montagu's 'The Lady's Resolve, Written Extempore on a Window' (1724), l. 11. In context, the verse reads:

> Let this great maxim be my virtue's guide;
> In part she is to blame who has been tried;
> He comes too near, that comes to be denied.

148. *the meeting immediately followed my consent*: Both the second and the fourth penitents consent to private meetings with their lovers, indiscretions which ultimately compromise their reputations (p. 58).

149. *Anger ... to be priz'd. WALLER*: Edmund Waller, 'Of Love', ll.1–8, 11–12. The lines, with the omitted couplet, should read:

> Anger in hasty words or blows,
> It self discharges on our foes.
> And sorrow too, finds some relief
> In tears which wait upon our grief.
> So every passion but fond love
> Unto its own redresse does move.
> But that alone the wretch inclines
> To what prevents his own designes:
> Makes him lament, and sigh, and weep,
> Disordred, tremble, fawn and creep,
> Postures which render him despis'd,
> Where he endeavours to be priz'd.

150. *A woman who hopes to preserve her virtue ... strongly engaged*: This simile, comparing the assault on a woman's virtue with a siege laid on a town, inverts the metaphor used by the second penitent: here, the woman is figured as the town; but in the earlier narrative the town represents the young men whom the Magdalen's ugly sister attempts to coerce into marriage by granting them sexual favours: see note 51 above.

151. *virtue followed my prudence*: At this point, the penitent indicates that she has had sex for the first time with Captain Turnham.

152. *no such piece of furniture ... thought necessary*: When the eponymous heroine of Fielding's *Ophelia* is abducted by the jealous Marchioness of Trente, she too is initially placed in a room without a bed (vol. 1, p. 266).

153. *I was with difficulty able to go thro' it*: The difficulty that an imprisoned heroine experiences reading her lover's letter becomes a convention of Gothic fiction. In Ann Radcliffe's *The Italian* (3 vols, London: T. Caddell and W. Davies, 1797), Ellena accidentally extinguishes her only lamp while she is reading Vivaldi's letter, and must wait until an accomplice brings her a light before she can learn the details of his plot to help her escape from the convent (vol. 2, pp. 10–11).

154. *There is a lust ... born to die. HARV. JUV*: from *The Satires of Decimus Junius Juvenalis. Translated into English Verse by Mr Dryden and Several Other Eminent Hands* (London: Jacob Tonson, 1693), Satire IX, ll. 193–6.

155. *to shed poppies ... to their rest*: The poppy is often used to figure 'the narcotic or sleep-inducing qualities of the plant' (*OED*).

156. *the highest ladder he could get was not quite long enough*: Fielding echoes this detail in *Ophelia*; when Ophelia schemes with the gardener to escape from the Marchioness of Trente's mouldering castle, she is informed that he has no ladder long enough to reach her room; a carpenter is called in to join two ladders, and Ophelia is forced to use this ramshackle piece of equipment: see vol. 2, pp. 71–2.

157. *thirty pounds*: Equivalent to approximately £3,720 in 2005, this was an enormous amount of money in 1759.

158. *Tunbridge town*: Four miles away from Tunbridge Wells, Tonbridge – or Tunbridge according to its eighteenth-century spelling – is a much older market town, mentioned in the Domesday Book.

159. *While our former flames ... power to sin. DRYDEN*: John Dryden, 'Palamon and Arcite' (1700), part III.12–13. The line should read 'my former flames'.

160. *a separation, and some allowance*: The penitent would like her father to arrange a separate maintenance contract for her, that is, an agreement stipulating that the husband and wife will live apart, and that the husband should provide the wife with a yearly allowance. As a private method of separation, often organized with the participation and thus the support of the wife's family, this would allow the wife to maintain her reputation in society. For further discussion of the separate maintenance contract, see Susan Staves, *Married Women's Separate Property in England, 1660–1833* (Cambridge, Mass. and London: Harvard University Press, 1990), pp. 162–95.

161. *Reading*: a town forty miles west of London.

162. *before my confinement was over*: In the eighteenth century, women were typically confined for a month after childbirth (*OED*).

163. *my fits returned, and I was not sensible*: This is the typical feminine response to abduction: in Richardson's *Sir Charles Grandison*, describing her kidnapping by Sir Hargrave Pollexfen, Harriet Byron writes, 'I pierced the night air with my screams, till I could scream no more. I was taken out in fits' (vol. 1, p. 210); and Fielding's Ophelia remembers, 'I exerted my Voice to its loudest Key …. But this effort only served to spend my Spirits the more entirely' (vol. 1, pp. 258–9). Significantly, Clarissa does not lose consciousness when Lovelace tricks her into eloping with him, and this could signal her sense of culpability for her predicament: see Samuel Richardson, *Clarissa*, vol. 3, pp. 1–22.

164. *I have been … overspread with damps!* DRYDEN: John Dryden, *The Spanish Fryar; or The Double Discovery* (1681), III.iii.177–9.

165. *till law had procured a divorce, and left me to starve*: In the eighteenth century, divorce on the grounds of adultery was obtainable in the ecclesiastical courts, in the Court of King's Bench, and in Parliament. According to Lawrence Stone, 'If the husband sued the wife for separation on the grounds of her adultery and he won, the court would not allocate alimony to her, and she was consequently left penniless' (*Road to Divorce*, p. 193).

166. *half of it was already fallen … were to sustain*: The mouldering state of Mr Merton's country house is similar to that of the Marchioness of Trente's castle in Fielding's *Ophelia* (vol. 2, pp.17–24).

167. *The ground round the house … howled without ceasing till morning*: Compare the description on this page with the following from Fielding's *Ophelia*: 'With the Twilight our concert began. The first Performance was a great House-Dog, that would suffer no Noise but his own, incessantly howling or barking. Every Hearth was full of Crickets, who chirped the live long Night, but had none of those lively Notes, which *Milton* celebrates as the Sound of Mirth. The old Towers of the House were filled with Owls of every Sort, who, by their hoarse Hooting, and their shrill Shrieking, bore no inconsiderable Part of the Concert, of which the Froggery made the Base. These vocal Performers were accompanied by all the Modulations of a bleak Winter's Wind, which gathering in various Passages of that rambling House, made a continual Whistling, even in the mildest Weather, roared in the Chimneys, and blew in at a thousand Crevices in the shattered Wainscot' (vol. 2, pp. 20–1).

168. *as hard as so many tennis-balls*: Fielding also uses this image in *Ophelia*: 'all the Furniture large and clumsy, except the Chairs, whose Seats were stuffed with admirable Art, being harder than a Tennis-Ball' (vol. 2, p. 19).

169. *Tho' he posted … left behind.* HUD: Samuel Butler, *Hudibras* (1677–8), Third part, canto III, ll. 63–6.

170. *the law might esteem Mr. Merton and I one*: see Blackstone's *Commentaries* for an extended discussion of this principle: 'By marriage, the husband and wife are one person in law:

that is, the very being or legal existence of the woman is suspended during the marriage, or at least is incorporated and consolidated into that of the husband: ... Upon this principle, of an union of person in husband and wife, depend almost all the legal rights, duties and disabilities that either of them acquire by the marriage' (vol I, pp. 430–3).

171. *the girl ... commanded them*: The sympathetic jailor is also a figure in Wollstonecraft's *The Wrongs of Woman; or, Maria* (1798), which like the fourth penitent's narrative includes the imprisonment of the heroine in a Gothic ruin at the behest of her tyrannical husband.

172. *the design I had on this young girl*: This language is uncomfortably similar to the language of seduction; for example, in act two, scene one of Colley Cibber's *The Careless Husband* (London: William Davis, 1705), Lady Easy says, 'to be in Love now is only having a Design upon a Woman, a modish way of declaring War against her Virtue' (p. 13).

173. *ten guineas*: equivalent to approximately £1,300 in 2005.

174. *twenty pounds*: equivalent to approximately £2480 in 2005.

175. *Man is but man ... mount aloft. DRYDEN*: John Dryden, *Cleomenes, The Spartan Heroe* (1692), IV.i.15–20.

176. *Mr. Merton had just brought his cause to a conclusion ... over me*: As Mr. Merton can prove that the penitent has had three children since leaving his house, and she does not contest the case, it is comparatively easy for him to divorce her. See Stone, *Road to Divorce*, for more information on the complex, and sometimes contradictory, divorce procedures in the ecclesiastical courts, the common law courts and Parliament.

177. *if I lost his love, I lost my all*: Alexander Pope, *Eloisa to Abelard*, l. 118. The line should read, 'if I lose my love, I lose my all.'

178. *And as pale sickness ... soul, appear. WALLER*: Edmund Waller, 'A la Malade' (1645), ll. 21–4.

179. *In owing, owe not ... indebted and discharg'd*: slightly misquoted from John Milton, *Paradise Lost*, IV.55–7: 'a grateful mind / By owing owes not, but still pays, at once / indebted and discharged'.

180. *Gibraltar*: A strategic base between the Mediterranean and the Atlantic at the tip of the Spanish peninsula, Gibraltar was captured by Britain in 1704, a situation that was formalized by the Treaty of Utrecht in 1713.

181. *As th' Elm ... torment the air. DEN*: John Dennis, 'Upon our Victory at Sea, and Burning the French Fleet at La Hogue. In 1692', in *The Select Works of Mr. John Dennis* (2 vols, London: John Darby, 1718), vol. 1, pp. 30–5.

182. *a French man of war*: 'a vessel equipped for warfare; a commissioned warship' (*OED*).

183. *administrator*: executor.

184. *that would have obliged the person who put me there, to maintain me*: Debtors were, in fact, expected to pay their own fees for admission and accommodation within prison, although the expectation was that they would work to pay these fees. In Sarah Fielding's *History of the Countess of Dellwyn*, for example, Mrs Bilson, a gentlewoman and wife of a debtor starts up a millinery business in order to hire a room with two beds in the Fleet and to pay off her husband's creditors. Her business is so successful, that she is able to find work for other prison inmates (vol. 1, pp. 180–8).

185. *Death only can be dreadful ... appear a friend. DRYDEN*: John Dryden and Nathaniel Lee, *Oedipus* (1679), III.i.74–7.

186. *to Him, who had so loved the world ... everlasting life*: John 3:16.

187. *He should feel great joy ... in him to pretend*: By implication, the child has not yet been confirmed; and according to Robert Cornwall, in the eighteenth century 'there was a

general recognition that confirmation should precede the first communion': see 'The Rite of Confirmation in Anglican Thought during the Eighteenth Century', *Church History* 68:2 (1999), pp. 359–72; p. 366.

188. *not fit for so solemn an act of devotion*: The issue of preparation for communion was much discussed by Anglican divines in the seventeenth and eighteenth centuries: see, for example, Richard Allstree, *The Whole Duty of Man Laid Down in a Plain and Familiar Way for the Use of All, but Especially the Meanest Reader* (London: T. Garthwait, 1659).

189. *the offspring of penitents ... received into the Magdalen-House*: This is a fantasy; no such institution ever existed.

190. *those who save a soul ... stars in heaven*: Daniel 12:3: 'they that be wise shall shine as the brightness of the firmament, and they that turn many to righteousness as the stars for ever and ever.'

191. *more blessed to give than receive*: Acts 20:35.

For Product Safety Concerns and Information please contact our EU
representative GPSR@taylorandfrancis.com
Taylor & Francis Verlag GmbH, Kaufingerstraße 24, 80331 München, Germany